Juli Zeh was born in 1974 in Bonn. She studied European and International Law in Leipzig and has studied and worked at the UN in New York, Crakow and Zagreb. She lives in Leipzig.

Christine Slenczka worked in publishing in London for four years before moving to Frankfurt, where she is now a full-time translator.

FROM THE GERMAN REVIEWS

'Bret Easton Ellis and Michel Houellebecq have already made a bitter and chilly criticism of our times, now Juli Zeh walks right through in her own way . . . she has succeeded in writing her novel with imaginativeness, a contemporary feel and high intelligence' *Die Zeit*

'The most beautiful and wild German prose published in recent years. Literature with the figurative magical power of Gabriel Garcia Marquez and the pitiless realism of Raymond Carver. Zeh is Zadie Smith's equal in every way' *Die Weltwoche*

'Juli Zeh's poetic images are terrific, reminiscent of a Quentin Tarantino movie' *Abendzeitung*

'Hits you right between the eyes . . . a literary trip, which takes your breath away again and again . . . written in excitingly precise prose this is a passionate epic full of anxieties and torments, a drug-saga, a heart-wrenching love story, all in a language which can't be compared to anything else published' *Hamburger Morgenpost*

'This is an unbelievable book: a love story without hypocritical romance, a crime novel without an enthusiasm for explanations, a drug story without moral condemnation. It is a piece of real politics without fanatical partisanship, a modern novel without navel gazing. And, along with all of that, it's the significant debut of a self-assured writer . . . you follow the story of Max and Jessie breathlessly through the book. You are a hostage from the first to the last page' *Sachsische Zeitr*

D1297507

Eagles and Angels | Juli Zeh

Granta Books
London

Granta Publications, 2/3 Hanover Yard, Noel Road, London N1 8BE

First published in Great Britain by Granta Books 2003
First published in Germany as *Adler Und Engel* by Schöffling & Co.
Verlagsbuchhandlung GmbH, Frankfurt am Main 2001

Copyright © Juli Zeh 2001
Translation copyright © Christine Slenczka 2003

Juli Zeh has asserted her moral right under the Copyright, Designs and
Patents Act, 1988, to be identified as the author of this work.

All rights reserved. No reproduction, copy or transmissions of this
publication may be made without written permission. No paragraph of
this publication may be reproduced, copied or transmitted save with
written permission or in accordance with the provisions of the Copyright
Act 1956 (as amended). Any person who does any unauthorized act in
relation to this publication may be liable to criminal prosecution and
civil claims for damages.

A CIP catalogue record for this book is available from the British Library.

1 3 5 7 9 10 8 6 4 2

Typeset by M Rules

Printed and bound in Legoprint S.p.a., Italy

Contents

1	Whale	1
2	Tiger (One)	8
3	Hole	17
4	Moths	24
5	Piglet	31
6	On Birds Flying South	39
7	Yellow–Red–Blue	46
8	Shooting Pigeons	54
9	Vienna	65
10	Yellow	72
11	White Wolves	86
12	Snails	98
13	Bari	106
14	Handles and Steps	116
15	First-term Stuff	123
16	Sacred Cows	133
17	Waltz	145
18	Half-sleep	154
19	Flies	165
20	Counting Fish	175
21	Pigskin	190
22	Rice With Kant	203

23	Goldfish	213
24	Tiger (Two)	220
25	Eagles and Angels	237
26	Tough	249
27	Justifiable Defence	258
28	Shershah Is Dead	268
29	Earthworm	278
30	Baumgartner Hospital	290
31	Europa	307
32	Rain	324

1 | Whale

I recognize her voice through the door. She always sounds half-pouting, as if she's just been denied her heart's desire. I look through the peephole, straight into a giant pupil; there seems to be a whale in the stairway peering into my flat. I step back, and open the door in surprise.

I was sure that she had black hair, but she is blonde. She's standing on the doormat, her left eye screwed up, leaning toward where the peephole had been a second ago. She straightens unhurriedly.

Shit, I say. Come in. How're things?

Good, she says. Do you have any orange juice?

I don't. She looks at me as if I should be rushing off to the corner shop to buy three cartons of the stuff immediately. It would probably be the wrong brand anyway, and she'd pack me right off again. I watch her walking around the flat. She doesn't come with a user manual as far as I can see. She rang the bell and I opened the door.

She sits at the kitchen table and waits for me to play host. She really does exist and now she's here. I'm paralysed. She doesn't bother to introduce herself; she assumes that a voice like that could only belong to a girl like her. Despite the long blonde hair, which she tosses behind her chair, I'm annoyed that she's right.

After just two minutes with her, I find it hard to remember the image of her that I'd had in my head while listening to her crappy programme on the radio. A little like Mata Hari, I think. She seems too young, like she's her own younger sister. But she does have that voice – impossible that it could belong to anyone else – full of affront and hurt, embracing every injustice in the world as her callers tell their stupid stories. They're mostly men. She listens and says *hmmmm* from time to time, the same deep, vibrating *hmmmm* that their mothers must have sounded as they rocked them in their arms. Some of them start crying. I didn't. I'd always loved the incredibly cold way she cut off the tearful outpourings mid-sentence when three minutes were up. She was worse than the Inquisition. I'd been tuning in every Wednesday and Sunday for months, long before I had a crappy story of my own to tell.

They probably keep all the callers' numbers on file. I'd given them a false name, but anyone can trace an address from a telephone number. So this is what I get for calling in.

I look out of the window. The moon is reddish and much too big against the sky; one side of it has been eaten away. It looks like a bad omen, and I suddenly feel afraid. I haven't been afraid for weeks – why now? But I'm behaving strangely. I must offer her something.

I'm out of orange juice, I say, but you can have apple.

No, thanks, she says. I don't want anything, then.

There is contempt in her eyes. I'm Max-the-depriver-of orange-juice, and will have to watch her dying of thirst. I start shaking some coffee into the espresso machine just for something to do. When it's ready, I put a cup in front of her. She sniffs it and makes a face, as if it were pig's blood.

Speaking of blood, she says.

I haven't said anything about blood. Perhaps mind-reading is part of her job.

Where did it happen?

*

No one is allowed to ask about that. I really ought to grab her by the hair and drag her through the hall, kick her if she tries to resist, throw her out. But I don't. I haven't spoken to anyone for a long time, apart from the cashier in the supermarket and the fairy who brings the pizza. He's always staring at my jaw, looking to see whether my beard has grown again. Whenever I let him into the kitchen while I look for change, he gets all excited about the sink hanging from the ceiling by chains, and the stove being made of sandstone. He tried to grab my butt in the stairwell once, and fell down the stairs when I pushed him away. He still comes, though, every day except Sunday. I don't know how many times he's been here.

Hey, she says. Where did it happen?

She smiles. Her smile goes with her voice, which travels through the room and taps me on the shoulder. Now I feel it too; I want to cry, just like the others. But no, no more, not again.

I have cried. Two days and two nights, howling on the floor. Every few hours, eyes dry like broken blisters, I drank from a half-full bottle of water that Jessie must have drunk from before she did it. I'd heard her swallow on the phone, her throat muscles working on water from this bottle.

A mouthful of water was all I'd needed for each fresh bout of tears. When the bottle was empty, I thought I would go blind. But I welcomed it. I never wanted to open my eyes again. I was already half-deaf. I pressed a hand against my left ear constantly, knowing that the tatters of my burst eardrum were fluttering like curtains at an open window. I carried on howling, racked with dry sobs. I lay curled up on the floorboards, rigid as a block of wood at first, then limp as clothes tossed onto a bed. I hoped desire alone would bring death, but sleep came instead. When I woke up I groped my way to the fridge and took a gram of coke out of the freezer. My nose was completely blocked, so I forced my mouth open, tossed the charlie in, and swallowed quickly before my throat seized up. I stumbled out of the flat, leaving the door open, and left the building. That was eight weeks ago. I haven't cried since then, nor felt the need to, until now. There's something about the girl from the radio. For a moment, I think everything's going to be all right.

In the study, I say.

She looks across the hall. One of the two doors is boarded up. Her gaze rests on it and she sips her coffee for the first time, absent-mindedly. She hooks three of her fingers through the handle of the mug. It seems an eternity before she speaks again.

How did you meet? she asks.

I found her in the rubble of a destroyed city, I say.

She looks me in the face. Her eyes are blue, one like water, the other like the sky.

You really *are* a bit strange, she says.

You have no idea what goes on in this world, I say, and you wouldn't believe me if I told you.

Noooo . . . she says, ironically. After all, I'm only twenty-three.

She's told me how old she is: ten years younger than me. If she's telling the truth.

You live another life, I say. You wouldn't understand.

Perhaps you should talk about it, she says.

And maybe you, I think, need to be thrown face down over the coffee table and thoroughly fucked. Not by me, though. Someone else can do it.

I'll explain, I say.

She fumbles with my pepper mill. She's probably imagining that it's a microphone because she can't listen properly without a microphone in front of her. Then I remember that radio presenters use headsets that don't look anything like pepper mills.

Do you see most of Europe devastated by war? I ask. The survivors betrayed, discredited and amnesiac?

No, she says.

I do, I say.

Another eternity passes. We might as well be sitting in different places altogether – she in her kitchen, me in mine, staring into the air, minds busy or vacant. We would have just as little to do with each other then. She pushes as many fingers as possible through the handle of her mug and I trace escape plans on the checked tablecloth with a teaspoon.

What's her name, then? she asks.

I start, even though I'd been expecting her to speak first.

That's fuck all to do with you, I say.

Show me the room where it happened.

I'll show you fuck all.

Please, she says.

I'll never go into that room again, I say.

You live in a two-bedroom flat, and you're saying that you never want to go into one of the rooms again?

Shut up, I shout. I bring my palm down hard onto the table and a teaspoon clatters to the floor.

Then you'll only have your bedroom and the living room, she says.

Only the living room, I whisper. It happened in a connecting room.

You should think about that again, she says.

I sit up so that I can take a deep breath, and slap her in the mouth with the back of my hand. Her head is knocked to one side. Her hair, which she had braided loosely just before, flies through the air and lands in tousled strands on her face and shoulders.

It would have looked good in slow motion, like a shampoo ad. I stand up and walk over to the window, to give her time to tidy her hair. In the lower right corner of the windowsill, three insects have died in the tulle of a spider's web; all three have the same number of spots on their backs. I wonder if spiders ever get to the soft, edible insides.

When I look at the girl from the radio again, her face is blotchy in places I hadn't touched, and a little red spot is swimming in the watery blue of her right eye, like a victim. I'm reminded of the moon. I look up at it again to find it recovered from its haemorrhage. It is smaller now, and light orange. Its contours are clearer and it has risen towards the stars.

She says something, and I hear the word 'dissertation'. I wonder fleetingly whether I should hit her again, but the thought holds no appeal. I sit down instead.

More coffee? I ask.

Orange juice, she whimpers.

I'm reminded of Jessie, who whimpered like that when she didn't get what she wanted. To take my mind off her, I concentrate on the inside of my mouth. It tastes sterile, like a hospital waiting room. My taste buds, tongue and lips are numb; I'll only be able to mumble when I try to speak. I hope I won't dribble. Everything's fantastic. It's going to get even more fantastic. It's only a game, after all, everything is all there is. And memories are really just like television.

I smile at the woman sitting at my kitchen table. It's an honest smile. When she smiles back – cautiously, because of her swollen lip – I start beaming: a thousand watts, halogen. I'm terrific, I am. I wonder if I should call her babe.

What did you just say, babe? I ask.

Orange juice, she repeats.

No, I say in a friendly tone. Before that.

You could be the subject of my dissertation.

Oh, I say, you don't just work, then, you're acquiring an education. That's great. Have you got a cigarette?

I'm getting talkative. She looks at me suspiciously.

Are you being sarcastic?

No, I say, I really think it's great. Studying is terrific. What degree are you doing?

I look at her face, interested. Her lip is still swelling, but it looks good on her. My lips might be swollen too. They're drooping in any case. I touch them with my fingertips. Completely numb. When I speak, my lower lip gets caught between my teeth all the time. It feels like rubber, and I have to spit it out. We look at each other.

Sociology and Psychology, she says.

Of course, I say, excellent. It goes with your work.

I'm going now, she says.

And stands up.

No no no no!

I grab her to make her sit down again. She shrugs me off. I want to talk.

Don't go, I say.

The thousand-watt smile dazzles her. She retreats into the hall and tosses me a pack of cigarettes.

Let's have one together, I call.

I don't smoke, she says. The station gives us the cigarettes for visits like these.

She picks up her jacket, and I hear myself babbling on to make her stay, speaking quickly despite the half-paralysed mouth. I have to speak to someone. There are so many marvellous, beautiful words in me – and they need a listener. I feel like a glass jar full of wriggling glow-worms. I want to give them away. I'm done for if the girl from the radio leaves now.

Bye, she says. I'll come again.

The door clicks closed behind her. I collapse onto the cool, tiled floor and start singing the national anthem. I can't think of another song.

2 | Tiger (One)

The alarm wakes me. I'm clutching the lowest of the boards nailed across the door frame. The electronic tone swells and cuts through the walls of the flat at seven every morning and evening – the time at which Jessie and I were woken by it on her last morning. I hear it from the kitchen, the living room, and now in the hall. Thank God for the voice control.

Quiet! I shout.

No reaction, so I clear my throat, lift my head slightly, and shout again, as loud as I can.

Shut up!

It stops.

I'll have to shout at it four more times at three-minute intervals, maybe bang my fists and head against the boarded-up door. If I have anything to look forward to, it's the day when the battery will die.

Dried sweat has left a brittle salt crust on my upper lip and forehead. When I rub it with a finger, it crumbles white and fine before my eyes, creating a micro-environment, a snowscape, on the floor. I have drooled a lake, and a dust-ball is the forest. It is snowing. I rub away at my face until the snowstorm stops. Then I take a deep breath and get up.

The hall is long like a train carriage, and empty, except for the aluminium telephone stand next to the front door and a narrow, hand-knotted runner. The runner leads to the door in a dead-straight line, as if you would lose your way without it. The **hair** scrunchy the girl from the radio left clashes with the cordless telephone. I pick it up gingerly and drop it behind the cabinet. When I touch the telephone, the hairs on my arm stand on end. There must have been blood and brains all over it, the girl from the radio said on the phone. Her name has escaped me all this while, but now I remember it: Clara.

Or so she calls herself on the programme.

Someone cleaned the telephone up. I was amazed how easy it was to use it again. It had remained neutral somehow. That night, I stood in the living room, holding the phone, staring at it. I often lose myself this way. Everything blurs in front of me, I hear voices and see things in my mind's eye. It's my way of remembering. That night, after I finally tore my gaze away from the telephone, I stared fixedly into space. I knew Clara's hotline number by heart, since it was repeated every ten minutes in an insistent jingle. I heard the tune in my head as I dialled the number; I seemed to be singing along rather than dialling it. I pressed the phone to my good ear. The radio was off, but I knew that her show was on. It was Wednesday, between midnight and one. I knew exactly what I was doing. When someone answered, I jumped, but I managed to explain why I was calling. I was put through immediately.

She began with her standard spiel, but I cut her short. I said I wanted to tell her about a conversation that had been conducted from the telephone I was using now.

How long ago was that? Clara asked.

Eight weeks. Now shut up and let me talk, I said.

OK, Clara said.

I got upset saying Jessie's name, so I decided to say 'my girlfriend' instead. To me, it felt as if I was talking about a stranger.

It wasn't me who was using this telephone; it was my girlfriend. I had called her from the office to tell her I would be home late. My girlfriend didn't say much – she just grunted.

One or two hours, my sweet, I said.

Hmm . . . hmmgh, she grunted.

Come now, don't be like that, I said

When are you coming, then? she asked, dragging out every vowel.

Soon, I said. In a minute.

It had been worse than usual for a few weeks, almost impossible to get a word of sense out of her. Of course she was sweet. And tiring. But I was worried.

Coooooper, she said, I think the tigers are there again.

You know that's nonsense, I said. Stop it.

You are coming baaaack, aren't you?

Of course I'm coming back, I said. Don't be silly.

I'm not being silly, she said.

Then came the shot. I didn't recognize the sound at first. It cut into my left ear like a knife, short and sharp, and there was a whistling noise. I had the presence of mind to press the receiver quickly to my other ear, just in time to hear the dull thud of a body falling to the ground and, a split second later, the hard clatter of the phone as it slid across the floor. Then nothing. The line wasn't dead, but all was quiet. There was a faint dog-whimper. I shouted her name a few times, half-heartedly. Sometimes shock clouds understanding, but I knew immediately. I knew it was too late. What I didn't know was why she had done it.

I found her at home. There wasn't a scratch on the telephone.

And you're calling me from that telephone now, said Clara. Surely there must have been blood and brains all over it.

10

She seemed unusually interested.

Yes, I said. She shot herself in the ear.

Then I put the phone down, so I could throw up.

The alarm goes off again and I shout at it. Now that the scrunchy is gone, I hurl the telephone to the ground, so that it bounces and slides over the floorboards into the kitchen. The battery-compartment lid and the rechargeable battery fly into different corners of the room. I've done this many times, but the phone is indestructible. Only the battery rolls out, and sometimes even that doesn't happen.

I go to the fridge and snort so hard that my nose begins to bleed. I let the blood trickle past my chin onto my collar. Another three minutes have passed. I shout at the alarm clock again, from the living room this time, where I throw myself onto the mattress, hang my head over the pillow, and listen to the whistling in my left ear that tells me Jessie is thinking about me.

I look at the wall calendar and at my watch to get my bearings. It's Monday, the beginning of a month I thought lay far ahead. The company is bound to call in a few days, perhaps even in a few hours. Then it will be official that I just can't get it together; that – without Jessie – a job, earning money and a normal life are things of the past. To think that when she came into my life, I thought a normal life would no longer be possible *with* her. That's fate for you. What a sense of humour. I force myself to laugh.

When the girl from the radio turns up again to pick up her scrunchy, my mind is made up. I will not try to start a new life. I don't have the imagination to do what Jessie did, but if I just let things continue the way they are, it won't be very long before I go, too. I'm comforted by the thought. I greet the girl from the radio with a wise smile on my dry lips.

*

Your fucking scrunchy, I say, went out the window, caught the rear tyre of a truck and is on its way to the Bosphorus now, unravelling in threads, so you'd better get moving, pick up the threads and knit yourself a new scrunchy. Come again when you're done.

What a long sentence, she says.

She marches past me into my kitchen, and sits at the same place as before. She lays her hands palms down on the table.

Orange juice, she says.

I have some. I wonder if I should lie, but it's too much bother. I pour her a glass. She gives me a look of helpless thanks, which makes me think that I should go back on my decision and just do something active, like stick my head in the oven.

It's not about the damn scrunchy, she says.

She pours her juice back into the bottle without losing a drop. She brings the bottle to her lips and drinks until it is almost empty; only a finger-width left.

I wanted to tell you something, she says.

Go on, then, I say.

I've got a new supply in, and the fridge is full, so I'm ready to listen to anything.

I had a dream last night, she says. You were in it.

I nod, smile, fetch another bottle of juice for her from the fridge and a gram of powder for myself.

You were the director of a film, she says. It had just ended. You wanted to show me the film. It was about a woman betrayed by her husband.

That's original, I say, speaking through my nose.

I tip my head back and tap my nostrils.

She was pregnant – in her last month, she says.

Go on, I say.

I walk into the living room to look for a cigarette. Back in the kitchen, she really has gone on talking.

The gynaecologist's chair, she's saying. A doctor is busying himself with a pair of forceps. You say it's your favourite scene.

12

The woman is screaming and writhing in pain from the contractions. Finally, the doctor pulls something out from between her legs and holds it up to her. It's a blown-up photo of a newborn baby, all wrinkled and bloody. There are flies swarming around it.

I remember that she doesn't smoke, so I exhale into her face. It doesn't seem to bother her. She opens the second bottle of orange juice.

What do you think? she says.

It's not important, I say.

It was your stupid film, she says. I couldn't even think up something that sick.

Maybe that's why it's not important, I say.

Anyway, after this dream, I knew the answer to a question that had been bothering me all week, she says.

What? I ask.

I wanted to know why you called, she says. Now I know. It's because you're going to tell me the whole story.

There's a moment of silence. Then I sit up. It's time to hit her again, and this time I'll only stop when she's lying on the floor.

The telephone interrupts me. I'm relieved, actually. She hasn't made the slightest sound of protest. I'm so touched that I can't bring myself to carry on. Apart from that, it's hot – the hottest day of the year so far. While I look for the damn telephone, Clara crawls into the hallway and leans against the wall. I find the phone under the sheets on my mattress. The ringing makes me nervous, so nervous that I answer without thinking who it might be.

Rufus wants to speak to you, the secretary says.

It's the office. Not the branch here in Leipzig, but the head office in Vienna. I collapse onto the mattress. A few seconds to take a deep breath while I'm being put through.

Fuck, I whisper, fuck.

Maaax, says Rufus.

He's American, and I've never dared to stop him from pronouncing my name the way he does. After I celebrated winning my first cases, he sometimes called me Max the Maximal. He's one of the top experts on European and international law; I had worshipped him from the day he first gave a guest lecture at the university. The day after my last oral exam, a woman rang to offer me a job in a matter-of-fact way. To work for Rufus in Vienna. The monthly salary was an amount I could have lived on for half the year. I would have worked for him for board and lodging. He's a genius. And he has no idea what's going on with me.

Rufus, I say.

How are you? he asks.

His American-accented Viennese sounds as cute as ever. Those who don't know him underestimate him.

Fine, I say.

Then I wonder why you're not at work, he says.

All right, I say, I'm not at all fine.

I thought so, he says. I heard something about an accident, but I don't know enough to offer my condolences.

Don't worry about it, I say.

Maaax, he says, you know the firm needs you. I'm calling to remind you that you need the firm.

I can hear from the way his voice is echoing that he's in the conference room. That room is the size of my whole flat: the ceiling is twice as high and the windows reach from top to bottom. The first time I saw it, I thought Rufus had achieved everything in life, and I thought I would too.

I'm sorry, I say, but you're wrong.

No, he says. You know yourself how calming the workings of the law can be, Maaax. Use it for yourself.

Rufus, I say, I'm a cokehead.

The line seems to have gone dead for a minute. Then he roars with laughter.

Maaax, he says. You know that thirty per cent of all hotshot lawyers are junkies. And one hundred per cent of them work in our firm.

It takes a second or two for his joke to sink in. Of course I know how it is. Everyone's stressed. But I didn't know he knew.

I can't come back, I say, I've given up.

What have you given up? he asks.

Trying to do something about the crumbling walls and bridges, I say.

Maaax, he says, have you turned to poetry?

No, I say.

You know, he says, that countless young guns would give anything for your job?

Yes, I say.

You also know, he says, that not many people are asked to come back after nine weeks' absence?

Only people who work for you get asked that, I say.

I picture him in my mind's eye – shorter, more tanned and more leathery than he already is. His office in Vienna is the smallest of all the offices, the only one furnished with antique furniture rather than minimalist Zen-style wooden fittings. I see him in the office, stacking ten thick, red volumes into a pile for him to step on, so that he can reach the early NATO documents from the 1950s. He's phenomenal.

The girl from the radio crawls into the living room doorway. Her cheeks are wet, but nothing else shows. She sits a suitable distance away from me. It's good to look at her.

And, Rufus says, you earn a bundle.

Yes, that too, I say.

Are you sure, asks Rufus, that you're not hankering to be a poet? You never know with Germans.

Quite sure, I say, smiling.

You're asking me to let you go, then?

We both know what this is about. I take a deep breath.

I'm asking you to make me redundant, and to give me a huge pay-off.

You've only been with us for three years, he says.

I don't reply. I know he's struggling with himself. He likes me, but I've gone too far.

We'll continue this in writing, he says in the end. Good luck, Maaax.

Good luck, Rufus, I say. You're—

He's hung up. I drop the telephone and decide to get rid of it, once and for all. I don't need it any longer. I stuff some bedclothes under my neck, and try to find somewhere cool to lay my face.

Well then, the girl from the radio says suddenly in a quiet voice. Now you have lots of time.

3 | Hole

I have kicked her out, but the doorbell rings again ten minutes later.

Before I go, she says, I really would like my scrunchy back.

I'm tired. A cool draught comes in from the stairwell. Her hair is hanging over her face. I point towards the aluminium stand and go into the kitchen. I hear her pushing it aside. It's a long time before she speaks.

Is it normal, she asks, for the floorboards in your flat to be sawn apart?

I peer into the hall. The telephone stand is still pushed away from the wall, and the girl from the radio is kneeling on the floor. She's found her scrunchy, and she's put her hair in a ponytail again. I don't want to go over at first; it's clear that she'll use any excuse to get on my nerves for just a few more minutes.

But then I go over anyway.

We stand next to each other companionably and look into the hole. It's rectangular, with roughly hewn corners, like a schoolchild's woodwork. A few holes have been drilled into one corner; they must have been the starting point for the saw. Beneath the two shorter sides of the rectangle are the narrow strips of cardboard that had supported the sawn-away lid, and a piece of floorboard about forty centimetres long that Clara has lifted away. She must have strong nails. Jessie had strong nails too. I try desperately to remember the last time the telephone stand was moved, but can't think of any occasion. So perhaps the secret compartment has been there since we moved in two years ago. I see Jessie's naivety in it — her belief in the safety of such a badly disguised hiding place. A naivety that was corrupted into guile by chance.

I was sure that I had locked away everything of Jessie's in the two rooms, erased everything without a trace. But here is something that is unbearably typical of her, something that can't be put away. A hole. It hurts so much that I have to turn away. I leave it to the girl from the radio.

I go into the living room and start picking up balled-up tissues and cigarette butts from the floor. Out in the hall, Clara is pulling something out of the hole, making a rustling sound that won't stop. I open the window, throw the tissues and cigarette butts out, and lean on the windowsill so that the sound of the traffic fills my ears. When the tram passes, or a loaded truck rattles past, the windowsill vibrates, and I vibrate with it. For a few moments, I revel in not having to feel my own trembling.

It's a lot hotter outside than it is in the flat. I wet my lips so I can push an unfiltered cigarette between them. I light it and try to take it in my hand, but it sticks to my lower lip. I burn my knuckles on the ash and rip the cigarette away from my lip. A shred of skin hangs from the paper. The smoke scorches my lungs and my eyes are smarting with sweat. Two skimpily dressed thirteen-year-old girls are looking at the carpet of tissue and cigarette butts on the pavement. They look up and see me and I spit. It's hot.

On the other side of the road, the outline of chimneys, bay windows and antennae with scattered lights in between could almost belong to an ocean steamer. Behind it, the sun streams red into the sky. But I'm the one who has the nosebleed. The world is about to lean back and press the cool cloth of night against its neck. I slap myself lightly, right and left. Lit from the inside, the trams wind their way through the rows of buildings. Maybe I even fall asleep for a while, leaning over the windowsill.

In the hallway, I see the girl from the radio crouching on the floor. I thought she'd gone long ago. I see the telephone stand pushed to one side, and the hateful hole in the floor. The girl is stacking banknotes into tidy piles of ten per row. Half the floor in the hall is covered with them. She turns when she hears me.

Just finished, she says. Five hundred thousand schillings, fifty thousand dollars and a hundred and thirty thousand deutschmarks too. What's that altogether?

I feel my eyes filling with tears.

Divide the schillings by seven, I say. You work it out.

Over three hundred thousand deutschmarks, she says. Do you know whose it is?

No idea, I whisper.

It must have belonged to your girlfriend, she says.

Very clever, I say. And now listen to me. I want to be alone. Take the money and go. Enjoy it.

A present? she asks.

Yes, I say.

She stuffs the money back into the plastic bag wordlessly. She puts the floorboard back into place and pushes the stand over it. The door closes behind her.

I go back to the window. This time I sit on the ledge. The moon is rising, pale and round like a giant aspirin.

The traffic wakes me. I must have been listening to it for a long time, half asleep. Adrenalin surges through my empty stomach and my diaphragm flutters. It's my standard reaction to the world outside. The window is open and the curtains are drawn – perhaps sleep overcame me on the windowsill and it's just bad luck that I tumbled backwards onto the mattress in the flat rather than out onto the street. Before I open my eyes, I know that it is light, and a horribly beautiful day. It's hot and children are walking to school. I hear their voices and those of their parents under my window. Cars stream past, on the way to work, off on holiday, or perhaps on the way to the doctor's. In the fifteen minutes I spend listening to the traffic, so many cars pass that I get dizzy. Extended over a whole day, all those cars mean an overwhelming weight of human activity: work, shopping, school. It oppresses me, drains me completely. The hustle and bustle outside seems to be feeding off the destruction of my body and my spirit.

I can't escape the noise from the street by burying my good ear in the pillow with the bad one facing upwards. Even if I closed the window, drew the curtains and piled a mountain of pillows over my head I would still hear cars, footsteps and voices. They'd be muffled of course, but they would have the same effect on my guts and my overloaded brain. I place my arms across my body and, clasping my hands, I pray for a poison attack that will bring everything outside to a standstill, stop all that loud bustle and finally bring me some quiet.

Then the telephone rings. Through half-open eyes, I see the white-blond of my floorboards, the peaks and troughs of the crumpled sheets, dust-balls like tumbleweed on an American highway, scrunched-up tissues held together by dried snot. Then my gaze lights on the telephone. It's out of reach, with the battery compartment gaping wide open. I'm sure it's the girl from the radio and I want to take the call. After five rings, the machine kicks in before I have the chance to reach for the phone and the battery. I can't even stretch my arm out.

The machine is on speakerphone mode, so I'll be able to listen to the call. *Beep.*

Max, a woman's voice says, that's it, I've had it.

It's not Clara. It takes me some time to work out who it is. Maria Huygstetten appears in my mind's eye, sitting at her desk just as I used to see her in the office when my door was open: pale porcelain face, reddish hair piled high, turned towards the light from the window. Sometimes, staring into space, I imagined a fat brown turd pushing its way out of her face through her perfect pink mouth.

She's speaking with that pink mouth into my machine.

Rufus rang to say you won't be coming in any longer, she says.

She was always unfailingly formal with me in the office. I've spent maybe ten nights with her, no more. Ten nights in two years, and those were the times when I just couldn't hold out any longer. Afterwards, I was racked with guilt every time, with a physical pain. Maria very reasonably pointed out that what I was doing was perfectly normal, but she was wrong. I only needed to listen to Jessie for ten seconds, her face anguished as she worked herself up to assure me that it wouldn't be long now before she could do it, not long now, very soon; I wasn't to hold it against her. Then I put my hand over her mouth and forced her to shut up, and I knew that Maria was lying – I was evil. Maria was the only one who knew about Jessie, and I was always a little afraid that she would call her, for whatever reason, and tell her that I hadn't been working in the office those ten nights.

Of course I know why she's calling. States of mind can be suppressed, but not Jacques Chirac.

Listen, says Maria Huygstetten. I know that we're not going to have anything more to do with each other. No worries. But you have to come and get the dog.

If I'd thought of the dog at all, I'd probably hoped secretly that Maria would get used to him and want to keep him. Of course I love Jacques Chirac, but he's Jessie's dog, and he should be dead too. I think of how he used to lean over us in the morning, teetering on his long legs, and how his hanging jowls gave his face an aggrieved, despairing look. I think of how Jessie had laughed over his expression – not really an expression at all, but a function of anatomy. She took his big head in both hands and shook him, and I leaned on an elbow and watched them. Jacques Chirac rejoiced to find us alive and awake every morning. He must have thought of our sleep as a temporary death, one that he was never sure would really end at daybreak. But now I can't bear having him around. I know he thinks that Jessie might come back. I can't stand the hopeful way he lies in front of the boarded-up door to the study and the way he pricks up his ears when the alarm clock inside starts beeping. Jacques Chirac is waiting.

I crawl over to my jacket, dragging the blanket with me. I find the coke and take it, lots of it, and fast. Then I lie back in bed and wait. But nothing happens. Practically nothing, anyway. Just a rising panic. There are times when it just doesn't kick in, when you have to take a break for three or four days at least. What lies ahead is clear.

I slide into my suit trousers, which stick to my thighs, put on sunglasses and leave the flat. It's an odyssey. Despite everything, I look forward to seeing Jacques Chirac. Thinking of him helps me cope with the roaring noise and the stares of the people on the street. It helps me through paying for my tram ticket and finding the right station on the map. I couldn't feel more alien if I were on the planet for the first time.

Jacques Chirac storms past Maria as soon as the door opens and jumps on me. He paws my chest and licks my face. I can't hold my balance with his weight on me, so I kneel in front of him. Standing up again, I hold on to his back and realize how thin he's grown, skin stretched over bone. I'm sure Maria has done her best for him.

I continue leaning on his back; he's stronger than me even in this state. A wave of weakness washes over me. I'm short of breath and I lean over, gasping. When Maria touches me, I shake my head. I can see what I look like in her eyes. She starts speaking, quickly and quietly, says something about me staying, that she can protect me. I don't take my sunglasses off, nor do I thank her. Before she can kiss me, I'm gone.

In the evening, I realize how good it is to have Jacques Chirac with me again. I stop him from lying in front of the study door. He won't have anything to eat, but I feel that he's happy to be with me. He lies on his side panting, stretching and contracting like a pair of bellows, drooling puddles. I wish I could do something about the heat for his sake, but I can't. There's no relief for either of us, so we go for a walk. He doesn't enjoy it, doesn't run ahead happily, doesn't want to play. But it distracts him, and me too. It helps me to pass the time until the coke kicks in again. We go for a walk every time this happens, just before I'm about to lose it completely. Back in the flat, I stand in front of the telephone stand for a moment. There's absolutely nothing remarkable about it. I don't think it's ever been moved. I don't believe the girl from the radio was ever here either. In my mind, I've been living like this for weeks: a short walk with Jacques Chirac, then lying down and trying to sleep until the sound of his panting gets me up again. Now and then the alarm clock goes off behind the closed doors, and I holler something.

Then we go for another walk.

4 | Moths

The Shell station casts a reddish-yellow light on the hollow. I lean over the ornate railing of a small bridge. Heating pipes lie like two fat snakes beneath me, bedded in weeds and undergrowth. They go towards the town centre: pale grey, writhing in great loops, some like gateways a man could walk through, some lying sideways in the grass. Jessie always used to ask me why the pipes were formed that way. I would mumble something about allowances for heat expansion. Who knows? Perhaps they just loop and curl the way they do for effect.

The plastic cooler bag I'm holding in my left hand is silver, decorated with blue snowflakes. It contains an ice-cream bar wrapped in gold foil. I bought it at the petrol station on a whim, even though I didn't want it. I'll look like a fool if I bring it to Clara. It would be completely inappropriate unless I wanted friendship, a fuck or a business deal from her. I don't care if she gets the ice cream or not. But the thought of eating it repulses me, and I just can't throw food away. Clara is the only person in the city I can bring an ice cream to late at night. On Wednesdays and Sundays, anyway. I get moving. Jacques Chirac follows me, teetering on his long legs. He gets livelier and trots ahead of me when we leave the orange glow of the street lights and enter the park. The ancient trees tower over us, looking in their blackness like the legs of a herd of elephants whose bellies are the night sky. I hear crickets chirping and the murmur of students lying in the grass with their bottles of wine.

It's warm. I'll be arriving at the radio station with a handful of white slush.

Nightfall always brings relief. The traffic ebbs, the streets are clear and I can wander aimlessly. It's not as if anybody else has anything better to do; they're at home watching TV. I see the bluish reflections of the screens against the windows and on the ceilings of the flats. From the colours and the frequency of the changing images, I can guess if they're watching the news, an action film or a documentary. At times like these, I don't mind the presence of others at all – their existence is as pointless as my own. As far as I'm concerned, daybreak need never come. The Earth could leave its orbit and fly into the eternal night of the universe, surrounded by the stars. Perhaps we'll take the Moon with us, a fingernail crescent hanging pale and slender in the sky. I'm feeling better. Perhaps because it's Wednesday. Wednesdays and Saturdays are the only days I'm aware of. Like a birthmark on a face, there's something that sets them apart from the other days of the week: Clara's programme. Perhaps the biochemical balance in my brain is improving . . . perhaps I can start coking up again soon.

Swarms of moths have found their way into the street lights. They are dying a slow death, clustered thick and black against the glass. A marten crosses my path like a salami on legs and disappears between the parked cars. I swing my plastic bag. On a night like this, I would have come home to find Jessie at the kitchen table by the window, her legs wrapped around the legs of the chair, her finger tracing the lines of a letter from Austria. There was never a return address on those letters; I sometimes found their ashes in the sink. But I would never have thought of trying to read one of them. I was sure that they were from her brother Ross and that she never replied to them.

I would have suggested going for a walk and she would have sprung from her seat immediately, face glowing, framed by an untidy yellow hairband that made her look like a little sun. She would have gone to put on her shoes and got Jacques Chirac up on the way with a nudge in the ribs. Out in the street, in the mild air and orange glow of the dusty city, she would have taken my hand and played with it, closing her fist around my middle and ring fingers, shaking off any other grip. We would have walked hand in hand. When we came to a petrol station she would have begged for an ice cream and I would have bought one for her. I feel it in the plastic bag. It's still solid.

Jessie used to practise eating an ice cream as slowly as she possibly could. She never bit a chunk off, just licked. It drove me mad. I couldn't bear to watch. It was ridiculous to lick an ice cream that had a chocolate shell. At some point the vanilla ice cream would dribble down the stick and large, smooth pieces of chocolate would break off and fall to the ground. When Jessie was finally finished with it, her whole face was sticky, not to mention her hands. Dust, pollen particles floating through the air and sometimes an insect would stick to her skin. She was happy then, or at least she looked it to me.

I stop and grab at my throat. For a moment, I can't breathe. I know this feeling, a stabbing pain just above the larynx, then an overwhelming urge to cough, but no breath to cough with. I force myself to stay calm and try to relax my throat muscles. It works. Then I lean over with my hands on my knees and cough fit to burst. I feel as if my lungs are being shaken out like socks that have got twisted in the wash. Jacques Chirac watches, unmoved. I reach for a cigarette in my back pocket and light it. The burn of the smoke on the tender surfaces of my lungs does me good. It jolts me back into the present, away from ice cream and happiness. Tonight, I have to get rid of an ice cream bought in a moment of stupidity. I have to stop walking aimlessly if I want to find Clara's radio station.

I try to turn my thoughts to Clara: she must be the type of girl who prepares her own breakfast muesli the night before, who goes to techno parties at ten on Sunday mornings, who doesn't add softener when there are jeans in the wash. But I can hardly remember her face. I've spent days sweating and moaning at home, listening to the sound of the traffic. Every hour seemed like a week.

I climb down the embankment to the railway tracks. There's a footpath cutting through hip-high dry yellow grass. Hemlock sways overhead. There must be at least ten different tracks here, most of them overgrown. Next to them, yellow and blue refuse sacks lie decaying in the bushes. The smell of rotting meat overpowers me. Jacques Chirac and I walk close together. I quicken my pace under two of the heating pipes, afraid they will collapse and squash me to a pulp. When the confusion of undergrowth ends to form two clear tracks, I climb back up onto the street.

The big square in front of the radio station is empty apart from two parked cars. One of them is conspicuously green, like a plastic frog; definitely not a standard factory colour. At the other end of the square I see a porter sitting behind glass in a lit entryway. As I approach the green car, a decrepit Opel Ascona, I notice even from some distance away that the number plate isn't just black and white – there's red on it, too. I don't want to believe it. I get closer and lean down to look at the sticker. I was right. The car is registered in Vienna. And why not? But it unsettles me, and then my disquiet begins to turn to rage – an inexplicable, unreasonable rage.

The porter looks at me suspiciously. It's two am, and I don't really expect to get to see her. I say my name through the glass, then hers. He gets on the telephone and the door hums open. He even smiles at Jacques Chirac as we go through. He opens his cabin door and calls out 'Second floor' after us.

I look at myself in the mirror in the lift. I don't have a very healthy colour, even without the neon lighting.

The doors open and an electronic female voice announces the second floor.

When the lift doors close behind me, it's dark and completely silent. I stand still, holding Jacques Chirac by the collar, waiting for my eyes to adjust so that I can somehow get my bearings. I finally see a glimmer of light to the left, and walk towards it. I enter a room and walk right into something: a console. I make out another open door, through which greenish light is falling. It's from a computer monitor. Clara is sitting in front of it with her back to me, a dark silhouette. A window is open. Moths, flies and bugs of all sizes crawl over the computer screen like punctuation marks that have come to life. I lean against the door frame.

Hey, she says.

She doesn't turn around. There's really nothing to say. I light a cigarette. Apart from her tapping on the keyboard, all is quiet. She types quickly, like a secretary. I don't bother to try to read what she's writing. It's enough to see the line of text extending: a worm expanding, stopping and starting again from the far left-hand side half a centimetre below, growing from a single letter, a tiny black egg. It's hypnotic.

The room is small and crammed with equipment that I don't recognize. Everything, including Clara's back and my body, looks unreal in the light of the screen. The glowing tip of my cigarette seems to be the only natural thing in the room. I don't know this girl. She was only in my flat twice. Jacques Chirac has stayed in the doorway and he's breathing more quietly than usual. I rustle the silver cooler bag.

I've brought you something, I say.

I'm out of breath before I finish the short sentence. It sounds even more stupid than I thought it would.

What is it? she says.

Beads of sweat form on my forehead. Just being in this room requires three times more energy than usual. I look into the bag.

An ice cream, I say.

That sounds not only stupid, but desperate. Perhaps this is it for me, really it. I take two steps forward and shake the ice cream out of the bag onto the desk next to her. She doesn't turn, but she does stop typing; the worm freezes in the middle of the screen. Her hands pause expectantly over the keyboard like a spider awaiting its prey.

The only thing I want from you, she says quietly, is your story. I'm not interested in anything else.

We are both stock-still for a few seconds. The bugs on the computer screen crawl on undisturbed. If only she would move, turn around, show me her face; if her voice had even a flicker of warmth in it, I could cope. I could laugh then, or shout, I could make her pay for the bugs, the green car, the traffic, the screaming children and the bad lighting in the lift. All I need is the tiniest of signs. But she stays still, completely motionless. She doesn't turn around. She doesn't even breathe.

Making a strangling noise in my throat, I grab the ice cream – it's all soft, and it belongs to Jessie anyway – and charge out of the room. I drag the dog along by his collar. He resists at first, sliding over the hard floor, but then he trots along beside me, paws clicking. We lose ourselves in the dark corridors. The small reddish light of the lift is nowhere to be seen, but we find a green light over the door to the stairs. I don't think Clara even noticed Jacques Chirac.

In the courtyard outside, I hurl the Magnum to the ground and grind it into the dust under my heel. It feels like slush. The foil bursts and vanilla ice cream spurts out all over my shoe and even onto my sock. I feel the stickiness seeping through to my ankle. In Vienna, when I was sometimes at my wit's end at work, I used to close my office door and pretend to be a statue: one foot pointing forward, right hand raised slightly with a copy of the most important international laws of Sartorius II lying open in it. Without looking down, I could see the bronze lettering on my pedestal: Max the Maximal. I knew I was being ridiculous. But it helped.

Clara could be watching me from an open window. There's no reason to break into a run. But I can't stop myself. I get to the street, force myself to slow down to a walk, then start running again after a few yards. The clock at the crossroads says that it's after three. It'll be three-thirty by the time I get home. The first birds will be twittering when I throw myself down on the mattress and I won't get any sleep. It'll get hotter and the traffic will start again, I'll toss and turn and beat myself about the head and then it won't be Wednesday any longer, it'll be Thursday or something else, a Tuesday past or the coming Friday or some other day – any day in my life.

There's a strip of paleness showing on the horizon over the rooftops, but it's completely dark in the hall of my flat, making the red blink of the phone message on my machine especially conspicuous.

Thursday, 12:32, it announces.

How pedantic these machines are. 12:32 for me was still Wednesday. It's a man's voice, one I don't recognize. But the accent is clear enough. Viennese.

When he's finished, the answerphone beeps and I yank the cord out of the socket. Without switching on the lights, I go into the living room, grab a few clothes and stuff them into a plastic bag lying on the floor. Then I shove Jacques Chirac out of the flat in front of me. I double-lock the door and run down the stairs. It's over.

5 | Piglet

Having a hot shower when the weather's warm is pure masochism. I start sweating and red blotches appear on my thighs. I'm dizzy. The air between the tiled walls is thick with steam and the visibility through the glass of the cubicle is poor. I feel as if I'm in an aeroplane breaking through a cloud bank.

This isn't my bathroom. I squirt generous amounts of shower gel out of a red plastic bottle without a label. It's got a masculine smell. Toiletries are arranged in a veritable skyline above the bathtub but none of the bottles are labelled. I'd opened a few to sniff the contents. It's all women's stuff, with edible odours: vanilla, peach, apple, coconut, kiwi fruit, strawberry.

I wonder if the men's shower gel that I'm using belongs to a steady boyfriend. I picture them sitting on the edge of the bathtub in the evenings, scratching the labels off shampoo bottles with their fingernails.

Rooting about in my nose, I get hold of a piece of snot that trails a long strand of mucus; it's blood red in places. It washes off my finger and whirls down the drain. She can't have a steady boyfriend. He would have come and beat me up long ago. Unless he was the intellectual sort, that is, but that wouldn't be her type. She either uses the men's shower gel herself or has bought it specially for me. I turn the hot water up. My insides feel like they're pressing against my skin, everything's streaming out of me towards the numbing pain of the hot water, which wraps around me like a bodysuit. For a moment, I'm glad that I'm even able to remember whose bathroom I'm in, and I look forward to finishing off with a cold shower. She probably gave me a drink, but I can't remember. At least I can be sure that I haven't slept with her, since I haven't been able to get it up for weeks, that much is certain.

The mirror is all steamed up: the tiles, the sink, the toilet and all the plastic surfaces too. The toilet roll is beginning to curl. It's all fucking amazing.

Then I remember the dog. I can't think where I saw him last, where I left him. I freeze for a moment and water trickles into my mouth. I spit it out, scramble out of the shower and throw the door open. A huge cloud of steam billows out. I look into the hall, conscious of it this time. It's laid with pale carpet. This must be an Ikea-flat financed by the parents. Four doors of white veneer, all closed.

CLARA!!! I shout.

One of the doors opens. Clara sticks her head out and there's Jacques Chirac, drool dangling from his left jowl.

I dry myself but get clammy all over again with sweat and steam. I can't put on the same boxers, so I slip straight into my trousers. A few pubes get stuck in the zip. The shirt sticks stubbornly to my arms and back; I do it up wrongly twice and swear.

Where'd you get the beast from anyway? asks Clara.

I start at the sound of her voice right behind me, barely muffled by the door.

I'll use your toothbrush, I say.

Why's he called Jacques Chirac? she asks.

Jessie named him, I mumble.

I bite my tongue. There's complete silence on the other side of the door – and then the crowing starts.

Hah! she calls. Now I know her na-ame, her na-ame, now I know her na-ame.

I can't step out of the bathroom with the toothbrush in my foamy mouth.

You could have asked me, you know, I say weakly.

And you'd have given me one again, she says.

Quite right, I say.

Why is Jacques Chirac so big? she asks.

Probably because he wanted to grow and grow, I say, until he could look Jessie straight in the face. He loved looking at her.

I rinse my mouth and run my fingers through my hair. With one of her lipsticks I write on the mirror: *Objects in the mirror appear further away than they are.* The door opens and the dog pushes his way in to paw at me playfully. Clara squishes her face through the opening. I smell coffee. Right now, I need coffee more than anything.

Hey, I say, have you made coffee?

Of course, she says, come into the kitchen.

The flat is small and we cross the hall in three steps. The carpet doesn't feel so bad under bare feet. Everything is extremely clean and the ceiling is too low. White kitchen, a stove with a ceramic top. There are two mugs of coffee and a DAT-recorder on the table.

So, I ask, who are you thinking of interviewing?

She looks at me with raised eyebrows.

Don't you remember what you promised this morning?

I run to the bathroom and find a bottle of aspirin in the cupboard. I empty half of it out. Then I walk over to the kitchen window. Above the rooftops, I see a hazy strip of light on the horizon, nowhere near turning pink. I look at the shadows cast on the pavement by the street lights – how they spin around their centre when disturbed by the headlights of passing cars.

You insisted on moving in, says Clara, so we struck a deal.

I press a hand to my right ear so I only hear the whistling of the left; the whistling and the silence in my head.

Did I tell you, I ask, why I wanted to move in with you?

She shakes her head. Maybe she's lying. There's an empty vodka bottle on the floor. I'm sure I must have drunk it all. The mug warms my cold hands. Clara tosses me a cigarette. She seems to have decided to mother me.

There was a message on my machine last night, I say, telling me that it was high time I sent the number, and over three hundred thousand marks with it.

How exciting, says Clara.

Plus the funeral costs, I say.

Your own? she asks.

I wish, I say.

She thinks for a moment, then she gets it.

You didn't bury Jessie yourself? she asks.

I slipped away, I say, until everything was over. Her father probably arranged for her to be collected. And taken to Vienna, maybe.

He lives there? she asks.

He had a house there fourteen years ago, anyway, I say.

And now? she asks.

How would I know? I hiss. I've only met him once.

But, asks Clara, what kind of number?

I DON'T KNOW, I say.

What else did they say? Clara asks.

That they're going to report me for murder if I don't cooperate.

Why? asks Clara. Did the police suspect you of murdering Jessie?

I wasn't asked anything implying that, I say.

That's strange too, she says. That kind of thing is routine.

I turn and grab her by the collar.

Look, I hiss. I only have a matter of weeks, three months maybe. And I want to be left alone in that time, for whatever reason, do you understand? I want to die in peace.

She looks at me disbelievingly.

You don't seriously think, she says, that you're going to snuff it from a few hits, do you?

I shake her.

That's *my* problem!

All right, she says, that's great. You're dying and you can tell me everything in that time. It's not as if you have anything better to do.

I look at the tape recorder. From this distance, it looks like the dictaphone Maria Huygstetten used to work with. She worked it with a foot pedal, like a sewing machine, and when I stood behind her, I could hear my distorted voice squawking into her ear. I think about my airy living room. Perhaps it would be better to lie there, looking at the stucco detail trailing across the ceiling and down the walls, turning its leaves towards the window during the day.

I have to go now, I say.

Nonsense, she says. And if you're worried about your coke, there's a whole bagful in one of the jackets you brought with you.

I put my mug down and rub my hands over my face.

I hope you don't bring the police here, she says snidely.

Lovely, I say, leaving the room.

I'm no desperado like Mr Barrister here! she calls after me.

I have no idea how she found that out. Perhaps she asked around, but obviously not thoroughly enough. Not every lawyer is a barrister.

The hall is empty: no coat rack, no shoes, no telephone, just closed white veneer doors, a lot for such a small flat. Kitchen, bathroom, living room and front door, I guess.

And where are my jackets? I shout.

She walks past me, smiling. She opens the door that I thought led out of the flat. It's the bedroom. About twelve metres square: a single bed of light-coloured wood, a matching wardrobe, a sunny-yellow cotton blind. Yellow and white stripy sheets.

Jessie's favourite colour had been exactly this shade of yellow. I groan.

Headache? she asks.

No, Ikea, I say. This must be just like the room you had at home as a girl.

Go ahead and imagine whatever you want, she says.

She holds my plastic bag upside down by the corners and shakes the contents onto the carpet: three crumpled suit jackets and no trousers, underwear or socks to change into. I could hardly have packed less sensibly. She picks out the packet of charlie at first go.

Well done, I say.

She takes it into the kitchen and puts it next to the DAT-recorder.

I have to go out for a couple of hours, she says. Have fun in the meantime.

She wipes the sideboard with a damp cloth. I'm not sure if it's getting dark or light outside.

Is it morning or evening? I ask.

She gives me a contemptuous look, tugs at her tight jeans and tosses her hair back.

Bye, she says.

When she's gone, I snort my first line in at least five days off the kitchen table. Fireworks go off in my head; the chemical reconstruction of my personality is beginning. I look around happily. Everything in the room is in exactly the right place, proving that all is right in the world. It's a world in which I have my place, in which everything has its place – even Jessie's death and a pain in the neck like Clara. A world in which everything can be explained, as long as one is intelligent enough to understand it all. As I am.

I'm going to pull myself together and get the hell out of here. Maybe go off to Guatemala. I stand up and sweep the mugs off the table, and coffee splashes onto the floor. Effortlessly, without losing momentum, I grab my jackets off the bedroom floor and open the front door. Nope, bathroom. Then I remember which door it is. I try the handle three times. I can't believe it. She's locked me in.

Back in the living room, the first thing I notice is a shelving unit at least two metres wide, completely filled with records and CDs. I don't know how many there are, but they must weigh a tonne. Perhaps being petit bourgeois isn't the only reason Clara lives in a brand-new flat. I once read about a DJ who lived in a converted flat in an old building. His record collection crashed through the floor, taking him with it. I pull a few records out at random. They all have Post-Its with a date and the number of beats per minute: 70, 45, 210.

Something is unsettling me, something in the corner of my eye. It's a newspaper lying open on the desk. Before I can turn away, I recognize the man in the photograph from several feet away.

I drop the records and go over.

'Marc Bell, British correspondent for the Balkans, meets Zeljiko Raznatovic in London. The Serbian folk hero denies the existence of the paramilitary group known as the "Tigers".'

Raznatovic is Arkan. Also known as 'The Cleanser'. It's a good photo. He looks healthy and happy, a broad smile on his porcine face. I know how he loves media attention, especially in the West – the enemy camp. I find it immeasurably irritating that there's space for a large photo of the grinning madman, but not enough for a detailed report. I'd be able to pick Arkan out even in a crowd. I had found pictures of him in the investigative file at the International Tribunal in the Hague, and pored over his features as if I was deciphering symbols from a foreign language. I was probably looking for an answer.

In any case, the newspaper has to go. Off the top of my head, I can't think of anyone I hate more than Arkan. Not even myself.

I grab the paper and even though I don't plan to clean up I take it into the kitchen and wipe up the spilt coffee with it. While I'm doing that, I wonder if it's pure coincidence that it was lying open at that page on Clara's desk. When the paper is soaked through, I toss it into the bin, wash my hands and return to the living room.

I sit on the floor between the glass coffee table and the blue sofa, and set up the DAT-machine close to my face. Jacques Chirac is lying next to me. He thumps his long thin tail twice against the floor and spreads himself out so I can scratch his belly.

I turn the recorder around in my hands a few times before I realize how it works. There's a new tape in it, and Clara has even laid out two more, still in their packaging, next to it. I find a note under the machine with a single sentence written in the same scrawly handwriting as on the records: 'The first time I saw her.'

I press the button to record.

Saw, saw, I burble, saw.

As if the word was something special. But it's not. It's nonsense, a completely ridiculous word, meaningless really, more a sound than anything. I can't think of anything, so I press 'Stop' and rewind the tape.

Saw, saw, burbles the recorder, saw.

It sounds awful, like a baby trying its first words: saw-saw-saw. Of course I know how my voice sounds on tape, I used to hear it every day in the office after I'd dictated notes. But it's still a shock every time, taking in this disembodied voice. It's sluggish and inarticulate, with an undertone of aggression. I rewind the tape again. I instinctively avoid people who sound like this. They are unpolished, devoid of all style, uneducated and dangerous. I press 'Record'.

The first time I saw her, I say.

6 | On Birds Flying South

She was perched on a desk, one of those much too small, battered children's writing desks we had in boarding school.

What does that have to do with it? What does anything have to do with anything anyway? I let the tape run while I light a cigarette.

The desk Jessie was sitting on was Shershah's. She was wearing a long faded green cotton skirt and no shoes. Her hair was short and blonde, sticking out in all directions. It reminded me of sunbeams when I first saw her. Her posture was so bad you immediately wanted to shout 'Sit up straight!' at her.

I like that. 'Sit up straight' encompasses everything. It suited Jessie from the very beginning, right up to her twenty-eighth year, her last. I smile and tip glowing ash onto Clara's carpet, singeing it. There's a smell of burnt plastic.

She must have been thirteen. It was one of the first few weeks of term, and we were all new. Shershah was there because he didn't want to follow his Iranian diplomat father around the world any longer. I was there because I didn't want to be packed off to a home for people with eating disorders by my mother; it was almost all girls there. Where Jessie came from, and what she didn't want, I didn't know. She looked a bit lost. We all looked a bit lost, like birds flying south who'd missed a connection and had lost all sense of direction.

Jessie was sitting on the desk, smoking. Next to her was a pile of roll-ups. She wasn't able to roll her own yet, so they were from Shershah. He introduced us.

Jessie, he said, Max.

He hadn't told me anything about her before. I had no idea how he had got to know her. She wasn't in our class and she was five years younger than I was.

Which house are you in? I asked.

Shershah answered for her.

Morningside, he said.

This is Dusklands, I said, unnecessarily.

Shershah put his hand on my forehead.

Max, he said, is my personal philosopher.

Jessie was tiny, that was what jumped out at you. The halo of hair made her face seem bigger, but her hands and feet were like a child's. She'd propped her feet against the back of Shershah's chair and the layer of dirt on her tiny soles was a few millimetres thick. She never grew much bigger than that, perhaps because she had started smoking at ten. Her eyes were adult, hard. Staring at me fixedly, they didn't seem to be part of her at all. I felt uncomfortable under her gaze.

Do you always go barefoot? I asked.

She didn't reply.

At least since I've known her, said Shershah.

Shershah amazed me. We had been living in the same room for a couple of weeks, had sat in the same classroom and eaten at the same table. He'd never displayed enough consideration for his fellow students even to pass the salt when asked, let alone answer a question for someone else. Since I'd known him, he'd already had three girls in and out of his bed. It wasn't like those girls were shrinking violets, God no, but he'd never even thought to ask them their names. There was just one striking thing about Shershah – a problem, even. He was beautiful.

When I need to pee, I hurry, barely waiting for the last drops to fall before I return to the recorder. I consider rewinding and listening to what I've said. But then I remember something else.

One night soon after I met Jessie, I began to understand what her attraction for Shershah was about. Long after curfew time she walked into our room without knocking, though she couldn't have known that neither of us was jerking off or leaping around naked playing air guitar to The Doors. She probably wouldn't have taken much notice anyway. I'd just had a joint, so I was lying in bed contentedly, reading. Shershah was sitting at his desk, painting a cardboard box with watercolours. He was taking care to get as much paint as possible on his hands and clothes so that tomorrow everyone would know he'd been painting. Jessie stood a little way into the room.

Knock, knock. Want some? she said.

We looked up.

I'll only ask once, said Jessie. There're loads of other rooms here. Do you want some or not?

Some what? I asked.

How much? asked Shershah in the same breath.

A hundred and fifty marks, Jessie said.

It was only then that I realized this wasn't about hash.

No, thanks, I said.

No dosh, said Shershah.

Jessie shrugged and left. She couldn't simply have walked in through the main entrance of Dusklands after ten. It would definitely have been locked. Later I found out that she climbed up the balustrade, took the top off the ventilation shaft and crawled in that way. None of the housemasters would have dreamt that any one of us could have passed through the shaft. There were ventilation shafts like that in every house, so Jessie was the only one who could move freely. She did it once a week, making her rounds conscientiously, selling coke to everyone who could afford it.

I'm beginning to be lulled by the sound of my own voice. I close my eyes, lean very close to the microphone and speak quietly, almost in a whisper.

But most of them could afford it, apart from Shershah and me. All my mother had was me and an S-class Daimler whose running costs used up the money from my father, which was meant for the school fees. The car made it easier for me, though. Whenever my mother came to visit, she drove the silver car right up to the building, and everyone saw me getting into it. That was important. The others wouldn't have known how to treat me otherwise.

Shershah's father was an ambassador in Ethiopia, and had broken off all contact with his son. He thought of Shershah as a curse, was ashamed of having fathered him and never sent any money. But Shershah didn't want for anything. He wore the same pair of greasy black jeans all the time, tight enough to show his cock and his leg muscles. He had shoes that he exchanged once a year, and he wore T-shirts or sweatshirts that he scrounged from the others' rooms. All his books and tapes were borrowed, and were never returned. Shershah's not having any money didn't bother anyone. His father had given him something more important: thick black hair and exotic features that blended perfectly with the genetic inheritance from his gentle, polished French mother. He didn't need anything else.

I open my eyes to find Clara sitting cross-legged opposite me, her hair hanging loosely around her. She looks like a ghost. I scream, try to get up and bash myself against the sharp corner of the glass table.

Relax, says Clara, calm down.

Her voice sounds as if she's speaking to livestock, an ox that is refusing to get into a truck. It soothes me. She's grinning from ear to ear and she looks happy. I don't know how long she's been sitting there, though it's probably quite late. It's dark outside.

Go on speaking, she says. Please.

I rewind the tape a little, to see where I left off. The sound of my own voice almost makes me sick. There's something unbearably corporeal about the way I speak. The slightest click of the tongue leaving the palate can be heard; the grinding of molars and the friction of dry lips parting. It sounds like I'm eating language. Clara puts her hand out and presses 'Record'.

Then we went to Holland together quite often, I continue.

No idea what I'm trying to say. I close my eyes and fumble for a cigarette. Clara hasn't said anything about the holes in her carpet. I inhale deeply, close to the microphone. There'll be a loud rushing sound on tape.

You mean, says Clara expressionlessly, you wouldn't have had much to do with each other otherwise.

Yes, I say, Jessie was Shershah's girlfriend, not mine. I liked other girls, tall, clean-cut types who transferred from the convent when they got sick of the nuns in their black and white sacks. I worshipped those girls from a distance of anything from five to five hundred yards. I was fat, and some of my pimples were as large as small grapes.

Jessie stuck to Shershah like a burr. Every minute he allowed it, she spent with him. And that was surprisingly often for him, though I don't think he ever laid a finger on her. She'd certainly have let him; she'd have let him do anything. It was strange to watch them. It was as if something had clicked contentedly into place in her head from the very first day. Whenever I saw them together, her metallic stare made me think of a machine gun with the safety catch off, constantly trained on Shershah. She barely spoke, just followed his every movement with her eyes. Coldly. She didn't react to the way he tugged at his bottom lip and leaned his head sideways, nor to the way his hair fell in his face, moving slightly with his quick, short breaths. The way he sat, legs spread wide, thigh muscles showing, didn't affect her. She just stared at him. Her gaze was welded to his face.

Out of consideration to Clara, I stub my cigarette out on the coffee table, not on the floor. Now that my eyes are open, I see the way she's looking at me: her eyes are fixed on my face. She's still smiling.

One night I thought it had finally happened. The smell woke me. The fishy smell of sex and wax. Forcing myself to continue breathing evenly, I blinked a couple of times and turned my head so that I could see Shershah's bed on the other side of the room. I imagined I had heard Jessie's voice, and was surprised at how the thought filled me with aversion. I didn't want him to sleep with her. It seemed completely perverse, much worse than the other things he did. There were quite a few Iranians at the school; we called them the Perverse Persians.

Oh! a girl's voice called. A bit more! A bit more!

It wasn't Jessie's voice, and I relaxed. The voice was high and false, so it wasn't one of the convent girls either. There was a certain type of girl at our school, pulled from turning tricks in Düsseldorf and packed off to boarding school. They were bored.

The girl began to moan affectedly. Shershah pulled the duvet back and positioned himself so that I could see his hand between her legs. She started saying fuck me, fuck me, deeper, faster, more, and so on. It was ridiculous, but I got a hard-on anyway and came even before they'd finished. Shershah threw her out.

How was it for you? he asked, smiling.

We shared a joint and he told me about Bakunin, and his radical left-wing friends. I fell asleep while he was still talking.

I've grown nauseous without realizing it. Now I have to throw up, and I know it's because I've been looking Clara in the face while talking.

Come on, let me help you, she says.

She comes round the coffee table and helps me into the bathroom. I heave all over her bathtub. It'll be hard work getting it clean again.

7 | Yellow–Red–Blue

The table is too high for me to rest my legs on comfortably. Nothing worse than a failed attempt at casualness. I ignore this, and the fact that my trouser legs slip back to display strips of pale, almost white skin with scattered black hairs. As I pull at the elastic of a sock with my index finger, the skin below begins to itch unbearably. The imprint of the sock feels like the grooved pattern on the edge of my desk. It's an antique desk, with a leather surface in the middle, bright green and rectangular like a tennis lawn, fastened by brass rivets round the edges. I've run my fingers over the ones in front so often that they shine. I've fingered the grooves often, too; I don't know if they ever made me think of the marks socks left on skin.

The more I scratch, the worse it gets. My desk is in the study. I haven't set eyes on it for over two months. Right now, I miss it. It's the right height, unlike this table, which is too high, too smooth and covered with an ugly grey patterned linoleum.

I lift my other hand to scratch my other leg, and just manage to resist the temptation to close my eyes and groan. The sound guy stares at me.

Does he have a problem or what? he asks.

I can't make out his accent. I'd passed the row of parked cars in the square before I entered the radio station. The bright green car was there.

Quiet now, soundcheck, he says, just as I'm about to reply.

He puts his finger on his lips and turns to the console. I stop scratching and lean back more comfortably, tilting the chair on its rear legs. When I light a cigarette, he makes a face and starts gesticulating wildly. 'No smoking', he mouths. I exhale in his direction a couple of times, flick the ash against my thigh and rub it into my trousers. Then I stub the cigarette out and toss it towards him. He catches it before it can land amongst the console knobs.

It looks like a bird's nest is resting on his head, but I suppose it's just his hair. His jaw is lined with a sparse, trimmed beard ending in a long pointy wisp under his chin. It bristles and slants forward every time he speaks, making his face look unnaturally long and goatlike. His nose is pierced with a silver stud on either side.

I get the feeling that I've seen him before. I look at the thick, gleaming chain leading from the heavy wallet in the back pocket of his baggy trousers to his belt and suddenly remember the two guys that our IT company used to send over whenever we had problems with the Intranet in the office. They carried wallets in their baggy trousers like that too, and wore short black T-shirts emblazoned with heavy-metal symbols. When they sat down, the cracks of their behinds showed above their trousers. They slammed their CD Walkmans down next to our computers and put on headphones as big as earmuffs while they tapped away at the keyboards. They only took them off to shout the odd comment about the music to each other. The screens took on an unusually dark colour and letters and numbers scrolled over them, to which they paid little notice. They hunched in their seats and didn't drink the coffee that Rufus had specifically instructed should be made for them. After three-quarters of an hour, the computers would be running more quickly than before the crash, without a single letter begun by a secretary having been lost, let alone any data. These guys could probably have accessed our entire databank by crooking their little fingers. It was pure luck that they weren't in the least interested. When I asked Rufus about it once, he laughed and said that the best form of security nowadays was not to set the hackers a challenge by having too good a system. Most of them, he said, were artists. They weren't interested in money, only in honour. I didn't know if he was right.

This goaty fellow here could be a computer genius too. The thought of it makes my skin crawl. He looks up from the console from time to time and grins at me as if he knows something I don't.

Clara is sitting behind the glass partition and leafing through some papers as the hands of the clock above her creep towards midnight. The lights on the switchboard in the room next door have been blinking with incoming calls for the last half-hour. Two men and one woman are taking the calls. The microphones at the ends of their headsets look like fat black leeches that have fastened themselves to the corners of their mouths, fitting snugly. Clara has a headset on too, slung around her neck. She hasn't introduced me to anybody. She's acting as if I'm not here at all. I like that. She's braided her hair into a thick plait, is wearing knee-high motorcyling boots and a strange, very short, red skirt.

Suddenly a bright red light over the glass partition lights up. The sound guy tosses a baseball cap over his bird's-nest hair, turns it back to front and falls onto the console with both hands. Clara starts talking.

She sounds like she always does: insulted, defiant, speaking through pouting lips. I feel as if I'm finally making a full connection between the voice I've known from the radio for some time and the voice she uses to speak to me in person. It really is one and the same.

*

Suddenly the other image comes to mind, the raven-haired woman I'd imagined, leaning over a microphone; this was Clara, before I met her. Now, watching the real Clara tapping at a keyboard as she talks, the other one finally dies, is superimposed on, driven out. I feel a tiny sense of loss, like a twinge in my stomach.

OK, says Clara, it's time again, you know what I mean. Just look at your watches — you do have watches, don't you? — everyone here has a watch. I bet there are what, five, nine watches or clocks around you, so just look at one of them. See: midnight. And who talks to you every Wednesday and Sunday at midnight? Who? Whoever guesses right gets a point, and the person who collects one thousand points tonight gets my telephone number. For the others, well, it's coming right up. It's midnight, I'm here for you, and whoever needs advice can call in. This is the programme for the desperate, the nihilistic, the ones left behind and the lonely, for atomic scientists, dictators and any jerk off the street. We're talking about a BLEAK WORLD here. You know who I am.

Like a pianist striking the last note of a difficult passage, she presses a button with a flourish and music fills the room. She throws herself back in her swivel chair, nodding to the rhythm, not changing her position even when one of the switchboard operators comes in. The door stays open.

Lines one to three suicidal, says the operator, because of love-life problems; then two eating-disorder types; one guy in love with the neighbour's ten-year-old daughter; a prospective bank-robber and someone who claims to have just raped his sister with an electric bread knife.

Oh, him again, she says.

Without looking up, she stretches her arm out and he puts the note in her hand.

Eight, four, eleven and five, in that order.

He nods and leaves the booth to take up his place at the switchboard again. He speaks to the other two, who nod, press buttons and speak into their headsets.

The sound guy is still staring at me.

He's on her specimen slide now, he says suddenly.

What do you mean, mate? I ask.

Let's see, he says, how far she gets with him.

Before I can reply, the red light comes on again, and he sets about regulating the first caller's voice. I wonder if I should get up and pace about for a bit, just to annoy him. I could peer at the switches on his console and even press a button or two. He doesn't have a hand free to push me away with. I could walk up to Clara's booth and knock on the glass partition, or go into the other room and put my hand down the woman's top. None of them can defend themselves – they're all hanging on to their equipment like intensive-care patients on a drip.

As Clara talks, her collar gets pushed up against her ear and she lifts her headset slightly to adjust it.

Her chatter bores me. And the way she lounges about in her chair, arm slung over the armrest like a CEO, gets on my nerves. Maria, I'm on the other line, what do you have those indicator lights on your telephone for? Sorry, Max, I didn't notice. That's fine. Close the door, please, and get me a coffee.

I was once young, like Clara is. After the first few weeks in Vienna, I stopped sorting the plastic cards in my wallet by colour. Some of my colleagues had 'Hello God' displayed on their mobile phones for a year. Once I bumped into Rufus in the foyer with my Ray-Bans on. He didn't say anything, just smiled. But the sunglasses and the mobile stayed in the drawer after that, for emergencies.

What am I doing here anyway? I feel myself slipping into one of those brief, deceptive moods, in which I find myself thinking the

50

way I did two months ago. I find myself missing Rufus, missing the ordered routine of the office. Everyone there, including the secretaries, was very good-looking. I don't know if that played a role in recruitment. Rufus probably saw unattractiveness as a sign of inconsistency.

There's a rushing sound in my good ear, as if I'm plunging from a great height. I close my eyes and force myself to think about how I found Jessie lying on the floor, how I didn't dare to lift her up because I was afraid that she'd blown one side of her head away and that her brains would spill out if I moved her.

Suddenly it's clear to me again, what I'm doing here. Nothing. Nothing, absolutely nothing. I force my eyes open.

My gaze falls on the pen that the sound guy is twirling in his fingers. He's looking at me again, but his expression has changed; perhaps I've grown pale and he's wondering why. I wipe the sweat off my brow. The pen is thick as a hot dog, made up of garishly coloured sections: yellow–red–blue. I had exactly the same pen at home ages ago, a freebie or something. I liked writing with it because the ink flowed easily. I can't remember where I got it. I squint, trying to make out the lettering on it as the technician twirls it round and round. I can't, which gets me on edge. As far as I can remember, mine didn't have an inscription.

I suddenly realize that he's looking me in the eye and moving his lips exaggeratedly. He's trying to tell me something.

I only wanted to help, I read from his lips.

I furrow my brow, so he mouths a few more syllables.

Jessie, I read.

Of course it's a mistake. I hear Jessie's name everywhere: rustling between the telephone operators' papers, singing against the tarmac with every passing car. Why not read it on this dolt's lips? It's paranoia. I'm proud of it. I jump when Clara shouts.

*

Maybe it's because you just talk too much!

She pounds a switch and shakes her head angrily. The sound guy is unsettled too; he stops twirling the pen and I lean forward quickly to read the lettering before he puts it down: *I love Vienna*. The word 'love' has been replaced by a red heart-shape.

Great, I think. The world has been laid out just for me, and in such detail too.

I have to laugh, and I slap my hand against the table as I do so. When I look up, Clara is standing in front of me.

I'm glad you find it funny, she says.

There isn't a trace of irony in her smile, which is pleasant and one-dimensional; it makes me think of simple things, like popcorn and the movies.

Yes, I say.

The headset is hanging from her neck, the cord trailing to the floor. She looks like an electronic toy come to life, making a bid to escape. Just a few more steps and she'll pull the plug out of the socket and freeze: dream over. Music is playing in the background.

I'm going to get a coffee, she says.

The sound guy jumps up.

I'll get it, he says, you stay here.

He leaves the pen on the console. I grab it and put it in my jacket pocket.

Any requests? asks Clara.

Music means fuck all to me, I say.

She nods.

I'm going, I say.

Clara is still nodding. She takes the mug from the sound guy and disappears into her booth. I take the lift down, wave at the porter, walk out into the street, then come back to ring for a taxi.

I suddenly feel like going for a run, and set off just as the taxi rounds the corner. I speed up, fumble in my pocket for a cigarette and try to light it while running, but don't manage to. When I come to a stop, I hear the taxi coming up behind me at a walking pace. I wave, roll my head back and feel the cool night air against my face. I start running again, laughing. I wish this road could go on for ever, not a single lampost in the way.

8 | Shooting Pigeons

I stop on the bridge. Beneath me, the railway tracks run in a straight line towards the old trade-fair grounds. Boxy buildings, with the occasional tower here and there, spread out before me in a field of grey concrete like a scene from an apocalypse film. The radio station is the only building with lit windows.

The street light above my head flickers at irregular intervals. I jump up and down a couple of times, to see if it makes any difference. It doesn't. If I knew Morse code, I could probably decipher a message. The same message that's in the spiral pattern that forms as cream is being whipped, in the position of satellite dishes on buildings, in the street maps of the big cities of Europe.

The taxi waits a few metres away. As the driver gets into gear to drive off, I wave at him again. He rolls down his window. He's so short that he can barely see over his steering wheel.

Are you getting in or not?

I can tell that he's afraid.

Turn on the radio, I say, I'll tell you which station. Leave the passenger door wide open, switch on your meter. You're going to get a huge tip tonight, more than you'll get for the whole of next week.

I hand him a twenty through the window, which calms him down. The radio comes on.

Turn it up, I call, more, a little more. Now stop, that's fine.

Clara's voice floats out of the taxi. It's a good sound system, amazing.

I know this programme, says the driver, it's *A Bleak World*.

Shut up, I say.

He pushes his seat back and props his legs against the dashboard. He's wearing sandals with white socks. He seems to be getting used to me.

I lean over the bridge. The overhead cables for the trains look like threads spun by a giant spider that has crawled over the city unnoticed.

I press a button, and the face of my digital watch glows a deep blue, a clean, virtual world of liquid crystal. The watch is called 'Cockpit' because of its many buttons. It's Jessie's. I'd carefully taken it off her wrist because I knew that she wouldn't have wanted Cockpit to be buried with her as long as it was still working. It was a present from me. Jessie used to walk around the flat with it and press the buttons without knowing what they did. She never learned how to set the alarm or use the date function. But she was always delighted when it beeped on the hour. She'd reply 'Hello, Cockpit', and I had to do the same so as not to annoy her.

I once gave my mother a watch for her birthday too. She was horrified, and said that giving someone a watch meant that their time was up. I laughed at her.

It's twelve-thirty.

Halfway through, says Clara. I can't be bothered today, you can probably tell. It's sticky, in here at least. What do you all want from me, anyway? You always want to know something, but what? The weather? OK: it's dark. The forecast: it'll stay dark till about five, and then grow lighter, then there'll be daylight. And it'll get even more humid than it is now. I think.

She pauses for much too long; you can hear her picking her teeth with something. She's breathing heavily, like a Bunsen burner roaring into the microphone.

OK, she says, we'll get through the rest of the programme somehow.

I wonder which of the lighted windows she's sitting behind. If I had my binoculars with me, I could at least make out the green Ascona in the parking lot, maybe even find the right window. The binoculars are compact but very powerful, almost impossible to hold in place with one hand despite the stabilizer. I carried them around with me for fourteen years, a lucky charm of sorts, and now that I need them, they're not here.

The binoculars were on a stand in the hall of a flat that belonged to Jessie's father. The building was near the Hohen Markt, barely a minute away from Stephans Platz, and was a whole storey higher than all its neighbours. Instead of a front door, it had a gated entryway through which horse-drawn carriages had entered in former times. The gates swung open noiselessly when you pressed a remote-control button.

We climbed up wide stone steps inlaid with marble, with a broad stone banister. The steps curved against their will up to the first floor, and seemed ready to spring back into a straight line at any moment. We stepped into a gallery, at the end of which was a small modern lift that we took up to the top floor.

In the hall mirror, I looked at my acne with repulsion. I longed for a shower. Jessie stood behind me. She had pulled a green felt hunting cap down over her ears, and tipped her head back against her neck to peer under the brim. She took the binoculars, grabbed a corner of my shirt and dragged me along. A highly polished walking stick clattered to the floor behind us.

We crossed a squarish living room with a Persian carpet lost in the middle like flotsam from a shipwreck in the open sea. Chairs and sofas blurred into the edges of the room. We stepped out onto the balcony through a door in the outer wall, which was almost a metre thick. We were high above the city.

Jessie passed me the walking stick and hoisted herself up onto the parapet. When she swung her legs over to dangle them over the top, I caught hold of her shoulders in a reflex action, but she shook my hands off as if they were an animal that had jumped up on her. She'd turned fourteen about six months ago.

She pushed her cap back so that she could see properly and lifted the binoculars. I twiddled the walking stick.

Your father hunts, I suppose, I said.

She mumbled a reply through clenched teeth, barely moving her lips.

Of course he hunts.

With her index finger, she twisted the dial between the eyepieces to focus on a particular point. There was a creaking sound in the room behind us and I turned to see Shershah creeping alongside the walls like a panther, looking at the pictures suspiciously. He tried the door to a cupboard and stroked the armrest of a chair.

Give me the weapon, Jessie murmured.

I didn't get her meaning immediately, and she reached out impatiently. I gave her the walking stick and she passed the binoculars to me.

Don't change the focus, she ordered.

She pressed the stick against her right cheek, and closed one eye. I looked through the binoculars in the direction she had been pointing them. The dome of the Karlskirche jumped into my face and I stumbled backwards. It was incredible. Seen with the naked eye, the dome was a small green semicircle, like the top half of a patinated coin, stuck somewhere among the buildings spread out ahead, almost hidden by the large, ornate roof of the Stephansdom in the foreground. But with the binoculars, I could trace the etchings on the bottom of the dome and watch a group of fat pigeons bowing jerkily to each other, their neck feathers all fluffed up.

Ping! Jessie shouted.

She swung the stick upwards, imitating a retort. The pigeons flew off. Through the binoculars, I watched a few down feathers floating down onto the ledge.

What can you see, what can you see? she shouted, laughing. Did I get them?

I turned to see Shershah by the balcony door. He'd obviously been standing there for a few seconds. He was holding an angular brown bottle, which he'd probably found in one of the cupboards.

Oh man! he groaned.

He met Jessie's gaze. She stopped laughing and slid down from the parapet. She took the binoculars from me and put them, the cap and the stick back in place. At the next opportunity, I planned to take the binoculars back onto the balcony and spend a whole afternoon there with a thick joint hanging from my lips.

I took them with me at the end of our stay. They were nothing to Jessie's father.

Two callers are dealt with, but I don't really take it in. I can't concentrate. I snort dust off a pocket mirror, and my head opens up into big wide space in which swallows hunt midges and midges hunt amoebas. The taxi driver is laughing, Clara must be funny. He's even slapping his thigh.

Before we go on, says Clara, I have an announcement about a missing person.

I turn around.

Nothing to do with you, she says, it's personal. If there's someone out there called Shershah, please call in. It's not a very common name, after all.

She's mad, I say. Blessed are the poor in spirit.

What did you say? the taxi driver calls out.

She may think I'm listening to her from somewhere. But she probably isn't directing this at me at all, but at Shershah himself. The whole thing doesn't really have anything to do with me. In her opinion I don't even seem to have much to do with myself. It's about something else. Now there's music again. It's fantastic.

Listen, man, I say, you have a telephone, don't you?

He stops nodding to the beat of the music.

I do, he says.

A car drives past. The guy at the wheel is hanging an arm out of the window. From the tapping of his fingers against the door, I can tell that he too is listening to Clara's programme.

How much? I ask.

I shove him another twenty, and he passes me a flat phone attached to a thick spiral cable. I dial the number of the programme. The music stops mid-beat.

Enough, says Clara. It's definitely too hot for music, in here anyway. Let's talk a little about our problems instead. Like, about the fact that I hate summer. I like autumn, especially when it's stormy, when the trees lose their leaves all at once, as if Mother Nature has peeled off a green mask. The sound guy is signalling that I should take calls, not blabber on. But he'll be sacked if he interferes.

Good idea, I say, give him hell, the Viennese fucker.

I try breathing deeply, but the air gets stuck at the same place in my lungs every time, never reaching the very bottom, never bringing any relief. I give up and take shallow breaths. Holding the telephone, I walk as far away from the taxi as I can. The driver is staring at me. It's unnerving.

This is Shershah, I say, the woman in the programme was looking for me.

OK, she says. I'm putting you through, don't hang up.

I'm put on hold; the jangle of the recorded music reminds me of the gypsy children who sit in front of department stores with mini-synthesizers, running their fingers over the keyboards wildly, pretending to be playing the tinny tunes themselves.

Want one?

The taxi driver leans through the open passenger door, offering his pack of cigarettes. I'd completely forgotten to smoke. Some things look different with a lit cigarette. I finally manage to take that deep breath, inhaling into the very bottom corners of my lungs. The smoke stings the soft membranes there; they're probably still pink, not yet coated with tar.

Clara's on the line.

Hey, she says, who's that?

Me, I say.

The screech of feedback slices into my right eardrum and I scream hysterically, then calm down immediately. Overreaction.

Turn the radio off, man! she shouts.

Turn the radio off, man! I call to the taxi driver.

Right, who? she says.

Me, I say.

She's definitely recognized my voice.

So they tell me you're Shershah, she says.

Shershah, I say, is dead.

What, him too? she whispers.

She catches herself.

Who was he?

A friend, I say, or an enemy.

Very mysterious, dear, she says.

She's trying on the irony, nice. I don't need to try to be funny any longer, and it's liberating. Rufus always said it wasn't who won that counted, but how much the other party lost. I wish I had my ISDN button here, the one I used to play around with endlessly while talking, like Pac-Man in a labyrinth looking for big red cherries.

Clara speaks at last. Perhaps it would help you to talk a bit about Shershah?

Nope, I say.

I'll help, she says. He died and left unfinished business?

Nope, I say, I killed him.

Now there's total silence. A couple more seconds and the producer's going to step in.

I have to stop, I say, the three minutes are up.

Wait! she calls.

Luckily, I find the button to hang up right away.

When I get home, she's slumped on the sofa like an empty sack and her eyes are small and reddish like an albino rabbit's. Jacques Chirac runs up to me and whips his thin tail against my legs. I put my hand on his head. Clara's smoking from a porcelain pipe. She offers it to me.

I thought you didn't smoke, I say.

Not tobacco, she mumbles, but weed, yeah.

I walk over to stand right in front of her.

Why? I ask.

She lets her head drop back against the sofa.

You're asking? You of all people? she asks, laughing. I think better this way.

Think about what?

I don't believe, she says, that you killed Shershah. You just haven't got the guts.

I shrug.

Whatever, I say.

But you have wondered, she says, if your girlfriend was murdered, haven't you?

You're completely stoned, I say.

Nooo, she says, seriously.

I don't want to talk about this at all. I take another step forward and my knees touch the edge of the sofa. I'm towering over Clara.

You mean, I say threateningly, someone crept into the flat while she was on the phone with me and shot her?

There could have been someone in the flat already, says Clara, when she called you. Perhaps someone she knew, someone she had let in.

Jessie didn't know anyone in Leipzig, I say. We only went out at night.

Someone from before, then, she says.

I hesitate. I remember Jessie saying *Cooper, I think the tigers are here again*.

That's ridiculous, I say to Clara.

It's just as ridiculous to shoot yourself in the ear while on the telephone. I've never heard of anything like it before, Clara says.

I know, I shout, IT IS RIDICULOUS! NOBODY does things like that, it's UNHEARD OF! I have NO idea why she did it.

Perhaps, whispers Clara, you should try to find out.

I sink to my knees. Sometimes my own height makes me dizzy. Clara doesn't seem to have taken my shouting seriously. She has to lift her head a little in order to continue looking at me. It's difficult. She has to hold an arm behind her neck.

Maybe she was threatened by somebody, she says.

You read too many lousy crime novels, I say.

I don't read at all, she says. I need books like I need a hole in the head.

Television, then, I say.

She shrugs.

Think about it, she says.

This isn't a game, I say.

She starts laughing.

Nooo, she says, it really isn't.

Your sound guy would say, I tell her, that I'm on your microscope slide.

She suddenly looks more alert. She even manages to lift her head properly.

He spoke to you?

Yeah.

What else did he say?

That he wanted to see how far you got, I say.

Anything else?

Nope, I say.

She sinks back into the sofa.

Tom's bonkers, she says. He's probably in love with me, that's why he thinks I'm thick as two short planks.

This is too complicated for me. I get up, go over to the shelves and idly tear yellow Post-Its off a couple of record covers; one of them has '60bpm' on it, the other '200bpm'. My pulse is erratic, moving between the two frequencies smoothly and quickly like it's being mixed by an experienced DJ. I stick the Post-Its to my front.

How far I get, what's that supposed to mean? Clara calls out. I get exactly where I want to get to.

She's really high. She doesn't even mind me messing her records up. I rip off another twenty Post-Its. They don't stick very well to cloth, and fall off my shirt onto the floor. Then I've had enough.

I'm sure you do, I say.

When I was little, she says, I wanted a burglar alarm for my room, but my parents wouldn't get me one. I decided to fill the bath with ice-cold water and lie in it until they gave in. My mother said I wouldn't dare do it anyway.

This was in summer, I said.

In winter, Clara said. They found me after forty-five minutes and took me to the hospital straight away.

And then you got your burglar alarm? I ask.

No, she says, but they apologized.

Her babbling really gets on my nerves. She probably thinks she's still on air.

Hey, I say, I want to record some more. Could you maybe go somewhere else? To a friend's place? Or for a walk?

It's three in the morning. Clara's eyes become more focused. We stare at each other like opponents in a duel.

The tape, I say, my life story. You DO want it?

Just when I think she's gone to sleep with her eyes wide open and staring at me, she gets up unsteadily. She holds on to the coffee table, to the shelves, to my shoulder. I take her to the front door. She reaches for the dog lead.

No, no, I say. Jacques Chirac stays. I concentrate better with him around.

She pulls on her boots leadenly.

See you later, then, I say. In a couple of hours or so.

I haven't turned the stairwell light on for her. I hear a dull thud outside once the door is closed. She's walked into the wall. And I can't help myself – I cup my hand to my mouth like a small child and start giggling.

9 | Vienna

I'm going to Vienna with Jessie for the hols, said Shershah. Do you want to come?

The summer holidays were always difficult. I never had the money or the opportunity to go away. I was stuck at home with all the horrors of my childhood: the couch, the TV and my mother's desire to feed me junk food and ready meals all day long. It was compulsive: my mother pressing food on me, and me eating everything she gave me, until I was so stuffed that getting up from the couch was no longer possible. It was our only form of interaction. This went on for three weeks, until I started throwing up a few times every day, and eventually snapped, and started beating myself. Then she packed me into the Daimler and took me to a home for people with eating disorders for the rest of the holiday.

Of course I wanted to go to Vienna with them, even though I knew perfectly well why Shershah had asked me. Neither he nor Jessie had a car or a driver's licence. The others – sons of doctors, professors and carpet dealers – had cars, but they rented catamarans for the summer and split the cost. They certainly didn't go to Vienna.

It didn't bother me. I was used to doing what other people wanted. I lent them my stuff, I ran errands in town, I met girls at the airport and drove them to their boyfriends. In return for all this, the others were friendly to me. It was a friendliness that was no different from any other. I was part of it all. Many others weren't.

Jessie liked being driven around in my car. It was an ancient Fiat Uno, red. I'd got it and the driver's licence on my eighteenth birthday, and had covered twenty thousand kilometres with it in the eight months since. Weekends to Amsterdam, the Cologne–Bonn motorway on many evenings, days spent just driving here and there.

Going for a spin to Amsterdam meant driving in groups most of the time: a couple of black GTIs or GTEs with my old Fiat. Jessie painted her nails for these occasions: ten small, red, round beetles on the passenger-seat headrest, which she held with both hands during the journey. When Shershah remarked that she looked like a teenage hooker with those nails, I was the only one who noticed how she whipped her head towards the window. In Amsterdam he made her wait in the car while the others bought their stuff. They bought everything except coke, which they got from Jessie, even though it was more expensive. Then we drove to Ijsselmeer, where someone had a bungalow. I lay by the water for a day and a half, head fuzzy from the dope and the lapping of the waves, watching Jessie making shapes with pebbles. I watched her nail polish being gradually chipped away, bit by bit, and imagined taking her fingers in my hands, very carefully, to gently scratch the rest of the varnish off. Jessie was the only girl in the group. No one took any notice of her. She was simply there. Shershah had brought her along and that was all.

So I knew that Shershah probably had a specific reason for going to Vienna, and I knew that I had only been invited along because of the car. I was happy about it all the same.

Shershah slept in the back seat on the way there. Jessie climbed into the front, rolled a couple of cigarettes for us and allowed me to complain jokingly about how crooked and limp they were. We listened to music. All the windows were wound right down, since it was thirty degrees Celsius in the shade. I confessed that I'd always wanted to be called 'Cooper' but hadn't managed to convince either my mother or my classmates to call me that. She begged to be allowed to braid my ponytail. I finally gave in and she set to work, knotting my hair together rather than braiding it. At the border, the guards made us get out of the car, and they inspected our luggage. I was shitting myself. But the bags were clean, all of them. I began to understand that Jessie was a professional.

It was sweltering in Vienna. The city was suspended like a man dying from a fever: motionless, dehydrated, hallucinating beneath the surface. Big black billboards with skulls and crossbones hanging from a few buildings in the Stubenring warned against driving. There were ozone alarms on the radio every fifteen minutes and afternoon curfews were being discussed. The incessant wail of ambulance sirens cut through the city. The old were dying from the heat.

Despite this, we hung around on the balcony. I leaned over the parapet, holding the binoculars, scanning the city methodically, absorbing it in tiny squares that expanded right up against my eyes. I had begun with the far right, with the steeple of the Votivkirche and part of the university, then I inspected the intricately worked towers of the Rathaus, the back of the Burg Theatre, and of course the gate to the parliament building. I wanted to get all the way to the left, undeterred by the Dom, which blocked part of the view. I wanted to look over Belvedere and the train station into the south-east, where the central cemetery is located. I couldn't see it, but I knew it was there because of the lack of rooftops. I looked at everything: windowsills, antennae, the angles of leaning chimneys, gables, the

Hofburg, various different kinds of cupola. Sometimes, where the buildings thinned out, I could see a distant street corner, empty in the heat. Then I stopped and waited for a few minutes to catch someone walking by. I saw the pigeons' nesting places, students in attic flats, and some tiny patches of forest in the far distance. I looked at every square centimetre of the city.

Jessie sat on the shorter side of the parapet to my right, leaning back against the wall. She always wore small white cotton shorts with the outline of a black bulldog printed on the left and a tiny sleeveless top, which she pushed up just below her barely-there breasts. She soaked up the sun, even though the radio intoned warnings of skin cancer, heat stroke and circulatory collapse on the quarter-hour. Her skin didn't grow red, but darkened in shades of grey, as though her whole body was being covered with ever thicker layers of dust. Two ties that I'd found in her father's wardrobe and knotted together were looped round her waist. I tied the ends to one of the metal struts in the wall that were probably meant to support climbing plants. I liked to think that this would stop her from falling five floors down into the alleyway below. I hadn't been able to talk her out of sitting there. I stood my ground until she'd at least allowed me to fashion a security harness.

We had tossed the pillows and duvets aside and dragged the huge double mattress off Jessie's father's bed into the middle of the living room, ten steps away from the balcony door, right beneath the silent, sluggishly rotating blades of a ceiling fan. Shershah lay on the mattress, arms and legs stretched out like the perfect human being Leonardo da Vinci had drawn in a circle, a cigarette in the corner of his mouth, ash breaking off and landing, glowing, on the sheet close to his neck. We had taken the entire stereo system out of the cupboard and put it next to the mattress. We'd found the CDs on the first day, and Shershah and I had spent half an hour sitting on the edge of the mattress, admiring the shimmering surfaces. Only after we'd seen enough did we let a couple of the CDs glide in and out of the player before we played the first one and closed our eyes.

At some point we stumbled upon a collection of baroque music, and found a piece that we all liked. Pachelbel. The first few bars made my heart explode like a supernova every time. It was about five minutes long. We set it on repeat, and played it for two whole days. Whoever wanted to sleep turned it down a bit. Jessie started crying after it had been played fifty times, her face crumpling like that of a small baby waking in the night and wailing for its mother. The sun devoured the tears off her face almost as soon as they appeared. I pretended to go on looking through the binoculars and said nothing. She stopped after half an hour.

Whenever my headache got too bad, I left the balcony, put the binoculars on the stereo, and pushed Shershah to one side so that I could lie down on the mattress. He was constantly rolling toothpick-fine joints with a mixture of tobacco and weed, which tasted good and made my brain feel as if it were going to spill out of my ears and vaporize. I sank into a state of sleeping wakefulness during which the fan moved nearer and nearer and ended up inside me, whirling around the images of the city that I'd seen. Sometimes, Jessie's impatient squeals as she tried to untie the sailor's knot cut through the mist of colours. Then one of us would get up unsteadily, tug at the knot with a limp index finger and finally pull it apart with our teeth so that Jessie could get up. Small and hot, eyes fiery red, she sometimes crept onto the mattress between our legs, plucked at the hairs on our thighs, tickled our toes and babbled incomprehensibly, non-stop.

After four days, Jessie got pushy. She repeated a sentence over and over again: get up and go to town, get up and go to town. Shershah was able to hold her in check for a while with his 'Shut up, for fuck's sake.' Then he struggled to get up and tried to hit her. She ducked out of his way and threw herself onto one side like a puppy, giggling and paddling her arms and legs. She rolled over my shin and the pain forced me to sit up as well. It was high noon; the sun was directly overhead, the city seemed to have no shadow.

I stood under a cold shower until I felt my blood drain away; to ever feel warm again seemed impossible. I got out of the bath, tied my hair in a ponytail on top of my head and held on to the sink until the wave of weakness passed and my vision cleared again. I followed my trail of sweat back into the living room. Shershah had tidied the mattress and was standing on the balcony squinting into the sun, looking out onto the city as if it were wilderness. Jessie was sitting on the mattress with outstretched legs, a hunched back and a hanging head. When she saw me, her face lifted. She pointed at my ponytail and started snorting.

We finally dragged ourselves into the lift and down the marble steps. Somehow, Jessie managed to get the gigantic gates open. We crashed into a wall of heat that was like an invisible defence shield. Vienna didn't want anyone in it. Such silence in the middle of a big city was absurd. It was as quiet as an open field in the country, only there were no crickets.

The ground was soft where the cobblestones stopped: the tarmac was melting. Jessie walked close to the buildings to stay in the shadow. Now and then she slung her arms across my shoulders and I carried her a couple of steps because the ground was too hot for her bare feet.

We walked towards Hofburg, so that we could take a dip in one of the fountains on the Michaelerplatz. The small group of tourists at the monument looked lost, as if they'd just made an emergency landing. Jessie urged us on, and led us across the Heldenplatz, along the Ring, burbling something about what a nice walk it was. Shershah and I leaned against each other from time to time. Then we got so sweaty from the skin contact that we pushed each other away again. Suddenly, Jessie signalled to us to wait, and disappeared into a building on the Opernring. We watched her through the display window of a gallery, surrounded by brightly coloured paintings, as she spoke to a fat man who listened, nodded and looked out at us. He stared at me insistently, as if he was trying to remember my face for later. Then Jessie came back and said we could go home.

As soon as we entered the flat, we knew that something had changed. There was a whiff of an expensive male cologne in the hallway.

Whaddya know, Jessie said, I think my father and brother are here.

She was right.

10 | Yellow

Clara's bought some dog food. Panting, she heaves the heavy sack into the kitchen and leaves it behind the door. When she comes into the living room, I feign sleep. She raises the blind, opens the window and leaves the room.

The last rays of sun fall onto my overflowing ashtray, onto my pallid, puffy skin, the hairs sticking to my arms and legs, onto the bottles I've emptied, the glass surfaces I've been snorting off, the crumpled newspapers and the cushions that have fallen off the sofa.

When the phone rings, Clara comes back into the room. She answers in monosyllables, staring at me all the while. I wrap the blanket around my waist and disappear into the bathroom. I leave the cubicle door open while showering, to get a bit more air. When I'm done, a shallow lake with Clara's and my hairs swimming in it covers the floor. I wonder what I should wear. More than anything, I need to get a fresh supply of underwear from my flat, urgently.

In the living room, I look for something that I can focus my thoughts on for a few moments, something I haven't already felt, or turned over in my mind countless times already. There's nothing. Clara walks in with a cup of coffee and sits at the desk. I lean against the shelves and look at her. She's been wearing her hair down for a few days and it looks straggly. Her legs are straight and white, without a trace of muscle or bone, as if they're made of wax. Her socks flop way past her toes, making her feet look grotesquely large. She's got rings under her eyes, of course. She doesn't sleep well at night, and when she does, I bang about the place until she gets up. I can't stand someone else sleeping peacefully in the same flat when I'm too restless even to lie down.

According to the clock on Clara's computer, it's only eight, but it's already strangely dark outside. The cassettes are in a small box, neatly labelled in my handwriting. Next to it is a pile of books with the yellow spines of the university library. I hear the scraping and crackling of my own voice coming through the headphones. Clara is typing professionally; her face is expressionless. I'm revolted by her. She looks busy and diligent, as if what she is doing makes the slightest modicum of sense.

I finish my coffee, step up behind her and look over her shoulder. My staring doesn't seem to bother her. She ignores me; it's as if the flat is some experimental lab and I'm a monkey running around in it, a monkey that has got used to studying the scientist more intently than she studies it. I drop onto the floor and, lying on my back, push myself under her chair like a mechanic under a car. I go so far back under the desk that I can see between her legs when I lift my head. There's not much to see. Just her boring cotton underwear, the red marks that the edge of the chair has left on her thighs, a vague intimation of genitals under the material. None of this interests me.

Listen, she says, there's a problem.

I'm hemmed in by the chair legs to the left and the right. I can't get up.

The professor doesn't like your stuff, she says.

What stuff? I gasp. What kind of professor?

He didn't say why, just: *That's not it, that's not it.* He probably doesn't quite believe in your psychosis. There're enough fakes about.

She stops and waits for me to reply, or maybe I'm supposed to burst into tears. Outside, a bolt of lightning flashes suddenly and I see a flickering blue reflection under the desk. It's quiet. Even the birds have finally shut up. It's strange how the traffic stops just before a storm and there's no wind and no telephone calls, either.

Are you listening? Clara asks.

Yes, I say.

What do you think, then? Clara asks.

She finally stops typing. When she gets up, I topple the chair and crawl out from under the desk.

What do I THINK? I ask. Are you completely losing it?

In the kitchen, Jacques Chirac is licking his bowl clean, pushing it around the floor with his tongue. The scratching of the plastic against the porcelain tiles gives me goose pimples.

You want me to blabber any old nonsense onto your cassettes, I say, and I'm doing it. That's all.

But if the professor won't accept it, she says, I don't you need to go on.

I walk over to the window. Summer lightning flashes. The sky hangs low over the town, looks like a pale blue and pink pasteboard construction into which the pattern of a skyline has been cut. The zigzag of the next bolt stays in the sky for an unnaturally long time, then smoulders and fades; though perhaps it only looks that way because of my over-dilated pupils, through which light is burning into my retina. The roll of thunder that follows is unbelievable. It sounds like a gigantic axe landing on a sky made entirely of wood.

Clara opens the kitchen window. A screen saver is building a system of three-dimensional tubes on her monitor. I find the files immediately: dipl.doc1 to 5 and max.doc, all organized tidily in a separate folder. Are you sure you want to send these six files to the recycle bin? But of course! I click on the mouse as quietly as possible. Then I open the virtual wastebasket, delete everything there too, pick up the cassettes and take the back-up disk out of the drive. I pull on my trousers and call for a taxi.

See you later, I call from the hall. I'm leaving the dog here.

While I'm waiting for the taxi, the first drops of rain start. They fall onto the street with such violence that I wonder for a moment if it's water or small jelly-like animals that are being hurled onto the tarmac from a high floor. I retreat into the entryway, lean against the main door and press my head between the cast-iron bars so that my forehead touches the cool glass. The storm is letting loose. Pale green leaves swirl through the air and are beaten down onto the street by the rain.

Just getting from the taxi to my front door is enough to get me drenched. It's dark. My mailbox is overflowing with bills and catalogues. I take everything out and throw it into one of the bins under the stairs without looking at any of it. Then I stop and listen for a moment before I go up to my flat.

The door swings open as I'm trying to get the key into the lock. I clutch at something in my jacket pocket. I wield the Viennese guy's brightly patterned pen like a knife in my fist. My eyes can't adjust; beyond the rhombus of light from the stairwell that is falling through the gap in the door, the flat is in total darkness.

At this, of all times, I don't have Jacques Chirac with me. This could be what Jessie and I had been half-expecting for two years. We talked about it once, right at the beginning, on the way from Vienna to Leipzig in a rental car, somewhere between Passau and Hof. Jessie had come to again, and the first words she said that I could understand had something to do with a dog.

I've always wanted one, she said. And a pony too. I'll have them both now.

What, I asked. A dog and a pony?

Exactly, she said.

I wrinkled my brow, and she stretched her hand out to touch my arm. Her face was pale, not quite itself after the long faint, but very earnest-looking. She didn't look childlike, but at least as old as she was. Moments like these were rare and they confused me. Her profile was reflected on the right side of the windscreen.

Well, Cooper, she said, Rufus will protect you. But not me. I'd feel safer with a big dog.

I didn't know what to say, so I remained silent.

That's a fact of life, she said. No one in the world can protect you when your own father has it in for you. Especially a father like Herbert.

She nodded, and carried on nodding. I stopped her by placing two fingers against her forehead.

I'll look after you, I said. I'll look after you better than myself.

You? she asked.

I was hurt by that. But of course she was right. I was a lawyer, not a hardened criminal like her father. And her. I shook myself.

Jessie, I said, it's really exactly the opposite of what you've said. It's been explained to me. They're going to leave ME in peace because of YOU. YOU guarantee our safety.

It was a great effort for me to confess this, but she didn't seem to understand.

I want a dog, she said.

We bought a Great Dane, and though Jacques Chirac has turned out to be a lovable fool rather than a killing machine, he does look impressive. If he was here with me now, I could rest my hand on his neck and we could walk into this flat together.

The timed light in the stairwell goes out with a horribly loud click. I make out the shadowy outline of the telephone stand in the hallway: it's lying on its side and the hiding place underneath is uncovered. Then I make out the double doors to the study, which are wide open. The planks that they'd been boarded up with are hanging loosely from the frame.

I stretch a hand into the flat and press the light switch. Suddenly, I don't care if anyone's here or not. I put the pen down on the telephone stand, take a deep breath and leap across to the study in three steps.

It's not as bad as I thought. Maybe I'd secretly expected to find Jessie's body still lying on the floorboards. The room is smaller than I remember. It feels like I'm back in a scene from my childhood. All the desk drawers have been removed and shaken out, and they're leaning empty against the wall. All that's left of my computer is the monitor. Three floorboards have been prised up. The door through to the bedroom is ajar.

I don't really care what they do with this flat; after all, it's not mine any longer. The floorboards have been ripped up in the bedroom too, and my wardrobe has been tipped over, its contents strewn everywhere. But I can't bear the sight of our bed: the sheets are messed up, the mattress slit all over like the victim of a bloodbath, some of the filling pulled out. A pair of sunny-yellow pyjamas lies on top of it all like a gesture of derision.

Something's ticking. It's our alarm clock on the nightstand. It's showing the right time. Somehow, the fact that it's carried on working disturbs me more than anything else.

I turn on my heel and start running. Out of the flat, down the stairs in the dark, out into the rain.

Jacques Chirac is waiting behind Clara's door. I shout. I shout again, very loudly. Clara isn't in. I stand in the hall for a long time.

The windows are still open. The rain has let up. It's just spitting now. In the living room, the clothes lying near the window are piles of wetness, with pieces of wavy, ink-blotched paper amongst them. Water has seeped right into the middle of the room; the stain on the carpet looks like a map of South America.

I tug all the towels off the hooks in the bathroom and throw them onto the kitchen floor. The bottoms of my trousers get so water-logged that the waistband gets dragged down to my hips. There's no message on the desk. The clock shows ten pm, but it's neither Wednesday nor Sunday. I find Clara's address book, and wonder if I should look up her friends' numbers. Hopeless. There are hundreds of names in the book.

I sit at the kitchen table, cover my eyes with my hands and try to think as intensely as I can about the carved-up mattress, Jessie's pyjamas and the alarm clock. One of Rufus's rules was: if you don't want something unbearable to plague you for ever, focus on it.

Immediately after we arrived in Leipzig, I'd bought the mattress, the pyjamas and the alarm clock, along with a pack of sleeping pills for both of us in the shopping centre by the train station. Thus equipped, we moved into the empty flat. The address was on a slip of paper I'd found the day before as I was clearing out my desk in Vienna. Two keys were fastened to the piece of paper with tape.

The next day, I overslept despite the alarm clock. I blamed the builder who'd started chipping away at the stucco at seven that morning. There wasn't a single building in that street without scaffolding over it. Instead of waiting for me to shout at it, the new alarm clock must have beeped twice and stopped at the next pound of the hammer. It cowered fearfully on the floor and didn't make a single sound after that. I went on sleeping and woke only when Jessie, in her sunny-yellow pyjamas, shook my shoulder.

Don't you have to get up? she asked.

I left the building ten minutes later. Jessie ran into the street after me, wished me luck, and promised to get something for dinner before I came home. I didn't actually need any luck, and I knew that she would never manage to get something decent together for dinner, but I was touched anyway. She pressed something into my hand. It was the yellow windmill I'd had to steal for her yesterday from a flower box outside a restaurant because she thought it looked like her. Yellow was her favourite colour. Cooper, she'd said once, yellow is the only colour that can freeze-frame time. You never know with yellow – you don't even know if you're allowed to stop or to go on. But it's the colour that hurts my head most too.

She could only bear yellow when everything else was fine. Looking at her standing there, her yellow pyjamas and the windmill competing for attention, I took it all as a sign. I kissed her and said, 'See you tonight' perfectly naturally, as if this farewell on the pavement by the front door was a part of our daily routine.

Not long after, I stood under the cream-coloured nineteenth-century façade in Mozartplatz, almost an hour late, and read Rufus's surname on the bronze plate. There was nowhere to hide the windmill in my suit. I was holding it in front of me like a rose for the hostess of a cocktail party.

The door on the second floor was ajar, so I simply walked in. The office was small; I counted only ten rooms. There was a strong smell of new carpet and of coffee. Maria Huygstetten came out of reception, introduced herself and held the windmill for me while I took my coat off. I looked at her, and she gazed just a moment too long into my eyes before turning away. Her perfume smelt of pepper and lavender.

She knocked on a door for me. The woman sitting behind the desk had such short hair that it looked as if she had just dyed her scalp. Her legs were so short that they barely touched the ground. She was dictating into one of those old cassette recorders, which she pressed close to her mouth. In Vienna we had tiny machines with a digital recording function.

Six, she said, the counter-party's statement on point two, Roman, one, Arabic, is being contested.

She stopped the machine with a loud click and stood up.

For God's sake, someone grumbled in the next room, is that shit going to work or what?

Max, she said, nice to meet you.

We started with an office tour, but though I'd coked up sufficiently at breakfast and was buzzing, everything seemed wrong to me, almost obscenely so. The office fittings were expensive but tasteless. The files on the shelves seemed to contain countless numbers of private cases and not a single document from an international organization. Even the ring of the telephone sounded like a local call. I saw everything perfectly clearly, as if looking through diving goggles under water. I was the new ornamental fish in the carp pond. The bristle-headed lawyer swam ahead of me, from the library into the corridor and in through the next door, followed by the windmill, then me. The sixty-eighth edition of the Staudinger civil rights commentary was arrayed behind me, though quite a few volumes were missing. I felt a sense of unease, as if the shelves would snap at me any minute like a large predator fish. I hadn't touched anything on German civil law since university. The work I'd done for Rufus had had nothing to do with either Germany or civil law.

You guys from Vienna are pretty dodgy types, aren't you? the lawyer said. Does all that chaos increase the number of lucky hits?

She cast me a derisive glance. She probably thought she was being incredibly sharp. She probably *was* incredibly sharp. Maybe I just looked silly: an ornamental fish with diving goggles and a windmill.

Do take your hands off your face, she said. Why are you doing that, anyway?

I pulled myself together. I realized that I hadn't actually given a thought to what these people here wanted from me in the first place. A man came in, wearing a polo shirt and linen trousers that made him look more like a golf pro than someone who worked for Rufus.

each animal. It can be reported that 40-hour fasting-adapted rats will survive in small cages of the usual type, but if allowed access to activity cages, they will all run themselves to death in 5–10 days, illustrating the breakdown of instinctive "wisdom." In contrast, the 36-hour fasting-adapted rats are able to survive and adapt to the regimen with or without exercise.

The 36-hour fasting-adapted animals ran an average of 15 km during the 12-hours of darkness when no food was available (19), and on the following day, still hungry, they slept much of the time and ran much less. The ad libitum control-rats exercised and ate at night and slept most of the day, with almost no day activity recorded.

We have studied a number of enzymes and have also studied nucleic acid metabolism, but data for only one enzyme will be mentioned here. Glucose-6-phosphate dehydrogenase shows great fluctuations and averages much higher values than the ad libitum controls (19). We feel that these data adequately demonstrate the fact that adaptive enzyme changes are part of normal physiology and that these changes can be exaggerated by increasing the time between meals.

The animals on this regimen have not been studied for longevity; but it is clear that obesity does not result during 30 days, and the growth curve during this period does not develop a steeper slope than the control curve, as in the case of rats fed two hours per day (12). The growth rate is quite similar to that of male rats studied by Berg (3) at the levels of 33 percent and 46 percent restriction of food intake and falls midway between the rates for his groups. Berg's studies demonstrated increased longevity and general health without evidence of immaturity. In the 36-hour fasted rats, it is as yet unknown whether the food intake would increase to the level of the ad libitum feeding in time, or whether in the long run, restricted feeding on a once-per-day basis would be preferable. It can be suggested, however, that the usual restricted food intake always results in fasting periods of 22–23 hours and that fasting may be partly responsible for the beneficial effect of the caloric restriction.

At this time, we can only speculate that the fasting-adapted animals derive benefit from the active use of their abilities to produce large shifts in intracellular enzyme patterns and leave it to the future to determine whether mental powers, motivations, and character would be helped or hindered in humans on similar regimens.

Definition of Optimum Environment

Turning now to the actual task of defining an optimum environment, I have tried to make the point that the culture in which we live is an important part of our environment. What we recommend as physiologists may become a part of our culture or it may be ignored, depending on the force of our logic and the force of counterpressures. A cogent example is the relationship between cigarettes and lung cancer, where the experts are pretty much agreed but the counterforces still prevail.

In the case of defining an optimum environment, I think it is essential to go beyond a mere consideration of toxic hazards and to recommend positive steps that could raise men above mere absence of disease to the concept of "positive health" mentioned by Dubos (8). My basic concern is that physiologists should be in the forefront of describing and analyzing the mechanisms of physiologic adaptation, not only in physiologic terms, but in behavioristic and molecular terms—not only in the academic sense, but also with the aim of guiding mankind during the next 20 or 30 years of rapid change to we know not what. If affluence is not conducive to an optimum environment, then what can we say to those who seek it? What are the minimum requirements for a world that physiologists could recommend and work toward?

I have made a list of seven points, not as a physiologist but as a scientist and a humanist. I present them as the whole package, recognizing that, as I am a physiologist, my main concern is the fourth point, which has to do with physiological adaptation. However, I might emphasize that, until we know more about the nature of adaptation and the molecular targets of toxic hazards, we can say very little about the problems of threshold and potentiation, which are the crux of the pollution problem.

My seven points are as follows:

1. I would begin with basic needs that can be satisfied by effort. These include food, shelter, clothing, space, privacy, leisure, and education, both moral and intellectual. [Regarding the ethical basis of science, see Glass (11).]

2. I would insist on freedom from toxic chemicals, unnecessary trauma (primarily war and traffic injuries), and preventable disease.

This is Dr Thomas Stickler, she said.

Hello, Max, he said. We've been dying for you to turn up.

Hello, Stickler, I said.

Something made me address him just as 'Stickler', rather than by his first name or with his PhD title. He obviously didn't like it. I knew that I'd continue calling him that, for the future anyway. It was a compulsion. While my thoughts were thus occupied, he continued speaking.

And the day after tomorrow, he said, you'll be called to the bar for Leipzig and Dresden.

Why would I want to do that? I asked.

These, my dear Max, he said, are barristers' chambers. Barristers stand up in court.

Stickler, I said, I'm a Balkan specialist.

Were, he said.

The plump trainee with the country-maid face moved out of the bare room into the library with her mountain of files, so I got my new office. I remembered Ricarda, the coffee-coloured trainee in UN City in Vienna. She earned 3,000 US dollars a month, and went jogging on the Donau island at lunchtime. She worked for Sachiko Girard-Yamamoto. Sachiko was the head of the Legal Department, earned five times what Ricarda did, and wore skirts so long that they covered her feet, which took such small steps that she looked as if she were being wheeled along the endless corridors. You only needed to look at her to get the feeling that you'd just done something terribly wrong. Sachiko almost always had something for me to do although I, like Rufus and the rest of us, didn't actually work there.

Dear Max, she would say, do you have a moment to spare for world peace?

Once, just when I was starting to become one of the employees whom Rufus trusted, one of those he talked to in passing about politics of the highest order, in the corridor or on the plane, he told me that this Japanese lady was one of the best friends of the small companies that were our bread and butter. Meaning that whatever Sachiko said got done – always and everywhere.

I didn't like driving out to UN City. Sachiko always caught me at the last moment while I was exchanging a few words with Ricarda, rolled ahead of me into some empty office and put a pile of committee-meeting transcripts in front of me. In the space of an afternoon, I would have to draft a complete resolution that would be presented to some working group as the result of previous negotiations. I did my best, and when Sachiko was satisfied, I rewarded myself by getting a couple of plastic packets of soy sauce from the sushi section in the UN canteen, then going to McDonald's for a portion of super-jumbo fries, which I drowned in the sauce and devoured on the way back in the U-Bahn. At that time, I thought Sachiko was about the worst thing I'd have to deal with in my life. A serious mistake.

Without knowing how I got there, I found myself in the woman lawyer's office again, holding a cup in my hand.

Max the Maximal, she said.

Stop it.

How the devil, she asked, does someone like you get a job like this?

I passed Rufus's entry test, I said.

What was it?

Rufus interviewed me in person, I said. At the end, he asked why German policy tended to support the interests of Ghana while the Austrians generally sided with the Australians.

She thought for a moment. I could practically see an outline of German colonial history spooling past under her forehead.

And? she finally asked.

It's all to do with the seating order at the meetings and working groups of the international organizations, I said. Germany always sits next to Ghana and Austria next to Australia, so the delegates know each other. They borrow pens from each other and bring each other coffee.

That was the correct answer?

It's not only correct, I said, it's true. Rufus even gripped my arm in response.

You're an eccentric lot in Vienna, she said. People working on international law aren't real lawyers.

Absolutely right, I said, and international law isn't really law. More like a religion.

It's going to be difficult to work out, she said, if you're a genius or an idiot.

Shit, I said.

Ah, come on, Max, she said, you'll cope. You'll get to work on some really interesting cases here.

What fucking interesting cases, I asked, can there be here?

At least, she said in a measured tone, we work with real people here.

I groaned quietly and thought again about how us young champions in Vienna had drafted rules for the whole of humanity; about how removed from everything I had felt, before the doubts set in. I decided never to think back to those times. Not to think about Rufus, either. I thought of Goethe: *And thee to scorn as I.*

Listen, I said, I've been transferred to Leipzig because they can't dismiss me, for private reasons. I'm here on a siding, not to be put to work.

She smiled for the first time.

You're wrong, she said.

I left early. On the street, I realized that I didn't have the windmill any longer. Jessie asked about it when I got home. I found it again months later when I went to Maria's flat for the first time. It was stuck in a vase between two dried flowers dyed dark-blue.

*

In the following weeks, I went to court often, and felt like a transvestite with leanings towards the priesthood. I learned how to decipher the entries that Maria made in the book listing petition deadlines. I tried to settle in, working my way through files containing badly copied contracts and correspondence between opposing parties that was filled with hatred and spelling mistakes. I coked up like there was no tomorrow. When I had a minute to spare I surfed the websites of international organizations. It was childish, but I felt like I was no longer allowed to play.

Until Stickler poked his head through the door one day. I'd come to realize that he was one of those people who said 'jet' instead of 'plane', and I was always happy not to have to see him.

Max, he said, it's time. In ten minutes the Minister of Home Affairs from Saxony will be here to talk about regional cooperation with Poland and the Czech Republic within the framework of EU expansion.

What, I asked, is it time for?

You're getting the stuff you're here for, he said.

Stickler, I said, I'm a Balkan expert. At least I was. Poland and the Czech Republic are not, as far as I know, in the Balkans. Why didn't you let me know before, so I could prepare myself?

You'll be fine, he said. Rufus rang specially. Most importantly, he said: Schengen first. Whatever that means. Anyway, bye, I've got to go.

The Home Affairs minister from Saxony was actually the Minister of Justice from Brandenburg, and I sketched an off-the-cuff plan for increased regional cooperation within EU guidelines for him. At the end, he shook my hand and dipped his head a little. It was a hint of a bow. I didn't understand it. It was only when more people started to come after him – people whose faces I knew from television, who needed help with the new European integration law, who treated me with great respect – that I began to realize that I was being seen as an expert in EU expansion before I had even begun to work in the area. I filled these new shoes easily. My one regret was being unable to lead my clients into the big conference room in the Vienna office, its walls dirty-yellow from the one thousand, seven hundred and sixty-eight volumes of the United Nations treaty, which diffused the light in the room and gave off the chemical, slightly resinous smell of preservatives. The faces of clients brought into that room took on the tint of the walls, and they posed their questions respectfully. But they listened to me even in my small Leipzig office, and on the day when the rough draft of EU institutional reform lay on my desk, I knew I had a life again. Sometimes Rufus rang and called me 'Max the Maximal'. I went home at seven and went for walks at night with Jessie, who had decided never to go outside in daylight again. I lived a normal life.

I catch my lips moving as I think. Now I can continue. I get up and fetch the DAT-recorder.

11 | White Wolves

Shershah kicked off his shoes in the living room and one of them hit the bottle of gin, its cap fortunately screwed tight, which rolled through the room with a bowling-alley rumble to land in front of the study door. The door flew open and catapulted the bottle back into the room, where it spun on its own axis on the polished floor. Spin the Bottle: whoever the bottle ends up pointing at has to do something embarrassing, something that will make him or her a laughing stock. I stared at the spinning bottle as if I was looking down at a roulette wheel, and already knew who it would point at.

The father was a giant, tanned and stout, but not flabby. He had black hair, which surprised me; Jessie's mop was yellow. He ran his fingers through his hair as he walked towards us; his hands were large and fleshy, like spatchcock. He'd be strangling us with those hands very soon for having laid his flat to waste. He was wearing light-coloured linen shorts and slippers; despite his size, he hardly made a sound as he moved forward.

A narrow-shouldered man with slitty eyes appeared behind him in the door frame. He looked at least ten years older than Jessie, in his mid-twenties. His trousers were a little too short; we'd called them 'floods' in school. I could see the word 'Victory' sewn into his socks. His acne was even worse than mine. It was impossible to look him in the face for long. He didn't notice me, because he was staring at Shershah. Then Jessie ran towards them both.

Well, my pet! the father shouted.

She grabbed him by the folds of his shirt and he lifted her up and swung her about as she squealed happily. He passed her to the brother, who snaked an arm around her briefly and smiled.

Hey, you, he said.

Hey, Ross, she said.

She stood on tiptoe to pat his shoulder and he laughed, though his eyes and the facial muscles around them seemed frozen. Perhaps it was a nerve problem – partial paralysis of the face, or something.

Shershah tried to light a cigarette, but his Zippo didn't work and he tossed it onto the floor. Jessie's father walked up to give him a light.

I'm Herbert, he said.

Shershah nodded and shook his hand without looking at him.

I'm glad, said Herbert, to be getting to know Jessie's friends at last. Even though I'd only expected one. But I'm happy you're having a good time in my flat.

He sounded as if he meant it. Shershah looked past him with the expression on his face that had made most teachers barely able to restrain themselves from laying one on him not too long ago.

There's a reason for us being here, at any rate, Shershah said absently.

You're having a holiday with my daughter, Herbert said. She looks as though she's enjoying it.

Jessie smiled oh-so-sweetly.

And we can talk about everything else in my study, said Herbert.

He let us go in before him. The study was the only room in the flat that had been locked. A blast of cold air hit me in the doorway. It was air-conditioned. The room was relatively small and was dominated by a large desk in the middle. For the first time in days, the beads of sweat on my forehead started drying off. I sat on the wide windowsill and clasped my hands behind my head to let the cold air blast under my arms. The rocky desert-world outside seemed a mere illusion.

Herbert sat at the desk, opened a notebook and took a pair of glasses out of a drawer. Jessie threw herself down on the carpet and plucked at her toes. Ross leaned against one of the bookcases and continued staring at Shershah, who stood with his arms crossed.

How long have you had a driver's licence? Herbert asked.

I don't have one, Shershah said.

The father pushed the notebook aside and took the glasses off. Ross finally stopped staring at Shershah and looked over at Jessie, who was bending over exploring her feet.

Jessie, Herbert said after a moment. Jessie, what's this supposed to mean?

She didn't reply and continued scratching her feet. Her fingernails were already quite black.

Jessie! Herbert shouted.

Ross exchanged glances with his father and raised a warning finger.

Sweetie, he said, how did you get here, then?

In the red Fiat, said Jessie.

And who drove?

He did, she said, and pointed at me.

And what's the other guy doing here? Herbert asked impatiently.

But that's Shershah, she said. You wanted him.

Herbert got up and crouched down beside her. She immediately rolled onto her side and curled herself up into a ball.

The Fiat is a lovely car, she shouted, a good car, we drive everywhere in it.

Despite the air-conditioning, my hands started sweating again, and I laid them against the cool stone of the windowsill. Jessie and her father were both scrunched up on the floor; they looked like two eggs, one upright, and one lying down. I didn't understand. I met Shershah's gaze. He had moved back to give Herbert room, and looked at me questioningly. I tried to shrug and shook my head. Ross walked over, pushed his father aside and kneeled down next to Jessie.

Outside, he said quietly, by the window, the yellow lions are grinning. Shall we wait for the white wolves together?

She sat up at once, wiped her hands over her face and pushed Ross away, an embarrassed smile on her face.

OK, she whispered.

Ross went back to his place by the bookcase.

Dad only wanted to know who'd be driving, he said.

Jessie jumped to her feet, ran over to Shershah and crashed into him. He was taken aback enough to put his arms round her. In his arms, she pointed at me again.

Cooper will drive, she said.

That was the first time she called me that in public. I knew she meant well, but I found it embarrassing nevertheless.

Max, I said to Herbert.

Aha, he said.

He waved at me with his large hand, as though I was standing at the railing of an ocean steamer that was just leaving the quayside, sounding its horn as it started its journey across the Atlantic. Sighing, he went over to his desk and scribbled something in his notebook.

Then you'll be doing it together, he said.

Ross stepped up next to him and they spoke quickly, and so quietly that I couldn't make anything out.

So, welcome, Herbert said at last. Jessie, do you have anything left?

Sold it all, she said proudly.

You're great, he said.

*

He pulled a freezer bag, fastened tightly with a red rubber band, out of a drawer.

Fuck, Shershah said.

Holy shit, I said.

$C_{17}H_{21}NO_4$, Herbert said.

I'd never said 'Holy shit' before. I'd also never taken coke before. There were at least two hundred grams in the bag. My tongue clicked dryly against the roof of my mouth. Herbert used a tiny spoon to shovel two little piles of powder onto a glass plate and laid a small gold tube next to it. He waved us over. I let Shershah go first. When he was done, I leaned over and saw my face in the glass, the white line cutting across the reflection. I held one nostril closed and snorted so violently that everything suddenly disappeared and my left eye began to water.

Sitting back on the windowsill, I dug out what was left in my nostril and stuck it in my mouth. It tasted salty, of snot, and bitter at the same time, sterile and chemical and uniquely delicious. My tongue and lips grew numb and the inside of my nose felt like an icebox.

What's with Jessie? I asked.

I pointed at Jessie, who was squatting on the floor again. Herbert misunderstood my question.

Not for her, he said.

OK, I said.

I don't need drugs, said Jessie. I'm sick in the head.

I was content with her answer, I was content with everything, because I understood it all. I understood the universe and the transience of life within it and the necessity of rising above it all for a time. I should actually have run out onto the street to enlighten everyone; maybe I really wanted to paint a picture or tidy the flat, clean it, put everything in order, into a geometric system in which the essential nature of it all would alone be visible. I knew the system. It was as if I was paralysed. Something had to be done, something I'd always wanted to do, and I finally sat down next to Jessie on the carpet, turned my gaze on her, a gaze that burned my own eyes, a gaze that I feared would fall on her like a two-thousand-volt blitz and reduce her to ashes. Nothing of the sort happened. I tried to sit down cross-legged, but ended up crouching in front of her, balancing awkwardly. Behind her small, bowed silhouette, the room shifted constantly. Walls slid into each other and apart again. She grabbed my hand suddenly. Her fingers were so small that she only got hold of my middle and ring fingers. It was the first time in my life that a girl had taken my hand in hers. We looked at each other and I understood Jessie too. I understood that things had to be rearranged in her head, according to a system that only I knew.

I realized that the other three were speaking amongst themselves in low tones.

But what's *with* Jessie? I asked.

Herbert misunderstood the question again.

She'll meet you in Bari, he said, give you the tickets and come back to Vienna with you.

OK, I said.

We'll go for a meal tonight, Herbert said.

But what's *with* her? I asked.

Jessie's coming too, he said.

OK, I said.

Shershah nodded too, grinning, face glowing.

When the telephone rings, I know immediately that it's her. I turn the recorder off. When Donald Duck gets a call from his uncle Dagobert, the cable jumps in the air with every ring, drawing the silhouette of the uncle with his beak wide open. I see Clara in front of me in the same way. I pick the phone up.

What, she growls, is that supposed to mean?

I can't think of anything to say.

Are you messing with me, you bastard? she asks.

I think for a moment.

No, I say.

Look, she hisses, you may be loony or not, but I'm not going to be fucked about with. NOT by YOU. It's IMPORTANT to me. VERY IMPORTANT!

She's started screaming, she sounds really worked up, her behaviour on the telephone contrasts brutally with my own state of mind; I feel empty, lost somewhere between Vienna, Bari and the sunny-yellow pyjamas.

Right, right, I whisper.

I don't want to fight, not now. I have to tell her what's happened to my flat. She's about to continue screaming, but her voice gives out like it's been shot in the knees. It snaps over and over again with a sobbing sound.

Look, she squeaks, you have to decide, and right NOW. Tell me straight, if you want to go on OR NOT.

She sniffles and I hear a faint cartilaginous crack that probably comes from her rubbing her nose too hard with the back of her hand.

Of course, of course, I say, anything you want.

WHAT!! she shouts.

Stay where you are, I say, I'll come over. Where are you now?

Café Josephine, she sobs, I'm standing at the bar and everyone's staring at me.

I suddenly feel sorry for her, more sorry even than I feel for myself.

Don't move, I say. I'll get a taxi and be with you in five minutes.

She hangs up. I grab the tape recorder and the dog and run down the stairs.

Clara is almost unrecognizable. Her mascara has run down her face in two uneven black stripes that fan out at the end like river deltas. There's another line running straight between her nose and her mouth where she's wiped her face with her sleeve. It's as if she'd wanted to cross her face out. Her ponytail is dishevelled, and hairs are sticking out all over her head. She must have completely lost it. The bartender casts meaningful looks my way as I walk over to her table. She's slumped over the small round marble surface that has an empty ashtray right in the middle. There's no sign of a glass or a cup. She doesn't even acknowledge Jacques Chirac, who turns away dolefully.

Just for something to do, I start stroking her hair. But a head of hair is actually the most repulsive part of the human body: a collection of dry, dead, keratinized cells; a mass grave. I pull my hand back, shaking a couple of static hairs off my fingers as if I've been touching a spider's nest. The vanilla scent of her shampoo clings to my hand.

I order a glass of water and a pile of paper napkins. We sit motionless until the waiter returns. I don't know what she's thinking. I don't even know what I'm thinking.

I dunk a napkin in the glass, turn her face towards me with one hand, and start rubbing at the black stripes. The serviette turns greyish-black immediately, but the stripes don't get any lighter. With more napkins and water, I manage to turn her cheeks a uniform grey. She is so limp that I have to hold her chin still, in order to keep rubbing and wiping at her face. When I'm done, her cheeks are fiery red, making her look more alive. I feel better.

Clara, I say.

She immediately starts getting worked up again.

The whole thing means fuck all to you, she squeaks, you've no interest in it at all.

You're right there, I say, but that's not so awful.

She stares at me; both her eyes, the left one like the sky and the right one like water, reddening.

Look what I brought you, I say.

I dig in my jacket pocket and put the disk and the tapes on the table in front of her.

I'm sorry, I say.

She shakes her head. Her eyes are filling again.

But I can't go on, she says, I really can't. My supervisor's probably right. I'm simply too weak.

Oh come on, I say.

I lift my hand, still looking at Clara, and order two double vodkas, straight up. And cold. The glasses are all fogged up. I feel my saliva running.

Lovely, I say. Drink up.

We clink our glasses. She gulps it all down at once, gives herself a shake and coughs.

I'll be back in a sec, I say.

In the Gents, I kneel in front of the toilet bowl, breathe on the lid, polish it with a bundle of toilet paper and lay a line.

She's ordered two more glasses, and smiles at me as I sit down. I beam back.

You see, I say, you'll be fine.

We raise our glasses and tip the vodka back. I'm going to make sure I don't cross the threshold into a blackout today. I want to stay with it. She signals to the waiter, then gets up.

Excuse me, Clara says. Back soon.

She comes back with her hair in a tidy ponytail. She can't have a comb in those tight trousers, so she must have yanked the knots out of her hair with her fingers.

If you'll listen, she says, I'll tell you what else my supervisor said.

Great, I say.

He's read my records a few times, she says, and he thinks I'm not ready for the full identification with the subject necessary for a study like this because of reservations grounded in the weaknesses of my ego.

Wow, I say, impressed, that's some well-chosen shit.

That's what I think, she says. He says he probably overestimated me, though I told him that you even hit me now and then!

And that's not enough proof of our unreserved commitment for him, I say.

Overestimated me! she shouts. It's impossible to overestimate me! I have no upper limits! I'm like a tower with strong walls but no roof!

That's a well, then, I counter.

He should take a look at the others, sitting in the Institute writing the hundred thousandth essay on C.G. Jung's image of women, she grumbles.

What does he want from you, then? I ask.

Good question, she says. I quote: Miss Müller, you want your degree and I want the essentials. The essentials of this man's story.

And those are?

Exactly, she says, only he knows that.

And why on earth does he call you Miss Müller?

Everyone calls me Lieschen Müller at university.

What the fuck is that all about? I ask.

She raises her bum from her chair and fumbles in her jeans pocket until she manages to tug her ID card out. Her hair is a little shorter in the photo, but apart from that, she looks pretty much the same. Lisa Müller, 28.02.1976, is printed next to it.

See? she says.

Was 1976 a leap year?

Why?

Forget it, I say. Simply hoping that you might just have missed being born.

What should I do now? she asks.

Lie in a bathtub of cold water again, I say.

It's all your fault, she whispers, you're just not crazy enough.

I pull my chair closer to her and take the DAT-recorder out.

I'm crazy enough, I say. Calm down and listen to the new tape.

I pass her the left earphone and take the right. I hear rustling and clicking sounds, followed by atmospheric roars from when I got too close to the microphone.

Max, she says, or Cooper, or whoever you are.

Shhh, I say.

I want to listen to the tape, and I want her to listen to it.

Don't you get it? she asks. There's no point if my supervisor doesn't think you're a suitable subject.

I groan and press the stop button.

Clara, I say calmly, or Lisa, or whatever. Have you told him that I've murdered someone?

She freezes in her chair, as if she's just been shot. You can practically hear the wheels churning in her head.

You haven't, then, I say. How thick can you get?

But, but, she whispers, I didn't believe it.

It's true, though, I say. Now be quiet.

She smiles at me, delighted, as if I were her bridegroom and we were standing on the church steps. Then she puts her hand over mine.

Thank you, she says.

The waiter brings more vodka and we raise our glasses.

She closes her eyes at last and leans back, stretching the earphones between us. My voice starts playing. The lamp behind me casts light over my shoulder. I tuck my thumbs in, spread my fingers out to form a spider with my hands and let its shadow run over the floor, trembling slightly, front legs groping forward, standing tall, body swaying. It climbs up Clara, up to her face, and her eyelids twitch as if she feels the shadow touching her. Clara starts smiling, as if she's dreaming something pleasant in her sleep. I tell myself that she likes hearing my voice on tape, the way people like a piece of music or a film. She's relaxing. Her head is full of the pictures I've put there: me and those who have died,

Shershah and Jessie. They must be very different in Clara's imagination, but there they are, and all three of us will still be there in Clara's head when I'm no longer here. My cheek muscles tug the corners of my mouth upwards. For a moment, I'm so close to Clara that we could be snuggled up against each other in the same armchair. For a moment, I'm happy, and so is she. Perhaps it's the vodka too. The waiter brings two more glasses. I lift one up to her nose, until she opens her eyes and sneezes.

When the tape's finished and I've pressed the Stop button, Clara lingers in her chair looking drunk and very sleepy. She opens her eyes and looks around the room, confused. I have to bend over and take her face in my hands. We lean our foreheads together and rub noses. Her skin smells of kiwi fruit.

I try to bundle her into a taxi outside, but she stops me.

Naaah, she mumbles, everything's fine, but I'll sleep over at a friend's for a while. Nerves, OK?

I didn't expect this, and it's not really a good time to admit to myself that I don't want to be alone. The taxi sets off, and I press my face against the glass to see Clara growing smaller on the street corner, as she raises her hand again briefly to wave me off.

12 | Snails

The doorbell frightens me out of my skin every time. Not hearing it for twenty-four hours is enough for me to forget how shrill it is. Jacques Chirac jumps up and runs to the door, writhing to the left and right of it, his tail wagging furiously. Clara drops by every evening shortly after nightfall to pick up the next tape. She rings to make sure I'm ready. Then she takes the dog for a walk.

It's still light – half past three, according to the clock on the wall. I get up and collapse again. My legs have gone to sleep and my feet are numb. I limp after the dog, a thousand needles pricking my lower legs. A figure with a shiny black page-boy, checked red skirt and knee-high motorcycle boots is standing outside. I recognize her by the boots. I leave the door open, turn and go into the kitchen.

It's a shock. So the first Clara exists, the favoured one of my imagination, who looks like Mata Hari. But I don't like this resurrection at all. She coos a greeting at Jacques Chirac, who keeps pushing his nose between her legs. I wonder how she got her long hair under the wig. Maybe the page-boy is real and the blonde mane has been fake all along. She follows me into the kitchen and sits down at the table.

What's up? I ask. Get lost.

Take it easy, she says good-humouredly. It's still my flat, after all.

What's with the outfit? I ask. Why are you so early?

I'm on my way to a party, she says, and some of the people who'll be there only know me like this.

You look like crap, I say.

I'm leaning against the fridge, because I don't feel like sitting down.

Is there anything to eat? she asks.

No, I say.

Please, she says. What do you eat?

What-do-you-want? I ask.

I feel my adrenalin rising.

OK, she says. I'll tell you. The party's HERE, at nine, because it's my birthday.

Your birthday's at the end of February, I say.

She throws her arms up in the air affectedly.

I just feel like it, she says.

Jacques Chirac's big head is lying on her left thigh. He's looking up at her imploringly, his lower lids are two white sickle shapes and his brow is crumpled in a heart-rending fashion. As she gets up, she pokes him in the chin, which serves him right. She puts a pot on the stove and I leave the kitchen. As the burner warms up, the pot begins to rattle and spit. I hear her opening the fridge, and her faint cry of delight at finding the bottle of orange juice. She's unnaturally cheerful. It makes me nervous.

I retreat into the living room with the recorder and the cassettes that I like most from the bookcase.

We went out for dinner, my voice on tape says, and Herbert made me learn the route. The others looked through the menu while I rattled off the towns and motorway exits by heart. When Jessie heard Ross ordering escargot as a starter, she grabbed the tablecloth and twisted it with both hands until everything on the table started sliding off: the cutlery fell to the ground and the people at the next table turned to look at us.

When, Ross said through gritted teeth, will you ever learn to pull yourself together in public?

His veins were showing. They looked as if they'd been laid on top of his skin, as if his body was held together by a wide-meshed net of thick twine. The waiter hurried off to get new cutlery and a cloth to wipe up the mess.

All snails are my friends, Jessie whimpered.

Good lord, Herbert said to Ross. Just have prawns instead.

Jessie smoothed out the tablecloth, the people at the next table turned back to their food and the waiter brought some whiskey. Vienna, A2, Klagenfurt, petrol, off at Villach, Plöckenpass, Tolmezzo, A23, Ùdine, A4 towards Venice, not Trieste.

Clara comes into the room, looking like she's about to tidy up. She's swinging her hips as she walks, in a way I've never noticed before.

Forget about wiggling like that in front of me, I say.

The words boom inside my head. With the headphones on, I seem to be alone in my skull with my voice ringing around me. I stop the tape.

Don't worry, she says. Relax, will you? It's the shoes that are making me walk this way.

She's lying. There's something different in the way she's moving about, as if something is about to happen. Perhaps it's just the stupid party. I hope she hasn't made any other decisions. I turn the volume up and rest my head in my arms so I can block out her existence.

We discovered the armour-plating at the petrol station, somewhere past Klagenfurt on the A2. We had to fill up one more time before the Italian border, because driving up to petrol or service stations after that was strictly forbidden. There were two full cans of petrol in the back seat. Shershah went into the shop to get provisions. He had a debit card from Herbert with a name on it I didn't recognize, and 0000 as a PIN. I walked around inspecting the car while the juice flowed into the tank. It was a black off-road hybrid that commanded a great view over the road and drove beautifully. I tried the boot, half expecting it to be locked. The hatch swung up. The boot was empty. When I looked again, I saw that the underside of the door was reinforced with a steel plate about a metre wide. God knows how heavy it was. I lifted the hood to find a similar construction. I pressed against the leather upholstery on the driver and passenger doors with my fingers, and I could feel a thick layer of interwoven steel cable. And all the glass was twice as thick as it was in normal cars. Bulletproof.

Shershah came back with two bags full of clinking bottles and rustling foil. I showed him the armour-plating and moved his hand over the steel weave beneath the upholstery in the doors. He didn't bat an eyelid.

So what? he said. Look what I've got us.

He'd bought loads of booze, although it was clear that I couldn't drink. I would have to drive while he had a good time in the passenger seat. It was about eleven in the morning when we left that petrol station.

We turned off onto the A2 at Villach to go through a quieter border-crossing and then returned to the motorway at Tolmezzo. I'd never driven through the Alps before. The steep mountain walls had practically no shade, so it just got hotter and hotter. The bulletproof-glass windows couldn't be wound down and there was no air-conditioning; only a sunroof, with the sun directly above it. I had to keep my hands in the same places on the steering wheel so as not to burn myself on the overheated black plastic. My fingers were sweating. Shershah lay groaning beside me in the passenger seat, which he'd tilted all the way back. His hair was tousled with sweat and it stuck to his temples. He rolled a pile of spliffs and stashed them in the glove compartment. Shortly before the pass he dug a tape out of his rucksack and played it. It was Beethoven. He turned it right up and tapped the beat on his thighs with his hands. I was getting dizzy. I turned the rear-view mirror so that I could see my own face in it when I looked up, and every couple of minutes I looked to see if I was still there. I was thinking about snails.

They waved us through at the border. The Customs officials were barely out of sight when Shershah, whom I'd taken for dead, reached up through the sunroof with his middle finger extended and shouted FUCK YOU!

Then he took out the first joint. I began to relax. The heat seemed to let up a little and the mountains conveyed some idea of the size of the Earth; the road sloped uphill steeply and I felt the force of gravity. Beethoven gave way to The Doors, and Shershah told me why he thought he was Jim Morrison reincarnated.

When Shershah had finally fallen asleep, I pushed my seat back a little and daydreamed about crossing the Alps in an armoured car on a secret mission to save two or three novice nuns from the Chinese. The nuns were wearing Esprit and Benetton gear and were to be sold to the Algerians. At Ùdine, I thought I could already smell the sea; at Mestre I did. The motorway swung away from the coast again and looped around Bologna. My eyes hurt from squinting, since I'd forgotten my sunglasses. I swapped the nuns for Jessie, who sat screeching and squealing in a cell, having bitten a few Chinese baddies in the hand. I dragged out the rescue scene, bringing Shershah into play and allowing him to fail miserably: it was six in the evening, we'd reached the Adriatic Sea at Rimini, a hail of fire from my machine gun had flung Jessie's brother – uncovered as a traitor – against the wall.

I was exhausted and needed a break. We'd come halfway and I had no idea how I was going to survive the rest.

*   *   *

I tear the headphones off my head with a cry. Clara has touched me on the arm; I really had forgotten about her. The living room is unrecognizable. It looks as if an army of elves has swept through it.

I have no idea how you did all that so quickly, I say.

I still have to buy some things and get ready, she says. It'd be good if you could disappear for a few hours.

Where to? I ask.

How about your own flat? she says.

Girl, I say, my flat has been ransacked. They're looking for me.

Astonished, she pulls her head back, creasing her chin.

I didn't know that, she says at last.

Yup, I say, I know.

Then go for a walk, she says.

It's still light outside, I say.

She doesn't get it. I pick up the tape recorder, leave the room and put on my shoes.

Is the spy from Vienna coming too? I ask.

What spy? she retorts.

But she knows who I'm talking about.

See you later, I say.

Jacques Chirac and I walk up the stairs. Four flights. When we can't go any further, I sit down on the marble tiles, lean back against the attic door and turn the recorder on again.

Apart from booze, all that Shershah had bought was crisps and chocolate bars. The melted chocolate oozed in the foil packaging like sperm in a condom. I was so hungry my stomach hurt. I polished off a jumbo bag of crisps and the stomach-ache got worse. The sea was dark blue, almost black. It promised a new life. I wanted to go swimming. I turned the car along the narrow coastal road with one hand on the wheel and looked out for a lonely bay to bathe in. There wasn't one. The hotels were so close to each other that they could have been a single kilometre-long building.

We can't stop here, Shershah said.

He suddenly sounded wide awake. The only sign of the booze and dope he'd been taking over the last eight hours was his fiery red eyes.

No sightseeing, he said, no petrol stations, no unnecessary delays.

I looked at him. Of course he was right. He grinned.

It's a job, he said, not for pleasure.

It's not a job for you, I said, but a driving holiday. I can't go on, don't you get it?

Only seven more hours, he said, and laughed.

SHUT UP, I roared.

I suddenly felt the blood rushing into my face. I even felt it throbbing behind my eyes. I could have killed him. I'd taken on too much and I had no idea how I was supposed to get us both to Bari. I was scared.

Relax, Shershah said.

He sounded well meaning and a little taken aback, which calmed me down. We approached a road sign.

Let's get back onto the motorway, he said, and stop at the first rest stop. You can lie down in the shade and sleep for an hour.

I didn't reply, but turned off at the next crossroads and sped towards the motorway.

It's warm and humid up here next to the attic door and I'm sweating as much as I was then. My sweat smells sour-sweet and it's leaving a burning sensation on my skin. Jacques Chirac is lying on his side and panting in fits, his paws clawing the smooth floor. I'd been at my wits' end then; I hadn't known how to go on, or how to stop. Now there's nothing in my life to stop, even if I wanted to. I was desperate then, but happy. Though I didn't know it.

Shershah woke me. I felt as if I'd only been asleep for a couple of minutes.

OK, he said. We have to go on.

I sat up and saw a gigantic ham sandwich in his hand. I felt sorry for having imagined mowing him down with a machine gun. He must have scrounged the sandwich off one of the families taking a break here. I saw folding chairs and tables at the edge of the rest area. Then my sight went blurry and everything danced in coloured spots in front of me. Shershah's face wavered against a green background. I ate the sandwich.

Shershah, I said, still chewing, I can't go on.

Stand up, he said. Get your circulation going.

He dragged me into a tiled building with aluminium doors and then into one of the cubicles. It stank. The ham sandwich heaved in my stomach. I avoided looking at the toilet, a mere hole in the ground. Shershah gave me a tiny straw. I bent over his hand like a horse carefully taking some sugar off him.

After that, I drove as if the car was an extension of myself. Gears clutch brakes gas – it was like dancing. I didn't stop smiling until two hours later, at Pescara. Now and then we got a glimpse of the sea with the changing colours of the sky above it; Shershah poked me in the side and gave a cheer every time. The moon rose to our left and flashed like a strobe light over the trees as they rushed by.

What time is it? I asked. Where are we? I have to piss.

Shershah struggled to sit up and squinted at one of the unlit road signs.

Twenty-nine kilometres to San Severo, he said.

That was one of the last towns I'd had to learn by heart. I tried to divide the stretch up into sections to estimate the total distance.

It won't take more than two hours, I said.

It's got to take no more than that, he said. It's just after midnight.

13 | Bari

As the next rest area came into view, my bladder hurt so intensely that I barely knew how I was going to leave the car. My stomach felt like skin stretched taut over stone. Bent double, I stumbled out of the car and unfastened my trousers at the first fence post I saw. Shershah stepped up next to me. The sound of piss falling on the dry ground seemed unusually loud. White-brown patches glimmered in the grass, trucker-turds on paper tissues. Shershah finished before me and zipped his jeans up. From the corner of my eye, I noticed that he wasn't wearing underwear.

Suddenly he straightened his back. He stretched his right arm out to tap me on the shoulder, but missed, and waved his finger up and down in space.

Hey, man, he said, you won't believe this.

I turned. The parking lot looked exactly as it had before, a broad stretch of asphalt without any markings, a trampled strip of grass next to a fence and a row of stunted trees. Only one thing had changed. The place where our car had stood a moment ago was empty.

You left the key in the ignition, Shershah whispered. You fucking dickhead.

I felt blood coursing down to my feet and then up again with an enormous whoosh, as if there was a fountain inside me. Then I looked down at the hand that was still holding my cock between thumb and index finger. The middle, ring and little fingers were curled into a half-fist, from which the car key was hanging like a beard. I fastened my trousers and held the key out to Shershah. Without the car itself, the key felt ridiculous.

Shit, Shershah whispered. Fucking shit.

Then he suddenly started laughing. He slapped his thigh.

Those Italian fuckers, I just can't believe it.

Do you have your passport with you? I asked.

We reached as one for our jeans pockets with our right hands.

Yup, he said.

They're going to stone us, I said.

But it's not our fault, he said. They'll treat us fairly.

I look forward to it, I said.

We were silent for a moment.

Man, he said suddenly, my tapes, my dope, my tobacco.

I lay down on my back. The tarmac beneath me was warm. I emptied my head of everything, separating soul from body, and let it fly wherever, back home to school, to my mother, to Bari even. Shortly after one, a car turned into the parking lot, sweeping the shadows off us into the forest. Shershah jumped up and raced towards the Italian getting out. The man raised his arms in front of his face, slammed the door and drove off with the tyres squealing.

Great, I said.

Shut the fuck up, Shershah said.

The next car had a woman driver. The interior light of the vehicle reflected against her thick black hair.

Well, now, Shershah said.

He rubbed his palms over his face. This time, he stayed where he was, waved, and waited for the woman to walk over.

Do you speak English? he asked.

Three minutes later, I was in the back seat, knees drawn up to my chest. It was a tiny car, a two-seater really. The engine was in the boot, right behind my back, and it droned so loudly that I couldn't make out a word of what was being said in front. Now and then, Shershah passed the filter cigarettes he got from the woman back to me to take a drag. She was only a couple of years older than us, just over twenty maybe, and she stuck to the slow lane, never doing more than ninety.

We managed to get into the city centre by half-past two. I saw a large lighted building, and realized that it had to be the station. So the girl had brought us to the meeting point. Shershah took her face in his hands to say farewell, but she turned aside, jumped back into the car and drove off.

It was a clear night. It had cooled off a little and the temperature was just about perfect.

Well? Shershah asked.

Get with it, I said. We've still lost the car. And where's Jessie?

A group of Interrailers was sitting in a row by the station wall, leaning against multicoloured backpacks. One of them had a guitar propped on his knee, and was playing 'Blowin' in the Wind'. We turned and walked around for a bit.

Is there more than one train station here? I asked.

Fuck off, Shershah shouted.

It was the first time that he seemed to be losing his cool. I suddenly began to suspect that he knew more about this whole thing than I did.

She's got to be here, he said. We're only half an hour late.

He went off to look on the other side of the station and in the building itself. My nicotine craving hadn't been satisfied at all by those few drags from cigarettes in the car, so I went over to the backpackers to bum a cigarette. They were German. I stood in the middle of the square, smoking and feeling the gentle summer breeze against my face. Every country, every town, has its own smell. So this was how southern Italy smelt – how Bari smelt.

There was a big crossroads at the end of the square. Just before it, the ground was swallowed up by a flight of steps leading down to an underpass. I saw a small park on the other side, which looked incredibly dark; it seemed to absorb every last glimmer of light. The wider of the two streets wound right around the park in a broad curve, like a roundabout. Jessie appeared in the mouth of the underpass like an apparition. Her yellow hair seemed to be glowing. She walked towards me unbearably slowly, holding a hamburger tightly in both hands. I was so happy to see her.

She stopped in front of me and sucked at the straw of the drink clutched in her elbow. Her dimples deepened, and the liquid spouted thin and yellow up the straw, like a plant growing in a time lapse. Her lips were lined with some pink stuff – it looked almost like felt-tip pen. The colour was smeared at the corners of her mouth so that she looked like she was smiling all the time.

What're you staring at me for? she asked.

She bit almost half her hamburger off and grinned at me, cheeks full. She sucked more yellow drink from the straw before she swallowed. I looked at her eating a mountain and drinking the sun with it.

Great that you made it, she said finally. Where's Shershah?

Looking for you, I mumbled. I have to tell you something.

I wanted to get it over with. Craning her neck, she looked around the square, at the row of backpackers, at the station entrance. I had to grab her by the shoulders to make her look at me.

Listen, I said, the car's been stolen.

There he is! she shouted.

She slipped out from under my hands and ran to Shershah. She gave him the rest of her hamburger and wiped her hands on her trousers. I suddenly felt a piercing sensation in my guts, like the twist of a knife, and I knew that I would need the toilet in the next few seconds. I ran past Shershah and Jessie into the station.

There was no toilet paper. But I had no choice; my guts were writhing like a nest of worms. I gripped the door handle in both hands, bent my knees, and leaned forward, my bum hanging over the bowl. The stuff that shot out of me was liquid and almost clear.

My thighs hurt when I stood up again. I took my trousers and boxer shorts off, used the boxers to wipe myself, and tossed them in the toilet.

Shershah and Jessie were waiting impatiently.

Are you crazy, man? Jessie said.

I apologized, and knew there was no hope. I'd need that toilet again in a few minutes. Jessie waved three plane tickets under my nose.

Don't you get it? she asked. We've just missed the charter flight.

I'm sick, I whispered.

We have to get back as quickly as possible, Jessie said,.

Let's go where you got the hamburger from, Shershah said.

Yes, please, I pleaded.

We rushed towards the underpass. I heard Jessie's bare feet pattering on the pavement behind us. She was panting.

You still don't get it, she said.

Her voice suddenly sounded deeper than usual, and calmer. Older.

We have to get back to Vienna now, she said, or we'll be in for it. All three of us. Do you understand?

We ducked into the underpass. The walls were so filthy that you could hardly read the graffiti. We rounded the park and I saw the lighted interior of the joint that Jessie must have got her burger from. I headed straight for the toilet, and got there just in time. There was even some toilet paper. I could have cried.

I came out to find them sitting at a table, a black plastic box lying in front of Jessie. For a moment I took it to be a portable heater. Then I noticed the cable spiralling from it up to Jessie's ear, where it ended in a normal telephone receiver.

The white wolves, she said into the mouthpiece.

Then she listened. A salad, two dry bread-rolls and a glass of milk had been laid out for me. I was touched. Even though milk's the worst thing for diarrhoea.

By train, Jessie said.

A sweetcorn kernel got stuck in my throat.

You can't be serious, I gasped.

Yes I am, she said. Change in Milan and then on to Paris.

Paris?? I asked. That's a hellish detour!

Jessie shrugged.

Instructions from the top, she said.

How long will that take? Shershah asked.

We leave at seven am, she said, and arrive in Vienna after midnight.

I won't survive that, I said.

Oh come on, Shershah said.

He had overcome his low. Three or four empty cartons in different colours lay in front of him, a couple of leftover French fries amongst them. He blew into his coffee, looking wide awake. He'd slept half the day in the car, unlike me. I had driven for thirteen hours, and had thought for two hours that I would be beaten to a pulp at the Bari train station because of the car being nicked. Jessie carried the mobile telephone over to the counter and exchanged a few words in Italian with the proprietor of the burger joint before he took the phone off her and stored it in the back room. The she went to the toilet. I leaned over to Shershah.

Listen, you bastard, I said. Why don't you just tell me what's going on?

So you won't fuck it up, he said simply.

WHAT? I asked.

What do you want? he asked. Everything's worked out. Perfectly choreographed.

WORKED OUT? I said. I'm practically dead with fright.

Lower your voice, he said. That's exactly what I mean. You're not laid-back. You kick up too much of a fuss.

I felt another stabbing pain in the guts and doubled up on the chair, unable to reply.

Maxie, he said, you have a driver's licence. That's it, that's all that distinguishes you.

He leaned back smugly in his chair.

You're having a holiday here, he said, like you would anywhere else. For me, this is about my future.

You want to work for Herbert? I asked tiredly.

The best job in the world, he said.

That's why you're hanging around with Jessie? I asked.

The girl loves me, he said, and love is always selfish. So we all win.

You're a damn pig, I said.

He laughed. As she came back Jessie looked happy to see him laughing.

At four am the man behind the counter shouted something at Jessie. She waved, and ushered us out onto the street. I could barely keep my eyes open as I walked, but my stomach seemed better for the moment.

I want to go to the harbour, Jessie said. Will you come too?

She meant Shershah. He rolled his eyes heavenwards.

I'm going to lie down with the Interrail cunts, he said. Wake me when the train comes.

I'll go with you, I said to her.

She reached for my hand, grabbed my middle and ring fingers and dragged me off, running. My feet moved themselves – I was hardly there – they stumbled forward, unbearably fast, it seemed to me.

The town flew past in patches, peeling away from us, I saw boxy houses painted yellow, some of them brown with age. I started sweating. My excess pounds felt like a thick ski-suit enveloping me. I had to strain with every movement, squishing my flab in order to move my arms and legs. I never had been able to run. Jessie showed some mercy, and we slowed down.

The buildings were larger now, greyer and newer, spread over the asphalt surface in an unusual pattern. This was the harbour, surrounded by wire fences. What I'd thought was a whitewashed block of flats was one of the ferries to Greece with its maw open. There were Interrailers here too, lying like a heap of old clothes in front of the locked passenger entry. Jessie led me along the fence. We passed some large corrugated-iron buildings and came up to the edge so suddenly that I almost took one step too many.

It was four metres down to the water. Big blue plastic hot-dog shapes hung from the algae-covered wall. There was a round black metal post next to us, thick as a tree; it almost reached my hips. Hardly anything docks here now, Jessie said. I come here sometimes.

She perched on top of the bollard, her legs not touching the ground. There wasn't room for two. I stood next to her. She simply sat there, back bowed, stuck two or three fingers of her left hand into her mouth, and started biting her nails. When I couldn't stand the sound any longer, I grabbed her hand and pulled it out of her mouth.

Jessie, I asked, what's with the wolves, the lions and the snails? She shoved her other hand into her mouth and starting chewing again. A few minutes passed. The sea lapped listlessly against the wall. It stank and it didn't look like much. The first light of day began to show on the horizon beyond the huge, steely body of the water.

I was very ill when I was little, Jessie said. A great big eagle brought me to a house where he kept his collection of children. I

sat by the window there, looking out at the weather and the seasons changing. I hated summer. It gave me a headache; too many sounds and colours. There was a patch of sunflowers growing below; the yellow screamed up at me. The snails didn't make it up to my window. They got stuck halfway up the wall and shrank back into their shells. Until it rained. Then they came to visit me again, and I always fed them well after their long journey. Do you understand?

I nodded. She looked up at me, her face like a small, flat, pale moon, in which the dust of the street had formed craters like Mare Crisium and Mare Nubium. Crisium: crisis; Nubium: clouds.

Ross came to visit me sometimes, she said. He explained that we had to wait and see how the animals changed. When it was hot, he used to say: Now the yellow lions are grinning and the white wolves are far away. We have to wait for them. And I waited. A long time. Until it got cooler. The snails came, and then the white wolves came, and smiled. They made my eyes and my head feel better.

When Jessie cried, she looked as though she just had conjunctivitis. Her eyes simply teared, but that was all.

I watched the animals changing many times, she said. Ross came now and then and helped me with the waiting.

I was silent. I couldn't bear it. She jumped up from the post after a while.

And why, she said vehemently, does Shershah not like me?

She looked into my eyes, expecting an answer.

He does like you, I said, better than any other human being. He can't do more than that. He's damaged that way, you know?

Damaged, she said. I understand that.

I threw up four times in the toilet on the train, then fell asleep. I woke up when we stopped at a station, but my eyes were so puffy that I couldn't tell where we were. I felt Jessie's head against the crook of my arm as she slept. I have no memory of changing trains

in Milan and Paris, but I remember Jessie bringing me bottles of water and me throwing the water right up again.

Ross was waiting for us at the station in Vienna. He handed Shershah a clear plastic bag containing our pouches of tobacco, Shershah's tapes, a pair of dirty socks, two misshapen chocolate bars and a few roll-ups. It was as if we'd died and someone had emptied our pockets of these meagre possessions before we were wheeled into the mortuary. I collapsed.

They put me on an intravenous drip in the hospital, and five and a half litres of water flowed into me. The doctor held a mirror up to my face; my skin was as wrinkled as an old man's. He told me that I'd almost died of dehydration.

My mother picked me up from the hospital in the Daimler a week later. When school started again, Shershah and Jessie weren't there, and it only took a few days for me to realize how deeply I'd fallen in love with Jessie.

14 | Handles and Steps

I see the moon through the small square window in the stairwell. It's lying deep in a swirl of clouds as if at the bottom of a bowl of cream. The sun got up and left its bed for a couple of hours, leaving behind a rumpled, sweaty sky; a few blessed hours of darkness and quiet.

I run my fingers through my hair, and feel the drool that Jacques Chirac left there when he woke me. An unmistakable red pattern has been pressed into my lower arm: it's the top of the DAT-recorder, with its Stop, Play and Record buttons. I decide to go for a walk until the pattern fades.

The kitchen looks smaller than usual, with four people squashed around the tiny table. The conversation breaks off when I appear in the doorway. I have difficulty telling them apart, these faces that are staring at me and blurring into each other. After a while, I make out Clara's wig and the sound guy's goatee. The cowshed smell of the university is hanging in the air. It's not so obvious when Clara is alone, but the four of them almost make up a seminar, perhaps about the social–ethical consequences of the collective entry into the post-material economy. Lawyers, on the other hand, never are students. They call each other colleagues from the first term onwards and are always smartly dressed because every day is an interview for them.

I bang the ice cream onto the table in front of Clara. Solero Forest Fruits.

Brought you something, I say.

It's almost a pity to have broken the silence. We'd just been starting to get used to it. Perhaps we should have simply let it go on and relished how it was becoming ever more impossible to say a word. The ice cream is from another petrol station, a different flavour from last time.

Happy Birthday, I say.

Great, Clara says.

The window behind her is open. She's lucky, because the ice cream sails right through it when she tosses it over her shoulder without looking. We listen to the soft rustle of the impact on the street.

Thank you, she says, her voice friendly.

The girl next to the sound guy pants squeakily a few times; she's probably laughing. I manage to look at her for a moment: she's pale and red-haired, and she reminds me of Maria Huygstetten. Behind her, there's a man's jacket hanging over her chair, it's as big as a sail, covering her back like a pair of eagle's wings.

That's Tom, Clara says, and the one who looks like your ex-secretary isn't called Maria, but Susanne.

Of course she's dropped in at my office, just to have a look. Maybe she even chatted with Maria. Who cares?

Hi, breathes Susanne.

She's twenty-two at most, and seems to be staring at me admiringly. Maybe she finds men in their mid-thirties erotic. For a second I wonder if Clara's introducing me as her boyfriend.

Got to go powder my nose, I say.

*

From the living room, I hear the conversation pick up again. It annoys me, and it continues to annoy me until I've snorted off a whole corner of the coffee table; then I feel friendliness coursing through me like water through sluice gates, buoying me up as I swim along into the open sea. Tom the technician comes into the room.

Hey man, he says. Long time no see.

Hey man, I say. Fuck off.

I know this room. I know it inside out and off by heart. I've scoured it for weeks like a catfish scouring the walls of its aquarium for food. This flat has become part of my head; my thoughts bend around the corners, dry on the tiles in the bathroom, condense against the windows, wrinkle the carpet, crunch under Clara's fingers on the keyboard when she writes. I've pawed everything in the room. Tom the technician wasn't part of it. He doesn't belong here.

Just as I'm about to tell him that, he pulls something out of his pocket and starts playing with it. It's a pen, a fat one, bright yellow–red–blue. I'm drawn to it as to a black hole that is about to suck all matter, all of existence, into it.

Why's he looking like that? Tom asks.

I don't have time to reply, because I'm waiting. I'm waiting for him to twirl the pen so I can see if it's got the inscription.

It has. *I love Vienna* – the word 'love' replaced by a heart shape. I remember exactly where I last saw it. In my former flat, on my old telephone stand, in the middle of the chaos after the thorough ransacking. I feel my features pulling apart, as if a thin layer of wax has been poured over my face and has hardened immediately. I can't get rid of the grin. It's like it's been carved into my face.

I walk out of the living room, trying to hold the grin before me like I'd hold a stinking cloth at arm's length. There's a grin on my face, but it doesn't have anything to do with me.

*

Did you have fun? Clara asks.

She and Susanne pat Jacques Chirac. Tom appears with a cigarette between his thin lips. The pen has disappeared.

What's the dog called? Susanne says breathily.

I tell her, even though I'm sure she knows already. The grin's still stuck to my face. Every time I look at the sound guy, I feel a twitch in my diaphragm, and I try hard to think about something else. My heart is pounding and sweat is streaming down from my underarms along my sides. There's a stool under the table, so I pull it up in front of the dishwasher. When I sit on it and lean back, the dishwasher starts. I turn around and pull the switch out again.

Clara is looking at me crossly. They seem to be speaking to me, and have been for some time.

Calm down, she says. Everyone wants to know why the dog's called Jacques Chirac.

We wanted to call him Giscard d'Estaing, I gasp, but we didn't know how to spell it.

Better?

Clara is kneeling next to me, wiping something over my forehead. I realize that no one else is in the kitchen. She takes the champagne bottle from me and puts it on the floor, where it rolls towards the wall, empty. I lean my head back, and the dishwasher starts up again. Clara heaves me up onto a chair. I feel pressure on my left thigh, and realize that she's sitting on my knee. The light is off, and the kitchen is peaceful, though there's noise from the living room, the buzz of people's voices.

Clara, I say.

I hardly ever use her name. It's uncomfortable having her on my knee, but I don't want to be rude.

I can't cope with all these people, I say.

My voice croaks. Clara nods and pulls her wig straight. Jacques Chirac is eating out of a half-full salad bowl on a chair.

Listen, she whispers, you're going to do exactly as I say now.

She strokes the top of my head. Her hands are slightly damp, and stick to my hair.

Just this one time, she says, promise?

OK, I say.

She pushes her face in front of me. Her eyes look funny, unfocused, more like pale blue shards of milky glass. Maybe she's turned her gaze so that she's really looking out in a completely different direction through her ears.

Go into the hallway with Jacques Chirac, she says, and wait for me at the front door. I'll come right after you, and then you'll walk with me, just beside me, OK?

OK, I say.

She slides off my knee and I grab the dog by the collar. Jacques Chirac and I go into the hall. I hear a blast of music as Clara opens the living-room door and slips in. I see curls of smoke intertwining in the beam of light through the door. My right foot crashes into a travel bag, I just stop myself from stumbling over it. Tom comes into the hall.

Hey, Max Maximal, is he waiting for a bus?

Dunno, Tom Tombola, I say. How many of them do you have, anyway?

Of what? he asks.

Pens, I say.

He stares at me for a moment, brow knitted so his face-piercing practically stabs him in the eye. Then he slowly raises his chin.

I see, he says languidly, the multicoloured ones. He grins at me impudently.

I've got tonnes of them, he says, huge vats in my flat, filled to the brim with multicoloured pens. From Vienna.

He pats me on the back and goes into the bathroom. I see Clara's back through the living-room doorway. She's speaking to Susanne, whose bosom quivers every time she laughs. Tom Technician comes out of the bathroom, scratching his balls, creating deep folds in his baggy jeans. He holds his hands up to my face, fingers curved into claws.

Sweetheart, he whispers. It's got to feel good when you've got something everyone wants.

He's probably tripping. I try to duck out of his way.

But he's got to remember, he says, not to do anything Jessie wouldn't have wanted.

This time I haven't heard wrong. That's Jessie's name he's saying, and for the first time in weeks I seriously wish that the fog in my head would clear just for a moment. I want to grab Tom by the arm, but he's already squeezing past Clara in the doorway as she comes into the hall.

Let's go, she whispers when he's gone. Susanne's got everything under control here.

She digs around in a pile of coats, something rattles, and then she takes hold of the travel bag and pushes me out the door.

You promised, she says, that you're coming with me.

The dog goes first. I suddenly realize that this is the last time I'll see the flat. That I'm looking at this stairwell for the last time, right now.

The dog was actually pretty happy here.

She's got me by the sleeve. I'm glad to be out in the fresh air. The moon has completely disappeared; it's smoothed the sheets out and pulled them over its head. There's a pale glimmer of light where it's hidden itself.

We run to the end of the street, turn back and go around the block.

Ah! Clara says.

I only see it when we're standing in front of it: Tom's green car. Clara shoves the dog into the back and pushes me into the passenger seat with the travel bag on my lap. There's a jolt as she bumps against the car behind us while getting out of the parking space.

On the motorway, she turns the radio on, and nods to the beat. I can see her smiling in the dark.

Life is strange, she whispers. It's really made up of handles to hold on to and steps to take. Everything would be different if there were fewer of them.

I feel it again – the twitching in my diaphragm.

15 | First-term Stuff

I don't ask where we are going, and Clara doesn't ask if I want to go. I would say no, but I wouldn't answer differently if I was asked if I want to go back to Leipzig, or head anywhere else on earth. The way I feel, everything except watching the green car bonnet rhythmically sucking in the white line flying towards us is impossible anyway.

The dog's got the runs from the salad. He's groaning, pushing his big head through the gap between my seat and the window, banging his nose against my ear expectantly. Every twenty minutes his whining gets so bad that we pull over to the side of the road. Then I open the door for him and we sit waiting, with the engine running, until he finishes and gets in again. In the meantime, I continue staring through the windscreen and try to imagine that we're still moving.

The constant interruptions make it difficult to sink into the particular feeling of limbo that overcomes me on motorways. This happens only at night, when movement seems to cancel itself out and it doesn't matter where I've been or where I'm going. I could be anyone and everywhere. I could dream of anything.

But of course I know where we're going. We're going to the city that sometimes manages to make me feel relatively alive – even when it is completely dead at midday, all the buildings like mausoleums, their inhabitants like zombies. Perhaps my return to Vienna right now has a certain force of logic.

Outside, the darkness looks more and more like southern Germany. Only a few lights shine through the trees; lit streets that make a whole village visible are rare. It's completely dark for stretches. It feels like humankind has been switched off.

In the distance, various shades of black part to show a panorama, a line of hills rising in black-black against the blue-black of the night sky. I've driven along this very road with Jessie, but on the other side, in the other direction, with the hills to our right, not our left. Now I have to look past Clara's cut-out profile to see the hills; back then, I was sitting at the wheel, and had Jessie's profile in view. It's hard to believe that these are the same hills and the same night sky – and that Jessie's profile has just been replaced by another. Then I felt I was at the beginning of something. Now I feel like I'm at the end, or even a little beyond that, like someone staying seated in the theatre after the play has finished, marvelling at it still going on, that there's no sign of anybody stopping.

Clara and I aren't listening to the radio any longer. We're breathing quietly, as light glints off the dashboard onto us. The darkness closes in on us. We're a capsule travelling through a hostile world, one that remains unchanged.

What I've always wanted to know, Clara says as we pass Nuremberg, is how one decides to study law.

I was so bored that I'd been wondering what she was thinking for a while, as she sat at the wheel, staring out at the empty motorway ahead of her. Was her head filled with words, sounds or maybe colours? Or was there just a roaring between her ears like inside an empty seashell?

I'm only asking you, she says, because I don't know any other lawyers.

I'm not typical, I say. I simply chose the course I was least confident about.

Why? she asked.

I thought it was my last chance.

And were you right?

You see the evidence, I say. After repeating two years at school, passing the exams was pure luck, and studying law was so ridiculous that I tried it for a joke.

She's got both hands on the wheel and is looking straight ahead. Her wig is lying on the dashboard like a dead black cat.

Then one day, I said, the state Minister of Justice presented me with a certificate for the best degree in my year. That was the punchline – the joke was over and it was time to laugh. I laughed in his face, he laughed with me, clapped me on the back and shook my hand again.

You were top dog, she says.

You don't understand, I say. When I left school I was still fat, had hair down to my hips and pimples the size of turtle eggs on my back.

Turtles come in all different sizes, she says.

Exactly, I say. I underwent a course of something like chemotherapy, the hair got shorn off for national service and the pounds dropped off on the training ground, helped by a little speed. I'd show you before-and-after photos if I had any.

Don't need to, she says. I know someone like that.

And what's he doing now? I ask.

He's still fat and pimply, has a lovely wife and child, and is very happy.

What are you trying to tell me?

She ignores my question and overtakes a truck, looking over her shoulder first in careful textbook style.

Have you never, she says, had a concept of fairness?

No, I say.

Of right and wrong?

No, I say.

Good and bad?

No, I say.

Are all lawyers like that?

Yes, I say.

We stop to let the dog out again and he disappears into the darkness immediately. I hear the liquid squirting out of his guts onto the grass. I stretch my legs, smoke a cigarette and look up at Cassiopeia forming a big M in the sky, M for Max. Clara is standing behind me next to the passenger seat, changing from her skirt into jeans.

The sky seems to pale a little on the horizon to the left, like a strip of faded cotton. Clara's noticed it too. She starts sliding from side to side in her seat. Watching her sitting next to me in the half-light without her headphones, microphone and cable, I realize how young she is. Even Jessie, of all people, was five years older than she is. Her hands look tiny on the steering wheel. For a moment, I'm amazed that someone with such small hands can even survive in this world.

Talk to me a little, she says.

I dig around in the travel bag lying at my feet. It's full of Clara's clothes. I recognize every item; I've even worn some of them myself. They're clean and neatly folded.

In the side pocket, she says.

My entire supply of cocaine is there, about a hundred grams, and a few lumps of chewed gum of different sizes.

Perfect organization, I say. As a reward, I'll help you choose the topic of conversation. Maybe you'd like to talk about what you've got planned?

Naah, she says. But have you ever asked yourself what they actually did down in Bari?

Who? I ask.

The silly cow's family, she says.

You constantly amaze me, I say. I wish I knew if you were brave or just stupid.

126

Why? she asks. Because I'm asking questions about a couple of small-time smugglers?

I revel in the view in front of me and the monotonous drone of the engine for a moment.

No, I say. Because you're talking about things no one should speak of, even in the tongue of angels.

I've done some research on the Internet, she says. I found an article headlined: 'Italian coastguard buys a jet-boat for 2.5 million marks'.

Interesting, I say.

Southern Italian, she says. It goes past Brindisi and Bari.

And why do you care about that crap? I ask.

I told my supervisor about the murder, she says.

It wasn't murder, I say. It was attempted manslaughter in conjunction with culpable negligence.

He got really excited, she says. Especially when I played him your latest Bari tape.

Thank you, I say, flattered. That's my favourite too.

He wants more of the background. Miss Müller, he said, you're on the right track.

Then everything's fine.

Only one thing worries me.

And that is?

Well, maybe filling my tapes with crap is having a therapeutic effect on you, and you might be normal by the time I'm done, she says.

It's a race against time, I say.

Seriously, she says. I know who you are now. In your law firm they told me that you were on the way to becoming one of the most important international lawyers in Europe. That together with your French and Polish colleagues you were really driving the integration of Eastern Europe forward.

Oh dear, I say, and have to smile. Maria still loves me, then.

Someone like you, Clara says, is out of action only temporarily.

Sweetie, I say, that's all over. The only thing that can happen is me dying on you in the meantime.

That wouldn't be bad, she says. I could write about that. But believe me, it won't happen. I know my stuff and your case is first-semester material. It's more likely you'll get rid of your guilt complex about the silly bitch's death and then you'll suddenly be ready to fly again.

I've got pins and needles in my arms and legs, as if an army of ants is marching through the corridors of my body. I need something to do. A strip of light appears on the horizon; night is slowly heaving herself up from the landscape. I wait a while longer and wonder if I should say something, but my lips are numb and lazy. They don't want to form the words. So I grab hold of the steering wheel and wrench it towards me.

The car swerves around and careers sideways across all three lanes. The shock seems to tear up Clara's face; one eye seems higher than the other. She's pulling the wheel back and there's a dull thump as Jacques Chirac is thrown against the side of the car. Then she starts screaming, the squeal of the tyres and her voice in disharmony. Outside, the forest, the hills, the crash barrier on the left, the road – everything revolves around us in slow motion before the car comes to a standstill on the hard shoulder. Facing the right way of course, absolutely unharmed.

Clara is leaning against the wheel, her face pressing the horn in time to the shuddering of her shoulders. The sound gets on my nerves. I grab her neck and prop her upright.

My love, which makes me so dangerous for you, I say, is the reason why I'm messing up my life and you're not. So watch the fuck out what you say.

She doesn't stop crying until after Passau.

The border post is still there, with signs indicating lanes for trucks, buses and cars, though the forest around it has been chopped down. But there is no light behind the windows and the cubicles are rigid shapes in the dark. Clara stays in the car lane obediently. The rest area is empty. We glide by at fifty without seeing a soul. That's Schengen for you. I like it.

When we stop for petrol, Clara gives me a wallet. There's a thick bundle of hundred-schilling notes inside; I'd blotted it out of my mind. I slide seven notes out to pay for the petrol and cigarettes. While the tank's filling up I walk around the car and look into the back. There's a box from a music mail-order company, big enough to have held at least fifty CDs. Now it's stuffed to the brim with banknotes. I wonder when and how she got the box into Tom's car. Certainly not when she ran off with me.

Though his accent is still faintly Bavarian, hearing the station attendant speak makes my stomach tighten. I love the Viennese dialect, and everything that reminds me of it gives me the jitters. The service area stinks of frying oil. It's six in the morning, and there's bratwurst on the grill. I wait in line behind a row of truckers in undershirts, rolls of fat bulging under the material. I'm standing too close to the man in front of me. He turns around and stares at me threateningly. In his unshaven, saggy jowls and the fine net of broken veins under his eyes, I see myself and my own defencelessness. The fat woman swims up to the lighted counter in her yellowish apron, as the neon light flickers and dies. I get coffee and two rolls for breakfast.

Outside, the sun immediately heats up every part of me not covered by clothing. Holding lit cigarettes, the truckers rub their bare arms with their hands. Having come through the night, we are all sore, silent and dehydrated.

Clara's walking the dog up and down the patch of grass behind the service station. She's digging her hands in her pockets and her shoulders are hunched. Her T-shirt looks grubby and she reaches up to scratch her arms and her face every now and then, leaving red lines on her skin. She sees the plastic cups and the paper bag

I'm holding, and smiles weakly. We sit next to each other on a wooden picnic table and prop our feet on the bench.

The new jet-boat can do fifty knots, Clara says. Do you know how much that is?

No, I say.

That's ninety-two kilometres per hour, she says. And even then it doesn't have a chance against the smugglers' speedboats. They have dinghies or light plastic shells, souped up like racers.

Yeah, yeah, I say.

She blows into her coffee, though it isn't even really hot.

The route goes through Albania or Montenegro, she says. They transport drugs and weapons mostly. Sometimes an illegal immigrant too. But the real people-smugglers use bigger ships. They're not so fast.

The sky above us is pale grey, lit from behind like a computer monitor. If there's a god up there, he's sitting behind it programming the second of August 1999 right now. I realize that it's my birthday. It looks like it's going to be a hot day.

The amazing thing Clara says, is, that they travel by night, but don't really hide themselves. Their success depends on speed. They give the police a good race, and they're kitted out to win it.

The piece of bread in my mouth expands to twice its size as I chew on it. I wonder if I should spit it out for the dog, but force it down anyway. It sticks in my throat and the pain brings tears into my eyes. I take a gulp of coffee to wash it down. I see Shershah and Jessie before me, clad in black, Jessie's yellow hair stuffed under a dark cap. It's night. She barely reaches his shoulder. They push their unequal shadows before them through a cobbled alley; it's so narrow that she could stick her elbows out and bump them along the walls of the houses. Their pace is leisurely, as if they're taking a walk, but they're not talking, not touching.

Bari must have a maze of really narrow alleys, Clara says. You probably know better than me.

Yeah, yeah, I say.

In one of those alleys, a getaway vehicle waits as close to the water as possible, some place just about manoeuvrable. The boat speeds up with as much of a head start over the police as possible. They throw the goods onto land, including the outboard engine, store it all in the car and drive off. They leave the empty boat behind. If a land patrol manages to get on their tail soon enough, they calmly let themselves get shot at and crash through every road barrier.

While Clara's talking, I see Shershah and Jessie next to each other at the stern of a dinghy that's practically vertical, a wedge-shaped fountain of water behind them, glinting snow-white against the dark surface of the sea. Her yellow hair and his black hair stream out horizontally behind them, their faces sharpened like greyhounds from the speed. Clara has finished her roll, and brushes the crumbs off her hands.

Can you guess how they did it, she asks, what kind of vehicles they used?

I stare into my coffee cup, as though I could dive through the smooth black surface of the liquid and escape. I finish the coffee and crush the cup with one hand.

Armoured vehicles, Clara says triumphantly. You can't spy it from the outside. They have heavy steel plates weighing over a hundred pounds behind every door. Does that remind you of something?

I leave her sitting on the table, go back to the car and place my hands on the warm, ticking surface. Clara steps up behind me seconds later.

The vehicles are imported for that purpose, she says eagerly, and often impounded at the border. There were pictures on the web; the police have collected fleets of them.

There was a time, I say, when I always wanted to know what Jessie had experienced, maybe at sea during the night, maybe in other places. For some time, I couldn't forget that she had seen terrible things and I thought it would be difficult to live with her as long as I didn't know what images she had in her head.

That, says Clara, can still be found out. Now, for example.

I feel her hand on my back, then on my head – maybe she's stroking me, maybe she's just testing the static electricity of my hair. Who cares? I turn and hit her hand so her arm flies off to the side and bangs against the windscreen. I hope it hurt. She sucks air through her teeth and walks back to the table, not even looking at me once. The dog is waiting, its stare riveted to the rest of my bread. She tosses it to him with her left hand.

16 | Sacred Cows

The padding in the hammock stinks of mouse droppings. It's made from a rolled-up acrylic sleeping bag. The shiny surface of the material has somehow prevented the mice from gnawing their way through it to nest in the filling. I wonder then why they come to the hammock at all. To get here, they have to climb up the beams and make their way along the angled rope like action heroes crossing a ravine.

I let one leg hang out sideways, so that my toes touch the ground, and I push gently to swing the hammock. The sweat on my back against the musty material of the sleeping bag has the effect of itching powder, but I'm too exhausted to scratch myself. I close my eyes and try to take the itching as a symptom of nerves, one of many, like the headaches or the burning in my eyes. I suddenly realize how much weight I've lost; my ribs cast shadows like mountain ridges, my stomach is concave, my knees are bony, my calves stringy. It looks good.

Clara is standing in front of the blackboard, looking at the pale chalk marks. She's taken her trousers off too. The door to the courtyard is open and a sharply defined beam of light on the floor stretches towards Clara's heels. When we arrived at the shack in Vienna, the thermometer by the door already read thirty-two degrees C, at ten o'clock in the morning. I had kicked the door right next to the lock a couple of times but nothing happened. Then I noticed the old slow-burning stove against the wall, and found the key in the connecting pipe for the chimney. It was damp. I can't get rid of the flecks of orange rust on my fingers.

Do you know what this scribble means? Clara asks.

She puts a foot on the edge of the wooden flooring and there's a rustling sound, then it's quiet again. Two-thirds of the cement floor is covered by planks, nailed to the beams laid crossways. The mice live in the gap between the cement and the floorboards.

As she steps over the dog, her knee bumps against mine, kneecap against kneecap. Her foot catches in the handles of her travel bag and she stumbles. There's a crackling sound, as if she's stepped onto a bag of rubbish. A yogurt container rolls out, completely black inside. Jacques Chirac jumps up and trots out into the courtyard. The floor area of the shack is barely twenty square metres; the hammock takes up the centre of the room and the corners are filled with cardboard boxes and a pile of computer manuals with covers that are all curled from damp. The only free surface is the bare cement floor between the door and the blackboard, on which there are two hip-high metal cupboards on wheels. One of them is meant to be a kitchen, the other a bathroom.

Clara pulls a single page out of the piles of paper that cover the entire desk and sits down on the edge of the floorboards in front of the blackboard. The fibres and splinters on the untreated planks must feel like an ants' nest beneath her bare thighs.

I'm glad she can't get comfortable anywhere. Apart from the hammock, there's only a wooden box upholstered with foam to sit on in front of the desk, which is really just a writing surface supported by two of the same boxes. If she were able to find a position to relax in, even somewhere to lean her back against, she would fall asleep immediately. My eyes are half-open like jammed Venetian blinds, and a chain of identical art nouveau U-Bahn stations is running through my head. After every fifth station, Schönbrunn pops up, followed by Schlosspark on the right. It would feel like a wake if Clara were sleeping next to me now.

She looks up at the blackboard and down at the piece of paper, copying the chalk figures. It's a senseless undertaking, as there'd certainly be nothing important left behind here.

It looks like programming code, she says.

I realize what she's writing with just as she says 'code'. It's as fat as a frankfurter, glowing in three bright colours: yellow, red and blue.

Where did you get the pen? I ask.

It was amongst the papers on the desk, she says. Why?

Clara must know if Tom and Jessie knew each other or not. But the thought of there being not only single events but possibly whole people in Jessie's life whom I have never heard of is so unbearable that I don't ask Clara about it. I prefer to believe in extraordinary coincidences and brightly coloured pens breaking the rules of space and time.

I feel a tickle between my fingers and lift my right hand up to the light. There's a hair sticking to the knuckle of my index finger, it's thick, black and wavy. When I pull it apart, it's as long as my lower arm. Arabic hair, unmistakable.

Look, I say.

Clara turns her head and looks at my raised index finger.

I don't see anything, she says.

You have to come here.

Her thighs have the imprint of the floorboards on them, every fine fibre and splinter delineated in red. She bends over me.

Present for you, I say.

She takes a moment to get it.

A hair? she asks.

Take it, I say, put it in your files. It's Shershah's.

Our fingers touch as she reaches for it, so I pull my hand back. The hair drops before she gets hold of it.

Doesn't matter, I say. You'll find a few others in the hammock.

Water?

My eyes are open, but I can hardly make anything out. I'm lying on my side against my left ear, so I can barely hear.

Water?? she asks.

In the courtyard, I say, my voice hoarse. There's a tap next to the door of the building in front.

When I wake again, the light is no longer falling directly through the window, which is made up of small squarish panes of glass. Somehow I've been dreaming of Herbert's air-conditioned study, four districts away from here, in the building with dungeon-thick walls in the Hoher Markt. A big dusty cooler box in the middle of the boiling city; a room of perpendicular lines and bright white pieces of paper covered with pale pencil marks, the papers rustling like freshly starched linen.

A shadow moves across the threshold and I hear the dog panting. It's an effort to sit up. I hear a faint splashing sound and try to unstick my tongue from the roof of my mouth; I have to drink something soon. There's a washbasin on one of the cupboards now; light is reflecting off the water in circular waves on the white wall. Something must be swimming in the bowl, because there's a faint scratching against the enamel every now and then. Definitely a mouse. It will hold out for half an hour and then drown if nobody saves it. I'm going to get up.

Oh no, oh no! Clara shouts.

I had fallen asleep again, though I don't know for how long, but it's almost dark outside. Clara has a towel tied in a turban around her head and her hands are pressed to her face. She's looking through her fingers into the washbasin. She seems to have

136

managed to wash her hair under the low tap in the courtyard. I put both feet on the floor and stand up. The hammock snaps up with me and swings back and forth, empty.

And what's in the other shed?

Her voice is still a little shaky. The paper hankies are completely soaked, making a formless, squishy shroud for the little body. I wouldn't have thought the fur of one mouse could absorb so much water. It's lying in my left hand, which I'm holding stretched out as I scratch a hole in the ground with my right. The hole is getting deeper, while I'm getting dirt under my fingernails. Clara's sitting next to me on the low wall, our knees are practically pressed against the wing of the Opel Ascona. I look up over the bonnet to see my face reflected in the glass panes that make up half the wall of the second shed.

That's for artists to work in, I say. It's a kind of studio.

The studio is no more than ten metres long, but it occupies an entire side of the courtyard. I remembered everything as being much bigger; I feel as if I've returned only to find a doll's-house version of the original. I find a rotten tulip bulb in the earth, scratch it out, and throw it aside.

What kind of artists? Clara asks.

I asked that too when Jessie brought me here, I say. She said, the artists who work for the gallery owner.

Which gallery owner? Clara asks.

You'll find out, I say.

She gets up, walks round the Ascona, cups her hands against the studio window and peers through it. I draw my arm back and hurl the dead mouse in the handkerchief into the bushes behind the chestnut tree. I wipe my hand against my boxer shorts while using the other to shovel earth back into the hole.

The Italian coffee pot with the narrow waist is on the electric stove, hissing like a dragon. Jacques Chirac has finally got up from the doorway and is sniffing around the chestnut tree. He can just about turn around on the patch of grass and the wall is barely a step away for him. In the squarish space between the buildings, a distant statue of Hercules is standing in the sky with legs spread wide.

Max, Clara calls, do you want some coffee?

I don't like it when she uses my name. I like it even less when she wants to play housemates. But the coffee smells good and strong, so I walk up to her and watch her pouring the black, oily liquid into small glasses. I recognize the glasses; they were nicked from Café Hawelka, where they serve water in them along with the coffee.

If you want sugar, she says, you'll have to pick the mouse crap out of the packet first.

I'm fine, I say.

Are you feeling OK? she asks.

Is that a joke? I ask.

We step out into the courtyard together. The darkness soothes me.

I want to go into the city, she says.

What for? I ask.

What are we here for?

You're asking ME?

We're standing close together, staring at each other. Her eyes – one like water, the other like the sky – are expressionless, like coloured glass.

Look, Desperado, she says. You coke up now and then we're going for a walk. As a reward, I'll show you something now.

She pulls me past the chestnut tree and, with both hands, parts the branches of a bush in a corner of the courtyard. I think it's a wild rose plant, without flowers; it's reinforced by the light green leaves of some parasitic creeper to form an almost impenetrable wall. I see the mouse in the handkerchief hanging at knee height in it, though Clara seems not to notice. She digs deeper into the bush and leans back to let me have a look. In the dark, I make out a couple of circle rocks, held together with cement in some places, with a sheet of corrugated metal on top.

It's a well, Clara says.

I squint at it. She's right.

Yes, I've seen it before, I say.

In fact, I'd only believed in its existence. Jessie told me about the well right at the beginning, when I'd thought that her stories were products of her imagination: meadows and fields that had to be stretched taut like safety blankets; travels to places where unused grandmothers were collected. I gradually began to recognize details from her babble in the real world and realized that she simply changed everything she saw and experienced so that it mutated into her own fairy-tale world. She never made anything up. Perhaps I'm here now to track down the last components of her inner landscape; perhaps then I'll feel complete; ready to go at last.

It's been raining, Jessie said on the phone. The slugs are lying all over the courtyard, like tongues that have been cut out.

Sorry, like what? I asked.

Tongues of angels, she said, that have come down with the rain. They're especially sticking to the well. I sit on the edge and throw stones into it, waiting to hear them land. But I hear nothing, absolutely nothing.

I fiddled with the stuff on my desk, fighting against the feeling that I ought to be saying something intelligent, trying to believe that she was just talking nonsense, though she sounded like an oracle.

Maybe you didn't wait long enough, I said.

I waited for hours, she said. The ground's all muddy. I've scratched all the pebbles out and thrown them in the well.

Just go on, I said. One day, you'll have filled it up and then you'll be able to see the bottom.

Then it'll be full inside, she said, like a chimney stack in a great big crater.

I said nothing, pushing the empty cart, on which the files were distributed to the offices every morning, back and forth in the middle of the room.

That'll be safer too, she said, when we have children. They won't be able to climb onto the well, and even if they were up there, they couldn't fall in.

Madly enough, the thought that she wanted to have children with me made me happy. Then I realized that 'we' probably didn't involve me, but Shershah.

The children could still fall into the crater from above, I said.

We'll have three, she said, so there'll still be two left if one falls in.

Is Shershah with you right now? I asked.

It was difficult for me to get the question out because I was afraid of the answer, but Jessie preferred not to react to it anyway. We fell silent.

I have to go, I said at last. Go and sit on the edge of the well again.

That's where I am, she said. I'm throwing another pebble now. This time I'm going to wait until I hear the sizzle of it burning up in the centre of the earth.

And if you have to wait till winter, I said, you won't hear anything because your ears will be frozen.

I put down the phone. Jessie might have been ringing from Mars rather than from the edge of a well.

And what's in it? Clara asks.

Nothing, I say. Whatever's normally in a well.

And what's that? she asks. I'm not good at wells.

The thing about this well, I say, is that you can throw a stone in and not hear it land.

What? Clara says. Nonsense. Take the lid off.

Fuck that, I say.

I go back to the shed and she comes after me.

Please, Max, she says.

Piss off.

Please!

I look her in the face. She's hopping from one foot to another, really getting on my nerves. It's as if she's one of Jessie's and Shershah's children, the one who didn't drown in the well.

I'll do it, I say, if you take off your stinking T-shirt and your bra right there and jump up and down naked three times.

She stops moving immediately.

What the fuck's that about? she asks. Is that supposed to arouse you somehow?

Bullshit, I say. You'd destroy all male potency within a radius of a hundred metres even fully clothed.

As far as I know, she says, that isn't even necessary in your case.

Exactly, I say. That's why I have nothing to lose. I just want proof that you really don't have the slightest shred of respect for yourself.

Oh, she says. That you can have, gladly.

I pour the rest of the coffee out for myself. It's only an inch deep, but strong as a packet of caffeine tablets. When I look up again, Clara's taken off her top. Her waist is narrow and her breasts are well proportioned, but the nipples look as if they've been borrowed from two different women. The left nipple is pale pink, small and flattish; the right one seems to belong to an older woman, because it's brown and slightly bigger, jutting out a finger's width ahead of the other. Her breasts seem to be staring at me. It's so strange that I have to turn away. I look through the open door, and I see Hercules' feet and Jacques Chirac sitting pensively

141

on the low wall. I hear her jumping up and down behind my back, her heels landing hard on the wooden floor three times. I cross the courtyard in a few steps and turn the tap on. I can't remember the last time I drank anything apart from coffee. Probably two days ago. I turn my head and let the water run over my face and into my mouth. It gets up my nose and I have to cough.

I'm getting dirt under my nails for the second time today, scraping the earth away from the handle. Then, using the whole weight of my body, I manage to pull the lid back a couple of centimetres. When Clara climbs into the bushes to help and grabs hold of the edge, the lid comes off easily. The well exhales cool air. Clara gets hold of a pebble immediately and throws it in.

That's unbelievable, she says.

See? I say.

She goes looking for another stone, and returns after a while. Jessie probably did use up all the pebbles in the courtyard two years ago. Clara puts her fingers on her lips, we lean over the edge, and she lets the stone fall. We hear a faint rustle, a whisper.

It's not water down there in any case, she says.

And not earth either, I say.

A cloud covers the moon. It's completely dark. The bushes around us stink of urine, since the dog's probably been pissing in here all day.

We'll do the rest tomorrow, Clara calls after me.

During the day, the sun casts the grid pattern of the window onto the desk and the wooden floor. Now the same pattern is thrown out into the courtyard by the light of the ceiling lamp, elongated and distorted against the low wall and the trunk of the chestnut tree. I count the boxes in the grid to pass the time and get a different result each try. Clara's shadow glides over the lighted rectangle of the doorway from time to time. When she comes out, she's carrying a small silver tray; that must have been stolen from a café too. There's a line of coke on it and a thousand-schilling note, not at all badly rolled up. She obviously learns by observing.

Life is like an Advent calendar where you open the twenty-fourth door and find another Advent calendar, I say.

Oh come on, Clara says.

She brings one of the cardboard boxes out while I snort. It looks heavy. The top is open and there's a number written on one side in thick pen: 1997. The one is a straight vertical line without a hook, and there isn't a horizontal stroke through the seven. Clara takes a single page out, then a few pages bound together, and passes both to me. I recognize the emblems on the papers' headings from a distance. One is blue against white, showing a laurel-wreathed map of the world with grid lines superimposed on it, as if it's viewed through a telescope. The other one is a white compass rose against a blue background.

Put it back, I say.

What is it? she asks.

You can see for yourself what it is, I say, and as for everything else, you wouldn't understand anyway.

She drops the box onto the ground. One of the sides collapses and the shiny, snow-white documents slide over the courtyard like a small glacier.

Is that the stuff you worked on? she asks.

Sort of, I say. *Inter alia.*

And why's it lying around here?

I can't tell you that either.

Yes, you can, she says. I'm sure you can. You just have to try really, really hard.

She's getting on my nerves so much that I'll do anything to stop her blabbering on. That's probably the plan.

That was probably information for the people who lived here, I say vaguely.

No one can *live* here.

You're proving the opposite.

I'm not living here, she says. I'm doing fieldwork.

She's veered off the subject, thank God. I stuff the documents back into the box as unobtrusively as possible. They don't belong here, they've been kidnapped, they're hostages from another world, a world in which they are spread out on polished conference tables next to carafes of iced water and a small receiver connected to the glass cubicles where the interpreters grip the corners of their desks, upper bodies swaying to and fro as they speak, as though they're trying to bow to the papers lying in front of them.

In reaction to a steady deterioration in the security situation, Clara reads out, we shall now go into the city. What are IDPS?

Internally Displaced People, I say. No joking matter.

Cool, she says. I'm going to work through the whole pile.

Don't touch it, I say.

I can't stand the thought of her leafing through these snow-white, perfectly neat papers, though she could easily download the contents of the documents from the Internet. It's silly; I'm defending the sacred cows of a religion to which I no longer adhere.

The dog is standing in front of the metal doors, his body and his larger-than-life shadow moving in time to his wagging tail. The chestnut tree spreads her fingers and lets the night breeze flow through. I stand up. It's not difficult. My head is cool and my feet are very far away.

Fine, she says. Let's go sightseeing.

17 | Waltz

I just have to tip my chin a little not to have Clara's head in view, with the hairs sticking out at her temples as they always do when she ties her hair back in a ponytail. Instead, I watch the curves of the Stadtbahn, which look as if the street is raising its eyebrows at our approach. I lift my head higher still and look at the upper halves of the buildings that we're slowly passing, the roofs bristling with a forest of antennae.

I try to imagine that the footsteps next to mine are Jessie's. The feet aren't bare, though it's summer and the tarmac holds the heat overnight for the next day, turning the street into a living thing that Jessie always wanted to walk on without shoes. She only wore them when she had got a glass splinter in her foot the previous day. Then she crouched on the floor at home, slit open the callus with a razor blade, and plucked the splinter out with tweezers. The next day, she would still want to go walking with me at night; she would just wear shoes and limp a bit.

Instead, now there's the rhythmic, singing sound of denim brushing against denim between Clara's legs. Jessie never made that sound. When I raise my hand to touch her shoulder, it's too high, and long, fine hair tickles my skin. I give up and shove my hand back into my pocket. Clara just won't be rubbed out of the picture.

I turn off to the left before we get to the first district of the city. We walk through the Josefstadt into the medical quarter, where the stones of the city are piled up in great towers and where every building is a discrete, rectangular planet of rock. We start walking around the old hospital but before we can circle it completely, the Josephinium leads us downhill and we follow gravity onto a new path. I've always been pulled through the city this way, meandering from block to block, never following a straight line, never quite in control of my own footsteps. Always straying off the path, in a constant state of half-confusion, getting to the right place in the end more by coincidence than anything else. I don't know if Clara feels it. Jessie did. When we went on our walks at night, we held on tight to each other so as not to be pulled in different directions by different groups of buildings. We held on so that we wouldn't lose each other.

I grab hold of Jacques Chirac's front legs, prop them on the wall and show him the water. He starts lapping it up greedily, his tongue beating a waltz. The sound echoes back from the walls, creating a momentary illusion; one of the carriages I used to hear every day from my office window seems to be clip-clopping up the lane. There's a thin growth of ivy on the winding steps and four-headed lanterns formed like gallows rise in between. All of us – Clara, the dog, the ivy, myself and the stone pillars – have four shadows, surrounding us in star shapes.

The moss-covered gargoyle with puffed-out cheeks spewing water still looks like an idiot. Next to it is a marble plate, smoothed by erosion. Clara squints hard as she wets her hands in the water and passes them over her temples, then cools her neck under her hair.

What does it say? she asks.

Old steps breathe autumnal when leaves lie, I say, all that's gone over them long past.

I skip the middle bit and jump to the last verse, which I recite smiling:

To our sorrow is much gone, things of beauty go first of all.

Don't you need to look at all while you read? she asks.

There's a light rattling sound above our heads: the midges are attacking the cloudy glass globes, which already have beards of dead insects lying inside – the corpses of those who got what they wanted. From the landing we look down at the dog at the bottom of the steps: he's curled around like a question mark, his tail held stiffly upright as he shits on the ground next to the low wall of marble.

We were eating down there one night, I say, when she pressed a sealed packet into my hand. I could see that she'd prepared her arguments. I opened it to find a little snowdrift inside. Close up, I could see the microscopic refractions of light like tiny points of colour dancing in the crystals.

That's impossible, Clara says. You were imagining it.

Could be, I say. But it was fantastic anyway.

Were you clean before that? she asks.

It's like with first love, I say. No matter how long ago it was, it still buzzes away in the background of your life.

That's rubbish, Clara says.

I hadn't taken anything since I started university, I say, and that wasn't at all easy. Holding Jessie's packet in my hand that night, I imagined someone spending years constructing a tall building out of matchsticks; when it's done, he stands twirling the last match in his fingers, heart slamming and mouth watering. He strikes the match and holds it to the bottom. There's a wonderful explosion, match after match going off, flames racing up the sides. I imagined this fire was the most beautiful light on earth. My heart was beating, my mouth was watering.

Jessie didn't need to wheel out a single one of her arguments.

You'd have to be really thick, Clara says, to start again after so many years.

I thought nothing was more pointless than matchstick buildings, I said, except when they burned up.

Very aphoristic, Clara says. I'll quote you. The truth is, your Jessie belonged to a group of drug dealers who got other people hooked so that they would work for them.

You make it sound perfectly harmless, I say. And what do you think I had to do for Jessie?

That's what you're going to tell me, she says.

The DAT-recorder bumps against the bench when I get up.

Be careful, Clara snaps.

She's cross because we aren't recording.

We always quarrelled here, I say.

The terraces of District Nine slope down in front of us. The city is steep here. A single storey can duck down to street level in front, basement windows staring out at the calves of passers-by, and rise three metres high at the back, looking out over a parklike courtyard through great panes of glass. Between the houses, the lanes lead down the incline step by step. I take hold of Clara's elbow; the bits between the steps are steep too and it's easy to stumble here.

Go this way, I say.

The black man is still the same. He stretches over the entire height of the wall, a heavily sprayed outline with arms thrown up high, and he's faceless apart from two violet eyes. His body gets younger-looking lower down and the legs trail off into a curving line that reaches the bottom of the wall and continues on the ground in an ever-tightening spiral until it finally disappears into a drain in the middle of the alley.

And? she asks.

Well, what's he doing there? I ask.

It's obvious, she says. He's running away.

Exactly, I say, but Jessie wouldn't accept that. She insisted that he was materializing from the drain like a genie from the bottle.

But he's got those panicky eyes, Clara says.

She believed it precisely because of them, I say. He's seeing the world for the first time.

We hear music, turn the corner and stumble into Café Freud. The last customers, a girl in a green wig and an old man, are dancing the tango to the strains of a waltz. When Clara goes up to the bar, the bartender stretches a hand out towards her hair.

For you, he says to me, we're all out of vodka.

Through a gap in the row of beer glasses, I see my face in the mirror behind the shelves; it's unshaven, shadowy and it could almost be the face of an Albanian. My stare is fixed like an axle on which I could turn, faster and faster, like a windmill, though not one that's yellow. There's enough action from the bartender as it is, since he's clutching my shoulder. The music stops. I lower my gaze and hear steps behind me – the couple are still dancing. Next to me, Clara downs the vodka that the barkeeper's put in front of her. Then he grabs her throat. I know that he'd have grabbed at Jessie too if she were here. My hand shoots out and grabs hold of his hair, I get a good grip – it's not a wig. I clench my other hand into a fist, just in case. The bartender's forehead knocks against the edge of the bar. Nothing happens. He's just bleeding. He looks up at me, horrified. He has violet eyes.

When he staggers forward, Jacques Chirac begins to growl next to me. It's the first time I've heard him growl. He doesn't manage to draw his rubbery lips back enough to show his teeth, but it's not necessary. I lean over, take the bottle of vodka and we leave the café.

Sorry, I say, a slip-up.

That's fine, Clara says.

She smiles, looking flattered. Maybe she's dim enough to think I was trying to defend *her*.

We get to the Donau canal and turn right. Jacques Chirac pads off into the bushes by the promenade. Clara drinks from the vodka bottle as she walks and it clinks against her teeth. The vodka trickles down her chin but she doesn't wipe it off; her wet skin shines when we pass a street light.

You all right? I ask.

The moon hangs in the black sky behind the canal, an open pot of cream in which fingers have left peaks and troughs. Beneath it, the treetops gather thickly like an audience before a stage. Freshly mown grass is heaped on the lawn.

Isn't there an inner city? she asks.

Of course, I say. Everywhere.

But in District One?

Not for us tonight, I say. That's for advanced learners.

Because of Rufus's office, you mean?

Her tongue is thick. I don't reply and she seems to forget that she's asked the question. She stops under a bridge.

I used to stand under bridges and imagine it was raining, she says. I waited for the rain to stop and got home late.

The light falling under the bridge lights up one half of her face and leaves the other in shadow. I take her hands and turn them palms up. They're black with dirt, even her nails. I pat her cheek and smile; you're doing well, I think, now get rid of the hair, saw a bit off the legs and we're nearly there.

Go on, I say.

I always wanted to have a horse when I was a child. To prove to my parents that I could take care of it, I hung a towel over the balcony rail and groomed it, fed and watered it every morning and evening.

And? I ask.

They thought I was playing, she says.

I like these stories better than the one about lying in a cold bath, I say.

I wasn't a happy child, she says. There'll be a towel on my balcony until the day I die.

Yes, I say, and you'll always have a balcony.

She's drunk and she looks as though she's going to start crying any second. That's Vienna for you: it grabs you by the shoulder and turns you around so you always look back into the past.

Let's go back, I say. It's stopped raining.

I slip the vodka bottle out of her grip discreetly. I've never been able to throw food or drink away, so I put it down by the head of a drunk lying on the next park bench.

She's swaying, so we walk arm in arm through the narrow lanes, silent. It's going well, as if we've always done this. It's like dancing, choreographed for hands and feet as we avoid things together: parked cars which leave a narrow space to walk in, dog turds, construction sites, potholes, rubbish, roots and uneven paving. We just have to hold on to each other, stay in step, keep up the pace, press our bodies together whenever we can. I think about dancing being nothing more than the art of avoiding rubbish together.

We're standing in Alser Strasse in front of the narrow piece of glass framed with iron that rises vertically out of the ground. This is the centre of the universe, my personal axis in the world. I realize what I really need Clara for tonight.

I put her on the other side of the glass sign. She's smiling and she seems happy; she's looking at me through the glass as if we're about to get married. Behind her is the house in which the poet was born, or, perhaps, as it's Vienna, died. I've always thought that there ought to be a shop-cum-café in places like this, and am always surprised that there isn't one there. I clear my throat and begin.

151

It is what it is, I read.

Our eyes meet through the glass. She's not getting it. The letters are pale grey, only legible if you concentrate and use the body of the person opposite as a dark background to read the words against. I pull at my cigarette and repeat the first line.

It is what it is, I say slowly.

I exhale. The smoke hits the glass and disperses like a mushroom cloud. Clara looks on. Then she raises her eyebrows and laughs.

Si ti tahw, she says, si ti.

I feel a pang in my stomach. I have no idea if it's happiness or pain or simply because I haven't eaten a thing for a day and a half. I drag deeply on my cigarette and the glow eats deep into the filter. Then I pull myself together.

It is what it is, Love says, I say.

Syas evol, si ti tahw si ti, Clara says.

We read through the verses this way. When we crouch down to read the lines at the bottom, I lean my face towards my knees casually and wipe my cheeks against my trousers. When we start reading it the second time, I have to stop halfway. I stay crouched on the ground.

That's enough, I say. That's fine.

Clara leaves her side of the glass and comes around to me.

Enif staht, she says quietly.

That's not written anywhere.

Then something clicks against my hips and I jump up. It's the button on the recorder that's snapped up at the end of the tape. I didn't notice her switching it on. Maybe she did it under the bridge by the canal. I feel like I've been shot in the back.

We're under one of the Stadtbahn's curving tracks again. I've been ignoring Clara for an hour, but when she falters and her knees buckle, I decide to catch her. I sit her on the bench against the wall of the passageway. It stinks of urine, so I stand off to one side, closing each eye in turn, making Clara and the bench jump around in front of me. The sky behind us is pale pink like a glass from which strawberry milk has been drunk. It seems inappropriate to me. The remains of the night are cowering over District Sixteen, which is where we're heading.

Thanks, Clara suddenly whispers.

She's probably delirious. Before she can fall asleep I grab her by her ponytail and pull her head up. She hardly notices. I don't want to touch her, but she can't walk on her own, so I have to practically carry her to the taxi rank. As I fumble for money in her right trouser pocket, I can feel her pubic bone. I get the taxi to stop two blocks before the entrance to our courtyard; I wish I could leave her in the back seat. She's as limp and heavy as a wet sack. To get going, I carry her in my arms. She puts her arms around my neck.

I have the feeling that she's wide awake and pretending.

18 | Half-sleep

It's wrapped in clear plastic. Clara's carrying it in her arms like a puppy that she's found by a river, an ill-fated pet which is bound to be thrown out of the house any minute by her mother.

I had to, she says, I need it.

You don't have to make excuses, I say. The money you're spending never belonged to me.

She doesn't reply, luckily. I don't feel like going into the subject. She tears the clear wrap off. The machine is incredibly ugly, made of plastic that tries, and fails, to look like silvery-matt metal, with completely pointless dark blue translucent bits at the side. It looks a little like a toy aquarium for Japanese kids – it's even got a display on which you can make LCD fish swim around and get killed by a virtual cat.

I haven't listened to music for ages. Jessie chose the stereo system in our Leipzig flat by pointing at it in a shop window that we walked past one night. She was the only one who sometimes put a CD on. I only used it when she barricaded herself into the bedroom and didn't allow me to go in. I'd sit in front of the stereo then and pass the time making faces in front of it, trying to catch the infra-red sensor that activated the sliding panel over the CD-player.

*

Clara finds the plastic corner to tear the wrapping off the CD right away. She doesn't even get near the point where you want to break open the whole CD like a bar of Rittersport chocolate. It's probably one of the things she learned in her job. Her fingers are damp; the prints she leaves on the gleaming surface evaporate immediately.

There's nothing for a moment, then comes the blast of a welding torch. The bass kicks in immediately after, like the sound of a metal press producing cars: there's the screech of a saw, the sound of rivets being shot in, hammering and screwing. I hear the wicked click of a gun's safety catch and a woman laughs quietly.

Then she starts singing; it sounds as though she's breathing out icy air like an open freezer, and I feel myself beginning to relax. Clara slides her back down the wall to lie next to the doorway, turns her eyes upwards and sighs. I sit next to her in the shade and stretch my legs out so my calves and feet are warmed by the rays of the evening sun.

I'll lay down in your ashtray, the woman sings, I'm just your Marlboro. Light me up and butt me, you're sick and beautiful.

Clara passes me a cigarette and lights it. In the last few days, she's been stretching two fingers out to me more and more so that I can stick my cigarette in between for her to take a drag.

Squeeze me like a lemon, the woman sings, and mix with alcohol, bounce me hard and dunk me, I'm just your basketball.

I squint, looking at the curls of smoke sliding along the beams of sunlight.

Watch me like a game show, the woman sings, you're sickeningly beautiful.

Beauty to throw up to, I say. Are you still feeling queasy?

I've been feeling nauseous for two days, Clara says.

Eat something, I say.

It's not that, she says. It must be the city. I think it's making me sick.

Don't you like it here? I say.

I do, she says, I really love it. Can't say more than that.

I let it drop. She presses the repeat button; the welding torch starts up, a gun's safety catch clicks, you're sick and beautiful.

When darkness finally falls, I walk to the petrol station with Jacques Chirac and buy red wine, water, two bottles of orange juice and an ice-cream bar.

The wineglasses balance precariously on the wool blanket. I coke up lying on my back, using the licked-clean ice-cream stick to shovel it down my nostrils. The stars look pale.

Full moon, Clara says.

You're looking at the lit-up signboard on the back of a building crane, I say.

A constant full moon, she says.

Only square, I say.

I sit up, drink some water, and hurl the plastic bottle towards the sky. The bottle's open. It rotates in the air and sprays its contents out in ever-widening circles. A few drops sparkle perfectly, hanging in the air for an unbelievably long time. The bottle doesn't even make it to the wall of the building in front. It hops over the cement and rolls away, empty at last.

Water from these plastic bottles always tastes a little like Barbie dolls, I say.

Jessie would have liked that expression. She'd have made a whole story out of it, about Barbie and Ken, how they blackmail the world with their threat to pee in every mineral-water bottle. Clara doesn't react; she just turns the stereo on again and turns the volume right up. I heave myself over to the machine, until my good ear is practically pressed against the plastic casing of the loudspeakers. The music pulverizes me, I let myself be blown away, whirling around the courtyard, the city, the country, the planets. All I hear is the sound of wind against my ear, the rushing sound of the Earth moving.

I only notice that the song's ended when Clara reaches over me to switch the machine off. Now it really is quiet.

A light breeze ruffles the dog's chin-hairs and wafts the smell of garlic over to us from the pot of pasta. It was difficult cooking on the small electric cooker; neither of us even touches the food afterwards.

Hands crossed behind her head, she's looking up at the Big Wheel, balancing precariously on its axis exactly on top of the next building's chimney.

Many of the stars we see up there have died thousands of years ago, Clara says, and their light is still speeding through the universe.

Yes, I say, and when we die, pictures of us will speed through space for a long time after, and they'll be able to see us from up there a thousand years later.

Sounds good, Clara says. Let's lie here for a while more and preserve ourselves for eternity.

I top up our glasses.

Have you ever thought, I say, that doing anything for other people is mad because we're human ourselves, so we know how little they deserve it? And, following on from that, doing anything at all loses its meaning altogether? Sometimes I think the Christians are simply being pragmatic with that 'love thy neighbour' stuff. They should just have left out the 'as yourself' bit. You know?

Huh? she says. No.

I should have expected that, I say. You're like a bag of peanut shells. Sometimes I dip in and think I've got one, but they're all really just shells, hollow.

I'm not hollow, Clara says, I'm concave. You see yourself reflected in me as much bigger and stronger than you really are.

And what am I really? I ask.

A pathetic jerk, she says, who's been waiting for weeks to be dumped into the sea.

At least a hole's got something around it, I say. You're proof of the fact that it's possible just to be the inside of a hole.

She shrugs.

You know, she says, I really don't care.

I've dozed off into a kind of sleep, though my eyes are open and I'm alert. The moon is round, patchy, like a plate that's been eaten from. Clara is taking spaghetti out of the pot strand by strand, arranging it by length on the concrete flooring. When she's done, she slides over to me and wipes her garlicky fingers on my T-shirt. I know she means to be tender. She lies so close to me that I feel her breath against my neck every time she exhales. A couple of her hairs move in the wind and tickle my upper arm. I don't do anything about it. It's like sleeping.

Don't you miss him sometimes, when you look back on the old days?

How did you know I was just thinking about the old days? I ask.

Do you ever think of anything else?

No, I say.

So, she says. Do you miss him or not?

Who? I ask.

Shershah, she says.

Who's Shershah? I ask.

She sighs and rolls onto her back.

Oh, come on, she says.

My clouds of cigarette smoke are suspended artistically in the air for a moment before a light breeze disperses them. I feel cradled by the cement floor.

When Jessie told me he was dead, on the phone, I say, I believed it immediately. But I didn't feel a thing.

Jessie told you he was dead? Clara asks.

She props herself up on an elbow and looks down at me. I blow smoke into her eyes but she doesn't blink.

Yes, I say. And Jessie thought she was next. She wanted me to protect her.

What was that about, then? Clara asks. Was she being paranoid?

It was mostly because she'd made a silly mistake, I say.

And you protected her?

Yes, I say, by killing Shershah.

She looks like she's about to explode; I can see it in the way she's looking at me. Her gaze is hard, as if she's wedged bits of steel between her eyelids.

Life is full of paradoxes, I say gleefully. I simply protected her from something other than she thought I did. From a much greater danger.

She's breathing quickly – perhaps it's a sign of her brain getting into gear.

I had a cat when I was a child, she says at last. I spent whole nights awake worrying that she would be run over in the street. When it really did happen, and we found her in the front garden where she'd dragged herself to die, I wasn't upset at all.

It was different with Shershah, I say. I was always sure he wouldn't see thirty anyway. He wasn't built for it.

Bullshit, she says. Adolescent romanticizing.

Could've been, I say, but I was right.

Doesn't count when you made sure of it yourself, she says.

I laugh. She's quick, batting her replies back before I've finished my sentences. Maybe she'd make a good lawyer, not in international law but cross-border corporate law; she could represent multinationals in cases where an amount the size of the Austrian national budget was at stake. She jumps when I sit up, loses her balance for a minute and almost falls backwards. Then she leans back on her elbow again.

I drink the rest of the red wine out of the bottle. It's not bad, but it doesn't take me back, as I'd expected, to one of the nights spent drinking a couple of bottles of this particular wine with Jessie. We crouched on the floor in an empty room and imagined pictures for her, images of dog sleds racing over an endless whiteness, giving off clouds of snow as high as houses, barely visible behind the blinding excess of light. We sucked tallow out of seagull-feather quills shaped like pens and killed seals resembling rolled-up duvets; anything to get through the critical time between two and five in the morning, when she got her attacks. If my tongue was capable of tasting this wine, I might be able to feel myself part of those scenes, rather than feeling like a spectator in front of a cinema screen. Maybe they fill the same bottles with a different wine nowadays.

Seeing him crumpled up on the street was one of the happiest moments of my life, I say.

He was your best friend once, Clara says.

Yes, I say.

You'll be punished for it, she says.

Already have been, I say. Jessie's dead. It's like she's gone back to him; she's reconnected with him. I can't even die myself without it looking like I'm trailing after them pathetically.

Tragic, she says ironically.

Maybe you're not really the right person to tell these stories to, I say.

She sinks down onto her back slowly, her gaze fixed on me. She simply stares at me in the face until I get it. I'm wrong. She is capable of something, something unique: she can put up with people like me. If I were wearing a hat, I'd raise it.

What about you? I ask later. Have you ever had a love life?

I already had five years of unrequited love behind me at twenty, she says. Since then, it's all been revenge, really.

Even with me? I ask.

WHAT with you exactly? she asks.

I nod and smile: fine.

And what about sex? I ask.

Well, she says, more like masturbation with both parties present.

Ah, I say. Family?

What family? she asks.

Do you want a family? I ask.

I had a family when I was little, she says.

Money? I ask.

You don't need much money when you're not a drug addict, she says.

What do you like anyway? I ask.

Radio, she says. One day I want to be transmitted worldwide by satellite. I want simultaneous translations in twenty languages. The Japanese need me too. I want to sit in my glass tower and scream 'Call me!' into the night along with the voices of twenty interpreters.

And then? I ask.

Then they call, she says. Everyone calls. You too.

A coincidence, I say.

No, it's not, she says. It's because I always get what I want. I just need to think it and it's done.

Every day a birthday, I say.

Exactly, she says. Boring as hell, really.

But why, I ask, are you here, and not at the radio station?

It's the summer break, she says.

Ah, I think. Learn something new every day.

Apart from that . . .

She's speaking quietly, so quietly that I have to turn my good ear towards her.

Apart from that, I have two sides. One side wants to work in radio and tell everyone that nothing counts for anything really. That only one thing relieves the boredom of it all: power over other people.

I'm afraid mankind knows that already, I say.

Then they should stop being hypocrites, Clara says.

And the other side?

The other side belongs to people like my supervisor at university.

What do you want from him?

I want him to put it in writing – that I'm not only just as intelligent as he is, but just as inconsiderate too.

To whom? I ask.

Myself, of course, she says.

You probably won't answer if I ask what the good of that is.

Quite right, she says.

When the sky begins to turn pink, I can't tell where my body ends and the cement floor begins. I feel a slight chill creeping over my arms and legs, almost like a piece of cloth, as if a second, very thin skin is being drawn over me. It's good to feel a little cold; I'm finally cooling down. At last, the dog's sleeping without panting. I feel drained and at peace, like I did after one of those nights with Jessie, when she was finally lying still on the mattress as a scattering of birds began circling in the soupy clouds. I forced her chin up then. Look, I said, look, it's getting light. She nodded and fell asleep. I loved daybreak then.

It's not as if I've never asked myself the ultimate questions, Clara says suddenly.

I thought she was asleep. Night has slowly retreated from the outlines of everything; the black column to our right has grown bark and turned into a chestnut tree.

And what are the questions? I ask.

Where am I going, she says, where have I come from, and what the fuck is it all about?

You're right for once, I say, those are the questions.

She gets up and walks into the shed stiffly. The door slams behind her. I feel a tingling in my diaphragm. It's fear. The sound of the door slamming means the end of the night. It's going to get bright and hot.

I want to see how Clara likes her new mattress; it's a thin, stinking layer of foam that I pulled out from behind an open door in the building in front.

She's lying on her stomach, arms stretched out ahead of her, fingers curled around the edge of the mattress. Her left leg is stretched out over the foam and her right leg is bent. If the floor was upright, she'd look like a mountain climber making her way up a vertical face. As if dreams had to be conquered.

They say that some people answer every question truthfully in their sleep, without remembering it the next day. It never worked with Jessie, though I had a whole list of questions ready.

Clara, I ask in a low voice, what about when you don't want to play this game any longer?

She doesn't stir. She doesn't seem to be one of those people. Or perhaps it was the wrong question.

I lie down in the hammock. Falling asleep now would be pure coincidence, a matter of letting myself be taken by surprise just when I stop thinking about the fact that it's going to be boiling in the shade in two hours, that the time of day has lost all meaning for me, that Clara's sleeping beside me as if she's been switched off. I'd be ignoring the fact that I'm completely alone; someone who doesn't even want to spend money on a long-distance call to people he's known for a long time, like his mother, for example.

I pick up one of the documents lying on the floor. It's a Resolution of the UN Security Council, file number 1101 from 1997, *adopted by the Security Council at its 3758th meeting.* The phrases sound comfortingly in my ear like a child's prayer. I am small and my heart is pure, *taking note of the letter from the Permanent Representative of Albania*, no one but Jesus should live inside, *reiterating its deep concern over the deteriorating situation in Albania*, if I've done wrong today, dear God look away, *authorizes the Member States to establish a multinational protection force*, your mercy and the blood of Jesus, *condemns all acts of violence and calls for their immediate end*, make everything whole again. The United Nations logo begins to swim in front of my eyes, the globe beneath the grid is a blue blur; this crap is sending me to sleep. I reach for another sheet. It too is about Albania. The sheet that follows is a NATO document about the unrest in Albania. I realize that the whole box is full of documents on the Albanian question. I look at the year written on the side of the box: 1997. An interesting year, as far as I remember: a couple of good wines, Kofi Annan became UN General Secretary, Shershah died, the expansion of NATO became fact, Jessie and I had to leave Vienna, the last Bosnian concentration camps were closed. Maybe I should be the one working through these papers, instead of Clara.

19 | Flies

The sound of a flame-thrower wakes me. I'm lying in the hammock surrounded by a pile of crumpled papers. Clara is standing in front of the desk, spraying a deodorant into the flame of a lighter she is holding in her left hand. The flame is horizontal in the air, almost invisible in the daylight, dispersing into a bluish cloud at the end. Just before it reaches one of the wooden stools, I notice the finger-length black spider sitting there. The two halves of its body look like they're about to burst. They hardly seem to be connected to each other; legs wave in the air around them. It's too big for Europe. It's sitting there as if it wants to point out a mistake in the system; like where the crack in reality is.

For a split second, it looks as if it's cowering before the blast, but perhaps it's just being moved by the pressure of the flame. Its legs whirr against its body in a blur, melting down like burning hair. Its trunk drops onto the floor, bounces twice and is still: a small black ball. But from the corner of my eye, I keep seeing the spot where the spider was sitting.

I hear a car door slamming in the courtyard. Clara enters the shed holding a file and a paper bag from a bakery. She's wearing the page-boy wig, a knee-length black skirt and lace-up ankle boots, which I haven't seen on her before. She must have gone shopping.

I don't know what she does all day while I lie in the hammock, moving time along by sheer force of will, second by second, so that the day creeps westward bit by bit. I can imagine Clara with a mini-camera round her neck, visiting the sights. But she's more likely to have been wreaking havoc in the city.

She tosses the paper bag onto my belly. Jacques Chirac is behind her, swinging my hammock by wagging his tail. The girl and the dog radiate energy in concentric circles; I feel like a cork bobbing towards the periphery.

OK, you've slept long enough, Clara says.

I think nothing of the sort, but I realize that the contents of the paper bag might take away the pain caused by the bloating in my stomach in a matter of minutes. I tear the bread rolls apart one by one, scraping the soft white doughy insides out and rolling them into ping-pong-ball shapes, which become grey in my hands. My stomach gurgles like a broken toilet. Clara is kneeling on the floor, punching holes into sheets of printed paper and putting them in the file.

What's that? I ask.

Your medical file, she says.

She opens a bottle of orange juice for herself and I shake the rest of the bread rolls out for the dog, who comes over immediately for them. When the car door slams for the second time and Clara comes in, putting the key in her pocket, I realize that she's using the Opel Ascona as a locker.

I lie in the hammock for as long as possible, not stirring. But I'm disturbed by the thought that there might be a basement below spanned by a spider's web, with fat, ticking spiders spread across it. And Clara and I are living here above the floorboards, as unaware as flies.

I thought I'd been awake all along with my eyes closed, but when I feel pain somewhere in a distant part of my body, I can't place where it's coming from. Waking is like surfacing from anaesthesia, fumbling my way back into awareness of my nervous system. It's not so much pain, more like being rubbed raw in a sensitive place. I open my eyes. Clara pulls her hand back from between my legs. She's taken my dick out through the slit in my boxer shorts.

Are you out of your mind?

She doesn't reply. I tuck myself back in and have to laugh when I look at her.

All in the name of science? I ask.

I get up, walk around her and stand with my back to the open door.

Didn't I tell you that Jessie took that with her?

Took fuck all, Clara says. It's the coke.

Cocaine, I say, increases sexual performance.

Yes, in the beginning, she says. But then it narrows the arteries and affects the circulation and then that's it.

The way you think about men is a bit clinical, I say.

People are always ringing me on the programme with the same problem, she says. And they're all cokeheads.

Then you also know, I say, that coke leads to pathological personality changes in the longer term. To uncontrollable outbreaks of aggression.

Scientific terms shouldn't be used by people who don't understand them, she says.

But they can be put into practice, I say.

As I bend over to pick up one of my shoes from the floor, she retreats into a corner of the room. She stands there, leaning forward slightly like a goalkeeper waiting for a penalty shot.

Right, I say. Let's make your supervisor happy.

It's great to see the way she gasps, ducks under the hammock and charges past me. Caught behind in the strings, the black page-boy wig swings back and forth wildly while Clara's ankle boots clatter over the courtyard. I don't try to stop her. The heavy door to the courtyard slams shut. I continue laughing for a couple of seconds, then I walk out holding my shoe and bash in the passenger window of the Opel Ascona, gleefully imagining the way that Tom the Technician's bird's-nest hairdo would stand on end if he were here now. Though it's not really necessary, I knock the last cubelike glass splinters away from the frame before I open the door from the inside.

Clara's file is under the passenger seat. When I pull it out, a piece of paper comes into view, dirty and crumpled like all things that have been inadvertently driven around in a car for a long time. It's a copy of a bill from two years ago, for services rendered as a system administrator, the expansion of the network and work on the SAP databank. There's nothing particularly surprising about this. When guys are as young, weird-looking, and at the same time as self-confident as Tom is, they're likely to be computer geniuses. But then I realize that the bill is for work done in Rufus's office.

I crumple the sheet up and toss it back into the car. I can't tell the difference any longer between what I should have known or guessed long ago and what I should still be surprised by. Best not to be surprised by anything and to forget about finding any logic in it all. I take Clara's file into the shed.

There's a yellow card index inside. Under 'Phenomenology' I learn, for example, that I mostly sleep on my back and cross my arms in a strangely challenging manner. The chapter on 'Dreams' is empty, most of the stuff is under 'Self-presentation': the transcripts of the tapes take up a good fifty pages. Then I turn to 'Background' and start reading properly.

She's obviously gone through a few of the documents after all, and she's been on the Internet. I find a copy of a tiny, barely legible map of Europe with 'The Schengen Area' printed over it, criss-crossed with the dotted lines of transport routes. One of them, the one from Russia through Albania, running straight across the Adriatic Sea into the south of Italy, is marked over in red felt-tip pen. There's a press release, from which a sentence highlighted in yellow jumps out: *The disappearance of Albania's police forces during the period of the worst domestic violence in March and April 1997 left the border-crossing points open to drug trafficking. The smuggling remained rampant until the end of the summer.* I read through the rest of the article, and a list of quotations in Clara's neat handwriting that must have come from me, although I don't remember most of them: 'It's only a matter of time before they pick us up here', 'She thought she was next', 'I can't really believe it's about money'. 'Conspiracy Theory' is written in square brackets, followed by a question mark.

Just when I've had enough and am about to close the file, I discover another section: 'Reflexes and Interactive Consequences'. There's only one sheet in it, with a sentence typed in the middle in large letters: 'I FEEL SICK.'

I nearly jump out of my skin when something crashes against the window from outside. It sounds like a brick wrapped in cloth. The glass is undamaged, but something falls to the ground outside. I sit quite still for a second or two, as if I'm in a trance. The dog lifts his head, but doesn't make a sound.

Of course it was just a matter of time before they came to look for us here; impossible to sit unharmed in the lion's jaws for ever. The thought of a hand grenade lying outside nags at me. I don't feel very happy at the thought of being blown apart in the next few seconds.

I step into the doorway. The dog gets up, and I hold him by the collar. The only thing I see is a fat blackbird sitting under the window, fluffed up into a ball of feathers with an orange beak poking out. It must have flown into the window even though the glass isn't clear, and the individual panes are so small. It's probably bashed its head in and is about to die at any minute. While I look at it, I feel a prickle in my neck. My skin feels like it's been rubbed raw and the tiny hairs are standing on end. Something's not right. Then I realize what it is: the birds are silent and it's unnaturally still, like before a storm. As I listen, the courtyard door opens a crack. I'm relieved to see Clara's face peering in, probably to see if I'm sitting on the ground biting the heads off little children.

A shadow suddenly comes into view. The blackbird screeches and spreads its wings as a large bird picks it up and hurls it against the wall of the shed. Its wings flap against the stone and the blackbird's body rolls sideways, wings breaking with the sound of snapping matchsticks. As the predator bird takes hold of it, I feel as if its pale yellow-eyed stare is fixed on me. Then it lifts off with a couple of wing movements, prey in its claws, and disappears over the roof of the house in front. A perfect bird of prey. If it were bigger, it could carry off a slithering snake or a princess. Or Jessie.

At the other end of the courtyard, Clara has tipped her head back to look up at the bird. For some reason, I'm glad that she saw it too.

It's a jungle out here, she shouts to me. Do you want to go into town?

We take the tram. I buy tickets for us and for the dog, which Clara finds hilarious. But I've never had the nerve to travel without a ticket.

People are obeying the ban on driving, so the tram is packed. Everyone under seventy is standing and it's warm and sticky like in a greenhouse. Clara's wearing the wig and is hiding behind sunglasses, but I notice that she's not well. Her limbs are limp and she's hanging on to the strap above with one arm, swaying like a marionette. It's anyone's guess which one of us – Clara, myself or the dog – will collapse first.

It's probably because of the falcon or hawk or whatever it was that I trace Jessie's name in the dust on the window, then look at my fingertip and try to make out what difference the name makes to it. Jessie often used to immortalize herself this way on windscreens, shop windows and mirrors. Most of these monuments must have been washed away by the rain long ago, but it's just possible that some of them have survived, in some hidden, protected corner of the city. The longer I stare at the dusty window, the louder the whistle in my deaf ear gets. I like that. In some way, Jessie shot us both in the head, and I'm almost as dead as she is. Through the window, the parliament building suddenly appears on the left and I stretch my neck to keep it in view for as long as possible. Rufus's office is behind it.

When Clara pushes past three rustling grandmas with their shopping bags to jump out of the tram at Schottentor, I'm not sure if we've arrived or if she simply can't cope any longer. I'm glad because I'm about to collapse. I can feel Rufus's presence within a radius of a few hundred metres. I try to tell myself he's away on a trip, working on the other side of the world, but I still feel him. I suddenly feel the presence of others too: Shershah and Jessie. And then I think I see Tom the Technician's red baseball cap in the middle of a group of tourists. I grab Clara by the arm and stand still.

Please give me the recorder, I say.

She's got it, with a new tape in it, too. She walks past the town hall into the park, attaching the microphone on the way. We sit down in the middle of a sea of white plastic chairs, placed ready for a philharmonic concert to be performed after dark. The space is glaring and empty now; the chairs reflect the sunlight like a snowdrift, dazzling the eyes.

Should I go? she asks.

That sounds as if I'm about to throw up and need to be alone for it.

Stay, I say. It's not so important.

She called me in the office, I say, and didn't give her name. I hadn't been expecting to ever hear from her again, so I didn't recognize her voice, and the conversation lasted barely a minute.

Clara has turned away from me. She's stroking the dog, who's half-lying and half-sitting awkwardly on his long legs. My sweaty hands are getting the recorder wet. I put it down on the chair next to me.

Jessie called again the next day, and this time I guessed who she was. She didn't seem to find it strange to be speaking to me again after twelve years, she just asked if someone had left a message for her, and then she hung up. From then on, she called often, mostly in the evening, when the secretaries had gone home and a law student was manning the emergency switchboard. She wanted to know if Rufus routinely recorded all calls, and I wondered how she knew Rufus. I switched the recording function off because she asked me to, though that was strictly forbidden. She always asked first if there was a message for her, and then we chatted a little. She told her strange stories, about transparent people standing motionless on their pedestals, or about fish, tigers and fountains.

I always pretended that it was a normal conversation, asked questions as if I knew exactly what it was all about. Though I didn't understand anything, her stories were somehow familiar to me. They could have been fragments of vaguely remembered fairy tales that had been read to me as a child. The more I listened to her, the more I liked it. I would stand by the open window with my eyes closed, pressing the cordless phone tightly against my ear in an attempt to implant her voice directly into my head.

Sometimes she didn't say anything at all, but just breathed heavily into the receiver. I got tenser and tenser as I listened to the sound that her lungs made and I couldn't think of a single word to say. When she finally hung up I couldn't work any longer, so I would go home and remain restless for a long time. But I got even more wound up when she didn't call at all. I worked on and on, waiting for the telephone to ring, and only left the office after midnight.

I don't know when it was that I finally asked what kind of message she was expecting me to receive for her. By this time, I'd long got used to the ritual of her asking for a message.

Oh, she replied. It's not going to arrive anyway.

Why not? I asked.

You were the emergency contact point for Shershah and me, she said. He wanted to get in touch.

There he was, finally. It wasn't as if I hadn't thought about him. I thought about him the whole time really; he lurked in the background like Fortinbras with Hamlet. But I'd allowed myself the absurd thought that Jessie could simply have lost touch with him after they'd both disappeared from school all those years ago.

But he's dead, she said. I just ask after a message to comfort myself a little.

My hand flew to my mouth, not in horror, but to stop myself from asking when, where, how. I didn't want to know, so there was no reason to ask. He was dead and I was alive. That was enough.

Do you know if there's any water around here? Clara asks.

I press the Stop button hurriedly. I don't want another voice on the tapes. I rewind: 'my hand flew to—' no, that's too much. Forward again: 'there's any water'. No, back. Now it's right.

The Donau canal, I say impatiently, but it's not very near.

Then I notice the dog, who's dragged himself off into the shade, lying on his side, his tongue lolling in the dirt, a couple of dry leaves stirred by his panting stuck to it. Looking at Clara, I can tell what his skin must look like under the fur.

I don't know how you can stand it, Clara whispers. We'll come back for you later.

But you have to cross the Schottenring to get there, I shout after her.

She doesn't turn, swaying over the Schottenring in the direction of the opera with the dog behind her.

I want to switch the recorder on again, but I stand up and follow her as if I'm being pulled by a string. Somehow I imagine she'll right herself round the next corner, straighten her back, and start walking differently, like an actor leaving the stage and assuming his natural gait on the way back to the dressing room. But nothing of the kind happens. She doesn't even tear the wig off; her brain must be frying beneath it. We cross the Rathaus Park in single file and leave it through one of the iron gates. I don't bother to try to hide. Neither she nor the dog turns round.

There it is again, the over-ornate Greek main entrance with the ramp and the ridiculous equestrian statues in front of it. My legs move more slowly, as if the pull of gravity is increasing the closer we get to the parliament building. Clara and the dog are almost run over by a tram, but they manage to get to the other side and walk along the north side of the building. Coloured flyers with dusty footprints on them are scattered over the ground. Police officers are leaning against the columns, guarding the entrance; a couple of Romanians in orange work overalls are picking up glass bottles. I recognize Jörg Haider's face with a Hitler moustache on it in the crude drawing on one of the flyers; the Austrians have been at it with politics again. I fight my way through to the other side of the road and make it to the beginning of Bartensteingasse, but then I have to stop. I have absolutely no desire to see anyone I knew from before. The thick-walled Habsburg building that Clara is walking towards glows in a fresh yellow; how nice, I think, they've finally had it repainted.

On the way back through the park I scoop up a couple of handfuls of water from the duck pond and splash them on to my face. The liquid stinks. I'm obsessed by the thought of what harm Clara could be doing to me. The realization that nothing in the world can harm me any longer doesn't comfort me in the least.

20 | Counting Fish

The first thing I thought when I saw Jessie was that she looked exactly the same.

I got there early and waited a few minutes, instinctively looking in the right direction so I saw her coming from afar. She approached the bridge from the other side of the canal, not from the city centre. I recognized her wreath of glowing yellow hair, the tips of which bobbed in time to her step, and her oversized trousers and colourful top. It seemed like I'd just seen her in the school courtyard or dining hall. I looked down at myself, to make sure that I, unlike her, *didn't* look like I had then. Most of the person she knew had simply ceased to exist, melted down years ago through a combination of speed, push-ups, forced marches, the barber's scissors, and the dermatologist's chemicals. Ultra-fine, practically transparent layers of skin had been peeled off my whole body, deep down to where every last pimple had been. Looking at myself in the mirror now had a calming effect on me.

But that didn't help. Jessie was standing on the other side of the bridge under the red traffic light and I stared at her as though she were a being from another world who had come to take me away. I hadn't expected anything in particular from our meeting. I'd looked forward to it, and thought it wouldn't make any difference seeing her in person after speaking to her on the phone almost every day for weeks. I suddenly realized that I'd made a fatal mistake. It didn't just make a difference – it was a shock. I felt my back curve, my shoulders sink and my arms suddenly hang uselessly by my sides. I felt patches of sweat under my arms and an unpleasant, cold dampness in my shoes: signs of a paralysis I had forgotten long ago. My whole body suddenly remembered the time I had lain in bed every day, reading a trashy science fiction novel, waiting for the heroine, breasts bound with ammunition belts, to turn up again; and how I had almost damaged my kidneys because I had often been too lazy to get up to go to the toilet.

The traffic light turned green. The closer Jessie came, the more I felt like an impostor, someone who had crept in where he wasn't really allowed. I thought about the flights in first class with Rufus, which were getting more and more frequent, stretching my legs out as he drank a coffee with Cointreau next to me; a mixture, he thought, that could only be drunk on a plane. He would speak in his abrupt manner on the point of the 'home call' we were making, oblivious to any reactions, as usual. I'd never been able to give a correct answer in class in school even when I knew it; now it seemed strange to me how much I enjoyed sitting silently listening to Rufus. Beside him, I looked at the world from above. He had a unique ability to see the planet as an interesting but completely manageable place. For him, the countries of the world in all their complexity were nothing more than individual persons with separate personalities and easily graspable characters. They were born and died, they had biographies, they were marked with certain qualities and had lived through traumatic times; they had memories, hopes and dreams, they were poor or rich, strong or weak, had friends and enemies. Rufus was their doctor, their judge and priest. Only countries themselves and a handful of other people worked on his level. And I was his assistant, looking over his shoulder, often dizzy from the view. Now I thought I knew why. The idea of that being my proper place in the world suddenly seemed completely wrong to me.

On the other side of the road, Jessie was getting nearer. I had a long way to fall. I felt myself pulled towards her, into an abyss without a safety railing. I wanted to turn before she spotted me, run back to the U-Bahn station and back into my office, where I would get all calls from her number blocked. I wanted to be back working with what I knew.

It was too late. It was busy on the Franzen Bridge, but Jessie had seen me over the cars. Our gazes met and the shock turned into pure fear when I realized that she'd recognized me immediately. She didn't stop short, but threw an arm up in the air.

Cooper!! she called.

I hadn't heard the name for twelve years. I waved back and Jessie ran into the road.

Look out! I shouted.

Brakes screeched. There was a stink of burnt rubber. One of the drivers couldn't stop himself from signalling are-you-crazy? – then she was standing in front of me, safe.

My God, I said.

Cooper, she said. I'm totally confused.

I worked out that she had to be twenty-six years old. There were a couple of fine lines running across her forehead and the expression in her eyes was too tired to be a child's. But everything else made twenty-six seem impossible: her tiny frame, her clothes, the way her hands constantly moved to touch her face or her hair, the way her arms dangled, how she hopped from one foot to the other. She could have been twenty, sixteen, even twelve, really; her age changed according to the way the light fell on her, perhaps according to what she thought or said in any single moment. She had the sun behind her now, and her eyes seemed to have got darker with the years, almost black. I couldn't tell if her pupils were unnaturally dilated – perhaps she had two holes in her face into which I could shout and then listen for an echo.

She was looking me up and down too, as though I was something she wanted to buy. She looked at my black suit, felt the lapels of my unbuttoned jacket and the light-coloured shirt beneath. I'd taken the tie off and stuffed it in a pocket, but Jessie's fingers found it immediately. My hair fell into my eyes as I looked down at her. I had a casually styled haircut that wasn't suited to looking at a small woman close up. I'd get it cut as soon as I could.

It's wonderful to see you, Jessie said. You look really professional.

And you're exactly the same, I said on impulse.

She hugged me slowly: slung her arms around my middle, leaned her head against my chest and pressed against me, probably as hard as she could. I smelt her hair, which had something of the sun-warmed street and the vertically slanting light in it, a hint of rain and the whole of late summer. I smelt her skin, sweet and clean, untouched. Jessie was tiny in my arms; I hadn't held anyone so small in ages. I suddenly realized that I'd missed her, that the life of titans at Rufus's side hadn't been perfect. Big things like Rufus or even whole nations could be marvelled at, listened to or fought against, but they couldn't be loved. I remembered that Jessie had been the first girl who'd held my hand of her own accord; it was a sad memory, in which I was a sad figure. But I recognized myself in it. Now it seemed to me that I'd always felt differently from the others in the office, though I'd never admitted it. They were completely absorbed in the big picture, while I had needed something small. The smaller, the better – and ideally as small as Jessie.

I pushed her away from me a little and pulled myself together.

I actually meant to be in Greenland by now, she said.

In Greenland, I said. That's far away.

You haven't been there either, have you? she asked.

I shook my head. She started walking down Radetzkystrasse and I walked next to her.

Jessie, I said, I don't have much time. My lunch hour ends at one.

It's because of the silence, she said, and also because of the cold. And most of all, because there are no colours there.

Don't you want to tell me what you've been up to in the last twelve years first? I asked.

Whatever, she said. I've got a book at home, with pictures of the Arctic. I'll show it to you sometime. The sea is dark grey: it gleams and looks all sticky. There are icebergs swimming in it, and proper castles and palaces, with towers and gables and balconies and battlements. The eskimo boats that float in front of them are tiny and colourful, like leaves in a moat. And the silence – do you know what the silence is like?

Total, I said.

Exactly, she said. Total silence.

She turned along the Vordere Zollamtsstrasse, running her hand over the metal railing on the three-metre-high wall at the foot of which the Wien ran. I knew what it looked like in full flood; it reached from wall to wall, flowed swiftly and could have almost been called a canal. Now it was a shallow stream of water flowing over the knee-high steps of a cobbled gutter.

Jessie, I said carefully, I have to be back in half an hour.

So white and still, she said. Can't you imagine it, Cooper?

The name was like a landing strip for memories. Every time she used it, I felt the next squadron approaching. I thought for a moment.

Yes, I said, I can.

Good, she said. I just want to show you something. We're walking towards the U-Bahn station anyway.

We walked the next fifty paces in silence. Then she suddenly stopped, tugged a corner of my jacket and pulled me towards her.

Look, she said. Do you understand that?

She pointed down at the river. There was a swarm of black fish in it at the level of the third underwater step. Their heads were against the current, and they were so closely packed together that the water sloshed off their backs over the sides of the gutter, flowing left and right along the concrete path. The wriggling of countless bodies, just short of leaping out of the water, looked like the trembling of a single large animal. They made up a huge mass of energy, ten metres long and three metres wide, probably weighing a few hundred pounds.

Isn't that beautiful? Jessie said.

It's repulsive, I said.

What are they doing? Jessie asked.

I don't know, I said. Exploring, spawning. No idea.

We stood there, elbows propped on the railing. The swarm of fish didn't move, but simply stayed put.

They've been here for days, Jessie said.

You live nearby, then?

She didn't reply immediately. As she paused, I looked at her sideways. There were shadows on her cheeks and the bones were prominent. She'd grown thin, not just lost puppy fat. A thin whitish crust covered her lips – some kind of secretion, or traces of saliva. There was a dark red scab bulging from the middle of her lower lip.

Oh well, she said. Maybe you really can drop in some time.

She gave me the address: 61 Praterstrasse, close to Praterstern, and we stood there a moment longer. A ladybug landed on my elbow, one spot on each wing. I'd been told as a child that the number of spots on its wings told its age, but no one had been able to explain why there were no one-year-old ladybugs. I touched it lightly with my index finger so that it would bring me luck, but it slipped off my elbow and dropped into a clump of grass below the railing where it also lost its grip and tumbled onto the asphalt. It lay on its back, paddling its legs, not managing to right itself. I turned away in disgust.

What do you want to do in Greenland anyway? I asked.

It'd be good for my eyes, she said, and my head.

She touched her eyelids, then her forehead.

It'd be very expensive too, I said. Do you need money?

I regretted the question immediately, but she didn't seem to notice.

I thought I had more than enough really, she said.

I realized that she was probably loaded. She'd certainly been working for Herbert all these years; I couldn't imagine what else she would have done.

Would you take me to Greenland with you? I asked.

Oh Cooper, she said. You don't really want to go at all. Don't treat me like a child.

She turned on her heel without casting another glance at the fish, and walked up the street in the direction we had come from. I let her go. I started counting the fish for fun, poking my index finger in the air, but I couldn't carry on; my gaze simply slid off the shining bodies. When I gave up and lifted my head, I saw Jessie standing a few metres way. She was watching me.

Come round tonight, she called to me.

Then she walked off, mingling with the people on the bridge.

Tourists are the only things still moving in this city, creeping with bowed heads like refugees. A flash of yellow hair in the middle of a group of dark-haired tourists makes me start. A second glance shows that the girl's hair is a very different blonde from Jessie's. As she brushes past me, I look into the wake she leaves behind; neither happiness nor pain there, just an exhausted blankness. I'm obviously getting to the point where I'm ready to believe that Jessie, whom I found in our Leipzig flat with a bullet in her head, will come back to me in the middle of a group of Italian tourists.

I stop the recorder for a moment to recover. I've been sitting here for half an hour at most, and there is already a light stripe on my arm where the microphone cord has been lying. The sun is deadly hot. I wonder if Clara and Jacques Chirac have found refuge in Rufus's air-conditioned offices, and if they might spend the rest of the summer there. I don't ask myself what she's really doing. I drop the cigarette after two drags. It tastes like exhaust fumes and the smoke is much too hot on my tongue.

Jessie was waiting downstairs for me. We greeted each other wordlessly. We took a cast-iron cage to get up to her flat; the lift itself was made entirely of wood, the walls covered with scribblings and carvings like the top of a school desk. There was an 'M+J' amongst them, but with a date from the Second World War.

Jessie was standing in front of me, and I looked at the shoulder bones and spine that showed through her thin T-shirt. She must have weighed barely 100 pounds. She whipped around when I put my jacket round her shoulders, looking for a moment as if she wanted to bite my hand; she drew her upper lip back in a snarl and her face filled with fury. The jacket dropped to the floor.

Cooper, she hissed, you can come over. But if you try to mother me, you'll never see me again. And don't touch me.

I didn't reply, since we had arrived. She opened the door to her flat and let me in first. The shiny floorboards in the hall stretched out like a still lake. Nothing disturbed the surface, not a single piece of furniture, no newspaper lying around, not even a pair of shoes. Without looking into any of the rooms, I knew at once that the flat was empty. It echoed the way an empty flat does and had the impersonal whiff of places that potential tenants viewed with an estate agent.

Have a look around, Jessie said.

The first three rooms were separated from each other by double doors. There were a couple of damp discoloured patches on the walls and ceiling; and the uninterrupted sheen of the blond wood parquet floor. On the other side of the hall was a fourth room with an armchair, a couch with a kind of night stand beside it and a bed, all in a strangely awkward arrangement. The whole space looked fake, like a bad imitation of a living space. I was sure that none of the objects were used.

The fifth room was more like a storeroom squeezed into the furthest corner of the flat. This was the only lived-in room. A few items of clothing hung on the walls, and other pieces of clothing were scrunched up to serve as a pillow at one end of a blanket spread out on the floor. There were a couple of empty bottles and a tin saucepan that was obviously also used to drink from; newspapers; and a cardboard box sealed with tape.

I stop the recorder again and sit thinking, looking at the air shimmering over the tarmac, making the street look as if it is partly covered with water.

What I thought of the small room, I say into the microphone, really should take into account the fact that the cardboard box was probably stuffed with banknotes in three different currencies.

I stop again, rewind and erase the last sentence.

Everything looked grotty and run-down, except a mobile phone lying open in the exact middle of the floor, its clean, functional black contours distinguishing it from the rest of the room's contents. It seemed to have chanced on the room by mistake, yet it was the most important thing in it. Jessie had obviously been calling me from it for the last few weeks. She stepped up next to me in the doorway and we stared into the room together.

It's nice here, I say.

They're going to cut off my phone soon, she said sadly.

I slowly began to understand that what Jessie was short of wasn't money itself but the ability to use money to get the necessary things in life. The empty rooms, Jessie's clothes and most of all her face told of deprivation. I tensed my shoulders with a jerk to cope with the sense of oppression that suddenly came over me.

Don't worry about the telephone, I said. I'll take care of it.

There was also a narrow bathroom with a toilet next to the fire exit, and a big kitchen with a balcony. All that was in the kitchen was a fridge with a hotplate on top of it, and a single chair. I put my briefcase down on the floor and took a deep breath.

She'd told me on the phone how she loved slitting open packets of boil-in-the-bag rice because the tautly stretched plastic gave way after very little resistance, like skin, letting the knife dig into the soft insides. Sometimes she stabbed at the packet until the entire contents lay all over the floor, grains of rice with shreds of plastic between them, no longer edible. Now I saw the knife that she used on top of the fridge and also a few grains of rice. I'd already realized on the phone that she was completely alone, for the entire day and the night too. And she had certainly been so for some time.

She let me look in the fridge: no food, just a few plastic packs of snow for selling on the street.

Do you want some? she asked.

I don't take anything any more, I said.

Oh, she said.

She shook her head, looking disappointed. Remembering that I had an apple in my briefcase, I took it out and offered it to her. She closed her hands around it absently and took a bite. I counted that as a first success. Then I saw how blood trickled from the dried-up ridge in her underlip when she opened her mouth, colouring the apple and running over her chin.

Tastes funny, she said.

I couldn't stand seeing the red against her pale face. I dug around in my jacket for a paper handkerchief and held her still by the hair on the back of her head as I wiped her mouth and chin.

From now on, I said, the rooms will be numbered from front to back so we can find our way around. OK?

184

She shrugged.

OK, she said. I don't care.

She stared into space for a while. She seemed to be preparing to say something important.

Cooper, she said, I've learnt.

Her voice echoed horribly against the tiled walls. I would have given anything for some noise from the street.

All my life I've been looked after by other people, she said. That's proved to be a mistake.

I waited for her to go on, but she had finished.

From the window in Room Two, you looked out on Praterstern. There were horse chestnuts lying on the street, most of them crushed into a pale pulp by car wheels. The few whole ones shone brown and white, not quite ripe yet. I wondered if Jessie thought of them as horse eyeballs, and decided to ask her sometime. Maybe it was possible to map out her inner landscape. I was beginning to feel cold.

The evening light slanted over the city, making everything seemed exaggeratedly three-dimensional. The rooftops overlapped with their own sharp shadows and illusory depths. I too felt incredibly three-dimensional, fitting somewhere into the panorama before me.

Oh, I heard Jessie saying, the ice-cream man is in the papers.

I turned and looked across the room and the corridor into the bathroom, where she was sitting on the toilet a good eight metres away from me. She was holding a scrap of newspaper and reading it. Then she shook her head and wiped herself with the piece of paper. I came closer.

What on Earth are you doing? I asked.

There's no more toilet paper, she said.

And you read the newspaper before . . .

I saw part of a newspaper lying under the sink, and my open briefcase next to it.

But that's my *Frankfurter Allgemeine*, I said.

Well, the *Spiegel* wouldn't haven't done, Jessie said. The shiny paper would just have smeared everything about.

I took the paper away from her and read the rest of the headline over the article that she'd ripped apart. She'd torn most of it, and the photo, too.

'Arkan the Cleanser interviewed in Belgrade. Serbian folk hero accuses new Albanian government of supporting the UÇK.'

A strange coincidence. This man's file had been on my desk not long ago. Charges had been brought against him in the Yugoslavian war-crimes tribunal a few weeks earlier, without the knowledge of the public or even the man himself. Louise Arbour, chief prosecutor in the Hague and a good friend of Rufus, had decided to keep the case a secret. There were people in high places everywhere who supported Arkan.

Louise had asked us to produce a report. Over the course of twenty pages, I set out the basic principle of territorial integrity, which forbids interference in the internal affairs of sovereign states, even in the cause of criminal prosecution. Then I pored over various commentaries, judgements of the international courts and the latest articles on international law on the Internet. In the subsequent forty-eight pages, I made a case for an exception to the basic principle being possible where there was grave violation of human rights. Rufus read it and told me what he thought, blunt to the point of rudeness. Max, he said, in international law – a field that is characterized by wooliness above all – there's only one thing to do: be a positivist, and only argue for what you can see. Otherwise we might as well call what we do politics, and leave it to the diplomats and moralists.

He was right, of course. But Arkan was one of the worst criminals on Earth. He had called Milosevic a softie, and regarded himself, on the other hand, as an artist. He had organized the cruelties of genocide with an almost loving imagination. Thinking about him always made me feel slightly ill. But I got rid of the last forty-eight pages and argued for Serbia's inviolability instead, thereby ensuring Arkan's freedom.

Jessie, I said, who did you call the ice-cream man just now?

She pulled her trousers up, flushed the toilet and tried to get past me.

Who was in the picture? I asked.

She shook her head left and right, then bent down and slipped under my arm.

A friend of Ross, she said from the door, my brother.

I know who Ross is, I murmured.

From the number of feet left at the bottom of the photo, I could tell that there had been five people in it. An absurd impulse prompted me to check if one of the pairs of trousers was too short, and if the socks beneath had 'VICTORY' on them, as I remembered Ross from years ago. Then I remembered that the person Jessie had recognized wasn't Ross but a friend of his. Besides, Ross would hardly be wearing the same socks twelve years later. One pair of legs belonged to Arkan, and there was really only a one-to-four chance that he was the man whom Jessie had meant. But she had said 'ice-cream man', and I remembered that Arkan had run a café in the early nineties, directly opposite the football stadium of the Red Star Belgrades, the team from which he had recruited men for his paramilitary units. I had no idea how Jessie could have known that.

This guessing game was making my head spin. I tossed the paper back under the sink and went back to stand by the window. The world outside was one I knew, one whose highest laws I was familiar with. This was a world in which someone could simply point at a picture of a perpetrator of genocide and say, 'That's one of my brother's friends.' It was getting dark. I stared at the reflection of my face on the glass, and tried to think of nothing at all. I'd mastered this art to perfection in school, and had been able to put on an interested expression as if drawing a curtain over the emptiness inside my head. If I was going to have to deal with the past anyway, I could at least make use of some of the few good things about it.

It didn't work, not the way it should have. I managed to empty my head of all thought, but I started longing for something instead. For something warm and living that I could take in my arms and hold on to. Maybe I just needed a hot-water bottle, or a cup of tea.

It was almost dark outside when I went to look for Jessie. I found her in the kitchen, sitting stiffly on the chair, her back straight, her calves parallel to the chair legs. It looked more like six legs standing than a person sitting down. She looked as if she was waiting for her own execution. I was suddenly gripped by a desire to leave the flat immediately.

Shall we do something? she asked, stony-faced.

I didn't know if she was looking at me or if her gaze was resting on me by pure chance.

It's too late for today, I said. I have to go.

She made small sounds with every breath. Her hands were trembling and she was clasping them tightly. I couldn't stand the sight of it, so I fumbled for the packet of cigarettes in my jacket, stuck two in my mouth in a V shape and lit them together. I passed her one. She had to untwine her fingers to take it.

Look, Jessie, I said. I'll come again tomorrow and then you can help me with an important project.

She took short puffs at the cigarette. Her eyes grew wider and they focused on me.

What project? she asked.

We're going to send letters to everyone in the world, I said. Everyone is going to step out of their houses on one particular day and start running in the same direction.

Everyone? Jessie asked.

Everyone, I said.

What for? she asked.

What do you mean, what for? I said. The globe is going to start rotating beneath our feet, isn't it, and we'll move forward like a circus bear on a ball into space to find a better solar system.

She started laughing, and crossed her legs.

Cooper, she said. You always have such crazy ideas.

I'd never had crazy ideas before in my life; I was just starting to have them. I leaned over her quickly, kissed her forehead, grabbed my briefcase from the floor and ran out of the flat without looking back at her once. I left her sitting on the chair in the middle of the empty kitchen, my cigarette in her mouth, still smiling faintly. I ran down the steps as quickly as I could, faster than the sound of my own footsteps, which seemed to be clattering after me, a split second behind.

Suddenly everything happens at once. Clara is standing next to me; perhaps she's been standing there for a while. The tape has ended, the Stop button snaps up sharply and once again I think I see someone I recognize on the street. This time it's Maria Huygstetten, and on second glance it still looks like her, just before she turns the corner with her pile of red hair. I want to go after her but Clara and the dog distract me. They are wet – the dog especially – and look as if they really have been to the Donau canal. I wonder if I dreamed that they went straight to Rufus's office. I feel disorientated, as if I'm waking up in the middle of the night to find the walls have been moved around and the night light is on the wrong side of the bed.

We can go now, Clara says.

What? I ask.

Back home, Clara says. Are you done?

I don't know what with, but I nod anyway.

How's Rufus? I ask.

The question doesn't surprise her.

Don't know, she says. He didn't let me in.

She takes the tape out of the recorder and stuffs it into her bag. That'll be ten more pages in her file. She walks off slowly, a little hunched over, and I follow her.

21 | Pigskin

I stamp on the mat outside the supermarket, right next to the sliding doors. They still don't open. I bang my fists against the glass and knock my head against it: bang, bang, donk; fist, fist, head. So it's Sunday. Who'd have known? The streets are always empty anyway, and the sounds that filter into the courtyard are neither softer nor louder than usual today.

I slap my flat palms against the glass one more time, kick it and nearly break my toes because I've forgotten that I'm barefoot. Jacques Chirac comes up next to me and butts his nose against my thigh. I look in at the empty checkouts: everything is dead and all the lights are off.

Young man, someone shouts, you're not going to get the door open that way.

He's sitting a few metres away on the single plastic chair in front of a small café, a latte propped on his lap. Some old geezer, still with it enough not to be sparing his breath and spit even in this murderous heat. One of those people who'd tell the devil how he should be turning the spit he's roasting them on. An empty travel bag lies at his feet.

I press my face and my throbbing foot against the cool glass. My head is pounding away as if two pistons are burning up my brain.

I'm supposed to make it to the next open petrol station in this state. And back too.

Good boy, good dog. You've grown thin.

I can't quite make out the old man's accent. He rolls his r's and his vowels are a little too clipped and a little too wide. I turn to face him. The dog is standing between his knees, dipping his head and wagging his tail as if he's greeting an old friend. The old man is holding his cup in the air with his left hand and stroking Jacques Chirac's head with his right, moving the dog's floppy ears back and forth. He catches my eye and stops patting the dog, who promptly sits down.

What do you need so urgently from the supermarket? he asks.

He rolls his sleeves up, exposing stringy arms covered with bright pink patches, as if there's a thin peeling layer of human being over pigskin. His hair is long and dark, greying only at the sides. It reaches his collar.

I walk past him and get a coffee inside. The shop is so small that it's barely possibly to turn in it, but it seems to sell a little of everything. Except for cigarettes. I lean against the door frame, holding the cup in my hand.

Cigarettes, I say.

I thought that they didn't have cigarettes in Austrian supermarkets, he said.

This one has a tobacco counter in front, I say, speaking slowly and exaggeratedly clearly.

Let me help, he says.

He pulls an unopened packet of filter cigarettes out of his pocket and hands it over to me. I tear off the cellophane wrapping.

Can I buy a few off you? I ask.

Keep them all, he says.

I take a fifty-schilling note out of my pocket and the banknote curls around my finger stubbornly. The old man has noticed. His face creases along his laugh lines and his smile doesn't need to carve out new paths as it would in the face of a younger person.

Leave it, he says. Keep the cigarettes. I don't smoke myself.

He's the second person I've ever met who offered me cigarettes without being a smoker himself. The first was Clara.

Maybe you can do me a favour instead?

I turn my back on him, drink up my coffee in the shop and walk back into the street. The old man has the travel bag on his lap now. He's giving Jacques Chirac some nibbles. The dog doesn't move when I turn to go. I decide not to call him at all.

Listen, the old man calls. I'm just looking for a particular street.

I stop, irritated by my own good manners.

What's it called? I ask.

I realize too late that he could have asked the shopkeeper long ago.

Römergasse, he says.

My hands fly up to my face.

What's wrong? he asks.

Which number?

Twenty-one, he says.

I should have known. Everything's been revolving around me for weeks, down to the smallest detail. And I never have time to prepare myself for it.

Follow me, I say quietly.

The travel bag yawns open as he bends over to put his cup down on the pavement. I see a glint of something metal in it. The saucer and spoon clink against the tarmac, then he sits up, his face red from bending over.

Where are you from? I ask.

I don't know if that's anything to do with you, he says in a friendly manner.

You're not from Vienna, I say. But with *that* in your bag you can't have come from outside the EU borders.

You know a lot, he says. That's great. Knowledge is the most important thing in the world. More important than money, love or cigarettes.

We get going. He's even slower than I am. After a couple of metres, I take the bag from him. We take ages to walk the few steps down the lane but I don't feel like holding his spotty arm to support him.

He leans against the wall while I open the front gate. I hear him panting behind me in the darkness.

Almost there, I say.

We walk past the green Opel Ascona. I fetch the only chair, a rusty construction of thin metal pipes, out of the bushes and put it under the chestnut tree. The old man drops into it.

Is that Lisa Müller's car? he asks, pointing at the Opel Ascona.

It takes me a second to realize that he means Clara.

You're asking the important, unresolved questions first, I say.

That means you don't know, he says.

On the surface, I say, it looks like the car belongs to one of Lisa's friends. But I'm used to the surface being deceptive.

A very important step, he says. Once you've taken it, you're closer to realizing that all truth, which we can reach eventually, really lies in the surface of things and that the core is empty. But one thing at a time.

I'm no philosopher, I say, and I don't believe in philosophy.

Doesn't matter, he says. Philosophy doesn't believe in you either.

That we can agree on, I say, and hold my hand out to him. Max.

Schnitzler, he says, not Arthur, but related in spirit.

But that's not your real name, I say, chancing it.

You know even more than I thought, he says. And you, do you have a last name?

Yes, I say, but I don't know if that's anything to do with you.

As you wish, he says. I normally only address students by their first names. But if you want to put yourself on that level, fine.

I disappear into the shack to take a ration of coke, leaving Schnitzler alone with his opinions for a while. I like him. Perhaps it's his unique arrogance, or perhaps it's the fact that I haven't spoken to someone intelligent for ages. I assume that Herbert's sent him, and feel glad that it's him, not someone else.

The coke is good. I smoke another one of his cigarettes before I go back out into the courtyard, looking at myself in the mirror I've just snorted off. It could be the moment when my whole life flashes before me, but it doesn't happen. Instead, my face slowly assumes a cubist aspect and begins to look like a collection of cut-out shadowy surfaces, something I've always wanted. In school, I had to press my finger into the flesh of my face to feel the bone beneath. Before I went to bed, I often imagined a tube being inserted under the skin of my cheeks and sucking the fat off into a bucket. I imagined the fat being cloudy and viscous, like heated dripping. The bucket filled up slowly, and my features slowly appeared, surfacing like a sunken ship at the bottom of a lake pumped dry. This fantasy made my heart beat faster and brought a smile to my fat cheeks. I fell asleep to it many an evening, happy thanks to the cannabis that I'd had just before that.

I'm smiling now too. There I am. I touch my jutting cheekbones with my fingers. I touch my eyebrows, which feel like hairs growing directly over bone. My face reminds me of someone. I think it's Shershah.

With another glowing cigarette between my fingers, I leave the shed, prepared to cede victory. Schnitzler is dangling from his chair as if he's secretly suffered a quiet stroke. Jacques Chirac is stretched out at his feet.

It's nice here, Schnitzler says as soon as he sees me.

Do you want a glass of water? I ask.

If it's no problem, he says.

He rights himself wearily. I walk over to the tap on the other side of the courtyard and fill a tin cup. He empties it in one gulp.

Aaah, he says, heavenly. Nothing like tending to a really urgent need.

Quite right, I say, the more urgent needs one has, the better.

If you think that, you really must be the one, he says.

I hadn't expected a platitude like that from him. It amuses me to be annoyed by it. Rather simplistically, I'd expected that when the end came it would be a tasteful one, carried out by a person of style.

Since you've struggled to come all this way, I say, I certainly am the one – for you, at least.

You know who I am? he asks.

I thought I did, I say. Looking at you, though, I'm not so sure.

His bag is lying within reach, but he doesn't seem to be making any move towards doing the deed. Realistically, though, it's highly improbable that Herbert would have sent such a wreck of a man to carry out a job like this. There would certainly be others.

I put a foot on top of the wall and stub my cigarette out on the roof of the Opel Ascona.

Where did you get the address? I ask.

He smiles.

You want to know everything.

Of course I do, I say. It's human nature always to want to know everything, and it really should be common sense to refuse to comply with that demand. I'm working on it.

He laughs.

God had to give man a sense of taste so that he would feed himself, and a sex drive so that he would reproduce, he says. From that, you can tell what kind of common sense there was to begin with.

Perhaps it would have been better to tell us what this whole fucking life is all about anyway, I say. Then we might have done something to hold on to it ourselves.

He's obviously highly amused.

God save us from understanding! he shouts. It takes the power from our rage, the honour from our hatred, the joy from our revenge and the blessedness from our memories. If you'll allow me to quote.

OK, I say, that's enough. Let's cut the crap.

We fall silent. The conversation has died. He bends over and pats the dog. His action transforms the rusty garden chair into a rocking chair, the Opel Ascona into a fireplace, and the neglected Great Dane into a hunting dog. Jacques Chirac spreads his legs like a practised whore.

Once you're done with the dog, I say, perhaps we'll finally get to the point?

And that would be? Schnitzler says.

I vaguely hope, I say, that you've come to carry out something that wasn't done two years ago for the sake of my girlfriend.

What's that? he asks.

My execution, I say.

You really are an interesting case, he says.

I suppose so, I say.

There's something rather irresistible, he says, about the way you carry the bag of your supposed murderer back for him and offer him a glass of water.

Faced with a wreck like you, I say, that was only the decent thing to do.

Exactly, he says reflectively, decent. But I have to disappoint you. I'm not kitted out for manslaughter.

With contract killers, I say, it's mostly a case of murder.

You're a lawyer.

It wasn't a question, nor a realization. He was paying tribute. He's beginning to get on my nerves.

So what's that in your bag? I ask.

It takes a few seconds for the penny to drop.

I see, he laughs. You're mistaken there. This should be familiar to you.

He unzips the bag, and this time I recognize the metallic object after one fleeting glance. It's a DAT-recorder, much like Clara's. I feel like an idiot.

OK, I say. You want to see Clara.

Who? he asks.

Lisa, I say.

Clara, he repeats. A role-play. Does she call you something else as well?

Come on, now, tell me what you're really here for, I say.

Your Clara called me almost as soon as she arrived here, he says, to give me the address. She was very proud of what she was doing, and hung up before I could let her know what I thought. I'm very glad to finally be meeting you in person.

You're glad, I say, that I've murdered someone.

I'm a psychologist, he says. I specialize in criminal pathology. A mushroom picker is glad when he stumbles across a mushroom.

I nod lethargically as I fumble in the packet for another cigarette.

And a newly classified criminal, I say, is always glad of a new victim.

I'm looking into his eyes, not really expecting him to take fright. He's obviously seen far worse cases than me. Nevertheless, I imagine that I see a reaction in his pupils, a rapid widening and narrowing, like something being pumped up. His sharpened gaze flatters me even though his mouth purses mockingly.

Max, he says. I'm sorry. I've read the first fifty pages of Lisa's work and it's a good story, but it doesn't have the slightest thing to do with my field.

Then Lisa will fail, I say.

Exactly, he says, but it doesn't work like that with us. The professor concerned has to make sure that the student writes an acceptable dissertation.

Be that as it may, I say, but she *wants* to write this. She wants to finish whatever it is she's started there.

Yes, he says, that's perfectly understandable. Besides, she's a bit stubborn by nature. But that's why I'm here.

No, I say, that's definitely not why you're here. No professor travels eight hundred kilometres because of a student's dissertation, even through Prague if necessary.

That was meant to be a joke about the bad roads in Eastern Europe, but he doesn't laugh.

I'm taking Lisa back to Leipzig with me, he says.

You can't do that, I say. She's needed here.

What for? he asks.

She's kicking up enough fuss in the city, I say, to attract the attention of the people who are supposed to find me here.

Do cut the crap, he says.

She's stirring up the mud, I say, and trampling the grass and getting on everyone's nerves until they realize that they really have to do something about it.

Do you take me for a fool? he says.

Schnitzler, I say, I don't want to go back to Leipzig, and I don't want Lisa to go.

What you're going through with Miss Müller, he says, lies somewhere in the field of symbiotic therapeutic relations. Just don't start thinking there's anything personal between you two.

Think what you will, I say, but you're wrong. Everything is perfect the way it is. If Clara is having fun crawling around in the destruction of my life, digging around in the ruins, then leave her to it. It'll all be over soon. Then you'll have Clara back.

That's not what it's about, he says.

He pulls his trousers up to his knees and rolls the cuffs until they stay up. Then he peers around the courtyard, looking as if he's having difficulty holding his temper.

I just happened to be in the city . . . he starts.

He's hit the wrong tone. It's obvious that he's lying.

Definitely not, I say.

Miss Müller, he says, is not going to get her diploma this way. And you can be sure that she'll follow me to Leipzig if I seriously ask her to.

That's what I'm afraid of, I say.

I should calm down and try to find out what this is really all about. The way he's looking at me tells me that he's open to negotiation.

OK, OK, I say. I was a bit slow there. You're threatening me, and you're probably offering a swap. Clara for something else.

He lets go of his trouser folds and sits up.

I'm currently researching the pathology of organized crime, he says. Public interest in this subject has increased enormously since the Balkan wars.

I don't give a fuck about your field of research, I say. I want to die here, with Clara beside me. I'm laying myself open to you.

He leans forward in his chair, suddenly seeming more agile.

I'm going to be quite open too, he says. There are very few people who can contribute to my research by making statements. They're either international criminals on the wanted list or their victims. Neither group is inclined to be very talkative in the service of mankind. You and Jessie, however . . .

Between my hands, his head feels like a great big fruit, perhaps a coconut with long hair. I press hard and tip Schnitzler and the chair towards the chestnut tree, until his head hits the trunk and the chair is balancing against my knee. It would be easy to bang him against the tree once more and topple him over, to leave him lying there and forget about him. At some point he'd be covered with moss and become part of the garden.

Schnitzler, I say, you're a tough guy, but you're past it now. Tell me, which country were you born in?

Young man, he says, nothing has been able to frighten me for a long time.

Fine, I say, let's put the question another way: was it Albania?

No, he says.

I let him go. The chair rocks forward violently, nearly throwing Schnitzler onto the lawn.

What was that all about? he groans.

I'm just trying to avoid the insinuations that I'm constantly encountering, I say.

He picks up where he left off, speaking quickly and interrupting himself after every second word.

You and your dead little girlfriend, he says, were in an *extraordinary* position . . .

I have *extraordinarily little* to lose, I shout. You'd better *fucking* remember that!

I assure you, he whispers, that you'll still have a long, happy life ahead of you when you've put all this behind you. It's just a matter of making a few right decisions.

I stretch my hands out to his head again. He's so damn ugly.

When Death approaches with countenance turned, I quote, we speak of recovery.

He doesn't seem to be taking it very well. His eyes widen a little, giving him a crazed expression. He changes tactics and both hands fly to his heart. It's obvious that he's play-acting. He looks like a corpse, but that's got to be the heat. He's a tough one.

I'm not impressed, I hiss.

He drops his hands, grips the armrests and kicks Jacques Chirac, who has got up worriedly to see if everything is all right.

Max, he says quickly. You've really had some incredible experiences. Tell them to a professional, not an amateur!

Hi there, Clara shouts. Look what I've brought.

I didn't hear her coming. She's suddenly there in the middle of the courtyard, holding a Shell plastic bag, probably containing cigarettes and booze. Maybe there's something to celebrate. Her face is animated, flushed and damp, almost feverish. God knows what she's been up to in the city and where she gets the energy for it. When she sees Schnitzler, a hand flies to her head and touches the black wig before dropping down by her side again. She stares at him, small and crumpled in the rusty chair; then at me, standing with a cigarette in the corner of my mouth, my hands resting on my hips.

Wow, she says. Cool.

Miss Müller, Schnitzler says. A pleasure, as always.

What are you doing here? she asks.

I'm off, I say.

I make it up to the Wilhelminenberg forest, supporting myself on Jacques Chirac's patient back from time to time. At the top of a gentle slope, a tree stump offers a surface of at least two square metres to lie down on. Amidst the lavender and high grass, the stillness is only interrupted by the rustling of insects going about their daily business. Time passes without a trace there, and basking in it is like lying in water that's exactly body temperature.

She's still there when I get back. I'd only half-expected it. She's cooking pasta for the dog on the electric stove, stirring the pot conscientiously. I walk up to her and she holds a rolled-up piece of paper out to me. It looks as if it's meant for snorting coke.

A letter for you, from Schnitzler, she says.

There's a telephone number on it, and a single line: 'Real conversation begins after the last word. Call me.'

Did he say you should give up on your dissertation? I ask.

Yes, she says.

And what did you say?

That he should leave me to continue in peace, otherwise I'd look for another supervisor.

I put an arm around her from behind and lean my forehead against her shoulder.

Good girl, I say. Well done. What's his real name?

Milan Kucia, she says. Everyone calls him Schnitzler because he's always quoting his work.

A Slavonic name, I say.

He comes from Belgrade as far as I know, she says, but he's not too popular there with his favourite subject.

Organized crime, I say.

Did you chat a bit? she asks.

He's got charisma, I say, in his own way. Now I understand a little more why you're so in awe of him.

No more than you are of Rufus, she says.

No, I say. Less, in fact. Did you never have a proper father or what?

She doesn't reply. I let her go, though it actually felt rather good to be holding her.

I've won today, she says, as far as points go. That's what he said. Miss Müller, go on, but work damn hard at it.

Fine, I say, work away. Are we eating together?

I'm not hungry, she says. I feel so ill.

22 | Rice With Kant

Fuck, I hear her say, just what I needed.

A dream recedes and the needle sinks down the scale back to zero. A vibration ebbs, the screaming of a great machine in which I was one of the rotating shafts dies down, the volume and tone dropping until all that's left is a monotonous whistling. Lying still, I realize that the whistling is coming from my left ear. I open my eyes and see a couple of flies circling the bulb on the ceiling even though it's off. I've been having a nightmare, though I know I will never remember what it has been about. Everyone knows that God has a warped sense of humour; he doesn't grant us peace from our own brains even in our sleep.

My body won't listen. Neither of my feet will leave the bed and my torso doesn't move when I try to sit up. I finally manage to lift my right arm. My fingers are hanging off the end like dead leaves on a branch but I still have to use them to peel the sticky viscose of the sleeping bag off my skin.

Shit, she says, it must be here somewhere.

I begin to realize what she's doing: she's looking for somewhere to plug in her headphones at the back of her CD player. As I turn, my hand bumps against something firm. It feels almost like an erection, but that's impossible. There's no time to worry about it.

It must be a mistake anyway. I watch Clara stick the plug into the back of the stereo. The big black headphones look professional, like something a DJ would wear. She takes a fat earmuff in each hand, spreads them wide and lifts them over her head.

No, wait! I call.

She listens and waits, hands suspended in the air. I can't stand up, so I wave her over instead. She comes over slowly, but she's still coming, obedient as a dog, lugging her CD player as if it's made of cement. She leans a hand against the hammock stand and passes me the headphones. She's bent over. It must be the stomach problems.

Where did you find them? I ask.

Under the table.

You'll get them back in a second. I just need to check something.

The air is thick around me. I bring the headphones close to my face and push my nose through the middle. Shoulders slumped, Clara waits, her gaze fixed on her new toy.

The headphones could hardly smell stronger if he was still wearing them. I feel a fiery explosion of adrenalin in my guts, shooting right up to my throat. Shershah had hardly ever washed his hair, so it had always smelt strongly. But this is overpowering. I breathe out and in again, and my head fills with another cloud of odour. I've stumbled across the traces of his immortality, found his hideaway between the black earmuffs of a pair of headphones, like a fleshy, boneless little animal in its shell.

I see him in front of me immediately, quite clearly, as if he's actually standing in the open doorway to the courtyard like a figure in shadow with his back to the light. Shershah had always known how to make the best of the light wherever he stood. I never knew whether it was intuitive or deliberate. His slim figure is slightly slumped and he looks sleepy. Like a wild cat's, his inert manner has something dangerous, deliberate about it; as if he is ready to spring forward and kill at any second, even if you have known him for a long time and he's never pounced before. His shoulders are slightly raised, his head bent forward as if he's constantly listening for something right under his feet. I watch the way he lifts both hands to twist his hair into a braid, which springs apart as soon as he lets go.

I used to braid his hair like that in school sometimes, when he was lying in the armchair in our room like a brand-new dummy, his head hanging over the back of the chair. His braid was as thick as an arm. Shershah never moved, and he didn't seem to be aware of what I was doing at all. Sometimes I'd stand still for a long time, holding his hair, waiting as the cigarette smoke curled up from his lips towards the ceiling, like a petrified Lot. Sometimes I got angry, overcome by irrational rage. I hated his casualness and his confidence, which he didn't have to lift a finger for. I got so angry that I wanted to wrap his hair around his neck and strangle him. It was impossible sharing a room with him. Everything focused on him: everyone's eyes, waves of music, the titles of the books lying around – it was all about him, but he remained untouched. Even my hatred rolled off him like drops of rain off a waterproof.

Killing someone is a lengthy business when you come across traces of him in the most absurd places. I'm going to finish the job and do the world a favour.

Music suddenly leaps out of the headphones. I lift my face and open my eyes. Clara looks at me accusingly, one finger on the stereo's volume dial. It's got a good stereo effect, because I feel as if I'm holding an entire concert hall in my hands. I sniff the sponge padding one more time before I pass it back to Clara. *Goodbye, stranger*, I think. I didn't have time to say farewell two years ago. The scent of Clara's hair will take away the smell. There will be no more resurrections.

She puts the headphones on immediately, wearing them around her neck rather than over her hair. She starts nodding to the beat so fluidly that her head looks as if it's only attached to her neck by a string. She looks good with the headphones – more complete, almost happy. I'm beginning to understand that she needs this stuff: to wrap herself in – matt-silver knobs and buttons and enough black cables and wires to trail around. Maybe she's imagining that she's in her glass cabin now, the city spread out before her in the night, a network of radios all playing the same music, Clara's music, chosen and played by her, the same music that she's rocking herself to right now.

But it's hot. She'll get a migraine if she goes on nodding that way, worse than a circular saw. Then she'll have to be sick and I'm definitely not cleaning it up. If there's anything left in her to be cleaned up, that is.

I find her in the courtyard in the afternoon, lying under the blazing sun. I heave her up and drag her over to the shade by the wall. Her eyes are half-open, but she hardly reacts. Under her mascara, I see a miniature reflection of myself in each of her pupils, a little distorted by the convex surface. My nose is much too big and my stubble looks like a smudge of dirt beneath it. Looking at myself in Clara's eyes, I don't get the feeling I normally do when I look into a mirror – that someone is looking back at me from the other side.

Max, she whispers, I'm not well.

That's obvious, I say. It's the heat.

You don't get it, she says. I feel like I'm dying.

I have to hold my good ear to her lips to make out what she's saying. Her breath smells like stale water in a vase from which old flowers have just been removed. Somehow, seeing her like this makes me feel better. I haven't felt so strong for ages.

You're overdoing the empathy a little, I say.

She doesn't get the joke, or maybe it wasn't much of one anyway. I get up to fetch my supply of coke. I take a tiny bit out with the tips of my fingers, open her mouth with my other hand,

and sprinkle it in as if I'm adding salt to some soup. She doesn't resist, but her tongue contracts and writhes like a slug poked by a matchstick. I pick up the glass nearby, dunk it in Jacques Chirac's water bowl and carefully pour some water into her mouth, closing it and tipping back her chin until I'm sure she's swallowed.

Well done, I say. Medicine.

Then I sit down cross-legged on the floor, light a cigarette and wait. Two minutes later, a smile spreads over Clara's face. After five minutes, I sling the headphones around her head and turn the music up. She smiles even more, then she sits up. I've just found out that, stripped down to underpants, it's possible to sit sideways on the moss-covered ground under the tap and let the ice-cold water flow over my stomach and my legs. It's almost comfortable. If I don't move, after four or five minutes the water might just as well be burning hot as ice-cold. The extremes of temperature can be felt, but not the relation of one to the other. I get a headache after ten minutes. And I'm dizzy when I stand up.

Twenty minutes later, we're making our way into the city. The music seems to be drawing every last spasm of movement out of Clara. It won't last.

Clara, I ask, what the hell are we doing in town again?

What we always do, she whispers. Trying to get you to talk.

The DAT-recorder bangs against my hip with every step. I'm going to get a black and blue mark there. I swing the strap over to the other side every once in a while to achieve some kind of symmetry of pain. There're hardly any cars on the street, just ambulances. The trams are overcrowded, with bodies pressed together thickly in the compartments. They're probably all dead, corpses travelling from one terminus to another. We walk on and the dog follows us, his head hanging.

Clara stops and doubles up for a moment in the shade of a hotel awning. I finger her ears playfully.

Shershah smelt nice, I say quietly, don't you think?

She doesn't reply. I think she's retching.

At the next telephone booth, I make her stop, and I call for a taxi.

There it is, I say.

Clara stumbles as she gets out. I take her arm, though the touch is intolerable. We're superheated, as if microwaves in the air are cooking us evenly from the inside.

Which building? she asks.

She's clutching her stomach with both hands; bent over so low that she has to tip her head back and turn her gaze up to see the other side of the street.

The corner building, I say. The flat was on top, on the fifth floor.

Nice area, she says through clenched teeth.

It's District Two, I say.

Then I help her to sit down on the steps of the building in front of us.

Darling, I say. You're not going to die. I'll keep talking and as long as you can still hear me, you'll know you're still alive.

Please, she whimpers. Blow the cigarette smoke in another direction.

The dog slinks as far back into the shade as possible. I sit so that my foot stops Clara from toppling over. The street is unnaturally quiet. There's a resounding click when I switch the recorder on.

I'd changed a few things in the flat and I was proud of them. I'd hammered a nail into the wall near the front door so that I could hang my coat up when I came in. There was an electric kettle in the kitchen, and two cups on top of the refrigerator. I'd bought a box of old books from a street stall at the Naschmarkt; they smelled musty, and were on completely random subjects, but that didn't matter. I'd found that reading aloud to Jessie sometimes calmed her down. It didn't matter what I read, as long as the words that came out of my mouth were exactly those on the page. She was a stickler for that, craning her neck constantly to follow the lines in the book as I read. The exact correspondence between the written and spoken word seemed to give her something to hold on to while everything else around her – myself, the ceiling, the floor, her own body, the book itself and what I said – was slipping and sliding around, changing from liquid to gas and back, leaving her tormented and alone.

I'd bought a pair of second-hand army boots for her, for the winter. She went to visit them in the hallway from time to time. There was also a roll-up camping mat from a sports shop. She'd never have let me into the flat with a proper mattress.

I found the most revolutionary of all the new things lying on the Stubenring. I heaved it onto my back and along the whole of the Praterstrasse right up to her building. I pressed the doorbell until Jessie leaned out of the window of Room One above.

Come down, I shouted. Help me carry it up.

Not on your life, she screamed. That's not coming up here.

Her voice reverberated down the lane. People stopped and craned their necks upwards like me.

Please, I called, trying to keep my voice down. I swear this is the last thing I'm bringing.

No, she screeched even louder. Take it away and don't ever come back yourself, either. I don't EVER want to see you again!

It was getting dangerous. When Jessie took against something, she could cross her arms, lift her chin, fall backwards onto the tarmac and hit her head, too stubborn to catch herself. She was still screaming. I saw her going wild with rage in the window. Above the roof, seagulls were circling in the blue sky as if the sea were nearby; they were just diving for rubbish in the street. I needed an idea, something quick, something amazing. As long as Jessie was still at the window, I had time. Then the Lord gave me inspiration.

It's old, it's dying!

I shouted so loud that she could hear me over the sound of her own screaming. She stopped for a moment.

I'll come down, she said.

The window slammed shut. The main door seemed to open the very next second. Jessie must have slid down the banister. I smiled, but she looked serious. The table was old and heavy, soaked with water, nothing more than the essence of a table: four legs and a top.

Table, this is Jessie, I said. Jessie, this is table.

Hello, she breathed.

It would have been much easier to carry it up the stairs myself. Jessie was so little, and she insisted on walking behind, so I had to bend down low and knock my shins black and blue. But she helped me enthusiastically, panting as she told me to look out at every turn, not to crash into the banister. I let her have her way. We put the table next to the window in the kitchen. Jessie stroked it.

It's beautiful, she said tenderly. Where did you find it?

In the rubbish, I said. It looked so sad.

She looked at me, downcast.

Good that it's here now, she said.

I nodded.

Look what I bought for it, I said.

A small bag dangled from my left elbow. It contained two packets of boil-in-the-bag rice. She understood immediately. The table would be happy to have a meal eaten off it. That was its job. From then on, it got easier to feed Jessie, and when we had to flee the flat a few weeks later, the table was the only thing that she said goodbye to.

She ran up to me when I came by in the evening. I brought some coffee and had a couple of sugar sachets in my pocket that I'd smuggled out of the office kitchen. I also brought rice – always rice. She was used to eating rice. It was more of a ritual to her than a matter of nutrition. We cooked it twice as long as the instructions recommended, then she cut the bag open, concentrating like a surgeon opening a stomach, and I tipped the lump out into the tin pot with a single shake. We sprinkled salt over it, and if I had a tomato with me, I'd squeeze it in my fist and dribble the juice over the rice. I was allowed to push the rest of the tomato into her mouth if I told her the story of the snake first. The snake that grew more and more colourful because of the things it ate, until it shimmered like a bird of paradise and the jungle all around it turned black and white. Then I passed her the pocket mirror I used to snort coke off, so that she could see her red cheeks. She sat down at the table, holding a spoon in each fist.

What's for dinner today? she asked.

It's not ready yet, I said. You don't need to sit down yet.

What are we having? she insisted.

Rice with Kant, I said.

Oh no, not Kant, she cried. Can't we have Nietzsche with it instead? We had Kant yesterday.

Exactly, I said. And there's still some Kant left. We have to use it up.

She groaned and let the spoons clatter onto the table as I went to fetch the book.

We ate out of the pot. I sat on the chair and Jessie stood next to me. The book lay open in front of me, and a few rice grains dropped off the fork and landed between the lines now and then.

The major works of Kant, I read, are not only some of the richest, but also the most difficult texts in world literature.

Ah, she cried. That's not real Kant, it's just Kant flavouring!

Of course, I said. You can't have real Kant with rice. It's too difficult.

Then we could have had Nietzsche as well, she said through a full mouth.

We only have Nietzsche flavouring too, I said.

I held the book up: *A Condensed History of World Philosophy*. She laughed so hard that half of what she was chewing fell out of her mouth. She laughed like this often while we ate, but what she swallowed was enough. It was her only meal of the day, but it was better than nothing. I was happy, and her colour really was starting to improve.

Clara is slumped back against the door. When it opens from the inside, she falls sideways, not managing to stretch her arms out in time to catch herself. I put the coke equipment I've just taken out back into my trouser pocket, prop her upright, then get the dog to stand up and shoo him onto the street. The woman who's trying to get past us with a pram pushes my hand away when I try to help her carry it down the steps. I realize that all we need are a couple of plastic bags, some bottles and a cap laid out for change to look like tramps. The woman marches off as quickly as she can. I make sure that Clara is in no danger of toppling over and the dog creeps back into the shade. I wait for the row of buildings in front of me to stop washing towards me like waves on a beach, then I switch the recorder on again.

23 | Goldfish

At the weekends, I'd leave the flat at the same time as I did on weekdays. I'd come back a little earlier, but never before six-thirty. I wanted to get Jessie used to a certain rhythm so I could be sure that she would get through the day without me when I was at work. I used the time to look in on my flat in Währingerstrasse, which had begun to smell musty. I got a change of clothes, picked up fresh shirts and suits from the cleaner's and went to the office for a couple of hours, to show I was willing.

But I knew that I was on the verge of cutting myself off. I'd heard rumours about a new contract, something to do with the Balkans – definitely my speciality – and Rufus had cancelled a couple of his lectures at the university to fly to Albania. He hadn't asked me if I wanted to go and I didn't even know what it was all about. When I made the mistake of thinking about what was happening to me, I started panicking. I resolved over and over again to concentrate on work, to stay late as I'd used to – until ten, or nine at least. But Jessie would pop into my mind's eye at six, sitting behind the door in the empty flat, waiting for me. Nothing could keep me at my desk after seven. I wanted to talk to Rufus about it, but it was obvious that Jessie was in hiding. As long as I didn't know what had happened to her and who was involved, no one else should know where she was. Ever since I'd heard her mention Rufus's name, I'd had the feeling, without knowing why, that I had to choose between them. For the first time ever, I found myself in a situation where it was impossible to trust Rufus.

The road smells of heated tarmac and chewed gum. I leave Clara and the dog alone for a few minutes, and buy a bottle of mineral water in the supermarket on the corner where I'd always bought rice for Jessie. I pour some water into my cupped hand and dribble it over Clara's face. The bubbles stay on her face like glass fleas for a second before they burst. I tip some water out into my hand for the dog too. Head bent, he laps it up vigorously with his large tongue. A few people walk into the buildings in front of me, disappearing into entryways that I know are tiled and cool, with junk mail lying on the floor beneath the metal mailboxes; a tricycle blocks the inner door to the courtyard. I feel quite alone.

Clara, I say. I've had this noise in my head ever since I was born. It exists purely because I'm alive. It's unbearable. Sometimes, when it's too quiet, the noise gets louder and louder and there's no escape from it.

I don't think she can hear me.

I had a maths teacher once, I say, who always wrote on the board with a pea-sized piece of chalk. I sat there hypnotized, watching the chalk between his over-long fingernails, sweeping round, left and right over the blackboard. The geometric figures he drew mirrored my consciousness. They were diagrams of tortured screams.

I want to repeat what I've just said into the recorder, but I've forgotten all but the last two words when I switch it on. They're stuck in my brain, repeating themselves meaninglessly: tortured screams, tortured screams.

Have you had something to eat? I asked.

Yes, Jessie said.

I lifted her T-shirt carefully and looked at the belly button beneath it for a few seconds, clean as the mother-of-pearl interior of a sea-snail shell. I sniffed the skin a hand's width above her trousers.

What are you doing? she asked.

But she didn't push me away.

I'm trying to find out what you've eaten, I said.

You're trying to smell it through my tummy? she asked.

Oh yes.

And I really did smell something: citrus fruit. It was lucky for me that she never managed to eat anything without dripping it onto her shirt.

Oranges, I said.

That's right! she said, delighted.

I nodded sagely, patted her T-shirt back into place and swaggered off to fetch my jacket hanging from the nail in the hall.

Rubber-nose, she said mockingly in colloquial Viennese, retard, idiot.

I metamorphosed into a pimply young dude in a leather jacket, pulled an imaginary can of beer out of the fridge, and climbed into my souped-up Escort by the door.

Bye, honey, I said.

I revved the engine and zoomed into the kitchen, where my briefcase was. There hadn't been any files in it for weeks. Today, it contained a bag of kiwi fruit. I took one out and gave it to her.

Take it, I said, and get in.

She stepped up next to me and slammed the invisible car door. We ran down the steps side by side. On the way, she bit into the kiwi fruit's hairy skin, with the fruit wholesaler's bright oval sticker still on it. She swallowed that too. Peeling the fruit was out of the question. The only reason that she ate kiwi fruit was because of their furriness, which gave her the sensation of biting into a mouse. In the same way, she only ate oranges because she'd found out that it was fun to pull off, strip by strip, the whitish fibres that were inside.

On the street, a cool wind brushed past our faces, tearing leaves off the trees. Now and then, chestnuts dropped to the ground like small spiked maces. With Jessie beside me, I convinced myself that autumn and winter had always been my favourite seasons. I imagined how we'd walk in the Prater Park, leaves crackling under our feet as the Ferris-wheel gondolas glided over the golden treetops, large and red like the tram carriages in the city. And how I'd bundle Jessie up in a thick bright fleece in December and roll her through the snow.

May I hold you? I asked.

No, she said.

OK, I said. Let's get something to eat.

At the Kebab Palace, she said.

And where's that? I asked.

Next to the Chip Temple, she said, opposite the Sausage Palace, just behind the Pizza Cathedral and the Gyros Villa.

I laughed. She didn't give a hoot where we went because she wouldn't touch a thing anyway, but I needed a decent meal at least once over the weekend.

She wanted to walk through the park first, though it didn't lead anywhere. The paths smelt of autumn, with a faint whiff of cotton candy.

Jessie turned her face to me, a trace of tears on her right cheek.

Why do you always want to touch me? she asked.

It was a difficult question, and one for which I didn't have a ready answer.

Because it's nice, I said lamely.

Maybe for you, she said. But not for me.

I'd known it deep down, but hearing it in so many words from her was a shock nevertheless. I felt terrible.

Do you *have* to touch women? she asked.

No, I replied. Not immediately.

That's good, she said. Because I just *can't* with you. You have to stay with me, though. Otherwise I'll have nobody.

Every word hurt, a series of cuts across my stomach. To try to explain anything to her now would be pointless. I cleared my throat.

And what about Ross? I asked.

Herbert and Ross will kill me if they find me, she said.

I was losing my grip on this conversation. Jessie's eyes were stretched unnaturally wide, and she was breathing too quickly. Suddenly, I couldn't get the thought of what it would be like to sleep with her out of my head. It was the first time I'd thought so baldly about it. Though she was twenty-six and no relation to me, I felt like a pervert.

Don't exaggerate, I said. That's your father and brother you're talking about.

No longer, she said. Unfortunately.

We sat down on the grass and listened to the birds, to the children shouting and dogs barking as they played on the lawn some distance away. It was a perfectly normal day.

You don't have to believe me, Jessie said at last. But they've killed Shershah. And they'll probably want you too, soon.

What have you both done? I whispered.

She didn't reply, weaving blades of grass instead.

Cooper, she said quietly. I can't cope alone.

I fell back and closed my eyes. What was really going on here was unimportant. I folded my hands together and swore to the grass, the sky and the trees that I would stay with Jessie for ever.

Stop it, Clara says. That's just so fucked-up.

I'm amazed that she's still able to take in anything, let alone speak. I'm annoyed by what she said. Her head is lolling so far back that her carotid arteries are sticking out like electric cables laid over a wall. I feel like pressing my thumbs against them and waiting to see what happens.

Did you just say, I ask, that I should stop filling your fucking tapes?

I feel sick, she whispers.

I know that, I say.

No, she says. Now I really mean it.

Darling, I say, let me finish telling my story and then—

Please, she begs, don't say anything. You're making me ill.

I'm not doing anything at all, I say.

It feels like a fade-out, she says, with your finger on the dial.

Man bears the burden of guilt, I say, and woman the pain. It's always been that way.

I'm begging you, she says. Spare me.

I turn away from her. She's gone crazy.

Do you know, Jessie said. Goldfish are so incredibly dumb.

I opened my eyes. Birds were flying high up in the sky, mingling like amoebas on a microscope slide. Jessie was sitting up, looking lively. I didn't know whether I had been asleep, dreaming even. We were still in the park anyway, and I remembered that we'd wanted to go to a restaurant. I also remembered that I'd wanted to ask her something.

Goldfish, she said, swim back and forth in an aquarium. On the way back, they've already forgotten the way there, and vice versa.

Still lying down, I pulled a folded-up piece of paper out of my bag. It was a colour copy of a newspaper page: a photo of the pop singer Ceca, who also owned a few Yugoslavian and Albanian financial institutions. She was surrounded by eight children, only one of which was her own, though I didn't know which. Her husband Arkan stood off to one side, grinning into the camera.

Jessie, I asked, have you seen this man in person before?

I watched her glance dart secretively towards the picture, eyelids lowered.

So they always think they're in a huge ocean, she said.

I folded the piece of paper up again.

Goldfish, I say, live in fresh water.

She bent over me, her hair hanging around her face.

You don't understand anything, she said huffily. Goldfish are so stupid that they don't even know the difference between salt water and fresh water.

But you do, I said.

She threw her head back and laughed, her mouth filling with the glow of evening light reflecting off the gold fillings in her teeth. The sky above her was pale and whitish. She stretched her hand out to brush a hair off my forehead, rested it on my cheek and leaned her head forward to kiss the tip of my eyebrow. But she lost her balance and her lips slipped over my temples to my ear. Keeping the rest of my body still, I crushed the paper in my hand and tossed it into the grass. To hell with it. And with the birds, the barking dogs, the children playing and the white evening sky too. To hell with Arkan and all the colour copies in the world. My mouth was grinning as if a banana had been wedged in it from left to right.

Max, Clara whispers, I can't stand it any longer. I have to go home.

I'm not done yet, I say.

I get another mini-portion of coke ready for her as I carry on speaking.

24 | Tiger (Two)

Sometimes Jessie had a way of fingering and chewing her lips, tugging her hair and pulling at the skin around her nails that I couldn't bear to watch. She searched out every little scab or bit of her body that could be picked off; she slid one fingernail after another to dig at traces of dirt, scratched off flakes of dandruff and picked her nose. She did all this with one hand while the other held a cigarette, fiddled with the candle or simply held on to the table. It unsettled me. I wished I could have tied her hands up. Every now and then I would lean across the table to pat a spot of blood off her face or her arms with a paper handkerchief.

Then they suddenly called, she said.

Who? I asked.

The grandmothers, of course, she said.

She stuck a hand into the tomato salad that she had ordered and stuffed a piece of red into her mouth. She didn't chew.

No one knows where they got my number, she said. Maybe from Herbert.

She mumbled through the slice of tomato.

Definitely, I said.

Herbert told me to go. He said they needed my help. Or perhaps it was Shershah.

Wait a minute, I said. Who called whom and said what?

The grandmothers called Shershah, she said.

Shershah or Herbert? I asked.

Yes, she said.

I pulled the tomato salad away from her. The people at the next table kept looking at us. The waiter brought some wine, and addressed Jessie with the formal 'Sie'.

Right, I said. You were told about a phone call. And that you had to go somewhere.

Yes, she said. Now listen, do you know what they wanted?

No, I said.

They had nothing, she said. No clothes, cutlery or paper. They didn't have any more blankets to keep warm with, no more forks to comb their hair, no margarine left for their skin. They couldn't bend over.

Jessie, I asked, why couldn't these women bend over?

I don't know, she said. They did everything standing up: talking, peeing, sleeping. One of them even died of shock while standing when a tiger tried to enter the room. That's what they needed me for. The grandmothers couldn't speak to anyone else but me.

I gripped the blood-flecked paper handkerchief in my pocket. It grew damp with sweat, and started to disintegrate. I pulled myself together and forced myself to fork some pasta off my plate and stuff it into my mouth. I reminded myself how to behave in a normal conversation, and propped my elbows on the table.

Was that around here somewhere? I asked.

Yes, she said. By plane first, then by jeep. A couple of tigers picked us up from the airport. Ross held on to my left arm the whole time. The first time, Herbert was there too, and he held on to my other arm. As if I couldn't walk alone. Ross's hand trembled holding my elbow and he didn't make any jokes, which meant that he was frightened. Of what, I don't know. No one said a word.

Were the tigers armed? I asked.

Of course, she said.

And what about you?

Not really, she said.

And were the tigers very young and well shaven? I asked. Did they smell strongly of aftershave?

Yes, she said delightedly. How did you know? Have you been there too?

Maybe, I said secretively.

She smiled at me and I congratulated myself silently. It was going well. I ate a bit more pasta but I could have thrown it right up again. I pretended to be busy eating, not listening.

It stank everywhere, she said. It was a lousy airport, not like the one in Bari. There were no shops and hardly any buildings. Just mud, really.

Not very nice, I said distractedly.

Yeah, she said. I just wanted to get into the car and go, but when we got in, they had put some awful music on, incredibly loud. Turbo-Folk. Do you know what that is?

Don't think so.

It's some woman screaming. And there's frantic sawing at a violin and a synthesizer.

Oh, I said.

That must have been one of Ceca's records. I knew that Arkan used his wife's music as a sign. It was all about getting as many people onto their feet as possible with very little fuss. It was done so well that people jumped up mid-meal from their dinner tables and fled into the forest through their back doors as soon as they heard the music on the street. Those who didn't run regretted it.

So I tapped the driver on the shoulder, Jessie said, and asked him if he couldn't turn the fucking noise off. He said 'Shut up.' The other person in front shouted at him and I grabbed his hair from behind and pulled hard. The jeep veered off a couple of metres to the right, towards the bushes, spraying mud, before they got it back onto the road. Ross pinched my arm, even though he'd smiled to himself. Now the music was off. Herbert sat there as if nothing had happened. He looked out at the landscape throughout the journey, and he was wearing a pale blue shirt, as if we were on holiday.

I really couldn't get any more pasta down, so I picked up a toothpick and started drilling into my teeth. The waiter came again to clear the table. I wished he would fuck off. We should have gone to a cheap restaurant with lousy service. Luckily, Jessie was in the midst of her story, so she wasn't distracted.

We drove into a city, she said, and stopped in front of a hotel.

I'd been waiting impatiently for the name of the place since she had started talking. I decided to hazard a guess.

Was that the hotel with a terrace on the pavement? I asked, chancing it.

Exactly, she cried. Do you know it?

Depends, I said. What's the city called?

Oh, it's such a long time ago, she said. I remember I had to think of Sunkist, the most orangey of oranges.

Sanski Most, I said.

That's right, she said.

Now I knew where we were, and also that we were probably talking about 1995, when an important HQ of the 'Tigers' had been in that city. Jessie had mentioned mud, so I guessed it was springtime, at least six months before the Dayton Accord was signed.

But no one was sitting at the tables on the terrace, she said, and the streets were empty too. There weren't even any cars. We sat down and a man about Herbert's age came out of the hotel a few minutes later. He was wearing a hat, and thuggish sunglasses. Raybans.

I didn't tell her that I also had a pair somewhere in a drawer. It was probably a disease that men all over the world suffered from.

The Tigers immediately jumped to their feet, Jessie said, and raised their fists to their chests. Even Herbert stood up to greet the man, though he hadn't taken off his hat and glasses, nor did he excuse himself for not doing so. He spoke German. Herbert said: Mister Simatovic, I want to assure you first of all that our being here has nothing whatsoever to do with politics. The man replied: Good, call me Franki.

I found it incredibly difficult to hide what I was feeling. There was nothing else on the table that I could fiddle with apart from the tomato salad, but Jessie needed that. She was arranging basil leaves into a wreath. I would have given anything to look into her head for a second to see how much she understood about what she was saying. Even in her isolation, she must have heard something about these events and people, at least through the radio, television or newspapers. I wanted to know whether her ability to remember and relay it all – without asking any questions about what it meant – was deliberate, or at least half-conscious. The only thing I knew for sure was that I couldn't give anything away if I wanted her to continue talking. I just had to sit there quietly. On no account was I to sweep the salad off the table and shout: Jessie, you've met Franko Simatovic! There's not one photo of the man to be had anywhere in the world. The people in The Hague would pay a fortune for a description of him.

Franki greeted Ross too, she said. Then he bent towards me, put two fingers under my chin and said: Well then, little one, how do you like it here? I shook his hand off and Ross said: Mr Franki, she's twenty-three and a half, and not slow. Franki apologized immediately and said that I would do well. Ross always took my side.

Yes, I said. I know.

Then they opened their files and unfolded maps. I knew I was free for a while. I walked down the street, followed by two Tigers. It didn't smell any better than the airport. All the windows in the houses were shattered and there was no one around. The sun came out and I wandered into an entryway because everything looked so green beyond it. The Tigers were standing to the left and the right of it, showing off their weapons. There were tall trees with light green leaves in the garden, and a swing in the shade. I wanted to sit in it, but then I noticed the big dog in it. Its body was all twisted and its tongue was hanging out of its mouth. White bone was protruding from its legs instead of paws. Butterflies of every hue clustered thickly over its body.

She started tugging at her hair again. I didn't stop her, but felt relieved that I'd trimmed her fingernails for the night before.

Do you know, she asked, what might have happened to its paws?

I scrabbled around furiously for a fairy tale or fable of some sort, any story in which a pawless dog let itself be run over because it had worn itself out running. I couldn't think of anything.

I think, I said carefully, its paws were cut off.

Yeah, Jessie said. That's what I think too. I went back to the hotel immediately. I didn't tell the others about the dog. I didn't want to unsettle them.

There was a pause. Jessie had stopped. She was twirling her hair round and round, unable to move on from the memory of the dog. I knew that she couldn't stop thinking about it. I opened the menu and started reading out the desserts.

Warm raspberries with whipped cream, I said thoughtfully. Wine jelly on a bed of fruit.

The meeting had ended anyway, Jessie said. Franki had disappeared. There was a stretch limo with blacked-out windows in front of the hotel. When I got in, I realized you couldn't see out of the windows either. I didn't want to see any more of the city anyway. Ross sat opposite me. We had a smoke and tipped our ash everywhere except into the ashtray. The ride took for ever.

Bavarian crème, I said.

When we got there, I saw that the building was really a school, she said, surrounded by men. They were wearing cowboy hats over ski masks. It looked ridiculous. Ross told me where I had to go, and pressed a huge bag of grapes into my hands. I had to go in while the others waited outside.

Chocolate-covered grapes, I said.

Each time, I always had to pass through a room in which a hundred faces looked up at me: men, women and children. Someone had thrown them down on the floor like a great big card game.

I looked up from the menu into Jessie's face. It was incredible to think that the images flickering behind her forehead were those that I had seen in the reports of human rights organizations.

Those were personal documents, weren't they? I said. Passports, ID cards, all sorts of membership cards. Like things you'd find in someone's wallet?

Once I stopped and took a better look, Jessie said. It felt strange. I took my own ID card out and tossed it down with the others, face up. Ross flipped when I didn't have it with me at the border.

I can imagine, I said.

There was other stuff lying around too, baseball bats with the word 'Cestitamo' carved into them. Do you know what that means?

Welcome, I said.

Yeah, she said. So you speak a few languages, huh?

Uh-huh, I said.

The grandmothers, she said, were crammed together in a room right at the back. Their stuff was lying on the ground. There were planks in between with long nails hanging from the ends. And beds with leather straps at the top end were standing against a wall. The grandmothers stared at me as if I was a ghost. I had to stand there eating grapes until they wanted some too and I had to talk about myself a little.

I slowly began to get it: they had used Jessie as a kind of messenger, a go-between. It was a crazy idea, but brilliant. If there was one person in the world even a victim of persecution wouldn't be afraid of, it was Jessie.

I always told them, she said, that I was the daughter of an important man. That I worked with him and that I loved someone else who I worked with too, someone very handsome. With long black hair.

By the way, I said, where was the bastard the whole time?

I clenched my fingers under the table. A slip-up. Thank God the word 'bastard' didn't seem to unsettle Jessie.

He wasn't there, she said. But the grandmothers liked hearing about him. Some of them even tried to stroke my head, as if I was ill. I slipped out from under their hands. Then I told them the good news. My father, who was very important, had made a promise. Whoever managed to swallow five grapes without chewing would be set free. That was difficult. I'd tried it myself every time I practised with them. But most of them managed it after a few attempts. They worked very hard at it. I told them that they would be taken over the border with lots of other people. They liked that. Then I helped them shave.

Why shave? I asked.

So that they could be found again. The fields and mountains were thronging with people in those areas, especially along the border. It was easy to spot a bald head amongst them from above. But I only helped to pick them up once. Ross did that with a couple of other people.

What was going on with the grapes? I asked.

Training, of course, Jessie said. So they would be able to swallow the plastic sachets after that. You know that Herbert deals drugs.

I lifted my arm and signalled to the waiter for the bill. I urgently needed time to think. It was obvious what would happen if I called Louise in The Hague and told her that I knew a girl who had not only met Franki in Sanski Most but was also an eyewitness to the Gunsfor drug operation, which had financed most of the Balkan war on the Serbian side. A neutral eyewitness, neither criminal nor victim. Someone from Western Europe. It would revolutionize the entire Tribunal. It would be a scandal, a sensation, and there would be a conflict of interests at the highest levels. It would force people to show their hands, to show how serious they were about bringing international crime before the courts. And the media would go wild. Bosnian rape victims abused as drug mules. The evacuation of refugees hand in hand with organized crime.

I thought about what Rufus had said: that the drug issue was a secondary problem and had to be kept out of the political debate; that it was difficult enough as it was to reach an international consensus on the question of the Balkans. Jessie's story would destroy all efforts in that direction with one blow. It would cast Rufus's clear segregation of the drug problem in a dubious light.

I thought I knew Rufus, at least a little, and that was important to me. He towered over national borders, over the bursting ragbag of humanity, and set up a new value system for all the pushing and clamouring within it, a religion in which 'non-intervention', 'national sovereignty' and 'human rights' were the highest commandments. But now it was getting difficult not to ask myself if Rufus had anything to do with Herbert. And if so, what?

Cooper, Jessie whined. Don't you want to know how the story ends?

I jumped, and signalled to the waiter behind Jessie's back to wait a little.

Of course, I said. I was just distracted for a moment.

A change had come over her. She had stopped sliding about on her chair, and was sitting quite still, her hands pressed between her legs. Her whole body was trembling – even the ends of her hair and her eyelashes were quivering.

It was all very quick, she said. Once, when I was telling the grandmothers about my work, one of them asked what we did. I said that we travelled by boat from Italy, for example, and she said that she'd always wanted to go to Italy. Her name was Marta and she was lovely. I promised to take her with me sometime. Then she suddenly grabbed my hands and shouted that I had to swear to it by what was most precious to me. She looked so terribly upset and serious that it shocked me and I swore on Shershah's life. Then I went out immediately and told Ross that we had to take someone with us. Ross said no way. Before I could reply, one of the men walked up to us and took off his hat and his mask. Oh – that was the ice-cream man, the one you keep asking about. He said, no problem, show me which one. We went back in together and I said, it's Marta. He grabbed her ear, pulled his knife out and cut it off. It came off easily. So then he did the other one too. Marta didn't scream once, she just tried to press her hands to her head. The ice-cream man tossed the ears at me and said that I could tell my lies to them from now on. Then he shot Marta in the face and she collapsed. One of the ears had caught against my top, and it fell into the dust when I ran off. Ross came up to me, pulled my sleeves down and knotted them together against my back. Then he carried me off to the next jeep and drove off with me. I screamed all the way, remembering that I'd sworn on Shershah's life.

It's a horror movie, I said, a fucking horror movie.

When we met up with Herbert in Vienna, I told him that I wouldn't be going on with it any longer. He said he'd sort it all out and that we would have to go on.

Fucking bastards, I said, goddamned fuckers.

I said no. Ross also said no. Then we all started screaming and I carried on after they'd both stopped. Herbert asked if I wanted to be locked away again, and Ross raised his hand as if to hit him, shouting that the whole Balkan thing had been crazy from the start. Herbert finally said fine, only boat rides for Jessie from now on.

I agreed, but only so I could leave. I didn't want to go on at all, I just wanted to get to Shershah and tell him that we had to leave. I couldn't take back my oath. I knew that Shershah was going to die, and that it was all my fault. I wanted to go to Greenland.

Jessie noticed the hate in my face when she looked up and immediately buried her face in her arms. I picked out a few strands of hair that had fallen into the tomato salad. The hate felt good; it was even better than coke. It had liberated me in one fell swoop from all thoughts of Rufus, Louise and the whole pantheon of gods and world politics. I suddenly saw everything clearly. I was filled with repulsion for the people who'd driven Jessie into this hell. I'd crossed the border with a single, measured step. I was no longer looking at everything from above. I was outside of that. And all it had taken was one small, painless jolt to turn me into a person again.

Can we go and do something nice? Jessie asked, her face still nestled in her arms.

And Shershah, I asked. Did he want to go to Greenland?

No no no no.

She raised her voice until everyone in the restaurant turned to look at us.

Psssst, I whispered. Jessie, did he want to go with you?

When she raised her head, I wished that she had continued lying on the table. The lines on her forehead ran as deep as trenches in the candlelight, her mouth hung slack in the middle of her drawn face and her eyes were blank. I was looking into a mask, a parody of Jessie's face, staring at me with a half-open mouth.

I wanted to go to Greenland, she said. Shershah wanted to go with me. He said we needed more money before we set off. At least as much as we'd always had in the boat.

She tried to smile.

And why didn't you make it to Greenland?

No no no no no no, she started again.

Looking over my shoulder, I saw a man walking over to our table; the owner perhaps, or the head chef or maitre d' for all I knew. I waggled my fingers in the air to show that we were going. He stopped and waited.

OK, Jessie, it's OK, I said. Let's go somewhere else.

She still had that pained half-smile on her face. It was so unbearable that I decided not to probe any further. It wasn't important anyway. Jessie needed rest, that was all, rest, and someone to look after her. I put a thousand-schilling note on the table, took her by the arm and propelled her out in front of me. She spat the slice of tomato out on the street. I'd forgotten all about it: it had gone pale from being in her mouth. She stood slumped and twisted, as if she'd been buttoned up all wrong. I felt incredibly sorry for her.

He didn't come because he's dead, she said. Because they killed him.

I said nothing, though I didn't believe it was true. Maybe Shershah really was dead by now, but I couldn't imagine him ever seriously considering emigrating with Jessie. Much more likely that he'd seen an opportunity to get out himself, sufficiently padded with cash, of course. Maybe he'd been afraid that Jessie would lose it completely and that he'd lose his job as her well-paid companion, without any compensation for it. Or perhaps he too had wanted to get out for a long time but just hadn't known what to do otherwise. Or maybe the Balkan thing was too much for him also. Everything had probably come together all at once. In any case, he'd left Jessie with the conviction that she was responsible for his death.

OK, Jessie, it's OK, I said. Stop now. Let's do something else.

She slipped out of my grip. She had slung one leg over the other, and swayed on them as though on a stem.

Maybe they already have a model of him in the gallery, she said.

I didn't know what she was talking about. I didn't know what to ask next.

The artist in the courtyard, she said. He does things like that.

Hic gaudet mors succurrere vitae, Clara says.

She must be delirious, or maybe there was something wrong with the coke, though I feel amazing myself, considering. Clara is still sitting slumped against the wall, speaking with her eyes closed, like a transcendental medium.

People know their Latin in the circles you move in, don't they? she says.

Here death serves the course of life, I say automatically.

That's what the statue's called, Clara says, the one they made out of Shershah. I already know that you didn't find it in the gallery.

Go and have a look, Jessie said. If you find it, you'll know.

Stop it, I said.

She lifted an index finger and tunnelled into her right nostril with it. Before I could yank her finger out, blood was flowing over her upper lip and down the side of her mouth, its course split by the dimple in her chin. There was a scab in her nose that she only needed to scratch with a fingernail to draw blood. It had been there for weeks, and she knew how to use it.

Go on, she said.

Now? I asked.

She didn't reply.

Do you mean the gallery on Opernring?

That was the gallery outside of which, twelve years ago, Shershah and I had waited for her while she spoke to the owner inside. She'd showed me her favourite paintings in the display window not long ago, loudly colourful portraits of women, exaggeratedly tall and slim, their heads dipped with modest charm and their faces horribly similar to ants. They were titled 'Uncommon Grounds', 'Fu loves Fula' and 'Kings and Planets'. I meant to buy her one when her birthday came up.

That's not very far way, I said. You can wait here.

I'm coming too, she said.

Put both feet on the ground, I said, and wipe your face.

She stuck her finger in her nose once more.

OK, OK, I said. Listen.

I propelled her into an unlit underpass, found an unused paper handkerchief, twisted a corner and pushed it into her nostril. Her right eye was brimming with tears.

You can't come, I said. You say yourself that they're looking for you. Do you know what you're going to do?

She shook her head.

You're going to jump on the spot, I said, so that the world can rotate beneath you. It will go some distance while I'm away, and you'll be nearly home when I come to get you. Understand?

She nodded. The handkerchief hanging out of her nose looked like the torn-off wing of a white dove. She looked as if she was waving it at me when she nodded.

OK, start, I said.

She started jumping up and down on both feet, her body visibly relaxing. The handkerchief flapped up and down against her cheek. She'd have been locked up if anyone had found her that way. For ever. But I ran off.

And? Clara asks.

They were just closing, I say. The owner was the same man I'd seen through the window twelve years ago. Of course he didn't recognize me. And there was nothing there that reminded me in the least of Shershah.

I know, Clara says. The owner told me that they'd only managed to get him in at the beginning of ninety-eight.

You've been there, then, I say.

Of course, she says, and you have too. I saw Shershah, completely see-through. He really was incredibly good-looking.

How did you know to go there? I ask.

Oh come on, she says. The gallery was on the Bari tape.

And where else have you been? I ask.

Ask instead where else I'd go if I had the energy, she says.

Where? I ask.

To see the artist who made the statue, for example, she says.

That night, Jessie had one of the worst attacks I'd experienced.

Do you hear that? she said.

She sat on the kitchen chair and looked over my shoulder into the hall, where her boots stood like feet cut off a child, slanted slightly towards each other.

I hear them coming, she said.

You hear nothing, I said.

I have the ears of an eagle, she said.

Eagles, I said, don't have ears.

Then she started wailing. Every breath she took made a sound, quiet to begin with, but insistent. There seemed to be in her chest an instrument that her breath set into action. I ran off to get a book and started reading to her, but her wails got longer and longer. They didn't seem to depend on her breath; they didn't seem to need air at all. I dropped the book, gripped her shoulders and shook her until the sound stopped. Mouth open, she gasped for breath as if she'd just been dragged onto land.

When I was little, she gabbled, Ross used to show me a tennis ball with a slit in it. It opened its mouth when you pressed it. Ross made it speak that way. It looked like Pac-Man and it said, Jessie, you talk too much. You're disturbing people. You should be quiet. Or something bad will happen. And then it said, look what's happened to me, and its mouth opened wide. The two halves of its face yawned apart. One day, it said, your mouth will reach right across your head if you carry on talking so much, and your head will fall apart. And I promised to be quiet. I wanted to be a fish. I promised over and over again, but I never made it.

Jessie, I said, you don't talk too much. I love hearing you speak.

She wasn't listening to me any longer.

Now I'll be punished, she said, punished terribly. I hear them coming.

I shook her and she started wailing again. I screamed into her ears, but she didn't react. Her body grew limp and I had to stop her from falling off the chair. I rushed off to get a blanket and bundled her up to her ears. You're a fish, I told her. Fish sleep, when they're covered up.

I was fighting against whatever it was in her head that I didn't really understand, and all I could think about was that I had to stay alert and well. I had to get through the night with her to first light, and not lose hope. The coke that I took from the fridge, over and over again, helped me. The coke and the hatred.

That Jessie of yours . . .

Clara's voice falters. I think it's the first time she's said 'Jessie' and not 'silly cow' or something like that.

You have to speak up, I say, I can't hear very well.

It's obvious that she can't speak any louder. I just want to make life difficult for her.

That Jessie of yours, she says, wasn't so crazy after all, maybe.

So you think it's normal to shoot yourself in the ear? I ask.

In some situations, yeah, Clara says.

She suddenly opens her eyes and struggles to stand up, swaying like a camel that's been kneeling for too long. There's a series of cracks from her joints, some louder than others, all in different tones. She looks really pale now, her tan like a layer of dirt on her skin. Her breathing is laboured and the sweat on her face looks as if it could be acidic. It's leaving red patches on her forehead, her cheeks and her upper lip. I get up too. My bones ache from sitting too long on the stone floor. The street is completely empty and the heat is drawing out smells from everywhere. The air smells of excrement, petrol and overheated garbage bins. I watch a marten dart under a car, and disappear beneath the next one.

Max!

She grabs my arm. When her knees buckle, I hold on to her by the hair at the nape of her neck. She gurgles in a way that reminds me of the water-cooler in the office, with its big transparent blue tank and stack of paper cups. When you fill a cup with water, a bubble wobbles upwards in the tank like a transparent jellyfish. Clara opens her mouth and retches; a little liquid comes out, clear like water.

Max, help me, she says, help me.

I take hold of her hand and look at the watch on her wrist.

It'll be dark in two or three hours, I say.

Yes, please, she says. Turn the light off.

We'll stay here till then, I say.

I lay her down on the ground again, deeper into the entryway. Bubbles of spit dribble out of the right corner of her mouth.

I should probably wash my hands every time after I touch her.

25 | Eagles and Angels

You were screaming, Clara says.

The hammock is swinging wildly – I must have been tossing and turning, or maybe I still am. Perhaps I'm still screaming.

Stay there, Clara says.

She puts both arms around me to stop the hammock swinging. I press my forehead against her breastbone, bone against bone; together, we're more like a bundle of brushwood than flesh and blood. Her chin is resting on my head.

Stop nodding. You're crushing my skull, I say.

Calm down, she says. I haven't been nodding. What's wrong?

I was dreaming, I say.

Or I still am. I fall back into a half-sleep, anyway. I hear a whimper and wonder what's up with Clara. Then I realize that it's me who's whimpering, and I stop by holding my breath. Clara is kneeling in front of the hammock.

What were you dreaming about? she asks.

Sounds, I say, pictures. I thought it was eternity. A nightmare.

I can't speak properly. It's dark and the half-moon fits exactly into one of the window panes. I wonder why I'm sleeping at night in the first place. It's my own fault if I'm dreaming then. My hand slips under Clara's T-shirt. Her stomach is hard; there's not a single fold in it, nothing I can hold on to. I don't want to touch her breasts. The thought of how they point outwards tickles and repels me at the same time. I give up. She's getting up, anyway.

I can smell it when you get an erection, she says. The foreskin retracts, and then it stinks. I can smell it from here.

I'm impotent, I say.

You wish, Clara says. Go back to sleep.

Strangely, I really do feel tired, in a good way, the way people normally feel when they're looking forward to a good night's sleep. Maybe I forgot to coke up in the evening, or maybe I'm able to sleep longer because I've been getting practice, stretching each session out longer and longer until I'll only be awake for five minutes a day, and finally not at all. That will be death.

I put one leg down on the floor and rock myself gently. Clara hasn't gone to sleep. Through the window, I see her standing under the chestnut tree like a ghost. I don't know what she's doing there and I'm sure she doesn't either. The tree leaves rustle. Or maybe a fat hedgehog is making its way through the bushes, plucking slugs off the stone well.

Huge dogs are hurling themselves against the wire netting from the other side. They're barking so hard that it would be impossible to hear ourselves talk even if we tried. They're barking at Jacques Chirac, who doesn't even glance at them. He's as proud as a baron. Or maybe he's playing dead. But Clara is fiercely determined to keep going; she leads and I follow, resigned. Before we left, she'd asked me for some coke to draw out her last dregs of energy, not knowing what on earth for, of course. I don't care. I feel unusually well, so I can walk anywhere. She looks really good from behind, her hair in a long braid over her back, great big baggy trousers hanging low on her hips with the stripy band of a pair of my boxer shorts peeping over the top. With fresh powder in her veins, she's moving fluidly, like a school of fish. As long as she doesn't turn around, she could be one of the female fighters in some screwed-up city; they're always attractive like she is. But her face destroys the illusion; it's not smooth and innocent, but is haggard and oddly distorted.

We press ourselves against the cool stone of a high garden wall at the corner, and wait for the barking to die down.

Have you been here before? she asks.

This place doesn't even have a postcode, I say. Are you sure we're not already in Slovakia?

Who cares? she says. He must be somewhere up here.

Sweat collects on my skin underneath the recorder strap. I really don't know why I'm the one who's always carrying the thing around, as if I have a kidney disease and it's my dialysis machine. Jacques Chirac presses his nose against my side. I know what he's trying to say: let's forget about all this and go home.

Whatever, I say. Where to now?

Straight ahead, she says, to the end of the development.

What development? I growl.

She sets off again. I can barely keep up. Maybe I should tell her that I don't have enough coke with me to pep her up for the way back. She seems to have forgotten that she was all but ready for the morgue yesterday. Besides, I don't know why she's walking barefoot.

Why aren't you wearing any shoes? I shout.

Didn't you know, she shouts back, that you can research someone's inner life by taking on their outward appearance?

She waits for me to catch up.

Is that one of Schnitzler's methods? I ask.

One that's been further developed by me, she says. Try to imitate the expression on someone else's face, as precisely as possible, and you'll soon know what he's thinking. And the clothes too. It's not difficult.

Strange theory, I say.

It's not a theory, she says. It's been proven.

I'd better not ask whose inner life you're trying to research today, I say, or we'll never get anywhere.

Yes, she says. Don't ask.

There haven't been any buildings in sight for a while now. I've given up anyway. There's something meditative about the motion of my arms and legs. *I've been through the desert on a horse with no name*: the sentence spools through my head again and again to the rhythm of my feet. I can't do anything about it. The sun's been directly overhead for ages. Maybe the Earth's stopped turning, and we've been racing towards a fixed star ever since lunchtime. That would explain why it's so unbelievably hot.

There, Clara says suddenly.

I see an old van in front of us, half-buried in the trenchlike hollow next to the path we're on. It's painted matt black and is so badly dented that it looks like it's melting. A path has been trampled from it into a meadow, which looks like wild bulls could be wandering loose in it. There's a very basic building at the end of the path, just a shelter really, like a magnified house of cards. The shingled surfaces lean steeply over two storeys to meet in a gable. I can't see a window. It must be pitch dark inside.

And you think someone lives here? I say.

Do you think cars grow in open fields? Of course he lives here. It's just a bit makeshift.

Whoever *he* is, I say, he needs an airlift to get his shopping done.

The dump we're living in isn't much better, she says.

We have access to the canal, I say, and the whole thing's still in the middle of the city.

Nevertheless, she says, we have something in common with him.

Great, I say.

We're all in hiding, she says.

*

240

We bang against the door for a while and then there he is, framed by the huge pointed roof of his house.

I know him, he says, pointing at me.

Shit, I say.

Clara's eyebrows shoot up.

You can't possibly, she says. My assistant's never been to Vienna before.

Come off it, girl, he slurs. I know the man.

He's right. I even remember his name: Erwin. I met him when Jessie showed me the courtyard one day, telling me that she and Shershah had lived there. She showed me the stove in which the key to the shed was hidden. They carried the oven indoors in the winter and stuffed it with woodchips from the sawmill until it was glowing hot. I asked why she and Shershah hadn't had a proper flat instead, and she said that they'd been comfortable here. Then I bumped head-on into someone standing in the door frame, swaying slightly. He was tall, dark and leathery-faced, and reeked of schnapps. Jessie said 'Hello, Artist' to him. He said, 'Where's the Adonis?' and she said she didn't know, then he slurred, 'Good, I'm goin' home ter wash m'self'. I recognize him. He looks as clapped-out as he did two years ago.

The sun may have set in there . . .

He slaps a hand against his head.

But I've always had an eye for faces. He's one of the fellas from the operation, he says.

We'll be gone in a minute, anyway, Clara says. It won't take long.

She marches past him into the house in her bare feet as if she's wearing heavy army boots.

Come back, girl! he screams.

And runs after her. I go in too. It's no cooler inside and there's a stifling stench of burning plastic. The dog decides to wait outside, collapsing into the narrow strip of shade right next to the wall. There's a door ajar at the end of the hall, through which bright electric light is streaming. I see Clara's shadow in it. The stench gets unbearable when I walk through, and I see immediately why the artist doesn't think his brain is up to much.

He gropes about in a drawer and tosses us two ridiculously flimsy smog masks; nothing more than a gauze bandage with two rubber bands to pull over the ears. Eagles don't have ears, I think. Erwin puts on a mask too, one with a yellowish stain in the middle, which looks like he's smoked countless cigarettes through it.

The room is smaller than I expected; the walls are vertical, despite the slanted roof sloping down to the ground. There are four metal constructions leaning against the wall next to the door, modern versions of the iron maiden. Another one is spread open in the middle of the room.

Don't be afraid, he slurs, I was just cleaning up.

What exactly should we be afraid of? Clara asks.

Why have you come? the artist asks.

I'm working on a report for the arts programme on Radio Central Germany, Clara says glibly.

Yeah, right, Erwin slurs. And the brother there is just here for the beach.

He's pointing at me.

Sorry? Clara says.

The small-time crook, I say, is here for fun.

She shrugs.

In any case, we'd like to know how you work, Clara says.

The artist lifts a knee so he can slap his thigh as he laughs.

Ah, he says. But you're fine apart from that.

Listen, I say impatiently, the girl is crazy about your crap and Herbert says it's OK.

He stares at me with his watery bovine eyes for a while. His brain is probably churning like a coffee grinder. Behind his back, Clara smiles at me and gives me the thumbs-up.

All right, he says. Ten minutes and you're gone.

Nobody could hold out in here for longer anyway. We squat down next to the open halves of the iron maiden.

This is a casting mould, he says. It'll do for a hundred and seventy-two to a hundred and eighty.

I run my fingers over the smooth surface. Inside, it's so shiny that the metal almost feels soft. I just manage to yank my arm back when the cover thunders down with a crash that echoes off the walls. The artist grins at me. He's completely mad.

The moulds themselves are works of art, he says. They'll be worth a fortune once I'm pushing up the daisies. A mate of mine makes them. He's a goldsmith.

What happens then? Clara asks.

You put the model in here, he says. The filler pipes are over here and there. And that's it. I mix up the plastic myself.

You pour hot liquid plastic over human bodies? Clara asks.

Well, it's more plexi-stuff really, he says. And that's just for the second casting mould.

He leads us to the back wall, where an assortment of what looks like dental instruments is strewn across a work bench. Next to it is a pile of translucent plastic bodies, cut lengthways. They are clumsy human figures with thick external seams.

The real figure is cast in these, the artist says. Once again in a special material, clear as gin.

He pulls one of the plastic half-bodies out of the pile; it's in the form of a woman's back. Holding my face a few centimetres away from the surface, I see the imprint of the woman's pores and a few blonde hairs melted into the plastic.

Yeah, the artist says. The moulds often have hairs in them. I have to pick them out with tweezers. The head and pubic areas are the worst.

We're especially interested in the actual models for these . . . experiments, Clara says.

These aren't experiments, he says. This works. It's an exact science.

So who are the models? Clara asks.

Look, darling, he says, have you seen the Bond film *Goldfinger*?

Maybe, she says. Why?

Then you know that no one can survive for more than a few minutes once their skin is completely sealed over, he says. Even a nose as big as a trunk doesn't help. They just suffocate. Get it?

No, Clara says.

It takes a good couple of hours for my plexiglas to harden, the artist says. No one can breathe through that.

I just don't believe it, Clara says.

No, I say, he means something else.

You there, he says, you weren't born yesterday. You have a nose for it.

'Nose' reminds me that it's high time for a line. I feel a little oppressed.

He uses corpses, I say.

I watch Clara's eyes narrow and blink above her face mask. I think she's laughing. We stand around the plexiglas sarcophagus silently for a while, like a team of defeated surgeons around a patient who's just died. The imprint of the woman's bum is as big as a salad bowl. She's probably been eaten up by the worms long ago.

God knows who she was, the artist says.

As if anyone had bothered to ask.

Do you mind if I have a line? I ask.

Go ahead, he says. D'you need a mirror?

I've got my set-up with me. Clara's eyes are closed. She doesn't look as if she hears what we're saying. I just manage to catch her.

It's the fumes, the artist said. They told me at the hospital that the stuff was highly toxic.

Nah, I say, she wasn't feeling too good before either. This happened yesterday too.

Maybe she's having her period, he says.

D'you want some? I ask.

No, thanks, he says. I make my own stuff.

He's propped open a narrow opening high up in the roof with

244

a pole, so that a square of light falls on us through the vapours, making us look as if we're in a Rubens painting. I sit down on a box. Behind us, the room stretches out across the full length of the house, narrowing to a point. Standing up straight is only possible inside the apex of the triangle that the room forms. There's a large freezer cabinet in the furthest corner.

You're probably not going to tell us where you get all those bodies, I say.

There really aren't so many of them, he says. I can't do more than four a year at most. Cleaning them up makes your sperm curdle.

And no one ever comes looking for them? I ask.

Well, he says. They're special cases. Anyway, it's not like I do anything to them. Apart from shaving them a little.

What happens if someone walks into the gallery and recognizes his brother on the pedestal? I ask.

That would be fucking awful, he says. That would be the end of all talk of my hyper-realism.

Clara is breathing very slowly and evenly, like a hibernating hedgehog. Maybe she's meditating.

No sign of life from the girl, he says. She needs some fresh air.

You've got to be joking, I say. It's sweltering outside. That's not fresh air.

Clara raises a hand, eyes still closed.

I'm fine, she whispers. Go on.

I pinch some coke off and walk over to her with the spoon.

No, she says. I don't want to.

Be quiet, I say, and swallow.

I trap her hands between my knees, force her mouth open and drop the powder in. Then I hold her tight until she swallows.

Wow, the artist says. You've got her under control.

I sit back down again.

Now let's forget about the body-snatching, he says. So you knew our mate here then?

Shershah? I ask.

I called him Adonis, he says. He was amazing. I couldn't wait to get my hands on him. He's my masterpiece.

I know, I say.

And his girl, he says. You know her too?

Who? I ask.

Now, what was her name? he says. Herbert's daughter.

Jessie, I say.

He lifts his leg again and slaps his thigh. His hand sounds like a whip against his jeans.

What's happened to her? he asks. I haven't seen her for ages.

She's dead, I say.

Holy shit! he shouts. Her too!

He looks genuinely shocked. Clara opens her eyes a crack and squints at us.

But Herbert wouldn't have done it just because of that one time, he said. His own daughter?

She shot herself, I say.

He clutches his forehead.

That makes sense, he says. She was a strange one. Stubborn.

I suck air through my teeth so that the coke tastes stronger. I have a slight headache, very pleasant.

What one time? I ask.

Come now, he says. You know better than I do!

I wait and watch Clara's eyelids move up a little more. The whites beneath are pinkish. The blood vessels in her eyes must have burst when she collapsed.

I heard something about it, he says. Adonis and the girl did something, and then the computer system crashed. The gallery owner was left with nothing and I didn't get any more cash. The operation seized up for a couple of months.

When was that? I ask.

He stops to think.

Ninety-seven, he says. Just before I got Adonis.

From whom? I ask.

From Herbert, as usual, he says. The ones from the hospital were like patched parachutes after the autopsy. Unusable.

And what do you do for Herbert? I ask.

He laughs.

I'm not going to tell you that, am I? he says. You might be undercover!

It's not hard for me to imagine. I look at the freezer cabinet again. He probably only needs it a few days a year for his corpses. The rest of the time, a few hundred kilos of stuff would fit in easily. An ideal transit point.

And you? he asks. What do you do for Herbert?

Oh, I say vaguely. I went down to Bari once. Apart from that, I'm not so sure myself who I'm working for any more.

I know the feeling, he says.

We fall silent, tired of conversation. He seems to have forgotten about throwing us out. I cast around for a reason to ask my last question, but can't think of one.

Just between the two of us, I say. Have you ever heard about links with the former Yugoslavia?

What? he asks. I don't understand.

About people getting involved in the business during the Balkan war, I say.

Are you paranoid or what? he asks. Herbert's operation is a family business. The stuff is sold on the street in Vienna.

I'll be honest, I say. Jessie was a good friend of mine, and she hinted at things being on a much larger scale. Dirty stuff. Very dirty.

You mean Jessie was caught up in things she couldn't handle? he says.

I don't reply. It's a sharp question. He's obviously smarter than he lets on. He waits for a bit, then shakes his big head and shrugs, looking like an unwieldy sack of potatoes.

I don't know, he says. I've known them for years and it's always been pretty harmless. Jessie talked too much.

No, she didn't, I say fiercely.

Come on, he said. With a hole in the head like that. You could hear grass growing in it.

Max, Clara says urgently. I can't hold out any longer. Let's go.

Wait, I say. Do you still have the mould from Shershah?

Of course, he says. I only destroy them once I've found a buyer for the figure. He's going to bring in a pretty penny, I tell you.

I come out to find Clara standing outside, holding on to the roof with one hand. Bet I'll be seeing one of you again soon, the artist had said. And Clara really does look as if I could leave her here already. She raises her eyelids slowly, her eyeballs rolling upwards. The blue of her eyes looks exactly like the cloudless dome arching over us. Eagles and angels, I think – it sounds better in English. She finally rolls her eyes back and looks at me.

He's in the gallery, anyway, she says. If you miss him, why don't you go and look at him there?

I prefer him as a hollow mould, I say. Will you make it back?

She looks over the fields in which the blackened heads of sunflowers are drooping like old people bending over the earth that they'll soon be buried under. They're all turned towards us; maybe they're nodding farewell or maybe they think we're alive.

I walk up to the edge of the field and lift one of the large sunflowers. Its black face is distorted by countless nodules, tightly packed seeds dragging the stem downwards. When I let go, it droops automatically.

I hear Clara's voice behind me. Max, I want a small house somewhere in the forest with a weeping willow rustling in front of it. That's all I want from life. Nothing else.

I think about plucking a few flowers and bringing them to her. Then I realize it'd probably take me half an hour of twisting the stems around and around to break off every last fibre. And I'd probably cut myself doing it, too.

My sweet, I say, that sounds wonderful, but it's precisely the simple things in life that we never get.

26 | Tough

Ever since I started giving Clara the stuff too, my supply has run down quickly. I came here with about a hundred grams, so unless Clara or the dog has been secretly lacing the coffee with it, at least three weeks must have passed. Three weeks in this shit-hole and at best all I remember of it is three or four nights, two colours in the sky, one meal, and a single, endless afternoon. The temperature doesn't seem to have changed in that time at all. All I remember of it now seems to fit into three full days at most. Yet I feel at the same time as if I've never lived anywhere else, as if everything else, my entire past, is something I've been dreaming during the countless hours of stillness in the hammock all those hot afternoons. Like dreams, memories have to be kept in a logical manner if they are to be retained; they need a beginning and an end, and events have to follow each other in a tidy chain of cause and effect. Anything that doesn't fit in will be forgotten. And, in the end, almost everything will be forgotten, I think.

Three weeks ago, I'd expected this time to age me by thirty years. I expected it to hunch my back, make the flesh fall away from my bones and suck every last bit of strength out of me. Thirty years in three weeks; that's barely a year and a half per day. That shouldn't have been too difficult. Instead, I'm sleeping better by the day, standing upright and, to be honest, feeling healthier than I have in a long time. Except for the pain in my nose that won't go away. It's telling me that a great big hole is going to open up in my nasal membranes soon. It's going to bleed, but I won't die from it. Right now, I don't feel as if I'm ever going to die of anything at all. I just hope that this is my final surge of strength, the last peak before the eventual downfall.

Instead, it's Clara who looks as if she's not got long for this world. Maybe she'll tell me how she does it before she goes. I turn her around and her shirt rides up. Her ribs form a staircase which I climb up, step by step, with my middle and index fingers.

Max, she says quietly, I feel sick. Have you got a cigarette?

I don't have any, so I have to go to the shop. When I get to the gate, the dog gets up from a corner. I'd almost forgotten about him. He totters towards me, stepping in one of his own turds on the way. The narrow strip of grass is covered with them. He follows me, leaving brown smears that grow fainter and fainter over the next ten metres. There's a pharmacy next to the supermarket. I think about getting something for Clara, but don't know what.

I come back with a bottle of Coke and a sack of dog food, which I empty out in a corner of the courtyard. Then I see him after I pass the Opel Ascona, and I drop the Coke in shock. The bottle will explode if anyone tries to open it later.

I've come to pick up my car, he says.

He's leaning against it, holding a roll-up in his fingers, thin as a toothpick. As I look at his profile, the sun glinting on his nose stud dazzles me, and then I recognize him. It's Tom. Jacques Chirac wags his tail at him tiredly before turning to his food.

I've thought of Tom often – because of the car, of course. I've bruised my shin against it every day and Clara has been crouching behind it to pee into the drainage hole in the middle of the courtyard. Apart from the nose stud, nothing else about him looks like Tom. He doesn't have a baseball cap with him and the bird's-nest hair is gone; his head is shaved bare.

It's right below you, I say. Have a good trip.

Lovely. Would he be so kind as to give me the key?

This reminds me that I hate the way he speaks, almost always in the third person.

I don't have it, I say. It's with the girl.

Clara.

He spits the name out as if he were talking about a deadly mushroom. I try to make out the expression on his face, but the sun is shining in my eyes and his head is moving back and forth, shaking invisible strands of hair away from his face.

Where is she, then? he asks. I'll take her with me.

Dunno, I say. She hasn't moved for days. She must be lying around here somewhere.

Look, he says. It took me ages to find you. Maybe I wasn't quite with it to begin with, but this shit has got to end now.

It takes a great effort not to jump into the shed with one leap. Clara must be in there – where else could she be? She can't make it into town alone any longer. If she really is gone, though, I've got a problem on my hands. I can't check while Tom's here. If I found her, and he tried to take her with him, we'd have to fight over her like two vultures over a carcass.

I take a step sideways out of the sun, and lift my hand to shade my eyes. His fist grazes off my hand. He stumbles forward with the momentum of the punch, almost crashing into the shed. I hadn't noticed that he'd wanted to hit me. The sun's at my back now. He's panting as if he's run a marathon.

Well done, he says. So he looks like Iggy Pop, but he's still got his reflexes.

Iggy Pop certainly still has all his reflexes too, I say.

I don't know what else to say. He walks over to the shed entrance, pokes his head in, sniffs the air and pulls his head out again, repulsed. He leans against the door frame.

The way you're going about it, I say, you can't have been sent to eliminate me by the HQ of some secret power.

He snorts derisively. I begin to find the silence embarrassing after a while, as if he's a pretty girl with whom I'm trying to strike up a conversation. I notice that the goatee has gone too. Suddenly I'm not so sure he's really Tom the technician after all. Maybe he's someone else altogether, and just has the same nose stud. Like Tom, the waistband of his jeans hangs down to his knees, but that doesn't have to mean anything. It doesn't really matter who he is anyway, as long as he doesn't cause any trouble and disappears before Clara appears from wherever she is. I point at the packet of tobacco he's holding, and he tosses it over to me. It's Van Nelle Red, the same brand Shershah and I always used, but the health warning is in Polish: *palenie tytoniu powoduje choroby serca*. I have to take out a plastic sachet of small shiny pills before I get to the paper and the tobacco.

Put that back in, he says.

How's Ross? I ask.

Fine, he says quickly.

Until my cigarette's lighted, we don't say anything more.

Listen, I say. Have you really come all the way here from Leipzig just to have a cigarette with me?

You don't seem to get it, do you? he says, furious. That it's my car you took off with in the middle of the night.

He's so worked up that he's forgotten to address me in the third person. I'm touched, almost. He must be at least ten years younger than me.

Look, I say in a friendly voice, that had nothing to do with me. You probably know more about Clara's plans than I do. I'm just a piece of shit without a will of my own. I just get shovelled into this or that corner.

You're right about the shit, he says, but . . .

He obviously wants to add something, but doesn't know how to start. He jerks his head back and forth like a madman, eyes darting wildly. Now I know why the golden rule has always been: take everything and lots of it too, but only within the range of what Mother Nature has to offer. No synthetic drugs. The good thing is, Tom's going to leave soon. In this state, he won't be able to stand being in one place for longer than a quarter of an hour.

You can wait for her here, I say helpfully. She'll definitely give you the key when she comes, and you'll have your car back.

He turns towards the shed and bangs his fist against the wall.

Fuck the car! he shouts.

Ah, I say. I see.

He comes a couple of steps closer and I try to prepare myself in case he tries to hit me again. But he reaches for his tobacco instead.

You've gone too far, he says. I had no idea that she wanted to drive to Vienna. He's fucking her head up with his damn psychodrama.

Who? I ask.

He points at me.

Him, he says.

I see, I say again.

He's fucking us all up big-time, he says. Both of you might as well be playing cricket here with plutonium rods. Does he get it?

I'm doing absolutely nothing, I say. But that's not a bad idea, about the plutonium rods.

He rubs both hands over his face. The roll-up he's just made nearly comes undone against his cheeks. His little finger hooks against the nose stud, bending his nose sideways.

Nobody believes he wants to die, apart from Clara, he says between his hands. But what does he need the girl for?

That's not an unimportant question, I say. But what's it got to do with you?

Clara is a friend, he says. I was stupid enough to tell her about you. She can be so bloody stubborn.

He's right there.

If only I'd kept my trap shut, he says.

I scratch my deaf ear to gain time. I trace my thoughts back a long way to try to find a connection. The image that comes to mind completely throws me. I see Tom sitting in the radio station, listening to my first call, saying to Clara afterwards 'I know who that was' or 'I know that guy.' Or perhaps he grew pale with shock first and said, 'Shit, Herbert's daughter is dead.'

Who are you really? I ask.

He looks at me doubtfully, as if he's wondering if I mean it.

I do the Polish stretch, he says. Doesn't he know that the south is long past?

Bardzo dobrze, I say. The past is my favourite time.

While he's fumbling to light his cigarette, I try to concentrate and remember the new, simplified trade and border treaties with the eastern states which I once pored over in the Leipzig office of Rufus's firm. Treaties that, in effect, extended the EU border outwards by five to seven hundred kilometres. A dim understanding of who I could have been working for, and to what end, begins to dawn on me, but I strangle the thought before it can fully take shape. I prefer to think about how funny it is to constantly be meeting people who know much more about me than I do myself.

When our gazes meet again, his face has changed. He looks calmer, even though he's still breathing too quickly. He's changed tactics. Maybe he's not even on anything, just incredibly jumpy. Maybe he's frightened of something.

He should look out, he says. After all, he's a cool customer. I know he's got it in him to fuck with everyone.

Or maybe the last jolts across his synapses have already rocked through him.

What's going on now? I ask.

Well ... he says, look ... He doesn't need to tell them that I helped her. A clever girl like her could have done it alone. Does he understand?

No, I say. Haven't a clue what you're going on about.

The cigarette has gone out. His cheeks hollow as he sucks on it in vain. I take a lighter out of my trouser pocket and toss it over to him.

That's it, man, he says enthusiastically. Always play dumb. Stay that way. He can tell them whatever he wants, but he'll leave me out of the picture. And not a word to Clara either, OK?

I clear my throat. He takes that as assent and gets all eager. He's standing so close to the shed's outer wall that I'm afraid he'll bash his skull in with one of his head jerks.

There's still some money left, you know, he says. I mean, if he needs money. Or anything else.

I don't need anything apart from Clara, I say. I'm here to end it, after all.

Great, man, he says. The earlier, the better. He can hang on to Clara. He's got us all under control anyway. And he'll simply keep mum as far as I'm concerned. I know he's a tough one.

He starts digging around in his trouser pockets, deep as potato sacks, and finally comes up with pen and paper. He lifts one knee to write on it.

If there's a problem, he says, it would be good if he could call me.

He passes me the piece of paper with the telephone number on it and the pen too. I'm thrilled to have one of these 'I love Vienna' pens again. He turns to go.

What about the car? I call after him.

He's already out of the courtyard.

I find Clara lying on the floor under the sleeping bag, which she's pulled out of the hammock to cover herself. It's difficult to see her; you have to know she's there to make her out at all. I push a lit cigarette between her fingers and she thanks me. I watch as the column of ash grows and finally breaks off. When the filter starts smoking, I take the cigarette off her again. She hasn't taken a single drag on it.

Max, she says quietly. I'm bored.

It won't be long, I say. Every dickhead knows we're here now. They'll come to get us.

What are you talking about? she whispers. Who are 'they'?

The people who are looking for us, I say. Ross and the others.

Nobody's looking for us, she says. We're about as interesting as a pile of old newspapers.

Even those need to be taken care of at some point, I say.

This place is nowhere, she says, godforsaken, it's the end of the world. All the sailors have looked for it in vain and we've found it, in the centre of a city, where no one would have suspected it to be.

The way she's lying there, slightly twisted and speaking so lyrically, I find her beautiful as never before. Her shirt is covered in patches of dust from the floorboards and there's dirt on her skin too, especially in the hollows of her knees and the crooks of her arms where sweat gathers. Her face alone is white and clean. I wipe it regularly. The skin is smooth and seems very thin, as if reddish hairline cracks could appear in it if she stretched her face too expressively. But it's been a long time since I last noticed any kind of expression on her face.

I'm going to tell you the rest of the story, I whisper, because you're so beautiful and so defenceless. And I'll always tell the truth.

Maybe I should have left, she says, when I still could.

Do you want to go? I ask.

I don't even have the strength to make it to the station.

Good to know, I say.

I haven't heard her speaking at length for some time. She too seems to be feeling better. I light another cigarette and push it between her fingers, pressing them together to keep the cigarette from dropping.

Max, she says. I know it's absurd, but I'm afraid.

She turns her eyes towards me and, with some difficulty, manages to focus on me. We look at each other.

I'm afraid, she says quietly.

Lovely, I say. You're becoming normal at last.

She nods, so slowly that it's barely discernible with the naked eye.

The shed door sounds like a forest full of birds in spring. No one's touched it for three weeks; now I'm swinging it back and forth for fun, listening to it creak and twitter. I see a vision of green grass and water gently lapping in the sunlight, glinting like a thousand silver pieces. I close the door and lock it from outside, closing the shutters and laying the bolt across them just to be on the safe side.

I open the car door and dig into the box of money. God, how long has it been since I last thought of my old flat. I pick out the dollar bills – they take up the least space – and stuff as many of them into my pockets as I possibly can without making myself look entirely misshapen.

27 | Justifiable Defence

I have to wait for Jacques Chirac at every corner, so it's twelve-thirty by the time I get to Renner-Ring. The square in front of the parliament is covered with grubby flyers; it looks like a funfair's just packed up and left. Jörg Haider's Hitler-moustachioed face is staring at me in different colours from all directions: from the ground, the flower borders, the car windscreens. I think about throwing my identity card face up on the ground for a moment, but decide I don't need to.

There are police, far too many of them. I take a detour through the Volksgarten, walk around the Justizpalast and approach Schmerlingplatz from the other side. Rufus once said that Austrian politics was of no more significance than a couple of children throwing sand into each others' eyes. I understand what he means now more than I ever did then. Even if Haider himself were actually part of the government, his antics would still be like a mothers' union benefit compared to the stuff going on behind the scenes on Rufus's Mount Olympus.

I position myself behind the Justizpalast just so that I can look sideways across into Bartensteingasse and keep an eye on the entry to the office. The junior lawyers leave the building between twelve and one every day, one by one or in groups. The men loosen their ties and the women throw on light jackets, lifting their long blonde hair over the collars. Cigarettes are offered around. Nothing will have changed. Anyone who can't spare an hour and a half for lunch isn't a lawyer any longer, but a slave. Law isn't just a profession – it's a lifestyle.

It's fifteen minutes walk from the Volksgarten to Singerstrasse. We normally walked in groups of six or seven, our shirt collars open and our ties tossed over the right shoulder. We crammed into Van Veinsten on the Franziskanerplatz, the most exclusive snack bar in the world. One or two people always managed to get a seat on the red leatherette bench, and could order carpaccio or at least a caprese. I hardly ever got the chance. The rest stood around letting their Tramezzinis get knocked out of their hands as everyone gesticulated and smoked more than they ate. When we wanted a bit of peace and quiet, and a proper meal, we went off in the other direction, to Skala in Neubaugasse. We threw ourselves into the René Herbst chairs and relished not being in Van Veinsten, not having to see any more ad executives or other idiots. The owner of Skala knew us all by our first names and he cooked us prawns or schnitzel – whatever we felt like.

I check my reflection in a car window while I wait. I had smoothed my hair back this morning, and shaken out my trousers. My T-shirt is black, and reasonably clean. My face is expressionless. The only splash of colour comes from a packet of Marlboros sticking out of my trouser pocket. It looks as if my heart's in there. Shades are definitely needed here but I didn't have time to buy a pair on the Hernalser Hauptstrasse. It's all Jacques Chirac's fault.

I see Kai first. He's alone, and I recognize him instantly. The car whose window I've been using as a mirror is a black BMW. I sit on the bonnet before calling out his name. Swinging his briefcase in a wide arc, he looks around questioningly, then begins to look annoyed. I call out again. He sees me and recognizes me after a double take. I don't move an inch. I let him cross the street and come over to me. I stuff my hands into my pockets and close them around the thick bundles of cash.

Maaaax!

He says my name the way Rufus always used to. Standing across from him, I see the entire street reflected in his sunglasses: a coach travelling into his head, shrinking and disappearing, someone walking past behind us, a wide-angle convex view of roof ridges against blue sky, and then myself in the foreground, stretched across the curved surface, nose too large.

Kai lifts his right arm and I meet his hand with a high five; we snap our fingers in exact time. He laughs; his teeth are as good as they used to be.

What are you doing here? he asks.

Bad question. I don't have an answer ready.

Just passing by, I say.

I heard you'd baled out, Kai says. Man, that's what we should all do, while there's still time, eh?

I shrug.

Man, he says, we all think about it. The old guys are still going strong, especially the chief. He'll outlive us all. One out of forty-five here has a chance of being made partner in the next fifteen years.

I'm relieved. He's talking such crap that I know he must be completely coked up.

Hey, I say, let's pop into Skala.

Naah, he drawls. Not today.

What, I say, no time for lunch?

I've caught him out. He shoves his hands into his pockets and I take mine out.

The beard looks good on you, he says, like the Gauloise ad: Liberté Toujours.

He laughs.

260

What are you doing these days? he asks.

Nothing, I say.

He laughs even more loudly, getting on my nerves. I want to get my order over and done with.

Nothing! he shouts. That's great. I guess that means you've joined the stock exchange. It's a good place for guys like us, it's in our blood. So where are you: Frankfurt, Paris or London?

I'm in Vienna at the moment, I reply, quite correctly.

Ah, he says. Specializing in Eastern Europe. I knew it the moment you let yourself be transferred to Leipzig. It's a dump, but we know which way the wind's blowing nowadays: Vienna, Leipzig and then Warsaw. You're not so dumb, Max, but then you were already dealing with Eastern Europe up there.

He gestures towards the top storey of the office building.

The time here must come in useful on the floor, eh? You just have to know where the next crash is going to be. That's all it's about, isn't it?

He's still laughing. It's amazing how he manages to talk at the same time. I can't seem to find the right moment to break in.

I knew you were in the city, he says. Rufus has been cursing like a whore around the office. He's furious that you're raking it in somewhere else. You're right, man.

He nods enthusiastically and looks at his watch.

Great to see you, he says.

No chance to ask him about his dealer. He waves as he folds himself into his Alfa Spider. He's always had a thing about Italian sports cars.

The next few people are clients; then I see a group of young lawyers but only a couple of faces I know from sight. I can't remember their names. Then I see Steve. I lean back on the black BMW again before I call his name. He sees me immediately but doesn't start to cross the street, so I have to grab the dog by his collar and walk over to him.

Hi, Steve, I say.

Hi, Max, he says.

He's actually called Stephan, but I address him the way Rufus always did. We shake hands.

I heard you'd left, he says. I barely recognized you.

He smiles, and I shove my hands back into my pockets.

That's right, I say.

Become an artist, eh? he says.

You could say that, I say. Now that the stock exchange has finally been set up in Warsaw, there are one or two things to do here.

Nice dog, he says.

Thanks, I say. It's my girlfriend's.

The girl who was here not long ago? he asks.

I clear my throat.

Could be, I say.

I didn't catch everything, he says. But I think Rufus was really worked up about something.

Listen, I say. I don't have much time. I need a contact. It would help me a lot.

What, he asks, a client?

Of course not, I say. I have to get some charlie quickly before I catch my flight.

I see, he says. Why didn't you say so right from the start?

Relief washes over me. I take my hands out of my pockets, stuffing the notes that I've accidentally pulled out back in. I watch him staring at my trousers.

It'll have be paid for by credit card, he says. It's the usual way, really.

I ignore him.

Could you ring? I say. I don't have my phone with me.

He looks really suspicious now. He hesitates, then pulls his mobile out of his jacket and flicks it open, his gaze fixed on me. Then he collects himself and presses a button. I hear an automated reply. Steve is silent for a while.

Two o'clock this afternoon, he says. Friend of mine. Black T-shirt, big dog.

He covers the phone with his hand.

Medium, L or XL, he asks.

Make it XL, I say.

XL, he says into the phone.

Then he hangs up and stretches his hand out to me.

Great to see you, Max, he says.

Where? I ask.

Schottentor, he says. Someone will come to you.

The dog can go in the back seat, the young guy says. Hey, did you hear me?

Shut up, I say. Stay cool.

Then I help Jacques Chirac into the Jag. The guy drives competently, even though he doesn't look old enough to have a licence. In a black Boss suit, he looks like a precocious boy dressed up for confirmation.

That's my supermarket we're approaching. But it only clicks when we pull up in front of the metal doors – to the courtyard.

You'll have to excuse us, he says, but you want an XL portion, and we're in the middle of restructuring. So you're getting some of the old stock. Do you want to wait in the car?

I get out, and Jacques Chirac positions himself in front of the metal doors, tail wagging.

Clever dog, the boy says.

I hold on to the dog firmly so he doesn't charge straight to the shed and start scratching at the door. The boy's got a key but the door swings open just as he's about to put it in the lock.

Uh-oh, he says. There's been a break-in. They really ought to get things under control around here.

I have to stop myself from laughing out loud. I hope whoever's going to get things under control is armed with a howitzer at least.

We pass through the outer building. The courtyard door is open. The bright green of the Opel Ascona hits us like a blast of peppermint.

Look, he says, and laughs. The fiery-green drug shuttle. I thought he was in Görlitz.

I wipe my palms on my T-shirt.

The new Poland–Leipzig route? I ask.

He flushes. He knows he's let his tongue run away with itself.

What do you mean? he asks sharply.

Easy, I say. I sometimes have business to do in Leipzig.

I don't do any buying, he says. If you need contacts in Eastern Europe, get in touch with HQ.

I nod. He crosses the courtyard in a few strides and starts to open the studio door.

God, it stinks, he says. And it must be at least five times hotter in here than it is on the street.

What's inside? I ask.

I'm pointing at the shed. With the shutters barred, it looks as if it's been abandoned for years. A sudden conviction that Clara isn't lying in there any longer comes over me. I'd always suspected that reality consisted of different layers that I slipped between from time to time and that those were the moments in which I just didn't understand anything at all.

No idea, he says. This was here before my time.

Looking through the window into the studio, I watch him pull away a large sheet, uncovering a perfectly modern refrigerator.

And how are Herbert and Ross? I ask, once we're back on the street.

Something relaxes in his face.

The operation doesn't go through southern Italy any longer, does it? I ask.

It still has over the last six months, he says, but that's finally coming to an end.

I swing the plastic bag I'm holding. It contains twenty decagrams of charlie. That was all that was left. It's enough to kill a dinosaur. As I sit down in the car to pay the guy, an image of the gigantic beasts snorting through an enormous bendy straw comes to mind. I can't help myself – I start laughing. The boy looks disgusted as I count out hundred-dollar notes. I tip him one and he doesn't refuse. He buttons his jacket up and gets into the Jag.

Where should I drop you off? he asks.

The farce is completely unnecessary, but I let him drive me to Hadikgasse and walk back immediately.

I half-expect not to find Clara when I open the shed door, but she is there. The air in the shed is stale. I fetch some water for her. I take the cold, crumpled cigarette filter out of her hand and help her drink. When I hold a pinprick of coke out to her, she opens her mouth so I can drop it in. Then I turn her. Lying on the same side all the time isn't good for the skin.

Max, she whispers. What time is it?

It's a strange question, but hearing her speak at all fills me with a childlike happiness. Moved, I watch over her for a while and consider carrying her into the car and driving off somewhere, anywhere as long as it's away from here – maybe even back to Leipzig because there's nothing she can do about it anyway. We've obviously been wired together since we arrived in Vienna. She's been my personal battery of sorts; the stronger I feel, the weaker she gets. The way it's looking now, I'll have used her all up in a couple of hours.

Darling, I say, just a couple of hours more. They're coming at last.

The dog trots up to us and drinks the rest of the water out of the pail. He looks livelier too, though emaciated. He settles down next to Clara and I lie down next to her too. Now we're all together like a small family. This city of stone is our fireplace and the hot summer air like the flames within. I'm going to continue my story.

I can't find the old tapes when I look for the DAT-recorder. I toss our clothes from one end of the room to the other and a lump of mouse excrement falls out from a pair of boxers. The dust I've whirled up into the air hangs there, glittering. It covers my lungs, making them feel like sandpaper. The smell of mice settles on my tongue.

Remember, I say quietly, how happy you were to find out that Shershah was dead. You wanted to know how it happened.

A little dampness is seeping out from under her closed lids. She might be crying. I wonder how her dehydrated body manages to gather enough liquid for even a trace of a tear. I open her mouth carefully and pour the rest of the water in to see if more tears will follow.

I went to Rufus immediately, I say. I didn't want to wait until he sent someone for me.

She turns her head to one side and tries to cover herself with the sleeping bag. I pull it off her. It's too hot for it.

Rufus wasn't in the office – he was in UN City. I took the U-Bahn to the twenty-second district and ran around through the thickly carpeted corridors of Block B for half an hour, getting a painful electric shock off every door handle. I hoped it would have a calming effect on my nerves. I finally bumped into Sachiko, her flat moon-face floating above a Chanel suit, looking as if she knew everything already. She propelled herself forward with tiny steps and led me to some conference room. Rufus came out, shook my right hand as usual, then held on tightly and laid an arm across my shoulder, hugging me briefly.

Maaax, he said, you haven't been granting us much of your time recently. Your sanity is at stake. And your job. And your life.

He slapped my back heartily, as if I'd just provided an opening for a great joke.

Come with me, he said. This way.

I thought we were heading for the cafeteria, but he led me out of the building instead. I looked out over the Donau as we crossed the parking lot. An unbroken stream of falling leaves floated past us. I wondered if someone was standing upriver pouring them in. We entered the next building, a curved multi-storey affair, and took the lift down to the basement, to the tiny room at the end of the hall between the telephone cubicle and an emergency exit with escape routes marked on it. This was the soundproof room. Suddenly, there we were, facing each other across a plastic table. I felt like I was in the visiting room of a prison. All that was needed to complete the picture was a layer of bulletproof glass between us, with tiny holes for us to speak through. Rufus went straight to the point.

We both know, he said, that incidents like this are commonly known as accidents.

It wasn't an accident, I said quickly.

Maaax, he said. You've studied all the different areas of law long enough to know how to classify the facts. It's a long time since I did all that. Isn't this sort of thing known in criminal law as putative justifiable defence? Or an excess of justifiable defence?

Putative justifiable defence, I said tiredly, is when you act in the mistaken belief that an attack is taking place. An excess of justifiable defence is when you go too far in acting on that mistaken belief.

28 | Shershah Is Dead

I had indeed wanted to turn over the legal ins and outs of the case, preferably right then and there in Jessie's flat in Praterstrasse, but we had to leave, and pronto.

Jessie was kneeling on the kitchen floor, clinging to one of the table legs and saying 'Bye, bye' to it, over and over again. I bundled her into a blanket, like a survivor of some accident at sea, and carried her down the four flights of stairs, running.

At the bottom of the stairs, I hadn't the faintest idea where to run next. I stood panting in the hallway of 61 Praterstrasse, thinking entirely pointless thoughts: how lucky it was that Jessie didn't weight more than forty kilos, that nobody had actually ever seen me with her, that I probably really loved her, that I was a loser, though I couldn't say why.

Standing behind the bright art deco window in the front door, I heard a siren: an ambulance, or maybe the police. They weren't normally so quick. With Jessie still in my arms, I charged out of the back door across Afrikanergasse into the courtyard of the building across the street. I nearly slipped on the flyers lying all over the ground, and I stumbled over a child's bicycle. I'd never taken any interest in the courtyards around here before. Chancing it, I heaved Jessie over my shoulder and climbed up onto the bins and then onto the wall, jumped into the next yard and climbed over more bins and another wall. I couldn't go any further – I'd reached the end of this row of buildings – so I ran out of the yard into Weintraubengasse leading down to the city centre. I stopped by the Donau canal and put Jessie down on the lawn. She sat there numbly, her eyes stretched wide open. A finger of the Wien flowed underground next to us. Trying to find our way through the system of underground canals occurred to me, but I abandoned the thought again immediately. I had a cigarette instead, tidied my hair and Jessie's too, and carried her back up to the street. We took a taxi to my flat in Währingerstrasse.

While Jessie lay in the tub humming hysterically and building castles of foam, I ran around the flat looking out of every window, expecting them to turn up at any moment: my pursuers, the police or even Shershah come back from the dead. I finally sat down at the kitchen table with my file of notes on criminal law and a stack of snow-white pieces of paper that I'd taken out of the printer. Occupying myself with the workings of the law always had a calming effect on me. Everything had its place in law.

In my best handwriting, I set down the first word, the first sentence, in a perfectly straight line. I laid out the bare facts. M, the respectable lawyer; J, his girlfriend; O, the victim and X, the man behind the scenes.

J seeks M out one day to ask for help. She thinks X is following her. X wants to revenge himself on her as a result of an underworld quarrel, and she knows that X will be sending one of his men to 'take care of her'. M doesn't know what to make of this story. He offers to spend some time in J's flat. J accepts gratefully.

M cooks for her, but she doesn't eat. She is even more restless than usual. She is constantly standing in Room One, pointing down at the street. Do you see that car right at the end of the other side of Praterstern, between the trees?

There are lots of cars there, M says.

Yes, J says.

I remembered then how Jessie's phone rang and she ran into Room Five. It was the first time someone had called since I'd been with her. She pressed the receiver to her ear, listening. Before I could pull it away from her she had hung up and fallen to the floor, stiff as a Parkinson's patient in the final stages. I dragged her back to the window. All was still in the street, perfectly normal, just as it always was, deathly quiet. It was late. I propped her up so that she could look out.

Look, I said. Everything's all right.

Just then, someone got out of one of the cars behind Praterstern.

No, no, no, no, Jessie screamed.

I let her go, needing both hands to open my briefcase. Jessie dropped back onto the floor and started whimpering rhythmically. It sounded even more synthetic than usual, and loud. I couldn't do anything about it. I took my binoculars out of the case – it was hard to make anything out with the naked eye. As I adjusted the view and focus, I thought about the last time I'd used these binoculars. That had been ages ago, at a time of my life that was more similar to the present than anything in between, because of the lead players in it and the atmosphere of confusion.

The man standing next to the car was stretching his back languidly. He was slim, with long wavy black hair. Then he stood with his shoulders slightly hunched and his head bent forward, as if he was listening for something. I watched him twisting his hair up into a braid that immediately sprung loose when he let go of it.

But it was dark, and I was watching him through binoculars, not some night-sight gadget. Then the figure took a few steps off to one side and disappeared behind a row of buildings.

270

No, no, no, no, Jessie screamed.

She flung herself from side to side on the floor, her eyes opened wide. I had to come away from the window to shake her until she stopped screaming. Then she suddenly grew completely still, sat up, pushed my hands away and looked me in the face.

Max, she said. In the night stand, in Room Four.

As I got up, I looked out of the window and saw the man again. He was crossing Helenengasse, walking towards the roundabout. I ran into Room Four and found the parts of a G4 rifle in the night stand, clean and neatly laid out. The telescopic sight was wrapped in a soft cloth. I wedged it under my arm along with the hand guard, the casing and the plastic shoulder rest, lifted the hem of my T-shirt and tossed the smaller pieces into the cotton fold. Then I ran back to the other room and sat down next to Jessie on the floor, my fingers flying to assemble the rifle the way I'd done in shooting practice during national service. Jessie watched me, whimpering softly.

Calm down, calm down, I said. We're going to solve this problem now, once and for all.

In the army, I had had eighty seconds to take the rifle apart and put it together again. But that had been ten years ago. Weighing up a nut and a screw in my hands for a moment before I attached them to the firing pin, my gaze met Jessie's. I wasn't a hundred per cent sure. Everything's fucked if the bits jam.

When I jumped up again, I saw the man by the red traffic light in front of the Tegetthoff monument. I heard the low rumble of a truck passing in the distance. The man looked down the street, and, it seemed to me, looked up to the top floor of 61 Praterstrasse. There were about two hundred and fifty metres between us. He started walking again. This was it. I cocked the rifle, and with no time to engage the muzzle-flash suppressor, took aim. I inhaled deeply, and felt my whole body relaxing. I felt happy, as if it were all a matter of breathing technique. I'd always done best at shooting in the army. I'd even outscored the instructors, which I'd been both glad and embarrassed about.

I had him perfectly in my sight in two seconds. Then the light suddenly came on overhead. I turned to look for Jessie. She was standing by the door, one hand on the light switch, looking at me like a dog watching its bowl being filled, drool running down her chin. I whipped my head back towards the street. The man had stopped where he was and was looking up at me, up to the only lit window in the whole building. Although I knew that my silhouette was all he could see, I felt our gazes meeting. I knew it was Shershah and I had the uncanny feeling that he knew it was me.

Then he jumped. He moved towards me, in the only direction that promised any cover. He landed in the middle of the street, hands held up as if to protect his head. I pressed the trigger as he was about to get up to run to the corner of the building. But nothing happened – just a clicking in the rifle's magazine, the firing pin shooting into nothingness. I only noticed the truck at the very last minute, its horn blaring like a fog alarm. Shershah was hurled to one side, and I whipped the rifle upwards in shock, as if imitating a recoil.

Bang, Jessie said happily. Got it.

The truck's brakes screeched. Jessie came up to stand beside me at the window and we stared down at the dark heap below, which the truck driver was running towards.

Is he dead? I asked.

Of course he's dead, Jessie said.

Arms resting against the windowsill, she was gripping the outside edge tightly, looking down. When I came back with a blanket, she was already in the kitchen, hugging the table.

Determine M and J's guilt.

I'd prepared for cases like this while studying for my finals. It was a problem of cause and effect. Despite the intent to kill and though, objectively, the situation hadn't been one in which M and

J had been under attack, M's mistake had in the end freed him from the burden of guilt.

I filled five pieces of paper and declared M not guilty.

Negligence, probably, I said to Rufus. If not, then putative defence of a third person. Saving the life of a third person. Jessie's life.

It won't come to that, anyway, Rufus said. It's almost certain that it was a normal road accident. And the rifle belonged to Jessie in any case, didn't it?

He repeated his question before I had a chance to reply, holding my gaze.

It *was* Jessie's rifle, wasn't it?

My head dipped slowly, imperceptibly. It could have been a nod, or something else entirely.

They were quick, by God. Under 'Miscellaneous News', I read in the morning paper about an unidentified man being run over on Praterstern; the circumstances of the accident were still unclear, but alcohol wasn't involved. There was a blurred photo, but it didn't show the dead man's face. I woke Jessie, who was by this time slumbering peacefully in my bed.

He really is dead, I said.

Of course, she mumbled. You shot him, after all.

I didn't shoot him, I said.

Maybe you didn't notice, she said. You were too wound up.

I didn't have the flash suppressor on, I said. There'd have been a yard-long flame if I'd shot. Unmissable.

Who on Earth would shoot without the suppressor? she said indignantly. You really are an idiot.

She dropped off again almost immediately, sleeping like the dead. When I couldn't bear being in the flat any longer, I called the office and found out that Rufus was in UN City. That was when I set off to talk to him before he sent someone to get me.

*

Rufus, unlike me, had sources other than the newspaper.

The man who was killed was a drug courier, he said. Someone who'd been making his money in crime for over ten years.

Rufus, I said, I know Herbert, and I'm quite sure you do too. The dead guy is one of his men. Herbert's going to be involved and the police are going to be involved. I've come to hand in my notice.

Now then, Rufus said.

But I'm a lawyer, I said. There's a man dead here!

Calm down, Rufus said icily.

I'd never raised my voice in Rufus's presence before. I'd always been smiling, friendly, in control, expressing admiration and gratitude. Even now, I didn't want to contradict him, but I had to say something, to shout at least once. Someone had to hear it. My head would have burst otherwise.

Shershah is dead! I shouted.

Then I sank my head down onto my arms against the small plastic table, waiting for a truck to run me over. None came.

OK, that's enough, Rufus said. Get a grip on yourself.

I thought about throwing all I knew about the business in the Balkans in his face, telling him all I'd heard from Jessie, and waiting to see how he would react. But I knew what he would say. He would shake his head in silent amazement and say, but Maaax, you work on that area. You're the last person who can claim not to know what's going on down there. That's what we're fighting, after all, together.

Pointless, absolutely pointless. When I sat up again, I had composed myself.

Good, Rufus said. Now let me explain something to you.

He pulled two Havana cigars out of his jacket. You weren't supposed to smoke in the soundproof cubicle. There was too little air in it. I took the first drag, inhaled and leaned back, clenching the cigar with my fist.

We work on international law here, Rufus said. And you, Maax, are a part of things. You know who got you this job. You should be grateful to him.

He paused and blew smoke rings over the table. I didn't realize that someone had got me this job. It slowly began to dawn on me, but I didn't want to know any more.

You don't like it, Rufus said. You've got yourself into something you don't understand. Herbert and I have been friends for twenty years. His trade isn't the point. Herbert knows a couple of people, and he knows how to handle them.

He caught the ash breaking off his cigar and tipped it onto the floor.

Let me say something about Herbert in my mother tongue.

He leaned forward and stared me in the face.

He did mankind a few favours, he said, which mankind never thanked him for.

He brought his hand down hard on the table.

Maaax, he said. You've got to understand me. We're keeping World War Three at bay here. Surely you don't think that mankind could have survived the last fifty years without international law, without the United Nations, without disarmament treaties and nuclear agreements, do you? These achievements allow us a certain moral emancipation. As long as someone contributes every year, every month, every day, towards keeping us from the worst, you don't look too closely. Herbert is a morally self-sufficient man. He could use his position against people, but he uses it for peace instead.

The air in the room was growing thin. I felt slightly dizzy. I stopped inhaling the cigar smoke.

Are you trying to say, I asked, that Herbert therefore has nothing to fear from the law?

Oh, no! Rufus cried. He's not untouchable. Let's say a young ambitious public prosecutor gets wind of Herbert's activities. He'd be rubbing his hands in glee. Up here, we could then turn this screw or that a millimetre or so . . .

He motioned in the air as if turning a radiator knob oh-so-carefully.

. . . And wait to see if the young guy gets pulled back in line by his boss. If the hotshot digs his heels in and squeals, the whole thing will quickly get political and we'll withdraw.

He drew both hands back quickly, as if he'd burnt himself on the imaginary radiator.

But Herbert is much safer, said Rufus, than, say, Al Capone was. And so this unfortunate accident will just blow over quickly.

I nodded and went to get up. I felt sick — I'd just killed my oldest friend and I hadn't slept at all last night. I had to do some thinking.

Patience. Wait a minute, Rufus said. I have a message from Herbert for you.

I sat down again. It was incredible how everything seemed to have been brought under control.

You're going to apply for a transfer to another office, Rufus said. You're going to leave Vienna. Don't think this is easy for me — I just couldn't refuse him. You'll understand that. And you really will be needed in Leipzig.

He didn't seem to expect an answer, so I didn't say anything. I wanted to get out.

Oh yes, Rufus said. And before you leave, you're going to drop Jessie off at the Baumgartner hospital. They know what to do there. If you're honest with yourself, you'll see how necessary this is. The girl is ill. Anyway, in your situation you'd best do what I've suggested. And none of these people . . .

My mouth seemed to have dropped open. He raised a hand to keep me from butting in.

. . . Shall be mentioned in this building again after today.

He stood up and smiled at me.

Maaax, he said. You know how sorry I am. It's like I'm losing a son. But the way you've been behaving over the last weeks makes me think that you want things this way too. I respect that wish. And now . . .

He stubbed his cigar out on the plastic table, took mine off me, put it out and laid it next to his.

. . . Let's get out of here before we suffocate.

He opened the door and I drank in the fresh air like water after a desert crossing. It really did taste like water.

I stayed in the basement of UN City for a while, on a chair in front of the computer terminals. I sat there simply breathing, hoping never to form another coherent thought again in my life.

29 | Earthworm

Clara hasn't been listening. All this time, she's not been there at all. I might as well have been telling all this to the dog, to a car, to a fucking wall. She isn't typing up transcripts of my tapes any longer and she simply isn't paying attention. I could kill her for that. And she'd deserve it, too.

I'm bored. I look up into the dark sky. I feel wide awake. It's hot, barely any cooler than it was in the daytime. It's a night for sitting in a shady beer garden with a group of friends, drinking Sturm. Only I don't have any friends, and have never been able to stand Sturm. The sulphurous smell of rotten eggs that fills the pubs when they open the bottles makes me sick.

Clara doesn't react to being kicked or hit and I don't want to hurt her. Maybe she's ill – maybe she has AIDS. It would be a good chance to infect myself, only I have no idea how I would manage it.

I've been wondering what she would look like with short hair, so I rustle around amongst the papers on the desk, looking for a pair of scissors. I find the 'I love Vienna' pen instead, and give up. I fetch a bucket of water from the tap, drink some, and pour a little over her, a very little, carefully. I don't want to startle her. I really do just want to help. I make sure that some of it trickles into her mouth and that she swallows.

Listen, I say right into her ear. I'll tell you everything. Right up to the end. But I've got to know that you're listening to me. Listening.

Her wet mouth opens and her tongue comes unstuck from her palate.

I'm listening to you, she says.

I can't concentrate. I'm half-listening for sounds from the street all the time. I don't understand why no one's turned up yet. I don't understand why they're leaving us in peace. It doesn't make sense and it makes me jittery. I need to do something.

Getting into the outer building is easy. The rotten wooden door frame doesn't even splinter, it just gives way. The room behind it is cloudy with spiders' webs, half-filled with old cans of paint, stacks of them; maybe someone wanted to repaint the place at some point. I find a few tools behind the door, including a rake, a pick, a broom and a sledgehammer. Their metal parts are so rusted over that, in the dark, they almost look the colour of their wooden handles. I pick out the most stable-looking of them, which is a spade.

Not a single slug is sticking to the well. It's either too dry or the angels have run out of tongues. I find it more difficult to lift the lid now than I did the first time, but I manage to lever it to one side with the spade. The rest is a matter of gravity; I pull my foot away just in time. The bushes have left red scratches all over my arms and upper body and they start itching immediately. A draught of cold mouldy air rises from the well. The shaft is uniformly black. I flick my lighter but the flame barely scratches the depths, and it dazzles me so that I can't make anything out at all after a couple of seconds. I have to wait for my pupils to recover, so I go off to coke up in the meantime. Whatever's lying down there won't be going anywhere any time soon.

The moon has crept up higher in the sky. I sit down on the edge of the well and break off a few branches so that the moonlight reaches the well. Shards of glass glitter all over the bushes, a copy of the stars above. I look down again. Now I can make out a couple of different shades of black within the complex weave of darkness below. That's all.

I tear some pages out of Clara's file at random, and turn them into thick twists of paper. I lay them on the edge of the well, where they glow whitely, as though they're giving off light even before they're lit. I light the first twist from below and wait until the flame has almost reached my hand before I let the makeshift torch fall into the well.

One thing's for certain: there's a blue rubbish sack down there, filled with something. With garden refuse, maybe. The courtyard is part garden after all, or at least it could have been once. Maybe someone once mowed grass here: weeded, lopped off a few branches and stuffed it all into a rubbish sack. The sack seems to be partly covered with mud, as if a few spadefuls of earth were tossed down after it, then got washed away over time by rainwater, making the sack visible again.

I drop eight flaming torches. As the last one reaches the bottom still burning, I see the ashes of the other seven. I see more than that. The rubbish sack is bulging, and something pale presses at it from the inside. The plastic of the sack is almost ready to burst. It's as if something has been vacuum-packed in it and has expanded over time, swollen. And that something really looks like a human face; or like a large, shaved head. I smell plastic melting. What I think is lying down there was certainly always slim enough to feel his own ribs when he crossed his arms. Now I'm the thin one and the thing down there is a fat white whale. Even if, in the end, it's an optical illusion or just garden refuse after all. A whale, and it serves him right. The flame goes out and the shaft of the well is black again, so black that the thought of lighting it up with anything at all seems quite impossible. Instead of lighting the last twist of paper, I toss it, white and untouched, into the darkness of the well. I think I see it down there, a patch of paleness, very faint. Almost indiscernible.

I stumble over the spade as I get up, and lift it on reflex. Holding the spade, it seems only natural to stick it into the earth. The ground is too hard and dry, but the earth must be a bit softer in the bushes by the well. After a few attempts, I fetch the pick from the outer building and set to work on about two square metres of ground. Swinging the heavy pick through the air feels good. The sharp sound of it hitting the ground echoes back from the walls with an infinitesimal delay. When I've done enough, I put a foot against the spade and shove it into the broken-up earth. Jessie would have wanted this. We're going to have three children, she said. If one drops into the well, there'll still be two left.

The earth gets softer about forty centimetres down. A pinkish piece of earthworm curls on the next spadeful, twisting around itself, looking for its other half. When I was little, my mother and I would go outside and pretend to do some gardening on the weekends, both for the sake of the neighbours and so that we would feel as if we had some kind of family life. That was when I learned that earthworms live on, even after being cut in half. I always wanted to know how many earthworms you could get out of just one, but I wasn't one of those children who tore the wings off flies or blew frogs up with a straw until they burst, so I never tried to find out. I was sure that I could do the same; that I could split up into a few Maxes and live on, probably more happily than before, no longer so alone.

I toss the spadeful of earth down the well. I find the second half of the earthworm in the ground and throw it down after the first. So they can live on happily. Not so alone.

My body is a bundle of aches and pains, like different notes combining to form a chord. My brain is slapping from ear to ear like water in coconut. The hole is big enough to bury a person in, but the well is far from full. I take a break and go to see if Clara is still there.

I sit next to her for while, perfectly still, cigarette hanging from the inflamed corner of my mouth. Clara is so beautiful that I could look at her for ever. I'm going to practise opening my left and right eyes alternately so that I don't miss anything of her. I push away the dog, who's been watching over her, and lie down next to her, fitting our bodies together like parts of a folding bicycle. I relax and enjoy the calming effect of her odourless skin.

Then I carry on digging. I don't see why I shouldn't work through the night. Jessie would have been happy. She would have jumped up and down and shown me how to enjoy life, the simple things in it: the night, the air, the earth, the earthworm. What more could a person need? It's easier to go on digging than to stop. Jacques Chirac wanders out of the shed to look at me. I'm finding my rhythm. The hiss of the spade slicing into the earth, the whistle of my breath and the plump thud of earth falling deep into the well – long free of the rustle of plastic – begin to form a hypnotic music. I start grunting softly every time I heave the spade over the edge of the well, simply because it feels so good. Somewhere inside me, I hear a trickling and dripping, the sound I always hear when I'm thinking about Jessie. It's as if I'm in a limestone cave full of stalactites and stalagmites. I think about Jessie a lot as I dig: the way she used to sit here by the well, dropping stones and waiting to hear them land. She was probably thinking about Shershah, whom she loved with her whole heart, who never came back to her. I know she wouldn't have been able to understand it, so she believed that her oath was responsible for his death. Nevertheless, she would never have stopped waiting for him without seeing with her own eyes that he was dead.

I think about how I don't have a single photo of Jessie, about how I'd love to give her something, but I don't know where her grave is. If she has one at all. With each hiss of the spade cutting into the earth, the notion that I can't be at all certain that the whale down there is Shershah grows stronger and stronger. It could be Jessie. Or both of them.

I have to stop digging. I'm going mad.

Lying next to Clara, my breath grows less laboured. I stroke her hair over and over again. It's because I can't stand the waiting. I'm overwrought. I lay a line as long as my lower arm even though my heart is drumming against my ribs in panic. It's pounding so hard that I can see it pulsing in my chest, my hands and in the hollows of my knees. When I'm done, I realize that I would certainly smell it if a body was decomposing in the well and I calm down a little but my heart keeps racing. I press Clara's head against my chest so she can hear it. I know she'd like it, 200 bpm. I've got to do something, I've got to move. My eyelids are twitching and my right leg is jerking spasmodically – I don't want to have an epileptic attack. I shoo the dog into the shed next to Clara and lock up from the outside.

Tonight seems to be a couple of degrees cooler than it was yesterday. That seems about right to me. It must be the end of August, so unless the Earth gets jammed in orbit the heat will let up and it will rain sometime, maybe soon.

I begin to suspect that Clara is lying in the shed waiting for rain, like one of those desert plants that curl up all brown and withered in a corner for months during the dry season, biologically dead. As soon as it rains, they bloom within minutes, expanding to ten times their size, turning green and almost beautiful. I can just see one of the plants before me; I even remember what it's called: Rose of Jericho. I imagine Clara creeping out on her elbows and knees as soon as the first drops fall, staying out in the rain until she's strong enough to get up and walk. She'll leave then, that's for sure. I'll have to listen to the weather forecast. I'm going to buy a garden hose for the tap in the courtyard and spray water onto the roof and the windows of the shed to see if Clara reacts, to see if she'll creep to the threshold after a while. Lisa of Jericho.

But right now, there isn't the time. I close the shutters. The air fanned by them really does seem suspiciously cool. It even smells a bit damp.

There are hardly any taxi ranks in this godforsaken corner of the city. I run down Ottakringer Strasse, past the digital panel displaying a temperature of twenty-eight degrees C. It's 2.43 am and pollution levels are all below the danger zone, even for ozone. It's all propaganda. It pisses me off. The digital panel is trying to tell me it's a perfectly normal night. I can't get it out of my head. And it's difficult running with a box under my arm.

Opernring, I say. Get going, man.

He stays calm; his unflappability does me good. I'm in no hurry, no hurry at all. Taxi drivers have seen all you can think of and worse. It's a Daimler, the same model my mother used to have.

Now slow down, I say.

We glide soundlessly along the Opernring. A couple of drunks are lying on the benches beneath the trees. I open the box, hand the driver a thousand-schilling note, and jump out of the car before he can even think about the change. But I see him starting at the open box. I see it's shaken his composure.

I stand still until he finally drives off, then I look into the gallery window to see if the paintings are still there. But there's nothing colourful in the window, just strange collages of grey cardboard from some other artist. It's difficult to make out the dark patches on the walls or the large object in the middle of the room, since light is reflecting faintly off of it.

I walk around to the side entrance and jam my finger on the doorbell. A couple of birds chirp in the tree above. They should all be poisoned. I don't have any reason to think that he really lives over his shop but it's worth a try. The intercom crackles.

A valued customer, I say, with a box full of cash.

As the door swings inwards, I see a hand around a Walther PPK, the same model that Jessie shot herself with. Herbert seems to supply his people with stuff he's bought from German police stock.

He puts the gun away as soon as he recognizes me.

Fuck, he says. It's Iggy Pop.

He starts laughing. For a moment, I think I'm hallucinating. I think I'm having a brain overload from excessive consumption; I've heard of it, but have never really believed it actually happens.

Why doesn't he come in? he says. I wasn't in bed yet anyway.

Vade retro [Get back/In the name of God], I say. What the hell are you doing here?

A holiday, sort of, he says. Waiting till it's all over so I can go on working in peace.

Explain yourself, you idiot, I say. What are you doing in this building?

Hey, he says. It's my old man's place.

Bad trip, I say. What a fucking bad trip.

I put the box down on the floor, fumble in my trouser pocket and take out whatever sticks to my fingers. I shove it up my nose more than snort it and lick the rest off my palm.

Heh, heh, he says. Take it easy. He's already completely based out.

My eyes are streaming, I can barely see him. Tom the Technician – the son of the gallery owner. And why not? Who the fuck cares, anyway?

Fine, I say. Thanks. Listen, I don't want to come in. I want to get into the shop. I want to buy something.

He's good at buying, isn't he? Tom says. Sorting out his snow in front of Rufus's front door really took the biscuit. I like it. But that nearly pushed things over the edge, I can tell him that.

Over the edge, I say. Speaking of which. You're a smart guy, aren't you? So tell me now: why the fucking hell is nobody bothering with us?

He shouldn't shout like that, Tom says. The neighbours.

Tell me, I say.

He should think about it, Tom says.

He stretches a hand out to touch me somewhere, but his fingers wave into emptiness.

They're nervous, all right, he says, but they're all lurking like wolves behind their rocks. To see if they're going to get it out of you or not.

WHO, I shout, wants WHAT out of me?

He grabs my arm, yanks me into the building and closes the door.

He's lucky that my father isn't here, he says.

Wolves, tigers, eagles, I say, lost in thought. Each in their own corner.

Exactly, he says. Now then, I know I owe him a favour, but this song-and-dance routine here isn't necessary. He'll get his own private viewing, OK?

I grab my nose with both hands; I'm getting a sneezing attack. Sneeze three times and you're in love, I think, but I sneeze at least ten times. When I'm done, I can't even remember what I wanted him to tell me. But then I remember why I originally came here.

To buy Jessie a present. I haven't planned to do anything so nice for a long time, something I could really look forward to. I have a feeling that Jessie's watching me from somewhere, watching me hanging around in the gallery hallway in the middle of the night. She's laughing her high-pitched laugh, shaking her head and whispering: Cooper, you always come up with such crazy ideas.

OK, I say. There's about a million schillings' worth in three different currencies out there in the street. Can you get it?

He carries the box in and leads me into the gallery through the staff entrance. 'TAVIRP' is printed on the glass window in the door. I stroll in, a special friend of the gallery who's come to buy paintings in the dead of the night. Then I see the statue.

Fuck, I say. I'd forgotten that this was here too.

Lovely, isn't it? says Tom.

He puts the box down on the sales counter, leans back against the counter and shoves his hands into his pockets. It's dim in here. The yellowish light from the street lamps slanting through the window in front is the only illumination there is. The air smells of scented oil. They probably burn some kind of musk oil to make the customers more receptive. The statue in the middle of the room seems to draw what little light there is. It draws the eye to it, too: everything in the room seems to be arranged around it. But that's nothing new to him.

I walk right up to the statue. It looks incredibly real. If he weren't as clear as water, I could practically convince myself that he was still alive. He's standing there the way he always used to, head bent forward slightly, as if he's listening for something. The receding hairline looks good on him.

Should I turn on the light? Tom asks.

No, thanks, I say. Don't. I can see.

I recognize the scar on the side of his knee from the operation he had for his torn tendon.

If he wants it, Tom says, the money he's brought must be just about right.

I had planned on buying Jessie one of the paintings: 'Kings and Planets' or 'Fu loves Fula'. I know how happy they would have made her, but this opens up a whole new dimension. I wonder if she would have wanted a glass Shershah as a trophy, as a remembrance, as a monument, as an angel over her grave; something she could destroy or embrace from time to time. I imagine her standing next to me right now, looking at him with her own eyes, but I haven't a clue how she would react. That gives me a jolt. I was sure I knew her better than anyone else because I never actually wanted anything from her, but I can't answer this crucial yet simple question. I turn away; I can't bear having him look at me.

Do you still have those paintings, I ask, with women who look like ants?

Only the larger ones, he says. The smaller ones went like hot cakes.

He points to three squarish paintings in the far corner of the room. There they are, all three of them, as if they've been specially kept for two years for Jessie. That decides it for me.

How much are they? I ask.

No comparison, Tom says. Three hundred thousand each.

If I take all three, I say, can I leave all the cash here?

No problem, he says.

Just when I'm sure that my decision is based on what Jessie would have wanted – the pictures, not the statue – I get the nagging feeling that the truth would have been otherwise. I'll never be free of this feeling. It spoils the pleasure I have in buying a present for her, something she wanted. He's done it again, the son of a bitch. He always does it.

Tom takes the paintings off the wall, carries them to the sale counter and packs them in brown paper. I feel like I'm at the butcher's.

What's the humming sound? I ask.

That, Tom says, is the Corpus Delicti.

He pulls back a corner of the cloth draped over the counter and shows me the computer beneath.

It's serving as a superior calculator at the moment, he says, to relieve the customers of their cash. It's as if someone were to take a Boeing round the corner to go shopping. But he's safe here. They want to keep him here awhile.

I don't understand a word of his babble. I don't care, anyway. He's standing with his back to me, so I stare at the heavy chain hanging from his wallet and the bulge of the Walther PPK in his baggy bum-pocket. I feel it coming; I know I'm about to flip out.

Because it hums so loudly, Tom says, Jessie used to call it—

I head-butt him when he turns round to give me the package. My forehead cracks against his – I think the impact throws us both equally – and then I have the gun in my hand. He staggers backwards. I'm only going to shoot once – him, myself or Shershah – and I'd prefer to shoot myself. Really, that's what I want to do.

The flash from the shot hangs in the air for much too long. I think of Clara with the hairspray Bunsen burner and the spider; I think of Jessie and the walking stick on the balcony in Herbert's flat; I think of myself on the phone in the Leipzig office when the shot came that splintered Jessie's head; I think of all these things, all at the same time.

I've missed. The gallery window collapses into itself in slow motion and the alarm begins to wail. My good ear begins to whistle like the other one. I drop the Walther and glance at Tom the Technician's uncomprehending face. In the very moment that I jump through the window frame onto the street, I see the box of multicoloured biros next to the door, all yellow–red–blue, freebies for the customers. I nearly slip on the shards of glass. The statue stands untouched on its pedestal, its smile imprinted on my mind for ever. I clutch the paintings more firmly under my arm and take off running.

30 | Baumgartner Hospital

I cast a fleeting glance at the well as I pass. Even after what I think was hours of digging, the hole doesn't look any bigger than a normal grave. Far from a crater.

Clara is lying in the shed exactly as I left her. Jacques Chirac wags his tail. I don't know why he's always happy to see me. Perhaps tail-wagging is just a bad habit. I pat his head.

Look what I've bought, I say.

I unpack the paintings and lean them next to each other against the boxes. I change them around three times until the ant-women are facing each other. They are incredibly beautiful, so gaudily coloured yet so modest. Jessie had good taste. They make up a perfect triptych for her altar – if only I knew where to build it. This isn't a good place.

Pity you can't get your eyes open to see this, I say to Clara.

I'm not in the least tired so I get the recorder ready. The last cassette isn't in it and I can't remember what I've done with it. It's not on the cupboard, not on the boxes, and is not lying anywhere amongst our clothes. Instead, I find my shaving stuff and a new cassette. I put it all down next to Clara and then I fill a bowl with water from the tap in the courtyard and put that down next to her too, with some blow and cigarettes. We are sitting, standing and lying in a circle: Clara, myself, the dog and the three ant-women. I wet the blade, foam up some shaving cream between my hands and rub it onto Clara's hairline.

I spent the afternoon in the office, looking through my desk for documents important enough to take with me, but I found practically nothing. There were no calls for me and no one asked for me. The secretaries seemed to have been told to shut me out.

When I left at around six, the outer office was empty. I picked up the key tagged with the unfamiliar Leipzig address and just left without saying goodbye to anyone, as if I was simply a visitor to the office or as if I was coming back the next day. When the heavy front door swung shut behind me, I realized that I was finally no longer a part of Rufus's Olympus.

Clara's hair is simply too long. It slips and slides constantly under the razor blade. I don't know if Jessie had needed to wet-shave the heads of the Bosnian women or if she'd had an electric razor. I had forgotten to ask. I keep nicking Clara's scalp accidentally because it's so soft, and a fat drop of blood oozes out every time. I catch each drop with my finger and lick it clean. It tastes perfectly normal, of blood, with a tinge of shaving cream. My mother always used to lick my blood this way when I'd fallen and cut or hurt myself. When I asked her why she was doing that, she said she could do it because I was flesh from her flesh, and blood from her blood.

This isn't working. I don't want to hurt Clara.

There's a scallop-edged kitchen knife lying on the floor not far from me. I grip her head between my knees, grab her hair and pull it taut like the strings of an instrument. The first handful is wrenched out by the uneven blade rather than cut off. Then I realize that I should be sawing more quickly, since every now and then her head knocks against the ground. Even though my knees are holding her head like a vice, the sawing motion of the knife makes it roll from side to side against the floorboards, as if she's lying on the bottom of a delivery truck.

Autumn was in the air and a strong wind was up. I wrapped myself up tightly in my coat and let myself be blown over the lawn of the Volksgarten along with the dead leaves and branches. I decided to walk back to the flat in Währingerstrasse – I had that much leeway, surely. I was frightened of course. A large, sharp-toothed circular saw was moving through my stomach, shredding my insides and whirling them around. I stopped by the gallery window in the Opernring to look at the portraits of the antlike women turning their pointy faces towards each other, smiling sadly, talking about me.

Before I put the key in the lock, I pressed my ear to the front door to listen for a moment. Silence. For a moment, I thought she might not be there at all. She might have run away, like one of those four-legged animal heroes when they feel that something bad is about to happen to them. Simply vanished, perhaps to Greenland. I opened the door.

The kitchen door opened almost the same instant and Jessie walked down the hall towards me.

Ud, ud, ud, ud, she said.

She stopped in front of me, one arm in a sleeve of her shirt, the rest of the shirt wrapped awkwardly around her torso while the other arm waved helplessly in the air. I immediately saw that the sleeve she'd got one arm into was inside out and the rest was all in a twist. She smiled at me, leaned against me and tried to hug me despite having one arm bound up in her shirt. I helped her into the shirt and kissed her. She held herself stiffly. I stroked her head until she relaxed and sank into my arms.

Cooper, she said. You're late.

It's not late, I said. It's just half-past six.

Still, she said.

She continued holding on to me tightly, walking sideways as I made my way into the kitchen. I dropped my bag on the floor next to the bottle of mineral water, instead of in its usual place. I wondered if I should search the flat the way I had searched my desk in the office, but I abandoned the thought immediately. What was the use, anyway? Jessie went over to the fridge.

What have you been doing all day? I asked.

Working, she said.

She waved her arms to indicate the flat around her.

Cleaning, tidying up, vacuuming, she said. Don't you notice at all?

I noticed it now. It was crazy, but I was touched and, above all, happy that she hadn't been out.

Great, I said. Thanks.

She poured wine into two water glasses and put one in front of me.

Cheers, she said.

She tipped her head back and emptied her glass in one go. She had tears in her eyes when she was finished. I drank a few gulps. We didn't say anything.

Jessie, I finally said, shall we go for a walk?

Oh yes, oh yes, she said.

She jumped up and ran into the hallway to put on her army boots, but ended up hopping around helplessly on one leg. I held her firmly and gently and made her sit down on the floor. She was quivering; even her legs were trembling. I tied her laces for her.

Are you cold? I asked.

Yeah, she said. I've been freezing all day.

I fetched her an old striped top of mine that I thought she'd like. It was the one I'd wanted to roll her through the snow in, right under the gazes of the smiling white wolves. It reached down to her knees. I rolled the sleeves up for her and told her she looked beautiful.

I couldn't be sure that she hadn't had any contact with her family during the day. They might have called her, or she them. I couldn't tell how much she knew. I couldn't even tell if she remembered how and why we had left 61 Praterstrasse last night. She could switch her ability to take things in off and on like a light. She didn't have to know anything if she didn't want to. Unless, of course, she was made to, every now and then.

We took the tram to the sixteenth district. We didn't sit down, but stood resting against the glass at the back of the last carriage. Jessie leaned into me like a weary child with each curve the tram took.

We got out in Wilhemstrasse and walked up the Savoyenstrasse to the Schloss. We walked side by side, not touching. The wind blew her hair sideways and she looked totally different. We didn't speak until we reached the forest. She perked up then and ran ahead to hide in the darkness. My striped top flashed everywhere amongst the trees and I had to lie when she asked if I could still see her.

We cut through the forest in a wide loop. I directed her back to the road unobtrusively, and we took the branch curving off to the left. We could smell the stink of the sewage-treatment plant half a kilometre away. A strong north-west wind was blowing. Suddenly, Jessie stopped, lifted one leg and put a finger to her lips.

Oh, she said. I've just remembered what I dreamed last night.

What, my sweet? I asked.

I longed to take her in my arms and bury my face in her hair, to inhale the fragrance of her vulnerable scalp instead of the stink of sewage.

Someone had made a copy of me, she said. A life-size statue, made entirely out of shit. He put the statue on the street and the dogs ate it up, smearing their beards with it. It stank to high heaven. Exactly like it does now.

She looked around uncertainly, as if this statue, a Jessie made wholly of excrement, could be standing around the corner.

That's just the sewage works, I said. Come, let's go.

She reached out for my hand and curled her fist around my middle and ring fingers. I wanted to hurry on, to run around the last bend and tighten my grip on Jessie's hand the moment she began to realize where we were going. I was hoping that she wouldn't start screaming. If I had to, I would twist her arms behind her back and knot the much-too-long sleeves of my top together.

She tugged me backwards.

I want to go up the observation tower, she said.

I pulled her on.

Nah, I said. The wind and the stink.

Oh yes, she said. Please.

I gave in. It didn't matter, anyway. She ran ahead again, away from the street and onto the narrow footpath that led to the small steep hill on which the observation tower was built. The path wound around the hill a couple of times in a spiral, but Jessie clambered straight up instead, her hands and feet squelching in the ground. The path was muddy; I felt water seeping up my trouser bottoms, weighing them down. Jessie was already on the viewing deck by the time I started climbing the metal steps that zigzagged between steel supports. The tower was a good thirty metres high.

I stroke the hair that I've cut from Clara's head and lay it out tidily beside me on the floor. Clara looks as if a cow has been grazing off her head; I have to smile. Her face is red and wet, I have no idea what with. I lather her whole scalp and dip the razor in water. It's easy now, gliding smoothly from her right temple to her ear.

When I'm done with the second round of shaving, I start plaiting Clara's hair into a thick braid. I'd liked it best when she wore it that way. Besides, a braid is a good token of remembrance – for whoever, for the survivors. Maybe I should attach it to my own head. Max, she had said, if you want to know what someone's thinking, you've got to take on their external appearance.

Only I've never actually wanted to know exactly what she is thinking.

The wind was whipping up a gale on top of the tower, hurling scraps of clouds across the sky, tearing loose the odd leaf. The round pools of the sewage works looked like a pair of spectacles pressed into the face of the forest. Seagulls circled above them like snowflakes, though what they were periodically diving for in the pools didn't bear thinking about. The wind sang through the steel; the entire structure was quivering like a gigantic tuning fork. Jessie was holding on to the railing with both hands, her face turned into the full force of the wind, her eyes streaming. I held on tight, too. I felt as if we were braving the whoosh of the turning Earth together.

I'm a ship foaming through the waves, Jessie shouted. We're going to Greenland!

She laughed and started throwing her whole weight back and forth against the railing. The viewing platform shook, the pipes sang and the joints creaked.

Stop doing that, I said.

I stood with my legs braced wide, like a sailor at sea.

Jessie! I shouted.

A ship! A ship!

She was putting everything into it. Her knuckles were white, her forehead beaded with sweat. She ducked when I reached out for her, lost her rhythm and crashed against the railing. I grabbed her and pressed her against the metal rod. Her elbows jabbed my solar plexus instinctively, knocking the wind out of me, but I didn't let go. I held on tight until she stopped struggling. Creaking and vibrating, the tower came to a standstill. Jessie's face was damp and I wasn't even sure if she recognized me. She searched my face, as if looking for something in my eyes, my nose, the corners of my mouth.

Jessie, I said, we have to go now.

Her gaze darted over my face for another second and then she threw me a right hook, slipped under my arm and ran to the other side of the platform. She hurled herself against the railing, swung one leg across it and was just about to climb over when I finally reacted. I leapt – I didn't know I could leap like that – and clamped one hand on her hair, the other on her shirt, pulling her back. We stumbled and she fell against the metal floor with the clang of a gong, probably hitting her head. I expected her to scream but she didn't make a sound; her lips were pressed firmly together. As I was bending over her, I accidentally stepped onto her hair and yanked a whole clump out. She clasped her hands together like a good Catholic and raised them to me.

You want to go away, she sang, go away-go away-go away.

She sang the words go away-go away-go away to the tune of 'Are you sleeping?' in 'Frère Jacques', over and over again. Her voice was loud and metallic, made resonant by the tower.

I-want-to-be – yo-ur – wi-ife, she sang. I'm-try-ing – so – har-ard.

Can't-you-hear-the – bells, can't-you – hear the – bells? Then she choked and turned her head to one side. She didn't resist when I lifted her up. With my fingertips, I carefully burst a bubble of spit by the side of her mouth and wiped it away.

I ran down the tower with Jessie in my arms, my feet sounding a different tone against each step. The metal vibrated, groaned and clanged: can't you hear the bells, ding-dang-dong, ding-dang-donnngggg.

Sshhhhh, I whispered into her ear, sshhhh. I'm not going away.

I ran through the stink of sewage, still carrying her; she babbled a stream of sounds and syllables and smiled from time to time. There was no reason to run, only I had seen the street lights through the trees, and I couldn't wait to reach their orange glow. When I got to the road, though, I didn't slow down. The longish multi-storey buildings of the Baumgartner Hospital seemed to appear ahead of me in time-lapse form. They lay white in the dark forest, ships in the Atlantic, going to Greenland.

The parking lot was empty. The gatehouse was lit.

I was out again in minutes. I had a handkerchief in each hand, and was patting my face, head and hands dry with them. Jessie had fallen onto her knees in the room behind the glass door, shouting my name – 'Cooper, Cooper', she had called, and it had echoed off the walls of the entire complex. I could still hear it as I ran down a staircase, got lost, bumped into a nurse and slalomed past stiff, swaying figures with heads twisted at awkward angles. Compared with me, they moved through the corridors so slowly that they looked like statues.

I stood out in the parking lot. Lukewarm saliva, which I had forgotten to swallow, pooled in my mouth. I spat it out. I looked up at the sky; it was a tinted windscreen with a patch of lightness in the upper right-hand corner, as if someone was holding a searchlight up to it from the inside. I looked at my hands, trying to make out anything familiar in them. My head was completely empty.

When I looked up again, I saw, at the edge of the parking lot a car that hadn't been there before. I squinted at it until I recognized the person leaning over the open driver's door. It was Ross. Panicked, I thought about running back to the building and hiding behind the small flight of steps that led up to it. But I knew it was pointless. If he was going to shoot me, he could do it anywhere in this wide-open space. He lifted a hand and waved. It looked as if he was hoisting a white flag – his hand was wrapped in a thick white bandage.

Max! he shouted. Hurry!

I was suddenly glad to see him, glad to hear a voice from someone who wasn't wearing doctor's garb. I ran over to him and he laid his good hand on my shoulder. He looked even more wiry and angular than I remembered, like a log on the beach weathered by a decade of sun, salt water and wind. He must have been nearly forty. His eyes were expressionless, but he was tugging at his lower lip with his teeth and chewing it. Standing there in front of him, I realized how quickly I was breathing: the creases in my forehead refused to smooth out and the corners of my mouth were quivering.

What have you done? he said.

I didn't know if he meant the murder or Jessie. He got a lighter out of his car and lit two cigarettes. I dragged heavily on mine, watching the glowing tip eating into the paper. Ross put his entire hand over his mouth and chin while he smoked. I was still waiting.

Fucking hell, he said.

It began to dawn on me that he didn't know what he was doing there himself.

Did Herbert send you? I asked.

Are you crazy? he said. I only just found out about this shit.

We fell silent. Thoughts of how I was going to go back to the flat in Währingerstrasse and then leave it again wandered into my head. I would get into the rental car, buy a map of Leipzig at the petrol station if they had one, and my life in Vienna with all its unfulfilled promise would come to an end. I didn't care about what might happen after that. I didn't want any part of it. A new flat somewhere, working in one of the branch offices – it all had nothing to do with me. It was simply an obligation, like a distant relative's birthday party, which I would try to leave as soon as possible. For a moment, I felt as if all light had gone out in the world. I found it difficult to breathe; even smoking was an effort.

I hate it all, I said.

Ross grabbed me by the collar.

I always thought you were a loser, he hissed. But this tops it all.

Rufus told me to, I said.

So? he growled.

My hand flew up to his lower arm; it was hard as rock.

I didn't even know, I coughed, that Rufus and Herbert knew each other.

How thick can you get? he hissed. Do you think those pretty blue eyes of yours got you the job?

I pressed the tip of my cigarette against his hand. He swore under his breath but didn't let go. There was a faint smell of charred skin. A spurt of adrenalin rushed into my gut and up my throat and I managed to loosen his hand and punch him in the chest.

Why, then?

You drove to Bari that time, he said. You belong to us. We would have needed you.

What the fuck! I screamed.

Hey, he said. We don't want to attract attention.

We stepped back from each other. He rubbed his scorched hand against his trousers and pointed to the building with the bandaged hand.

She can't do anything about it, he said. She'll break down in there. I thought you loved her, you prick.

Of course I love her, I said.

He snorted.

That aside, he said. If you can't do it for love, then get her out of there to save yourself. Take her to Leipzig with you. Then you have a chance of being left to live on in peace.

But, I said. Rufus said—

It's a bluff, Ross said. It's about something larger than that. Herbert and Rufus fell out. Shershah had chosen a bad time for his little operation, and there were plenty of people who never understood why Herbert had employed someone like him in the first place. And she . . .

He pointed at the building again.

. . . She was completely brainwashed by him. She would have done anything for him. I'd always warned Herbert about that. But Herbert wanted Jessie to be happy, at least for some time. For as long as possible. Whatever the price.

He flicked the ash off his cigarette.

Rufus wants to tidy up now, he said. Shershah's dead, she's in there and you can figure out what's going to happen to *you*, can't you? Think about it.

I didn't understand. All I knew was that somehow I'd been fucked with. By Herbert, by Rufus and now by Ross; maybe even by Jessie.

Can I have another? I asked.

He lit another cigarette for me.

You have to hurry, he said. Go in there and get her out. Don't tell her I was here. You have to stay together; it's best for both of you. If she wants to live with you, Herbert will make sure that there aren't any problems. As long as you disappear.

And if not? I asked.

Then she stays in there for months, Ross said, and you'll have to prove to Herbert and Rufus that you had nothing to do with that shit. The three of you have always been friends, after all.

Surely you don't believe that, I said.

It doesn't matter what I believe, he said. We have a problem on our hands and we're all climbing the walls.

He pointed at the complex of buildings for the third time.

What matters to me is this, he said. This time, THAT really is going to be the end of her.

I was starting to nod.

OK.

He laid his unbandaged hand on my arm for a moment in a gesture of camaraderie. I thought I saw something like affection in his half-paralysed face, or at least an attempt at something like it.

Love her, Max, he said. Don't let her feel anything else. She won't come back to Herbert and me.

Then he got into the car and started the engine.

Why did you hate Shershah so much? he asked through the window. Shershah was even more helpless than Jessie.

Dunno, I said. Maybe because he thought he didn't need to pay for anything in life.

He started driving off.

You're a psychopath, Max, Ross shouted. I'll call a taxi for you both. Good luck.

I walked off in the other direction.

Hello, it's me again, I said cheerily to the porter. I left my briefcase.

The door hummed open and we raised hands in greeting. I found the way as if I was being pulled along a string. Let her still be there, let her still be there, let her still be there, I chanted in my head.

The rigid figures on the benches in the corridors passed in a blur. I found the stairs; the glass door that only opened from outside was at the end of the hallway and I could see a striped top behind it. Jessie was pressed against the door from the inside, her arms raised, her fingers clawing at the glass. Her cheeks and lips were pressed flat, bloodless; her hair was damp and I could see her scalp. Her eyes were open but she wasn't seeing anything and she wasn't waiting any longer.

I yanked the door handle and she fell out towards me. She'd probably had an injection. I wanted her to walk – that would look less dramatic – so I laid her arm around my neck, but she dangled next to me, her feet not quite touching the ground. I forced myself to take it slowly. I spoke to her.

We have to finish our walk, don't we? I said.

I draped her on my back to take the stairs. The porter was looking straight ahead. I ran up to the door and let Jessie slide to the ground so that she was leaning against my shins like a dog, beneath the glass of the porter's cabin.

Me again, I said. Got it.

He turned and the door hummed open. I pulled Jessie up, my little sleeping beauty, took her in my arms and ran out across the parking lot. The taxi was waiting on the street.

It's too bad that I am not able to cut off the full length of Clara's hair with the blunt knife. The braid is much shorter than I'd expected. I stuff it into my pocket. When the nasty shaving cuts have dried, I wash Clara's scalp again and dab it with a corner of my shirt. I prop her up halfway so that I can admire my work. She looks even better than she did before. Exactly like a shop dummy: stick-thin, bald and half-naked. No longer like Clara. I think hard; though my brain is so sluggish, so fucking slow. I can't think of a single new female name. Clara. Klaus. Karl. Cain. I decide to call her Lisa from now on.

And now, Lisa, I say to her, you're going to ask me: And then?

The silence is like the hum of a refrigerator. I do an exaggeratedly querulous imitation of her voice.

And then? I whine.

And then, I answer in a deep bass tone, I packed Jessie into the rental car beside me. I could see her profile reflected in the window on her side. When she came to herself somewhere after Passau, she announced that she wanted a mixture between a dog and a pony and we bought Jacques Chirac a few days later. I went into the Leipzig office every day and worked on documents for EU expansion into Eastern Europe, not knowing that it served the re-routing of a drug-supply chain above all. Jessie stayed in the flat, cared for the dog, and looked forward to me coming home in the evenings. And I went to bed with my secretary now and then. All perfectly normal.

Silence. Absolute silence. I think about killing both Clara and myself with a cocaine overdose, like Romeo and Juliet. That would work for us.

And now, I say to her, you're going to ask the *key* question.

I'm standing in the middle of the room with one foot positioned in front of the other, like a statue without a bronze-lettered pedestal. I rub at the rash in the corner of my mouth as I stand there staring at the new Lisa. By the edge of the floorboards is a whole phalanx of abandoned cigarettes with long curved tips of ash. I'm restless. I itch all over under my clothes, as I sometimes do just before I fall asleep. I undo my trousers and go over to Lisa.

The key question, I say, approximating her whiny voice, is this: why did Jessie shoot herself? Why?

I try not to move her unnecessarily, just pushing her right knee a little off to the side. This rolls her body round so that she's practically lying on her stomach. A couple of shoves fail to get her back into her previous position so I just leave it. I should have chalked her outline on the floor so I can put her back into her original position later. She'd looked perfect that way, simply perfect. I spit into my right hand but it's not enough. I suck at the insides of my cheeks, thinking about a lemon, until I work up enough gobs of spit for the tips of my fingers.

It's difficult to get inside her. She doesn't make a sound, nor does she move. I move as little as possible too, just a fraction here and there. I wonder if I should just give up. It's all too allegorical for me: an impotent man trying to rape a woman feigning death. The ant-women are looking at me. Jacques Chirac is looking at me too, with what I take to be astonishment in his eyes. Lisa's left shoulder is poking my chin. And then, just as some fold of skin gives way and I suddenly slip completely into her, just as everything is easy and I can relax, I remember how I came home unexpectedly early one day and couldn't find Jessie in the kitchen or the living room, so I went into the bedroom. I only realized she was there on second glance as she raised her bright red face from the bed. She had been lying face down with one of the pillows wedged between her legs. I gripped the door frame and she rolled to one side. For a moment, I saw that she was trying to pretend that she was asleep, but then she realized there was no point and it was ridiculous anyway. So she half-raised herself and began burbling about how she had been dreaming, how she'd been riding a horse in her dream. For the first time, I felt real anger with her rising in me; in that moment, I felt like I really could have hurt her. I left the room and started preparing dinner. She came into the kitchen much later and sat on one of the chairs, her head hanging and her hair all awry. I racked my brains, but couldn't think of anything to say that would relax us both, give us the feeling that it was nothing. For it *was* nothing, really, only that I hadn't realized until then that she could satisfy herself. I suppose it was logical, but it just hadn't occurred to me. I couldn't think of anything to say, so we ate in silence.

All that goes through my head as I lie on top of Lisa, my stare fixed on the backs of my slightly shiny hands, my fingers curled around either side of her fleshless collarbone, which provides a handy grip. I lie on her limply. She's limp, too – we lie like two chops stuck together. In order not to slip out of her, I hardly move; and she doesn't move at all. I feel the awkwardness of the situation keenly. The back of her glossy baldness is right up against my eyes. Why is she taking this? I think. No one can be this weak when they're not completely dead yet, so there must be something else behind this – like the time she lay in an ice-cold bath as a child. Maybe it's a suicide attempt. She's probably incredibly grateful to me at the moment for giving her the opportunity to indulge her strange masochism. The thought gladdens me.

Think nothing of it, dear Lisa, I say politely to the back of her head.

It still doesn't work, so I give up and get up. I've grazed my knees on the rough floorboards and they hurt.

She's conscious, just as I thought. Beneath the pagoda curve of her lashes, her eyes are turned towards me. I catch her furtive look just as I'm about to step outside. She's lying right up against the dog. Thank God they don't cling to each other. I walk out into the middle of the courtyard and spread my arms like a preacher.

That's all, I shout. I've said it all! There's nothing more to tell. No idea how we're going to pass the fucking time now!

All. That was the magic word. Open sesame. Something clatters in the shed. There's a rustling sound and then she's standing there, clinging to the door handle, hunched but standing, the morning light reflecting off her newly bald scalp.

That's all? she asks.

That's all, I say.

And that's it. We obviously don't have much more to say to each other. She's just standing there, dazzled, blinking, sorting out her thoughts. It's nice to see her up, but thinking about what she might say about the pages missing from her file and what's going to happen when she realizes that she no longer has her hair fills me with unease. I leave the courtyard to stretch my legs. The night is over but the sky is milky and isn't turning blue properly. I can't even see the sun.

31 | Europa

In front of me, a mother pushes her two children back into the house that they were about to leave. I spread out my arms, waiting for the next passer-by to kill me in my craziness; but he just crosses to the other side of the street. I have Clara's blood on my shirt, and her fucking hair all over me. I pull the braid out of my pocket and toss it into the next drain. I have to push it through the grate with my heel. Then I turn and head back.

She's washed herself and put on a clean T-shirt. God knows where she stashed that. She's crouched on the low wall, elbows on her knees, chin resting on her hands. She seems to be white all over, like a bald baby Jesus or one of Jessie's tongueless angels. I wait for her to speak but she won't.

Lisa, I say finally, I feel as if I'm hallucinating you. It's not a nice feeling.

I've had a lot of not-so-nice feelings too, she says.

My voice is as sober as it would be if I were buying rolls in a bakery. It isn't coming out of me but from someone else entirely, someone invisible standing right next to me:

What's with the sudden resurrection?

You said you'd finished telling your story, she replies.

Let's try again, I say. What was all that Sleeping Beauty business about?

Oh, she says. You get along better with sick people. You only trust the weak and frail. It's one of the first things I noticed.

I don't believe that, I say.

Then don't, she says. Have you really told me *everything*?

I'm going to get you, I say.

I don't know if you've realized this, she says. But all your attempts so far to do people in, including yourself, have failed miserably.

The spade is lying behind her in the grass. She turns as I take a step towards it.

So the grave is for me, then? she says. And I thought you'd dug it for yourself.

I grab the spade and lift it up high. Clara's white skull gleams beneath me like a boiled egg at breakfast – but I know I can't do it anyway and she knows it too. Then a telephone rings. In itself, that's nothing unusual, but the ringing is coming from inside our shed. I drop the spade and it falls onto the cement with an ugly clang.

What, I ask, is that?

Phone, she says. You hear it, don't you? And probably for you.

She gets up and walks towards the shed slowly, her hands resting on her hips. She takes tiny mincing steps as if the air were made out of countless wafer-thin layers of glass and she's trying to destroy as few as possible. The ringing stops; she comes back with a mobile phone that I haven't seen before and hands it to me.

Hello, I say.

It's him.

Hi, he says. Max the Maximal.

Cut the crap, Ross, I say.

That's all there is to say for the moment. We fall silent. I listen to him smoking; I'm smoking too. I clear my throat.

Where the hell have you been? I say. I'm waiting for you.

I'm waiting for you too, he says.

Sounds like we should be getting married. He seems relaxed; he's only taking half as many drags from his cigarette as I am.

I hear you've finished your story? he says.

Who'd you hear that from? I say.

He leaves that for me to figure out.

Does that mean she's been working for you all this time?

No, he says, she only works for herself. But we had an agreement.

And that was?

For letting her do what she liked, he said, we got copies of your soppy tapes. She was sure that she was the only one who knew how to get it all out of you. She was very convincing.

I look at Clara settling herself down on the wall again; she's perfectly detached, still only half there.

Yes, I say, she was very convincing. Very successful.

But now I don't feel as if I really have it all, he says. I have a feeling there's an important bit missing.

Can you spell it out?

We should meet, he says.

Great idea, I say. Bring a gun with you.

Yeah, yeah, Max boy, he says. Easy.

He gives me the time and the place – in 'Europa' this evening – and then the line goes dead. I pass the phone back to Clara.

You're out of your mind, I say.

What do you mean?

You still don't get it, do you, what kind of people they are?

She's sitting with her knees pressed together, head down, speaking to the cement floor and not looking at me at all.

Why don't you just say that you're worried about me?

I hadn't thought about whether or not I was worried about her before; maybe I am, or maybe it's more that I feel I have an exclusive right to her. We made a deal: my story for her honour, her freedom, her health. In short, my story for her entire person. That's exactly it.

I'm worried about my property, I say. I bought you.

Wrong, she says. You rented me. And the contract expires now.

No, it doesn't.

Yes, it does.

We're getting nowhere. I try another route.

Clara, I say, do you love me?

She doesn't reply. I repeat the question and she crouches forward even further, pressing her forehead against her knee, and intertwining her fingers with her toes. I want to shove her, but something about her manner holds me back.

OK, let's try again, I say. Do you love yourself?

Yes, she says. Above all else.

And you think they're going to let you go back home, just like that?

Of course, she says. All I've done is record the ramblings of a psychotic junkie.

Ramblings?

Yours, she says. Stories trickle out of you like pus from a boil. I haven't ever met Herbert, Ross or Jessie; I can't even be sure that they exist. I've spoken to a stranger on the phone and taken a couple of tapes in to one of the most prestigious law firms in Europe. And what about it? What else could they want from me?

Lisa, Lisa, I say. Surely you can't be that naive.

She hugs herself, looking as if she's cold; a strange, thin, bald, freezing alien in a white T-shirt.

Look, she says. What do you really want from me now, for fuck's sake?

Excellent question. I feel that she's betrayed me, or fucked me up, but that isn't really anything new. It's worse feeling that I'm sitting here on the edge of sanity, on the outskirts of a city, with my legs dangling over a yawning abyss while all turns grey behind me. The streets are drying up and the buildings are sinking slowly into the ground. The last lights are already extinguished by a steady, unstoppable wind. I see myself skittering, antlike, over the emptiness, knocking against the ground with my hands and whispering: cement, all cement. What I want is for Clara not to leave me alone.

Nothing, I say. I don't know. Figure out what you've done and why.

She finally raises her face and looks at me. Suddenly, I don't know why I liked her bald; she looks terrible, not the Clara I know at all. Completely lifeless.

What would you say, she asks, if you found out that I didn't have long to live? That I'm ill? Infected with HIV?

I take a couple of steps back, look at the whole of her all sunk together, sitting there more like a parcel than a human being.

I would understand a bit better, I say.

See, she says. But I'm not. I'm fit as can be. That's why you'll never understand.

I'm overcome by something that I think is pure despair.

Clara, I say, do you love me?

She doesn't hesitate this time.

What I feel for you, she says, is contempt, pity, and maybe a little hatred.

Pity, I say. That's wonderful. It's the ideal basis for a long, intimate relationship.

She gives a bark of laughter, or maybe it's more of a snarl.

You're crazy, she says.

Somehow I thought we shared something, I say.

Mistake, she says. But I can tell you something else, something important, more important than all this shit here. It might cheer you up.

Please, I say, tell me.

Let's go back to Leipzig together, I think, let's go to South America, or Greenland, no, not Greenland. OK, whatever, Greenland too, God be my witness; let's pour wine out of a glass and see which continent the wine stain looks like and that's where we'll go in the end.

She pauses, then lifts her clear gaze up to me.

My dissertation, she says, is as good as done. Then you'll be able to get it off the Internet. Everywhere.

Fucking hell, I whisper.

She gets up and stretches while I sink to my knees; it's as if we're sitting on a see-saw together, and I'm heavier. I look up at her. It's not the baldness that looks so strange, it's the look of satisfaction on her face: calm and confident. Her face is clear, as if she's just come to a catharsis.

I've got something else that you might be interested in, I say.

She stiffens inwardly. That's the contempt.

Naah. Max, she says, you don't have anything else of interest. You're nothing but a phantom pain in your own existence.

I just want you to know, I say, that we do have something in common. We're both being equally fucked with.

Now comes the pity: her brows are drawing together and the corners of her mouth are turning down.

The difference is, I'm fucking with you, she says, but only God fucks with me.

I have a message for you from your supervisor, I say. I've got to act it out.

Her gaze is steady. I get up, clap both hands to my heart and do an impression of Schnitzler.

Max, I say, you've lived through some extraordinary things. Tell your story to a professional, not an amateur!

Her brain is certainly working all right. She gets it immediately, I can see it in her eyes. Something is breaking.

You had to tell me that, she whispers.

And here comes the hatred: she's going to get hysterical. She's been through a hard time and it's always been possible to break a camel's back with a straw. Her hands claw the air and I'm about to grab her, but it isn't directed at me. She's digging her fingers into her cheeks, barely missing one of her eyes. She pulls her face down until it looks like a Munch painting and then the scream comes out too. Her voice is shrill like the screech of metal on metal. But I'm at my breaking point too; I've hardly slept. I haven't slapped her about for ages, which I regret, since slapping her is good fun – and better than sex, much better. When the left side of her face is fiery red, I drag her over to her shed. The dog escapes as I push her in. She lands between the boxes. I slam the door shut and turn the key. She starts banging against the windows with something just after I've barred the shutters.

Max, she shouts. Max, you're going to regret this, MAX!!

His hand looks like one of those metal claws in a machine at the carnival. Put one coin in, press a button, and try to grab a stuffed toy, a watch or a cap out of the machine. He's holding his cigarette between the thumb and the little finger. I wonder why he's using his left hand, since it's ghastly.

What happened to your hand? I ask.

Got shot, he said. Funny business.

Where? When? I ask politely

Albania, he says. An accident. I got into a demonstration there two years ago, during the chaos. A couple of the guys had some old Russian sub-machine guns from some rediscovered bunker. They were shooting into the air. And a couple of the bullets came down again.

They weren't aiming at you?

Naah, he laughs. It was like being hit by a meteorite.

I look at the hand again, and feel like asking if he had it raised in a Hitler salute when the bullets fell from the sky, but decide to keep the joke to myself. He's dressed completely in black: on him, the clothes look as if they're borrowed. Just as I'm about to ask, I realize why. It's because of Jessie. Maybe he doesn't know that only bright yellow would be the right colour. He looks grotesque, more like the corpse than the grieving relative.

The waitress comes up to us. Ross orders two beers, holding the only two fingers on his left hand up to signal the number. The girl backs away from our table, only turning around when she reaches the bar.

Well then, Ross says. Let's chat a little.

Can't we get to the point straight away?

Sure. Tell me what the point is.

I don't know why you're here, I say, but I've come so that you can shoot me.

He taps his forehead with the little finger of his claw.

You're going to make me cry with laughter, he says. What would I get out of killing you?

I bang my fist on the table.

What else do I have to do? I shout. Shoot in a few more windows? Call the fucking police? Dance for you?

The waitress has taken my outburst for something else. She hurries with the two bottles of beer and puts them between us.

Glasses? she says flatly.

We'll do without, I hiss. Get lost.

Drinking from a bottle can be like kissing; there's a long narrow neck and a wet mouth. As Ross lifts his beer, I see the clear outline of a shoulder holster beneath his black shirt; he doesn't bother to hide it. He's probably even got a gun licence. I wonder if the holster is right up against his skin and if he would really take the time to unbutton his shirt to get the gun if it came to it. And why does he have it with him anyway, if he has no intention of shooting me? He's a strange one.

It's like this, he says. It's highly likely that you have something we urgently need.

What's that, then? I ask. The money?

He looks nonplussed for a moment, then he laughs.

Oh, THAT, he says. Of course not. There are three possibilities:

either you know what I'm talking about and have been playing innocent all this time. Or you have it, but don't know anything about it. If that's the case, we thought it would be better if you don't find out what it is at all. If you did, we either wouldn't get it, or it would get expensive.

That's why you ransacked the flat, I say.

Yeah, he says.

And that's why, above all, you needed Clara, I say.

Yeah, he says.

And the third possibility?

You don't have it at all.

And that would mean?

He thinks for a moment, and empties his bottle.

I'm not sure, he says. But then maybe Herbert would have to grant you your dearest wish. You really are a bit of a nuisance.

Great, I say immediately. I don't have it.

The bottom half of Ross's face is working on a grin; his lips are stretching, thin and pale, but without his eyes joining in, so all that comes out is a grimace. I notice now, of all times, that his eyes aren't dissimilar to Jessie's.

I don't think so, he says. That's very, very unlikely.

He wipes his mouth on his sleeve and signals for another beer.

So what do we do now? I ask.

Since Jessie's death, he says, we've been working on the basis of the second possibility.

And before? I ask.

As long as Jessie was alive, there was a stalemate, an agreement not to rock the boat. Herbert didn't allow anyone to get in touch with her.

We sit in silence for a while, as if we're demonstrating the impasse. The rise and fall of the Vienna dialect burbles around us, along with the odd burst of laughter. I begin to notice the background music; it's Clara's favourite song: *watch me like a game show, you're sick and beautiful*. I turn to the bar.

Change the song! I shout.

The waitress obeys. We seem to have attained the status of Special Guests.

Now that Plan A has failed, Ross says, Plan B kicks in. I'm going to tell you what we're looking for.

And you think where it is might occur to me?

We've got to try everything, he says. After all, you were living with Jessie for the last two years. And if you know where it is, by God you can name your price.

Whatever, I say. You know what I want.

You've really turned into a fool, haven't you? he says. Or an amazing poker player. You've worked for Rufus long enough. Probably enough for both to be true.

You're the only one who understands me, I say. Go ahead.

He leans back in his chair.

It's a number, he says. Fourteen digits.

My face obviously isn't displaying the reaction that he had hoped for. Maybe I should have slapped my thigh and shouted: Oh, a *number* – you should have said so from the start! He waits a bit longer, then gives up.

OK, he says. It all started in 1997. The banking system collapsed in Albania, remember? The people lost their money and it was total chaos.

He raises his claw-hand as proof.

I know all that, I say. I worked on that region.

Yes, I know, he says, but you have to listen to this in context. Jessie doesn't seem to have told you much.

I shake my head. No, she doesn't.

She really was a true professional, he says.

It sounds like the highest compliment he can pay to someone he loves. I wipe the sweat off my face with the hem of my shirt.

Nothing went through the Balkans for us after that, Ross says. The south-east route had always been one of the most lucrative, a real Park Lane. But a few things happened all at once. The Mafia had taken its money out of Albania, so a process of redistribution began to take place. The ports and airports were clogged up with the peacekeeping forces. And there were international warrants out for a few of our partners.

Arkan the Cleanser, I say. So you really do know him?

Jessie never talked crap, he says. Surely you know that.

But you profited from the Balkan conflict, I say, and Rufus could have prevented the charges against Arkan.

He shrugs.

I do the logistics, he says. Deciding when to pull out and what to do instead is Herbert's job. And Rufus's. It could have been yours one day.

I see bright spots whirling in front of my eyes, as if someone's tossed a can of glitter into the air.

You just have to know, I say, where the next boom will be.

Rufus decided on Poland, Ross says. Looking at the NATO war in Kosovo, I can only say he was damn right.

So they knew about that two years before, I whisper.

I almost tip my bottle over as I lift my hand to my forehead. Ross catches it.

Anyway, he says. We've been using other routes since then.

And I'm off to the toilet, I say.

I order a double vodka at the bar on the way. I hear my own footsteps with half a second's delay, as if I'm so tall that it takes that long for the sound to come up from my feet. A good noseful of blow in the toilet stall gets me back to normal height, and walking back to the table is pure bliss. I'm floating, not walking. When I sit down, my grin hangs in the air for a moment before it slides into place. I rest my chin in my hand.

OK, I say composedly. And what has all that got to do with Jessie?

In the last few weeks of the Balkan operation, Ross says, the incident you know about happened.

The refugee woman got shot, I say.

After that, Ross says, Jessie and Shershah just worked on the boat. They were at it almost every week. As long as the Albanian border was still open through the chaos, we gave it full steam.

He presses his lips together and holds them like that. They grow bloodless and pale. He passes his talon over his head; the fingers draw two thick grooves through his hair so that I can see his scalp.

It all went as usual, really, he says. Shershah, or whoever came from the Italian side, followed the passenger ferry route. The tiny Albanian boats came up from Vlorë and waited just behind the three-mile zone by Durrës for the exchange. I was mostly on the Albanian side. One night, we were crouching in a small wooden boat with a water tank full of cocaine on board while the international forces were flying overhead towards Durrës. The sea was choppy. It was almost suicidal to be out there in those tiny boats. I insisted on waiting, so we waited three hours. Jessie and Shershah didn't turn up and we couldn't get through to them.

My vodka arrives and I tip it back. Never drink after snow, I hear a sing-song voice in my head saying. Never drink.

I spent the rest of the night in a hotel, says Ross, glued to the radio and listening for news of an accident at sea. I prayed that they'd been caught by the harbour police instead. I cried along to soppy Italian love songs.

But neither of those things had happened, I say.

They'd simply taken off with the money, Ross says, and had landed somewhere else. Probably at the port in Genoa.

He stretches a hand out towards me; I don't know if he wants to pat me on the shoulder or grab my throat.

I never saw Jessie again after that, he says.

Take it easy, I say.

Do you know if she read my letters in Leipzig? he asks.

She did, I say. She did.

I try to work out how much money they must have had with them, based on a shipment of six hundred kilograms and a price of eighty marks per gram. I get muddled with all the zeros and give up.

Shershah had told her, I say, that they needed the money to migrate to Greenland.

That bastard, Ross says. To the white wolves.

Yes, I say, to the white wolves.

We fall silent and think about Jessie and the land of never-ending ice. The tension in the air pushes us together; we're bent over the table like two ancient tortoises, staring into the empty bottles between us.

That brings us back to the beginning, Ross says finally. Herbert had started changing our routes long before the ruckus in Albania. We started going through Poland instead. It was a huge operation. We had everything on the server; links, contact lists and bank details. But that was the least of it. You have to build roads for them, in order to drive your coke over borders and to your destination. They have to know what kinds of goods are let through the border. You need intermediate storage and partners in important positions. All those details were worked out under the terms of EU expansion into Eastern Europe and the new free-trade zone.

And were ultimately paid for, I say, with funds from PHARE and the IMF?

He ignores me.

So without knowing it, I ask, I too was working on the project when I was in Leipzig?

Ask Rufus, he says. All our crucial data was on the net in a separate domain, distributed across different sub-sites. Jessie got in there and locked it all off.

What do you mean? I ask.

The computer people said something about her locking out the root directory, and making herself the sole user. She'd secured access with a fourteen-character code; it could be made up of numbers, letters, or a combination of both. That's about six trillion different permutations. Even assuming that a computer could try out a million permutations per second, it would still take 190 million years to test all the combinations. That means that Jessie was practically the only one who had access to the data.

Practically, I say. Is that so?

Except Shershah maybe, he says, but he wasn't able to tell anyone, was he? That's why Herbert completely lost it when he found out that Shershah was dead.

So *you* wanted him alive, I say.

We *had* him alive, Ross says. We'd taken his passport off him, so he was running around Vienna like a rat in a cage. He'd have come to us sooner or later. Jessie would have calmed down and the code would have slipped out of one of them. But you had to go and kill Shershah.

It's my turn to ignore him. Jessie would never have calmed down, not after Shershah had left her in the lurch. But this isn't the time to tell Ross that.

But she can't possibly have done that alone, I say. She knew nothing about computers.

Who knows? Ross says. It was easy to underestimate her.

She always knew how to find someone to help her, I think. I reach for the multi-coloured biro in my trouser pocket, thick as a hot dog. Then I can barely suppress the urge to laugh out loud. No wonder Tom was neurotic with fear; no wonder he came to plead with me, in his own way, at least. Jessie must have paid him, though maybe he also did it to help her. If so, I'd have no reason to betray him.

She was a strange girl, Ross says. We all knew a part of her: you, me, Herbert and Shershah. But they didn't fit together.

He's nodding. And he's right. Jessie had been a small sealed chest beside me, even in those moments when I'd thought that I was holding her very core in my hands. I was wrong. No one could have known her the way that other people, a tree or even a dog could be known. At best, it was like knowing a school of fish.

I blow smoke rings over the table. Each one hangs in the air for ten seconds, filling in our silence. When I've finished the cigarette, I pick up the conversation again.

And why, I ask, did she do that?

Are you stupid or what? he says. She wanted to have something to bargain over, with Herbert and me. She was incredibly afraid that Herbert would take revenge on her because of the money. She felt safe as long as she had the code.

I recognize Jessie in this crude logic. The principle of it is as simple as hiding a plastic bag of money under a badly sawn floorboard in our flat. Maybe her tricks worked so well simply because her thought processes were less complicated than those of other people. She thought that whatever she hid wouldn't be found, and that was that.

The worst thing is, Ross says, she did all that even though Herbert would never have harmed her, whatever she might have done.

So you didn't even threaten her once? I ask.

Come on, he says. Herbert even stopped himself from seeing her for her own sake. I told you that already; it happened two years ago.

Cooper, I think, the tigers are here again.

What she did with the databank, Ross says, was completely unnecessary.

He doesn't get it, or maybe he doesn't want to. Unlike him, I know that she didn't do it to protect herself. And she certainly hadn't done it for me. She did it for Shershah. But he had left her, and when he suddenly turned up on Praterstern, she could no longer go on thinking him dead, so I had had to shoot him for her. She had built us into her world for a while and it had been working wonderfully. Just a small adjustment was needed to bring reality in line with her imagination. And I don't blame her. She had every right to want him dead. He had lived on anyway, through her breakdowns – large and small – and in her inability to lead an independent life. I only hope that he knew, in the moment of death, that it was her punishing him. I suddenly have the ridiculous feeling that I should be apologizing to her.

I light another cigarette carefully, as if it could be my last one ever. Every moment is choreographed, from striking the match to inhaling and exhaling the first puff. When the ritual is over, the cigarette is like a fuse burning between my lips with my head as the bomb. And it's going to explode any minute.

All right, Max, Ross says. Enough thinking. I've spelled it all out. Do you have any idea where Jessie could have kept the code?

I completely misunderstood her, I whisper. Maybe I still owe her something.

This isn't the time to cry, he says. It's not about us at all. There's enough stuff in the databank to create a huge scandal at the highest levels. If it gets out, it's the end of your beloved EU and the Balkans will suddenly be blown into the Atlantic.

And a couple of people will get jailed for genocide, I say.

Stop it, Max, he says. You may have had enough of life, but the rest of the continent hasn't.

Then destroy the server, I say.

Of course, he says. If we really can't get the code, that's the next step.

She was your sister, I say. She suffered. Now she's dead.

I'm not going to discuss that with you, he says.

Don't worry, I say. I have nothing more to say.

He traces a pattern through the wetness on the table with the thumb of his crippled hand. If he's nervous, he certainly knows how to hide it. He seems completely detached.

So, he says quietly. Do you have the code or don't you?

I don't, I say.

I think about the ant paintings, 'Fu loves Fula', and about how I have to talk to Clara, to ask her what to do next. We could get the number, call Schnitzler or The Hague, and Clara will get her degree, Jessie her revenge and Herbert, Ross and the others would get what they deserved. The world would be lanced of a boil and have one more international crisis, but what's an international crisis against Clara's degree or Jessie's revenge? I need time to think: about where Jessie could have kept a number and about what all this – the Balkans, Europe and humanity at large – has got to do with me anyway. What about Clara? And what would Jessie have wanted? I have to think.

What do you want? he asks. Money?

Actually, I say, I just wanted to be dead.

We're not speaking any longer. There's not enough air in this café to transmit the sound waves anyway. Somehow I didn't notice that it's become incredibly humid in here. We're just sitting and I don't think either one of us is thinking anything. Our elbows are propped on the table; now and then, the waitress brings new drinks without being asked, and we drink up. We're sitting together, wordlessly, like two empty buckets.

I start when the noise that's been on the edge of my consciousness for some time suddenly breaks through to me. There's a huge crack outside, as if giant hands are splitting planks of wood as large as aeroplanes over the rooftops. I blink rapidly and feel a fluttering in my stomach. I must be out of my mind sitting around here for so long; something must have switched me off. The drink.

Fuck, I shout. Clara! You don't need her now after all.

I jump up without waiting for a reply.

32 | Rain

Outside, I lean against the wall for a moment so that I don't crash to the ground. No one's following me. My field of vision is narrow, my temples are icy cold and my head feels lighter and lighter, as if it's going to detach itself from my body and rise like a helium balloon from a child's hands. The buildings fold around me and uncurl again; they're marbled with white streaks that glow unnaturally as though they're under black light. I'm going to faint. The next crash of thunder kicks me in the stomach. I feel incredibly sick and my knees buckle. If I collapse now, I'll never see Clara again.

Something lands on my head. It's the first drop of rain, as large as a tennis ball. I start running.

The rain makes people hunch down and tuck in their necks. It's suddenly growing darker and darker, as if the sun is sinking in abrupt jerks. The cars have their headlights on and are swimming down the streams of water on Burggasse. I run and run, moving my body as if it isn't mine. I swing my arms in time, making sure to keep my hands unclenched to avoid air resistance. Every step sloshes water up over my knees. Listening to the slapping of my shoes on the tarmac, I begin to hear irregularity in it, like the synchronized marching of an entire army. There are lots of us. We're running. We're too late.

*

The wind is up, swishing the thick curtain of rain beads behind which I can see people everywhere, hurrying towards the buildings; dark shadows sticking to every corner like dirt. They must have come out just in order to run from the rain. They cross my path from left and right; I'm the only one who's running along the street, not across it. This is no longer the same city, no longer the same dry, stony backdrop that my life has been played out against in the last few weeks. Everything is streaming and flowing, sliding and gliding under me and around me. I no longer recognize the street corners. I get into a panic imagining the buildings could sink beneath the ground and come up again somewhere else, changing places with each other. The streets could seek out new paths and I wouldn't find the way back to our courtyard. It will be hidden somewhere in this city, in this great big box of Lego blocks.

There's Lerchenfeldergürtel, so now I have to turn right. But I am sure I was much further along than that; I'm not even halfway there. The whole time, I'm thinking that Clara might be running as fast as I am right now, not far from here, cutting a straight path through the rain to the train station. Maybe she's even crossed my path behind me. I nearly fall when I turn into Thaliastrasse, crashing sideways into a bus stop, but I raise my arm over my face just in time, landing against the plexiglas wall: Liberté Toujours, the advertisement on it says. I run on, and even manage to speed up.

I haven't seen so clearly for a long time. I haven't had such a simple goal for ages. I have to go to her. I have to tell her it's all over, that we've made it. And that I'm sorry.

I stop at the district boundary and look down the street leading to the highway for a moment. My lungs hurt and they're rattling like they're slowly filling with water or blood. I'm drowning from inside. I shouldn't have stopped, because now I can't start running again. With my hands pressed to my sides, I struggle up the slope to the sixteenth district.

When I finally see the metal gate, I stop hurrying.

The chestnut tree is holding up its arms in revulsion over the mess of mud. The drainage hole in the middle of the courtyard is clogged and the water reaches up to the Opel Ascona's hubcaps. For a moment, I mistake the driver's seat for a human body leaning against the steering wheel in despair. Pages torn out of Clara's file are swimming everywhere, with ink running into watercolours on every page.

The shed door is wide open. The casing of the bolt has been torn out of the wood and is hanging from the frame, with nails protruding and the padlock dangling. I can't tell if it was opened from inside or outside.

I look in. It looks the same as before, but now I find it desolate, abandoned, as if no one's been here for years. The water has risen over the threshold and covers half the floor. I remember the mice, and wonder where they could have escaped to from their nests; their whole world is under water right now. Various documents and our clothes are scattered around on the floorboards. In the water, I see a piece of Clara's wig. There are books on the floor and in the open boxes, empty plastic bags, cups and glasses blackened with coffee, rusty cutlery. And there are crumpled cigarette packets everywhere, as if a swarm of red and white butterflies has settled on the room. It's silent apart from the rain, which is falling in the courtyard with a more regular drumming rhythm than on the street. The shed looks dead, like a film set of a city after a catastrophe. It looks like the place in which the last person died.

When I finally step in, the dog comes towards me from the corner. I push him away. He's alone. She's gone.

Clara is gone.

I say it out loud into the room a couple of times, shivering feverishly. My eyes are burning as if they've had acid dropped into them; I have to tell myself to keep breathing.

There's no message, not from her or from whoever could have

come to get her. Water squelches out of my shoes with every step I take. I sweep the papers off the desk with both arms and the DAT-recorder crashes down. Nothing. I look through the doorway into the rain. This is probably as much as a goldfish sees from its bowl. I could just swim back and forth for a while here – forget the way back on the way there and the way there on the way back – or imagine that I'm out in the open sea. Instead I pick up the mirror on the floor, look at my sopping face and comb my hair with a fork. I'm so disgusted at myself that I start to laugh.

I put the three ant-women under my arm, find the kitchen knife that I used to cut off Clara's hair, and go back into the courtyard. It's grown very dark, as if it's almost night. I have no idea what time it really is. I turn the paintings over and find the gallery's stamp and the artist's signature, but no telephone number. The rain is pearling off the oil paint; it looks like the women are sweating and crying. I kneel down in the water and start scratching at the paint, first with my fingernails and then with the knife. The blade turns red and blue and then I lose my grip and it slips into the canvas, slicing through an ant-woman's chin. I punch my hand downwards in anger and water sprays up. Jessie would have screamed, drummed her fists against my chest and arms, and not have slept for days. I rip the canvas, since now it no longer matters anyway, cut all the paintings out of the wooden frames and into narrow strips. They float on the water for a while, amazingly bright and beautiful, then get gradually soaked through and sink. Then there is nothing. I'm just sitting in ankle-deep water, surrounded by the colourful scraps of a large, rare flower, the scraps of Jessie's final resting place. Just sitting here.

The rain is hammering down on my skull. It's probably a light spray on Clara's baldness, wherever she is now. I imagine her out in the city somewhere, not far away, staring at the falling rain, probably from beneath a bridge where she's stopped to wait for it to abate. It's really up to me whether I want to think of her as dead or alive, though it's not an easy decision. If she's dead, she wouldn't have thought of me in her last moments, but of the towel on her balcony, the silence of those nights in her glass cabin, or maybe her dissertation supervisor. And that's fine. That's the great thing about her. Though some vague pain is tearing me in half, I feel a smile forming on my lips. It takes a long time to fade.

I'm lying on my back quietly when Jacques Chirac comes up to me. The water is cooling the back of my head; it's run deep into my ears and has turned my hands soft and spongy white. I'm cold; I didn't know how good feeling cold could be. The acid smell of puke fills my nose and I realize that it's coming from my own mouth, from my own shirt. The dog leans over me and the baggy folds of his face hang down, giving him that morose look that makes me laugh again. His ears are drooping forward in such a comical way, too; those soft, wet ears, velvety and pinkish-black on the insides. I fold one of them back and the dog snuffles happily at my touch. And then I see it. There's a tattoo on the inside of his ear, a fourteen-digit number. I'd forgotten that Jessie had it put there. Cooper, she said, it's safer this way, much safer. It's a very simple combination of numbers: three birthdates, with mine first and Jessie's last. I recognize the one in the middle too, as it's Shershah's. I was the oldest of the three of us and I've outlived them both.

The dog plops down next to me and the water ripples out in circles around him. I wait until he's settled down and then we stay like that for a while: me sitting, him lying down, close to each other like islands in the rain-dappled water.

I put my hand over his right eye carefully and he turns his face towards me, leaning his head against my leg. I stroke his forehead with my little finger while I position the knife between my index and middle fingers, so that the tip of the blade is pointing right at the closed eyelid. He doesn't move. I push his head down, look into the rain and ram my fist down on the knife handle. Jessie will be so happy to see him.

After I've heaved Jacques Chirac's body into the well, I wipe my hands on a towel and find Clara's mobile phone underneath it. Ross's number is saved in the directory.

He picks up on the third ring.

I'm going to name my price, I say.

You're always good for a surprise, Ross says.

You can find someone for me, I say. If you don't have her already, try the train station. You'll recognize her by her shorn head, which will gleam whitely in the crowd or in the dark. You've done this before.

And then? Ross asks.

You'll bring her here, I say, and then leave her alone. After that, you'll get the number.

See you soon, Ross says.

My skin is beginning to itch under the wet clothes, so I take my shirt and trousers off and sit naked on the wall in the courtyard. It's a good time to take a bath. I hold my hands together in my lap and look at them carefully. They look familiar, reliable. I clasp my fingers together to form an empty cup that stays empty, unable even to collect a small puddle of rain. When I've looked long enough and understood everything, I unclasp my hands again and stretch them out flat: upwards first, then downwards. Nothing falls in and nothing falls out. I sink down onto my back, relieved. The rain is heavy and regular. I reach out into the wet, formless air a few times. Then I lie there and look into the body of water. Staring at it, you would never know that it was falling down.

WITHDRAWN